PORCELAIN

PORCELAIN

JESSE SPRAGUE

Cursed Dragon Ship
PUBLISHING

To "Peter" a boy who doesn't exist but nevertheless saved me.

one

Gabrielle swayed in her too-tall heels beneath a bare bulb hanging from the stained ceiling in the bathroom of a man she barely knew.

Is this normal?

Through the thin door, Gabrielle heard Joe moving around and the sound of the snake habitat's lid shutting, followed by the refrigerator opening. A queasy tightness rolled in her stomach, and an impulse to run shot through her. Instead, she leaned over the running tap.

She wanted to be the sort of girl she always saw smiling and giggling around campus. Those girls didn't run away from being alone with a man. They were normal—unafraid.

Time to act like the sort of girl guys date.

Normal. It's time to be normal.

Gabrielle rested her palms on the stained porcelain sink and closed her eyes, trying to calm herself. The scent of cleaners hung heavy in the air, a soapy mint filling the bathroom. Rain drummed on the roof in a soothing rhythm. Though sparse and rundown, the room was clean; she'd guess cleaned in anticipation of her coming.

That had to be a good sign. Joe cared enough to prepare for their date.

Yet this experimental date night wasn't going as planned. If it had been, she would have been sitting in one of those ethnic diners that littered the university area, sipping from a frosted cup.

Gabrielle plunged her hands into the icy spray. As the water splashed, she repeated the affirmation her most recent psychiatrist had helped her create.

"The world isn't seeking to harm me." She kept her voice low, so it faded under the fall of water. "I trust myself to know the difference between real threats and fear. Good things will come to me if I open up and give the world a chance."

I agreed to come here.

Music started in the room outside, and the bass thumped into the bathroom. It drowned out the familiar sound of the rain. Gabrielle repeated her affirmation. Halfway through her fifth repetition, she stopped, heart still fluttering like a hummingbird in her chest.

It's just nerves. Sure, the whole situation is weird. What woman in her right mind goes to a man's house on a first date? To see his python, no less. I'm a mess. But I knew that. It's not like Joe dragged me here against my will. He's a nice guy, and I'm not going to ruin this night.

Gabrielle shut off the tap and stared at her reflection in the slightly warped mirror. The humidity of the drizzly Seattle day had brought her natural curls back, rather than the posh, straightened look she'd attempted. But other than the wild bounce to her dirty-blonde hair, she still looked put together, like the sort of girls she'd seen giggling as they waltzed into their dorms amid a troop of friends.

She wiped away a tiny smear of the thick, black eyeliner from around her wide brown eyes.

Normal. It's time to be normal.

The bathroom door squeaked as she opened it, and the pungent, earthy odor of pot swamped her. The living room and open kitchen were spartan, but she hadn't expected material wealth from a guy like Joe. Given that he had caught her eye because he brought his twelve-foot reticulated python to an overblown house party in Snoqualmie the weekend before, none of the signs pointed to him being an upstanding businessman. But he'd seemed so cool, so self-assured—everything she wasn't.

Joe sat on a worn sofa next to the snake's massive habitat on the far side of the living room. She'd found the reptile charming and exotic at the party. The snake still fascinated her, but its predatory eyes flicked over her. Its head moved along the glass as if seeking to get out, making her feel like prey.

Gabrielle stepped off the peeling linoleum. After a beer, the thick shag carpet was even more difficult to manage than it had been when she first arrived. Her borrowed heels proved impractical, but she'd have to make it over to the couch before removing them. No bending over in this skirt—also borrowed from her roommate.

Normal clothes. Normal life. Fuck it. Just go over there.

Joe scooted slightly to the side, a welcoming gesture.

Gabrielle sank into the couch and smiled at him. So what if they hadn't gone to dinner? Who said having a nice date required spending money?

"More beer?" Joe flashed a sweet grin that made Gabrielle want to smile back.

Her psychiatrist had warned her not to drink on her meds. But surely two beers weren't too much. And she was certain those girls in the dorms drank.

"Yeah, sure," Gabrielle said.

Joe got up and crossed the room to the open kitchen. He was short for her taste. Despite her own petite stature, she preferred big men, men who could protect her. But his build wasn't small. Sturdy and muscular worked too.

"How do you know Cinder?" Gabrielle asked.

"Lucinda? I don't. We have mutual friends, is all. She's your roommate, right?"

"Oh. Yeah, she is. I just figured since she's the one who introduced us . . ."

He opened the fridge and ducked down so he was hidden behind the kitchen island.

"I've seen Cinder around." Joe returned with the beer, popped the top off, and handed it to her. "I haven't seen you around, though."

Gabrielle stared at the bottle and gulped more than she intended. *Of course not. No one lets the crazy girl go to parties.*

Gabrielle motioned to the snake's cage. "How long have you had her?"

"A few years." Joe sat down right next to her.

Gabrielle resisted the urge to move away, though her muscles tightened and she felt herself drawing inward.

If Joe noticed, he gave no sign. "They start out small, and the guy that bought her from the pet store didn't realize she'd grow so big. I fell in love the moment I saw her, though." His voice gained a charming intensity when he talked about the snake.

"Doesn't it ever scare you having a predator like that living with you?"

"As long as she doesn't mistake me for prey, I'm fine. I keep her regularly fed. Once a week, she gets a rabbit or a bird. Unless I wear rabbit fur close to feeding day, there isn't a lot of risk."

"Still . . ." Gabrielle shivered. "She could kill you. That's part of what makes her so beautiful."

"That's what makes all women beautiful." Joe grinned and allowed the old couch to slide him closer to her. Its springs seemed intent on concentrating all weight in the center.

"Women?" Gabrielle said, affecting a flirtatious tone, though her hands trembled, holding her drink. Unable to restrain herself, she moved away from him, pressing up against the arm of the couch.

"People in general," Joe said with that same charming smile. "But yeah, women. We all pretend to be tame, but none of us are."

Gabrielle leaned forward to rest her elbows on her knees. The last thing she wanted to talk about was how dangerous people were.

Joe's fingers ran over the strap of her tank top and followed a curved line to the center of her shoulder blades. "Angel wings? Cool. What does it mean?"

Gabrielle shifted to allow him a better view of the tattoo across her upper back.

She stretched out her right arm, eyes tracing the many tattoos forming a partial sleeve that meandered over her skin. *The story of my life is etched here, where I can see and remember.* A doll occupied the central place among the other tattoos. It held a knife in its childlike hand. That had been the second piece of ink she got, after the massive work on her back. The angel wings between her shoulder blades hid from her, while her arm told of the life she remembered living.

"Gabriel is an archangel," she said. "Both me and my brother were named after angels. Michael and Gabrielle. Mom was huge into the religion thing." *I was her little angel.*

Joe ran a finger over the center of the wings. "So why the blood?"

"I thought it was cool." *Is that what I should say? That has to be a normal answer.*

Joe's hand stayed on her skin and slipped down the trailing wings of her tattoo. His fingers were now well inside her tank top, brushing over the edge of her bra. Gabrielle's stomach clenched.

"Bloody wings and a full-back tattoo," Joe said. "I'd love to see it all."

Gabrielle's vision went dark, and all she saw was blood.

Everywhere.

The tacky red covered her and the sheets around her. A cold hand fell on her stomach as she struggled to sit up.

Gabrielle took in a quick gasp of air as the room re-solidified. No red. Nothing except faded wallpaper, a snake under a heat lamp, and someone beside her.

"You okay, Gabrielle?" Joe asked. His fingers were still under the strap of her bra.

The tightness in her stomach rolled into nausea. "Yeah, sorry." She brushed his hand off and gulped from her beer.

She lost track of the conversation. Her answers and questions came out by rote. No matter how she tried to push the vision out of her mind, it wouldn't leave her be. One flash meant nothing. Steadying herself took a few drinks, and when she managed to drag her attention back to the world around her, she held a glass of vodka.

Joe's hand moved in a circle beneath her shirt. Gabrielle shoved down the urge to snap at him to take his hands off of her.

"Please, stop that." She twisted on the couch to create distance, using her legs as a barrier. Her back jammed against the armrest, which wouldn't let her get farther away without getting up. She doubted she could stand.

Joe ran his hands up and down her inner calf. Gabrielle's breath froze inside her panicked lungs as if saving air to scream.

That's what guys want. This is normal. She stared at the small hole in his T-shirt—the shirts branding was for the local garage band they'd chatted about at the house party. *Was that intentional, to impress me? He's broken, too, ragged around the edges.*

"I gotta run to the bathroom," Joe said.

She nodded.

The view out the window from the couch showed a patch of lit gravel driveway. The rain had picked up, blurring the view. Joe's blue pickup sat dead center in the porchlight's glow, and out beyond it, everything faded into black.

Once he was out of sight, she fumbled at her purse, her fingers feeling fat and unwieldy. Her phone glowed as she tapped the screen to find only one bar. Not enough to make a call, but a couple of texts from Cinder waited. Gabrielle didn't open them. Cinder would want to know how everything was going; Gabrielle didn't know.

I need to get out of here. Call someone who can help me. But how would they find me? She pulled up Google maps, but the GPS wouldn't load.

She opened a conversation with her brother and typed, then deleted, a message about the bloody flash. It had been three months since her last psychotic break, and that one had been isolated. Maybe this one would be too. Michael was out on a date with that older guy. No point spoiling his night with her worries.

I've ruined enough of his life. He deserves to be happy.

Her thoughts jumped, having trouble settling in any one spot.

I was trying to do something. Gabrielle stared at her phone and the single bar. The booze sang in her blood. No amount of staring reminded her of why she'd got out her cell.

She tucked the phone back into her purse as Joe returned. He plunked down next to her, close enough their thighs touched.

Gabrielle inched away, but the arm of the couch blocked her escape again. She heard the voice of her psychiatrist in her head, lecturing her about how she shouldn't ever overdrink. Not on her meds.

It's only one night. I'm in college now. I'm an adult. I don't have to be that girl anymore.

Reinventing herself as an average girl meant drinking, and it meant fending off handsy men. She'd overheard enough women talking about it. Normal. Society taught guys to push as hard as they could, hoping for a *yes*. As long as she remembered *no,* she'd be fine.

But with her head foggy with drink, she didn't trust her reactions.

Joe's arm snuck around her, his elbow resting on the back of the couch. He massaged her shoulders and leaned over, kissing the skin near her tattoos. His mouth moved up to her neck.

She pushed him away and glanced at his drink. He'd stopped refilling his a while ago.

"I should slow down," she said.

"No need."

"You have anything to eat? I sort of thought we'd get dinner."

"I have some snacks in the bedroom. C'mon."

Bedroom. Gabrielle stiffened, then inhaled deeply and carefully recited her practiced words inside her head. *The world isn't seeking to harm me. I trust myself to know the difference between real threats and fear. Good things will come to me if I open up and give the world a chance.*

Sex is normal. It's okay for him to try. Nothing is wrong.

At nineteen, Gabrielle was the only person in her circle of acquaintances who hadn't given in to those "base urges." Sex seemed so natural for everyone around her, like a dance they were born knowing the steps to. Yet she stumbled. Maybe it was time to let someone else lead.

She followed him into the bedroom and sat on the bed next to him. Her head spun with the sudden motion. The room's edges blurred and blended. If she focused on Joe, she was fine. He handed her something.

A packet of nuts. She opened it and ate. "Do you have anything like bread? Help me sober up?"

"I'm sure I have something. Let's sit a bit. Do you hear the frogs croaking?"

She did. "Sure."

"You seem nervous tonight."

"I don't date a lot."

"Yeah, you're a virgin, right?" His hand brushed over her sleeve tattoo, trailing across the golden eyes situated at the center of the doll's face.

Gabrielle tensed, body freezing even as her mind sloshed around the fact that somehow he knew her sexual history.

Did I say I was a virgin? I don't remember saying that. How else would he know? Did Cinder tell him? I'll kill her.

"It's just never worked out." Gabrielle shrugged. "I've done other things."

Stupid thing to say.

No harm in it.

His hand had moved up her arm to slide under the straps of both her tank top and bra. "Yeah?"

She took another sip from her vodka. It tasted awful, and she should stop, but the fuzzy edge to the world covered her like a blanket and smothered her fear. She was a gladiator in its warm whisperings.

"Yeah, a couple of times."

He leaned closer, and even her armor of drunkenness failed to fight off the underlying fear.

"*C'mon, put it in your mouth.*" The voice—tempered in the dust of time—ripped her armor with a flash of blood and her second foster father's face, gray stubble covered his chin.

Gabrielle downed the rest of the glass.

"Other things? Like what?" Joe asked. He plucked the cup from her fingers but waited for her answer.

Gabrielle clung to his hand, glad of any conversation to pull her from her memories—from her mind.

"Like?" Joe moved his hand, taking hers with it, further up his leg.

"Oh, you know." Gabrielle smiled. "Oral stuff." She looked down and realized where he'd positioned their hands in his lap. "Only a few times. I don't think I'm very good at it."

Is that supposed to talk him out of it? Did I go too far?

"I'm sure you're great."

I should've shut my mouth. I'm making things worse. Gabrielle giggled nervously but jerked her hand back into her own space. She tried to stand. Her legs refused her demand to transport her as far from Joe as she could get.

"Let me get you another drink," Joe said.

"No, I'm done. I don't want to go home blackout drunk."

"I'll get you another." Joe smiled. The expression struck Gabrielle as predatory, but it could be a trick created by the blur of her vision. "I've had too much to drive you home tonight anyhow."

He left the bedroom.

Gabrielle stood on wobbly legs, her brain fumbling to process the last exchange. Nothing was right about her situation. *I'm trapped here.*

Her heart raced, fluttering as only the heart of prey can.

She thrashed inside her purse for her phone. Halfway through a text to Cinder, she deleted it.

I can't tell Cinder anything's wrong. She doesn't know how broken I am. I can't mess that up. This is all normal and I'm overreacting. She'll think I'm insane.

Not Michael either.

I mean, yes, go ahead. Spoil tonight for him. It's not like he already gave up his childhood for you. No, no. And you don't even know where you are, idiot.

Gabrielle gazed out the window. They were well off I-90, buried in trees. Even if she made it to the road, she didn't know which way to turn. And it was dark.

I could just walk out the door. But how long would I have to wander before I got enough reception to get the GPS working? How much longer until anyone could come get me?

No.

I can't be alone in the dark.

Gabrielle scrolled her list of contacts, mostly doctors, to the one person other than Michael that she could trust. That was if Peter hadn't gone off the rails and stopped using his cell again.

Peter. The hammering of her heart eased slightly.

They hadn't talked in six months—had avoided each other on campus. Or Gabrielle had avoided him, and he'd let her. Maybe it was the other way around?

The urge to contact him overwhelmed her. Even if it didn't change her plight, just knowing he was out there, on her side, lifted some of the horror from the situation.

She opened a conversation and typed.

-Weird situation. You have access to a car? Call you when I figure out where I am.-

The message went to pending. Gabrielle dropped the phone back in her purse. There wasn't any more she could do.

Call the cops? Joe had done nothing wrong.

I could ask Joe for the address. Then someone could come get me.

She shivered and sat on the edge of the bed. *But he'll think I'm crazy. He'll get all insulted and—and he wouldn't tell me, anyhow.*

Joe reentered with another glass of vodka. She took it and lifted it to her mouth but didn't drink.

Am I imagining the threat here? Is this me?

Joe lay down on the bed behind her and motioned for her to come closer. Gabrielle's head spun, and she gave one last imploring look outside.

"You should try," he said.

She knew what he meant. His hand encouraged her to move down. She recoiled.

"I promise," he said. "There's no way you're bad at it."

Gabrielle laughed and shook her head. "I'm just tired."

"You can sleep here." He patted the bed. "I'll take you home in the morning."

He moved his hand up her thigh, his fingertips sliding under her skirt. Gabrielle moved away, down the bed, but he followed her, now tracing the skin above her hip bone.

"We can keep entertained until then," he said. "C'mon, I won't judge."

Gabrielle's blurry mind patched together the situation as he propped himself up and put his hand behind her neck, encouraging her to go where he wanted her.

All night was a long time.

She could keep saying no, fight him off until morning. But what if he got aggressive? She couldn't stop him. Even if he didn't force her into anything, it sounded like a miserable night, and she really was tired.

I just want tonight to be over.

It would be easier and safer to do what he wanted. She'd stay in control and keep the situation from violating more of her body than had already been sullied. It would start and stop at oral.

Then in the morning, I'll go home, and I won't be a victim. If I say no, he can force me to go all the way and I'll have no choice. If I choose this, I'm not a victim.

I'm not. Gabrielle's mouth felt dry, and her stomach lurched.

And afterward, he'll stop touching me.

I get to choose.

two

COLE PUT ON HIS SOCKS FIRST. SOMEHOW THAT SMALL ACTION MADE HIM feel less like he was sneaking out. The details were always what made or broke a moment, and this was a moment he had no intention of breaking.

Michael sat up in the bed, his bare legs tangled in the Egyptian cotton sheet. Only one bedside lamp was on, which was a shame; Cole wouldn't ever tire of looking at Michael. The king bed jiggled under them as Michael shifted over.

"I wish I could stay." Cole reached over and ran a hand through those glorious curls.

Michael tilted his head, his hazel eyes glowing golden in the light. The warm russet, tint to his skin always made the light color of his irises stand out, but somehow, it was more evident now—like a cat's eyes catching the moonglow. His expression was serious, but Cole didn't detect any anger at the attempted escape.

"I get it," Michael said. He slid to the opposite edge of the bed. Cole had a perfect view of the angel wings that stretched between his shoulder blades. Michael grabbed a robe he'd tossed over the metal footboard.

He's got to be the sexiest person I've ever dated. And this house? No way this belongs to a twenty-five-year-old social worker. If he were a horse, I don't think I could resist looking in his mouth.

"You're staring, Cole." Michael cracked a smile and ran a hand over his tight black curls.

"You're gorgeous." Cole leaned over and kissed Michael. The wine they'd ordered at dinner still clung to the inside of his mouth.

"Is that what you tell all the gals before you run off?" Michael asked, his smile widening.

"Oh, stop that." Cole rolled his eyes and reached down to pull on his boxers.

"Seriously, stay for coffee." Michael stood and slipped into a robe, belting it around the middle. "It'll feel less like you're sneaking off."

Cole gave a guilty smile. That was exactly what he'd been doing. "Wouldn't a nightcap be more appropriate? It's 1 a.m. Trust me, I don't want to go. Yolanda's already going to be worrying about me."

Yolanda would be plenty happy to stay with Isa all night, and Cole knew it. He hoped she'd gone to bed hours ago and wasn't even aware he hadn't come home. The lie had slipped off his tongue before he thought about it. But she worried about him like a mother —certainly more than his spoiled ex-wife ever had. Yolanda was Cole's live-in nanny and had been since his daughter was three months old.

Michael stood and crossed the room, flipping on the light. Cole grabbed his pants off the polished wood floor and pulled them on, placing his feet on the Italian wool runner that sat square under the bed, drifting out a foot on all sides. Before his ex-wife and her money, he wouldn't have so easily identified such things—he might not even have guessed Michael had money. He didn't act like he was somehow "above the little people" like Joan had. Then, as Cole swept up his shirt, he noticed something behind Michael.

A small wooden cross hung on the wall by the door. It didn't match anything else in the posh bedroom, nor did it seem to fit with the utilitarian appearance of the kitchen and living room beyond.

Yet, there the cross hung, placed right where Michael would see it every morning when he woke up.

"You religious?" Cole asked. *Add that to the list of things that don't quite match with this guy. I still don't even know what got someone like him into social work—it certainly doesn't fit with the fine furnishings. Though religious would help patch those ends together.*

"Ha! No." Michael glanced behind him, following Cole's eyes. "Oh, the cross? That was my mom's. If you want to know about it, I guess you'll have to stay for coffee."

As Cole followed Michael out of the bedroom, the bones of the house groaned around them. Old houses always had stories to tell, and this house's whispers refused to be ignored. Michael padded across the carpeted living room into the granite-tiled kitchen. Something he couldn't name bothered him, like a voice just out of earshot. Subconsciously his hand moved to where his firearm would be if he was on duty. Realizing he had done so, Cole dropped his hand.

Michael was an enigma; he seemed so open and friendly, but then there were so many gaps in Cole's knowledge of him. Michael steered any conversation they had away from his own childhood. They'd met in a boxing-gym almost a year before but hadn't really noticed each other until Michael was assigned as a liaison on one of Cole's cases. After that, they'd been tentatively dating for just over two months. Cole knew nothing about him prior to when he turned eighteen and went off to college.

Cole suspected abuse in Michael's past, and nothing made opening up tricky quite like that did. But the absence of facts was starting to feel deceptive. He had to know more about Michael.

I'll have to call Yolanda, tell her I won't be home for a while. If she's still up, she'll have half decided I'm bleeding in some alley by now and be planning the funeral. But I can't leave, not if he's finally going to open up.

"Just a second," Cole said and drifted over to the leather couch. From there he could see the stairs to the second floor. He'd never been up there, so it was filled with shadowy, unknown forces. Cole plopped down, putting his back to the stairway, and grabbed his phone from the coffee table next to the dregs of their after-dinner drinks.

In front of him, a sliding glass door provided a picturesque view of the night and the strip of preserved wetland that ran behind Michael's neighborhood.

Yolanda picked up on the second ring.

"Mr. Montez?"

"Yeah. Sorry, I know I said I'd be back earlier."

"It's okay, as long as you're safe." She sounded content, but she yawned. She'd definitely been waiting up, as he could hear the buzz of the television in the background. "You stay as long as you want. No problem. Good to know you're safe. Now I can go to bed."

Cole grinned. Yolanda had been living with them since his ex-wife, Joan, moved to Florida. Now that Cole had Isa for all but a few holidays, Yolanda seemed more attached to her than ever. Cole didn't mind—the girl could use a mother figure. He'd rather have a nanny who legitimately cared than one who was just there for the paycheck.

Plus, a stable house and stable home care would look good to a judge, now that Joan was back in state and seeking a parental agreement. The one good thing about Joan ghosting after their divorce was that he got to have sole custody of Isa.

"You have fun, Mr. Montez."

"Call me Cole."

"Okay, Mr. Montez." Yolanda giggled. The formal name bit was an old joke, and he doubted she'd ever tire of it. So he let it go on, despite not wanting the reminder of his ex's quirks. Joan's hardline attitude was the only reason that even a year after Joan cheated on him and then abandoned them—running off to Florida and her rich family—Yolanda couldn't break the habit.

"Thank you, Yolanda. If Isa wakes up, tell her I love her, and I'll be home in time for breakfast."

"Yes."

Cole hung up and turned his face toward the kitchen. Michael had leaned against the breakfast bar, elbows on the granite counter-top, watching him.

"In time for breakfast?" Michael's dimples showed. "We can do a lot more than coffee then."

"So," Cole said, getting up and walking toward the kitchen island, "you were going to tell me about the cross."

"Honestly?" Michael grinned and pulled down a French press from a high cupboard. "I'm surprised you don't know. I expected you to be snickering under your breath as I 'came clean.' Didn't you do your homework on me? All the police archives at your fingertips and you didn't find anything?"

"I don't research my dates." Cole wondered if that had been a good idea in this case. Michael's words smacked of a dark secret. His hand rested at his hip, touching the ghost of his firearm for comfort. "Though right now you're making yourself sound like a criminal."

"You're in homicide, right?"

Cole leaned on the counter next to Michael. He ignored the question as rhetorical. Michael knew where he worked.

"Even if you didn't research me"—Michael grabbed an electric tea kettle and filled it with water—"I figured one of the older guys would've told you about me or this house."

"I don't talk about you at work. It's not an *understanding* environment."

"I'd like to be offended, but I get it." Michael put the pot down on its base and flipped down the switch for it to boil.

As Michael stared at the pot, Cole gripped the edge of the counter and waited. The ramifications of Michael implying that Cole's homicide buddies might have information hit hard. If Michael was a danger, Cole really didn't know if he could win that fight. His mouth felt dry. None of this sounded positive. Part of him ached to turn and leave, to not find out whatever it was Michael clearly didn't want to talk about. But if him being in homicide was relevant to the story, he couldn't turn a blind eye.

"You didn't kill anyone." Cole broke the silence with his swift suspicion. "Right? That's all you have to tell me."

"They tried really hard to prove I did." Michael turned at an angle that Cole couldn't see his face and poured the coffee grounds into the press.

Well, that's cryptic.

Michael turned back, and his smile faded. "You look . . . Sorry. I forget that not everyone had to develop a sense of humor about this stuff. For me, there was no other way to survive."

"What happened, Michael?"

"When I was fourteen, I ran away a couple of times and accused my stepdad of abuse. The cops decided I was some punk kid and didn't do shit about it. Probably it had something to do with my stepdad being a wealthy white guy while I was just a kid." Michael shrugged.

"Did he abuse you?"

"That actually isn't important to the story. But when he and my mom turned up murdered in their beds with no signs of forced entry and multiple stab wounds, I looked promising as a suspect."

Multiple stab wounds meant a crime of passion. Cole had seen Michael fight at the boxing gym; he didn't seem capable of losing control like that. But he wasn't fourteen anymore either.

"But you were acquitted?" Cole asked.

"I was never charged. My stepdad was being a dick. I had stormed out of the house and stayed at a friend's."

"Wait, a murder in this house, the one we're in? How do you own it?" Cole glanced back at the bedroom. He'd been on plenty of murder scenes—that came with the job. But he'd never had sex at a double-murder site before, and it hadn't exactly been something on his bucket list. "Where did it happen?"

"Not that room." Michael chuckled and pointed up the stairs into the hungry darkness of the second floor. "I turned their bedroom into a home gym. And I own the home as part of my inheritance. Gabrielle doesn't want anything to do with it, so it's mine."

The water boiled, and Michael poured it over the grounds with graceful artistry.

"You guys lived with your biological dad after?" Cole asked, watching the steaming water streak from the pot to the press and the grounds swirling inside.

"No. Just me. He wasn't her dad. She went into foster care until I was old enough to get her out." Michael's smile died, and his eyes focused on the floor.

"I don't mean to interrogate you." Cole set his hand over Michael's. The robust smell of the coffee had already started to relax some of the edge from his worry, seeing Michael look so injured did the rest. No matter what had happened back then, Michael wasn't a criminal now. "Let's have our coffee and forget it."

"I haven't even gotten to the cross yet." Michael glanced at Cole with a weak upward quirk of his mouth.

"You don't have to." Even as Cole said it, he knew it wasn't true.

"I do. I like you, and this isn't the sort of thing that goes away. I don't enjoy talking about it, but if you're going to be part of my life, I need to know if this mess will be an issue."

"Okay. I'll hear you out. But I can tell you up front, as long as you didn't kill them, I'll deal with your baggage. I'd be a fool not to."

Michael nodded and pushed down the press. The grounds danced at the bottom of the glass. When he'd finished, Michael poured the coffee into two mugs.

Cole picked his up and sipped while Michael spooned in sugar.

"I keep the cross"—Michael strode over to the fridge and pulled out a small container of cream—"to remind me not to put my faith in intangible things. That the world gets better when we make it better. Mom died with that cross in her hands, same way she lived, trusting that some divine power would take care of everything."

"So you're an atheist?" Cole tried to remember if he'd ever mentioned attending church to Michael. Probably not. He didn't go often anymore, not since the divorce. People there hadn't known he was bisexual until Joan found out and broadcast her disgust. Personally, he thought her cheating was far more offensive, but he hadn't felt the need to inform everyone about it.

"I don't have an issue with God. What gets me is people attributing real-world events to God. Take responsibility and give credit where it's due. If someone's smacking your kids around, do something about it. Don't hide your cowardice behind 'God's will.' God doesn't cure cancer either. That's doctors and science. I don't know if I'm an atheist, but yes, I've noticed that little cross around your neck, and I don't care."

"I figured from the angel wings that you had some feelings in some direction." Cole motioned to Michael's shoulders.

"The tattoo? I did it for my sister. Mom named us after archangels—Gabriel and Michael." He took a long drink of his coffee. "So this whole conversation . . . It isn't how I want to end my night."

"Please don't suggest going to your workout room," Cole said. Michael was damaged, but that only meant he needed love more. Cole wanted to help push past his history.

Michael laughed, which made the joke worth telling. Cole took another drink of the near scalding liquid and watched Michael's sparkling eyes.

He's been through so much, and he still smiles more than anyone I know. How does he do that?

"You don't have an excuse to leave. Not until breakfast."

three

ORANGE EYES FOLLOWED HER. GABRIELLE REACHED UP TO TOUCH HER FACE. The unblinking eyes, too bright to ever be called brown, held cold laughter. The skin of Gabrielle's cheek hardened under her fingertips, and little cracks lined her flesh.

The eyes were closer.

Gabrielle extended a porcelain arm. The fissures along it spread, and chunks of porcelain plummeted into the dark. *I'm shattering. There will be nothing left.*

"*I can help you,*" the high, whistling voice said. Its eerily singsong quality did not convince Gabrielle of good intent.

No, no. Last time I asked for help . . . No!

Red swirled everywhere.

Gabrielle woke in Joe's musty bedroom. Her mouth tasted rotten, like vodka and other things she didn't want to think about. She kicked off the woolen throw and rose from where she'd slept on top of Joe's bare mattress. As soon as she sat upright, her head began to pound and her stomach clenched painfully.

"Want breakfast?" Joe asked from the doorway.

"I want to go home." Gabrielle grabbed her jacket off the chair and pulled it over her arms—noticeably uncracked arms made of flesh.

"I can make eggs."

"No. Take me home, now. I'll wait in the truck." Gabrielle stood and blindly passed through the house. Her ears rang, and in the buzz, she heard the offer of help again and again.

Would she *help me if I asked? How could she help me?*

Gabrielle tottered out into the cold morning air, the heels already making her calves ache. No direct sunlight reached her through the heavy cover of trees. Two options stood before her. She could wait in this sunless cold for Joe to drive her home, or she could try walking down the long gravel drive until she reached the road. With her stomach seething and head pounding, there was no real choice.

She stepped over to the rusty blue pick-up truck with her jacket pulled around her, like armor, and sat on the back bumper. On her phone she found a message from Michael. And a message from Peter.

Fuck. I texted Peter.

And he answered. That simple fact, that he'd answered, that he still even had his cell phone, comforted her. She held the phone to her chest and smiled. Maybe he was getting better. Maybe he'd listened and gone to see a psychiatrist.

But what had he said?

Her finger flicked over the screen and brought up the text.

-U OK? Where R U?-

Shame crept up inside her—he couldn't see her like this, couldn't know. She messaged back.

-Still don't know. Talk later-

Joe came out of the house before she got up the nerve to open Michael's texts. The keys were in Joe's hand, and Gabrielle stood and walked over to the passenger door.

"You're in a hurry this morning," Joe said.

"I drank too much, and I have classes to get home and change for." *And shower. And forget any of this ever happened.*

"Got it. Hop in."

The inside of the truck stank of tobacco, and the edge of the window was sticky. Despite the cold air, she rolled the window down and stared forcefully into the forest, trying to keep conversation at bay and the contents of her stomach from coming up.

He didn't hurt me. He didn't force me into anything. Am I being fair?

I don't care. I feel dirty.

I feel like a victim.

Was all the pressure in my head? A normal girl would know. She glanced at Joe but couldn't keep looking. Nothing in his face answered her questions.

A stronger person would have stuck up for herself. Would have said no.

"The world isn't seeking to harm me." She silently mouthed the words. "I trust myself to know the difference between real threats and fear. Good things will come to me if I open up and give the world a chance."

The scenery sped by. They passed into the tunnel on the I-90 bridge, and Gabrielle sank into the rhythm of the blurred lights and concrete. As the minutes passed, she was unsure if her hangover was what made her gut so tender or Joe's presence.

Blood splashed on everything, tacky in her hair and on the walls. The wooden cross clutched in stiff fingers, covering her mother's chest.

I can help you, the voice repeated.

Joe's hand fell on her leg, and for a moment, the bloody scene inside her mind mixed with the car's interior. With Joe.

Make it stop. Make him stop.

A tinkling laugh filled her mind. *"Just ask for my help."*

Then the worn interior of the truck returned. Joe's hand on the bare skin of her leg. Outside the window, the scenery was familiar. Her neighborhood. Her gut revolted, and she swallowed down bile. Even another moment here like this, with him touching her, was too much.

"Just drop me off here," Gabrielle said. If only she could get away from him and back to her life, everything would be better. Her hand pressed the release on the seatbelt and shot out to the door handle.

"What? Why?"

"Motion sickness." Gabrielle held a hand over her mouth, wishing it were a lie rather than a slight exaggeration. "I'd rather walk. Let me out!"

He shrugged, his expression informing her she was behaving like a crazy person. For once, Gabrielle didn't care. Every inch of her flesh was poised to run. She would jump from the moving vehicle if she had to. It didn't matter what he thought. All she wanted was for him to leave.

Joe pulled into a gas station, and Gabrielle scrambled out, practically tumbling to the asphalt and then backing away from the truck. Joe waited, his brow furrowed.

Make him leave. That's all that matters. Gabrielle forced a smile and waved him away before turning and wobbling up to the building, toward the lit interior and vividly colored snacks. After his truck drove away, she leaned against the dingy exterior window and closed her eyes, trying to push down the panic and nausea.

As soon as her spinning brain stilled and the fears and anger settled into the deep corners of her mind, Gabrielle pulled out her phone. There were only a few names in her recent history. She'd wait to talk to Peter until she'd thought of something to say. She couldn't lie to him—he could always tell. And in any event, if they were going to talk again, they needed to clear the air about other things.

Michael would already be at work.

That left Cinder, who was the best option anyway, as the condo she shared with Gabrielle was only a few minutes' drive away.

-Come and get me? Gas station by the pink house. Bring me a change of clothes, please.-

Gabrielle crumpled and sat against the building, staring out at the gas pumps. A little gray car pulled in, and a man got out to fill up.

He pointedly avoided looking at Gabrielle. *I must look like a homeless crazy person or a runaway.*

Her phone buzzed with Cinder's text.

-Be there in 10. Got class this morning so be ready. You owe me an explanation.-

Gabrielle tucked the phone away and buried her face in her knees. The gray car drove away with a squeak of tires.

Joe is gone. I'll forget this. It's over.

She hadn't had visions for years. Joe had caused them—pushed her to this brink. But she could step back. Sinking into her normal life would do that. She'd pretend it never happened.

The visions will stop.

College was supposed to have been her escape, her chance to be normal. This wasn't normal. No matter how her brain turned the night, she didn't understand what had happened. She didn't even know if Joe had known how she was feeling.

"I didn't even say no. Not once."

A car honk startled Gabrielle out of her thoughts. Cinder had pulled up to the curb in her red compact, and the locks clicked open. Then the window rolled down and a trickle of punk music punctuated the air. Gabrielle got up and moved the few steps to the car.

Cinder pursed her lips. As usual, her large breasts were on intentional display under a slinky, black top. Gabrielle envied how casual and easy Cinder was in her skin. She had pulled her blue hair back to show off the shaved sides of her head. This was normal, like a rope to pull Gabrielle away from her worries.

"Are you okay, Angel? I take it the date didn't go well?" Cinder's voice was as hard as usual but with a hint of tenderness and concern hidden underneath.

"Can we please not talk about it? Just pretend it never happened?"

"Sure, Angel." But despite the words, Cinder looked on the verge of continuing her interrogation.

"Clothes?" Gabrielle motioned to the gas station bathroom.

"Change in the car or I'll be late to my first class. Who goes on a date Sunday night, anyhow?" Despite Cinder's brusque words, her eyes moved over Gabrielle with concern. She started to say something else but stopped.

Gabrielle sighed but opened the door and slid into the seat. *At least the windows are tinted.*

"What happened?" Cinder asked. The radio underscored Cinder's words with grating vocals. "Seriously, are you okay?"

Gabrielle pressed her lips together, feeling the crack running through her throb. *The words would shatter me.*

"That adorable, red-headed friend of yours called me all panicked last night," Cinder said as she rolled the window up and pulled out onto the road.

Peter. I never should have messaged him. I'm not ready to deal with his issues. But I can't just let him worry either.

"I doubt *he* will accept not talking about it." Cinder stopped at one of the many red lights that dotted the drive to the University of Washington. "That boy thinks the sun rises out of your ass."

Hardly. "Please leave it, Cinder. It was a long night." *Could have been longer. Would I feel better or worse if I'd just stayed up all night fending him off?*

Gabrielle struggled into the long blue dress Cinder had brought for her and then out of the short skirt. With her legs covered and the soft fabric touching her thighs, the world became a little more manageable. Soon, tennis shoes eased her aching feet. But she didn't feel dressed until a duster jacket covered her arms and a gauzy scarf wrapped around her neck.

"Wash your face." Cinder shoved wet wipes at her and flipped down the passenger-side sunshade so Gabrielle could witness the faded disgrace of last night's makeup.

The first wipe cooled her skin as it lapped up the black smudges. Her brown eyes stared out, the dark irises becoming black pits as the darker makeup disappeared and left only pale skin. Eyes that could swallow her.

She scrubbed with a second and third wipe as if she could wash away the previous night along with the makeup. Her skin reddened at the rough treatment, but her stomach settled. Yet no matter how she attacked the last of the smudges, the rankness in her mouth didn't fade. Nor did the pounding in her head.

"You have any water?" Gabrielle asked.

Cinder shot her another pursed-lip look and motioned to the plastic bottle nested in the center console.

Gabrielle scooped it up and swished the water around in her mouth. She rolled down the window and spat out the water. Her second drink, she swallowed.

"Still going with 'nothing happened'?" Cinder asked as she pulled into the central plaza garage next to the Odegaard Library.

They rarely parked on campus because the price got astronomical quickly. The radio faded to static as Gabrielle dug around her purse for money. She'd been the delay, the reason Cinder didn't have time for street parking.

"Well?" Cinder asked.

"I didn't say nothing happened. I said I didn't want to talk about it."

Peter would understand. Her heart tugged. He'd understand that sometimes, problems are too big to face. The only way to move on was to walk in the other direction.

Cinder shrugged, but from her expression, Gabrielle could tell she wasn't going to drop it.

"I didn't expect you to stay the night. Dinner must have gone well at least," Cinder said.

"He didn't take me to dinner. He took me to his place."

Cinder pulled into an empty parking spot, then sat with the radio static droning.

"Did he hurt you, Angel?" Her voice cracked, her tough veneer slipping.

Red seeped in at the edge of Gabrielle's vision, spurred on by each buzz of static. Her head throbbed. Gabrielle rubbed at her eyes, but in the dark of her closed eyelids, the view was worse. Her mother's face carved with little bloodless lines, a riddle of cracks forming another cross—this one etched into her dead flesh. Her mouth hung slack, teeth stained a brilliant scarlet.

Gabrielle jabbed out at the radio, turning it off. Cinder grabbed her arm, and Gabrielle turned to face a mix of concern and anger.

"He didn't hurt me." *I am not a victim.* "We just had some drinks. He said he'd had too much to take me home, so I crashed there."

"Asshole." Cinder smacked the center console, rocking the water bottle.

"He didn't—"

"Bullshit. That is seedy as fuck. Any decent guy knows better than to get too drunk to get his date home on a first date. You don't force someone—"

"He didn't force me! I'm done with this." Gabrielle swung the car door open and bolted. Cinder wanted Gabrielle to face what happened. The only way to do that was to accept the voice's offered help, and saying yes to *her* never ended well.

Cinder called after her, but Gabrielle ignored it.

Once out of the garage, she dashed out into the quad under the sun. Other students dotted the walkway that wound through the cherry trees, which were just beginning to bloom. Several students sat in the still chilly sunlight or played hacky sack under the trees. The spring weather had yet to truly warm and many of the walkers hurried along on their way, making Gabrielle's half-run nothing out of the ordinary.

The peaceful scene enveloped her like a magic spell. She stepped into her student identity, leaving the scared girl behind. Out here, the previous night fell away—just a bad experience to be chalked up to lessons learned.

A quick look told her Cinder had not followed. Cinder's class was on the other side of campus. Still, Gabrielle knew she hadn't heard the last of it.

She picked her way across one of the patches of lawn to sit under a cherry tree. The buds over her head were nearly ready to burst open. Her class wasn't for another hour, but most of the students had disappeared inside the buildings, leaving the lovely courtyard empty except for a few stragglers and the hacky sackers.

"Gabs?"

Gabrielle didn't need to look to know it was Peter.

four

A LIGHT BREEZE RUSTLED THE BRANCHES OVER GABRIELLE'S HEAD AND MADE the cherry blossoms sigh. But it was not the tree that cast its shadow on her. She lowered her face to keep from seeing Peter there, framed by the jagged branches. They'd met here often enough. Deep down, she'd hoped he would know to find her in the quad.

She winced against the bright sunlight. "Come, sit, my head is killing me."

Peter sat next to her on the grass. The edge of his worn jeans moved her skirt on her leg so that it brushed against her like a caress. She forced herself not to turn to him. His expression might undo her.

"What happened last night?" Peter asked. He tugged at his messenger bag and pulled a small aspirin bottle from inside.

With him, it was okay not to be normal. She allowed herself to feel safe. "I got scared. It happens. Everything is fine now."

Peter opened the bottle and shook two capsules into his hand then offered them to her. Gabrielle took the pills and put them in her mouth. They stuck slightly in her throat going down, leaving a painful spot in her gullet, but at least the headache should go away.

"Hangover?" he asked.

She nodded and then relaxed back against the tree with her eyes closed. Peter leaned next to her, his warmth reassuring. They sat in silence until the pounding in her head eased and she opened her eyes to look at him.

"Gabs, I'm sorry."

"It's not your fault." Gabrielle smiled. He was the only one who called her that. The only one she'd allow to call her that since her parent's death. After six months of not hearing it, the sound of his voice saying her name reminded her of how much he meant to her.

"No. Not about last night," Peter said. "About last time we saw each other. Who knows how out of control I would be if you hadn't called me out. You were right. I wasn't ready to hear the truth, but you were right."

The deep emotion in his voice broke through the remaining walls she'd erected as force never could have. Peter had accepted his mental state back then hadn't been healthy—he'd accepted he needed help. That was all she'd ever asked.

Peter gave her a hesitant smile. "And sorry I broke your phone. I needed to let you know that—I never want you to be afraid of me."

Gabrielle's chin lifted to get a closer look at him. His bright blue eyes were clear and focused. He was different. How much of that was the past six months and how much had happened over the course of their six-year friendship? No longer a skinny, lanky boy, he'd filled out his frame. With his lean, strong body and well-muscled arms, he could have walked among the frat boys and fit in just fine. His were arms she trusted to protect her—or used to. His red hair was combed back from his face, but loose strands danced in the wind, tickling at his ears.

The flush of freckles across his nose and smattering over his arms kept him familiar. They belonged to the twelve-year-old boy who had let her sleep in his treehouse when her foster father was angry.

She didn't know what to say. Or even how to say it. She saw all she needed in those beautiful eyes. And she wanted to sink into his arms and let him shelter her. Of all the people and places in this world, Peter was her home.

Instead of holding her, Peter looked down and shuffled his feet against the grass. "I started going to a psychiatrist. The folks made me after you ran out of the basement screaming at me. They put me on meds. I blamed you for a while . . . but you had every reason to be concerned. I thought I was in perfect control of my mental state. I wasn't. Avoiding meds never did me any good."

"Peter." His name rolled off her tongue, sugar sweet.

"I think it's the best thing that ever happened—to my parents anyhow. They love having a mental disorder to pin on me. It's like they're cool kids in the put-upon parents' club. Like now they can blame how messed up I am on faulty wiring rather than their crappy parenting."

Gabrielle leaned against him, resting her head on his shoulder. The now-dull throbbing in her head faded more as she allowed her eyes to close. His shirt smelled of cologne, but his skin held the wonderful scent of soap and him.

"I wasn't scared of you, Peter. Never. I was scared for you and of losing you." *The last parts are true, but that first part is a lie.*

She shivered, not wanting to remember his frenzied face as he shook her shoulders. Not wanting to recall how his eyes had darted around, landing on things that weren't there—except in his mind.

"We good then?" he asked.

She looked up at him and felt the leftover fear from the night before loosen like muscles under a massage therapist's touch. "We're good."

"That takes care of me. Now you. What happened last night?"

Just tell him the truth. "I should have known you wouldn't let that go. I was at a party. Cops showed up, but I wound up with a ride home. No problems."

"If you aren't ready to talk about it, you could say that." Peter wrapped his arm around her shoulders.

"I tried that with Cinder. It didn't go well."

"I'm not her. I get it, Gabs. Sometimes you need to deal with something before you can open up and share. Just know that I'm here."

Gabrielle snuggled in under his arm—glad that his physical presence grounded her. Peter placed his chin atop her head and played with strands of her hair. They lingered under the tree, safely tucked together, and talked until students dismissed from classes began to flood the quad.

When Gabrielle stood, Peter scrambled up and pointed at her arm where her duster had rolled up.

"You got a new tattoo."

Gabrielle ran her finger over the spot. A gate—pearly white and gold. It was for him. She'd feared she'd lost him, and this was the only way she had known to keep a piece of him with her. The tattoos told her life story, and he deserved a place in that.

Peter stroked his finger over the gate. "I like it. It's more cheerful than the others."

"St. Peter and the pearly gates." She blushed and pulled the duster's sleeve down over the tattoo.

Peter smiled. "I'd always let you in, Gabs."

People started to trickle out of the surrounding buildings. The passage of time became acutely present in Gabrielle's mind. Her next class started in just a few minutes.

"I have to make this next class," Gabrielle said, carefully avoiding Peter's beautiful blue eyes. *I'd give anything to stay here with you.* "See you later?"

"Yeah. Call me. I'm using my phone again."

Gabrielle grinned as she spun and headed off to class. In all the distraction the night before, his responding to her text hadn't fully hit. Last time she saw him, he was too convinced the cops were tracking him through electronic signals to touch his phone. In fact, he'd freaked out and broken hers when she'd tried to use it.

She'd hoped his extreme reaction was the drugs, but her life was too filled with psychiatric institutions to miss that it could be something else, something he'd been showing signs of for years: schizophrenia. A scary word, a word without a cure. And yet, he was doing better. He had a handle on himself.

Peter made anything seem possible.

Either way, what mattered was he was back. His cracks hadn't spread too far. *How would I even survive if he broke?*

The whistling voice whispered in her ear, *"I'm not broken. I'm here to help you."*

Gabrielle dead-stopped on the path.

No, no, no.

The voice purred inside her, *"Peter can't protect you, not like I can. You asked for my help, and I'm here."*

"No!" Gabrielle ran forward a few steps, knowing she couldn't escape *her.*

A passing student gave her a dubious glance and moved onto the grass to pass her. The strands of normalcy frayed around her and broke, leaving her tumbling into the dark of her mind.

"He's not going to make it better," the voice said.

Gabrielle pulled out her phone. Her hand shook so badly she had trouble punching her code in to unlock the screen. Visions were one thing—a nasty part of her traumatized life—but the voice intruding on the real world?

Michael picked up on the first ring. His hello was cheerful. His night must have gone well.

I can't tell him. I can't ruin everything again.

"Gabrielle?" Michael asked. "Say something."

"Hi." Gabrielle stared out at the road past the angled pathways on the Parrington Lawn. The dotted yellow line carried her eyes into the distance. *Think of something to say. Something other than the visions and the voice. Something that won't destroy him.*

"You okay?"

A rusty blue pickup crested the horizon, driving along the road toward her—blue like Joe's truck. Darkness whirled up, and she was running through the woods. Her lungs burned for air, but something chased her. Her hands were missing, and the stumps bled. Cracks led up from the stumps, spreading with each step. *I'll never make it.*

She let out a sob as the street and the blue pickup came back into view.

Gabrielle clutched the phone. It was her only tether—a connection to Michael. He would make it better. He had to. "I'm scared. The visions are back. They won't stop, and I heard *her*. I'm sorry. I'm so sorry."

"Where are you? I'm coming to get you." Michael's voice dropped, sounding strained, desperate.

The blue truck slowed, pulling toward the curb.

The world isn't seeking to harm me. I trust myself to know the difference between real threats and fe—. Her mind refused to finish the affirmation. She didn't believe a word of it. The world was filled with danger, and she very much doubted good things were out there for her.

The voice whispered its offer again, *"I can help you."*

Gabrielle couldn't face Joe. The edge of the abyss reached for her, and she knew she was going over the edge. At least with the offered help, she'd be falling with a hand to catch her. *Yes, make it stop. Make him go away.*

Please, help me.

"I'm sorry. I'm so very sorry," Gabrielle said, but the request was made now.

Michael said something else, but she didn't hear. The world flashed red and then black. From a great distance, his voice reached her before fading into a buzz of nothingness. Like peaceful static, it rolled over her. Gabrielle let herself fade. As the jumble of signals ate away at her, she welcomed the oblivion.

five

Cole shoved his face into the stream of water from the showerhead. He allowed the comforting spray to absorb him, washing away the stress of the workday. Monday had been hard to face after his long night with Michael, but he'd made it through and back home.

He wondered what Michael's day had been like.

Coffee at one in the morning—bad plan. I'm not in my twenties anymore.

He lowered his face and watched the water swirl around the metal drain. The shower's frosted glass door made a haze of the rest of his bathroom.

No, I'm not in my twenties. But Michael is.

He smiled. It didn't matter how slow he had been today at work. The night had been worth it. Michael had finally opened up.

They might actually be able to turn their fling into a relationship.

Don't get too worked up about it. But god, would it be nice to have someone for emotional support.

"Daddy. Daddy!" Isa shouted, her voice echoing in his tiled bathroom.

Cole looked up to find her blurred, powder-pink form right

outside the glass. He grinned and waited for Yolanda's yell. It didn't take long.

"Leave your dad alone, Isa." Yolanda's voice was dulled by the walls between them. The nanny's accent obscured the words further. He couldn't make out her next words but pieced the scraps he caught into a meaning. "I'm almost finished with dinner. Go to your bathroom and wash your hands."

"I'll join you in a minute, chipmunk," Cole said.

"Come right away," Isa said before bolting out of the bathroom. She left the door gaping wide.

Time to get moving.

He'd made it home that morning in time for Frosted Flakes with Isa—a special "sugar cereal" treat they rarely allowed the four year old. But they'd barely had twenty minutes together before he'd rushed off to work. After struggling through the day, he'd headed home early. As the duty officer for the week, he knew anything really important would find him at home anyway.

Cole rushed through the rest of the shower. Still dripping and only wrapped in a towel, he darted across the space to close the bathroom door for a little privacy.

With the shower off, Isa's excited yammering trickled wordlessly through to him. This whirl was punctuated by Yolanda's laughter and clipped speech. Cole dressed while listening to the music of his family's voice.

It never failed to amaze him that they felt more like a family now than when Joan had lived here. Even Cole's sister had started coming around a few times a month—she'd never gotten on with Joan.

But Joan's back. And Isa has been so excited to see her mother. If only Joan weren't angling for more than visits. Why worry them? There's no reason for the mediator to side with Joan.

Except that Joan is Isa's mother and has all the money in the world.

But his ex wasn't being reasonable in her proposed parenting plan. No way he was giving her joint custody. He'd welcome her taking a larger role in Isa's life. He'd even offered overnights as long as Yolanda accompanied Isa, but Joan wanted what she wanted—and he was pretty sure it wasn't about Isa at all; she was getting back at him.

As Yolanda would say, "Just goes to show you, Mr. Montez, you can't fix people. They're gonna be what they're gonna be."

Cole exited the bathroom with his hair still wet and walked barefoot down the carpeted hall. A glance at the dining room showed him an empty table.

Giggles emitted from the family room. Cole grinned and headed over. Isa sat at a small princess table against the far wall to eat her meal. Her blonde hair, inherited from her mother, danced in its pigtails as she leaned in toward her spoonful of applesauce. Both she and Yolanda sat in the miniature chairs that came with the table. The tiled room around them was filled with scattered toys, and the countertop at the far end of the space gave a clear view into the kitchen.

Cole's smile widened as Yolanda shifted on the tiny seat, trying to make it accommodate her adult size. *Lucky she isn't overweight, she'd never be able to do that. Hell, she's lucky her back still lets her.*

"You didn't save a chair for me?" Cole gave Isa an exaggerated pout.

"I get you chair," Isa cried, her brown eyes wide with concern, and her long, blonde hair whipped around as she searched.

Cole and Yolanda repressed laughter unsuccessfully as Isa peeled from the room to retrieve a full-sized chair from the dining room.

"Here you go, Daddy." Isa grinned before she registered their laughter. She narrowed her eyes and planted her hand on her hip.

Reminds me of her mother.

"What's for dinner?" Cole asked before Isa could work up to being solidly offended.

"Quesadillas, Mr. Montez." Yolanda stood up. Her black hair was tucked up in a bun, and a red kerchief was tied around her head. A birthmark spread up her neck and tipped her chin like a tiny beard—but that was hardly her most noticeable feature.

Though they had faded since Cole first met her in the ER, the burn scars that puckered up over one cheek and down her chest to cover one arm were what caught people's attention. Those scars were what made people look away on the street.

"I can get my own," he said. "Don't get up."

Yolanda was already up, but the bags under her eyes made his guilt particularly prickly. *If I'd come home at a decent hour . . .*

"No. No. Daddy, I got you a chair."

"Sit," Yolanda said in a tone that brooked no argument.

Cole shrugged and sat, his knees too high to fit under the table. Isa burbled about something. The words passed by him, leaving a flurry of color in their wake, something about unicorns and taking turns on a rainbow slide.

The three of them ate together, though most of the conversation was stolen by Isa. When she finished, Cole gathered up the dishes and sent Yolanda and Isa off to watch some TV. He set the dishes in the sink and turned.

A stack of letters waited for him on the breakfast bar. Mostly unopened bills, but that didn't matter—he knew what they said. But the thick packet on top might be something he couldn't handle. Legal documents from Joan's lawyer. What had she added to her demands this time?

Damn you, Joan.

He couldn't last much longer. The house had been purchased under the assumption of two incomes to cover the mortgage. If he sold it now, though, it would weaken his case in court. But not as much as if the bank foreclosed on him.

And he couldn't fire Yolanda. She was family, plus no one else would take her in. Getting a job would be hard enough looking like she did. But once prospective employers discovered she'd been accused of the arson that killed her husband, no one would hire her to work in their home.

But Yolanda was a good woman who deserved a second chance. But, he knew, he worked for a system that didn't give out chances for free. Cole worked with enough bad people on a day-to-day basis to know she wasn't one of them, and she was someone who needed and deserved more than the system could ever give her.

six

A DIM LIGHT SHONE OVERHEAD. A SINGLE BARE BULB, HANGING FROM A ceiling that was just a little too low. Boxes lined the walls, and old furniture filled in much of the floor space. Gabrielle knew this room. She hadn't been in it since she was a child, and her mind spun, trying to decide how she'd gotten here.

But I'm not here, she thought as she looked down at her arms. They were the arms of a child, and in them lay the doll. This was before she became Gabrielle, back when she was still Gabi. *I'm not here, but I want to be here.*

She had a sense that where she actually was, wasn't as pleasant.

Gabrielle leaned into the memory. It was a soft one, a memory she was not afraid to face.

The doll sagged in Gabi's arms. Only the porcelain of her head had any real weight. Gabi wrapped her pointer finger around the doll's delicate hands. She was so fragile, so lost and stranded in the modern world. Despite her yellowed dress and myriad of cracks running like tattoos over her skin, she was precious.

Gabi felt strong and protective holding her.

"I can't believe you touch that thing," Michael said from behind her. His thirteen-year-old face was sprinkled with acne, and he was glowering. Still, Gabrielle felt a rush of fondness at seeing him treat her so roughly—this was before he became convinced she was breakable.

He'd been searching through boxes for some "Groo" comic he used to have. He'd gotten in a yelling match with Dad where he accused Dad of throwing his things away. Mom had cut in, insisting she'd accidentally packed the comic away in the garage.

Mom hadn't. Both Gabrielle and Gabi knew that.

But Michael's fruitless search for *Groo the Wanderer* gave her an excuse to play with the doll. Mom said she was too rough with the antique. But Gabi knew better. Dolls were meant to be played with, to be loved.

I'll love you, Gabi promised internally, staring into the doll's faded brown eyes. Mom said they were faded brown. They looked yellow. "She's not creepy when the lights are on."

"You're creepy sometimes." Michael laughed and ruffled her hair in an obnoxious older brother gesture Gabi secretly loved. Gabrielle missed the simple comradery between them.

"I think she's lonely," Gabi said, her little chin jutting out.

"*It* is a doll."

Gabi was old enough to grin at that. She'd caught the contradiction. "How can she be creepy if she's just a doll!"

"You're a brat. It is creepy. That doesn't mean I actually believe it's dangerous. It just gives me a weird feeling." He leaned closer to her, smile just a little too nice for Gabrielle's taste. "You know they used to make dolls with real hair? They took it from the little girls who owned the dolls. That could be from great grandma Tessie, kind of like touching a corpse's hair."

Gabrielle knew that factoid was true, but also that their porcelain doll hadn't had human hair. It didn't even feel the same, but Gabi hadn't known the difference. *I wish I still knew this version of Michael. This is what normal looks like. The small cruelties, the innocence of it.*

"Nu uh!" Gabi yelled at him and cradled the doll closer, hoping

Michael didn't notice she was avoiding touching the thin, patchy hair. "I like her, and if you're gonna be a meany pants, you can leave."

"Okay." Michael's eyes gleamed, and Gabrielle knew what was coming next.

He's going to suggest the game.

It was a game she remembered playing with Michael in that dingy garage. She'd called it the "If You're Not Afraid Game." They'd played it once when Gabi claimed not to be afraid of his bloody hand after Michael jabbed himself with a nail. They'd played it with the corpse of a mouse they found under a box. And they'd played it with the doll multiple times.

The basics of the game were simple, Michael turned off the lights and Gabi had to climb the stairs to the main house in the dark without running. If she ran or screamed, she was deemed afraid, and Michel turned the lights on. But then he called her a chicken.

Gabrielle had never told him, but sometimes Gabi played the game alone with just the doll and her gleaming yellow eyes.

Her gut clenched. This wasn't right. She didn't belong in this memory.

Gabi set the doll delicately back on its shelf. Next time, she'd come alone, and they would play longer. They would play pretend, and the doll would tell Gabi things about her great grandmother Tessie's times. Gabi needed to research the facts first, so she'd know what the doll needed to say, but she already had a plan in place when the lights went out.

No, Gabrielle thought. *No, I can't be in the dark with her.*

Wake up!

And she did. Her vision cleared, revealing a new scene to her. And then she doubted she'd woken up at all. Gabrielle sat on the floor. Blood was everywhere.

Gabrielle screamed and used her feet to propel herself backward. The fingers of her right hand stuck together. The room was splashed with red, though much of it had already dried into brown. She lifted her hand; partially dry blood covered her fingers.

Gabrielle rubbed her eyes with the side of her hand in an attempt to clear her sight, but when she lowered her hands, the room was still dotted with a crimson hallucination. Any moment she'd see her mom's dead body and know this was all in her mind.

Her left hand squeezed. She held a hard object.

No.

She looked down, terrified of what she'd discover clasped in her fingers.

But there was no gleam of metal—just her phone. A voice droned on, the words indistinguishable. Even under the veil of color, she recognized the snake habitat behind the ratty couch. Words couldn't penetrate the fear threatening to overwhelm her. This was Joe's house.

No. It can't be. I can't be here. I'm at school.

She turned to the right. The snake's cage was empty. The world seemed to slow around Gabrielle, with only the steady beat of her heart guiding her. She sank into the calm stillness of that, knowing if she allowed herself to think, to feel, she might shatter. Instead, she viewed the room around her with detachment, a haze of distance provided by her heartbeat.

This could still be a hallucination. Maybe nothing bad had happened. Gabrielle lifted the phone to her ear.

"Hello? Ma'am?" The voice reached her under a buzz of sound. The connection was bad, cutting in and out, but not disconnecting completely.

"I'll call you back." Gabrielle reached toward the snake's cage but retracted her fingers.

"Please, stay on the line."

Gabrielle hung up. Her phone had two bars, jumping up to three briefly. She had to pray it would make another call. She struggled to order her thoughts up inside the bubble of calm. The last thing she recalled in the real world was standing on the sidewalk watching a blue truck drive toward her. She'd been on the phone with Michael at the time. How had she materialized in Joe's house? And why was the room so dark? It hadn't even been noon. She called Michael. The air in her lungs was thin, and no matter how much she gulped, her chest burned—demanding more oxygen.

"Gabrielle!" Michael picked up on the first ring. In the background, she heard the murmur of a laugh track from a television. He was at home. Of course he was; it was dark. "Do you know how worried I was? I drove to the U after you called, but I couldn't find you. It's been almost twenty-four hours."

"It has?" Judging from the darkness outside Joe's window, it was just before dawn. That would make it Tuesday morning. She'd never lost so much time before. The shocked calm cracked, and she took in a desperate gasp of air. *Please let me still be hallucinating.*

"Gabrielle, where are you? I'm coming to get you."

"You can't." Gabrielle tucked her knees under her chin. The fragile calm engulfing her threatened to shatter. "Blood. Michael, it's everywhere. It's on my hands."

"Are you hurt?" His voice hinged on panic.

"No." *But I think I hurt someone. It's a lot of blood.* She rubbed her eyes again, hoping to clear the vision. The stickiness transferred from her hands to her eyelids, clumping in her lashes. The blood remained, and her artificial calm wavered.

"Take deep breaths. It'll fade. We'll get you in to Dr. White. These visions shouldn't be seeping over into your life. Where are you?"

"I . . ." Gabrielle braved the trail of splattered blood with her eyes. It wasn't real. She'd find her mother's body there and know the carnage was in her head.

Slowly she turned, observing more of the area. She saw through the doorway into the bedroom. The crumpled form inside was too big to fit her hallucinations. *That's not Mom.*

Gabrielle stood and crept forward until she had a better view. The twelve-foot snake lay curled under the window as if waiting for the sun. She focused on the body on the floor by the foot of the bed. The shirt was in tatters, ripped open by multiple slashes, and blood soaked the material against his skin. Two deep stab wounds pene-trated near the shoulder blades. But the face . . .

A squeak-like sob escaped her lips.

Beneath the splatter, it was Joe. His dead, hematoma-stained eyes seemed to follow her as she took one more step in his direction. The bloodshot edges of his sclera screamed into her mind, telling her to run. Raw patches spread from the corners of his mouth and matching rub-burn marks marred his wrists.

The python watched her with cold, black eyes.

"Gabrielle!" Michael's voice drew her back to the phone clutched in her hands.

"No," she whispered. "It's real. You can't help me this time. I think I killed him."

"Don't say that! Don't say that to anyone, you hear?"

She nodded, and a choked whimper escaped her throat. *Not saying it won't change the facts. It'll look like I did this, but I didn't. I couldn't have.*

"Even if they ask," Michael said, "you don't say that and you don't admit *anything*. Where are you?"

Gabrielle could barely force her voice out from under the weight on her chest. "I don't know. Joe's house. I don't know how I got here."

"I'm coming."

Gabrielle's eyes flicked to the window and the woods beyond, then back to Joe's filmy gaze. The long pause that followed burned through Gabrielle.

"How do you know where I am?" Gabrielle stumbled away from the body without breaking eye contact with Joe.

"Let it go. I'm on my way. Tell me what you see."

"Snake's cage, couch, snake, corpse. The fridge is open, and some of the beers spilled out." She crept closer to Joe and peered into the corners of his bedroom, leaning to keep her distance. Somewhere in her lurked a fear that his hand would reach out and grab her, pulling her into complete insanity. "It doesn't look good for me, does it?"

Then out the window, Gabrielle noticed a movement inside Cinder's car. Bewilderment at why Cinder's car was there was buried under the surge in her blood caused by the swift movement. It was hard to see much with only a vague pre-dawn light illuminating the area. Still, whatever was in the car seemed to be too small to be a person. An animal? Gabrielle moved across the blood-soaked floor to the glass, ignoring Michael as he rattled on. Out of the back windshield shone the eyes—golden and as wide as a baby's.

She's not real. She never was. I imagined her and her power. She was just a coping mechanism.

"I see *her*," Gabrielle whispered and then let the phone fall. There was the answer. Gabrielle hadn't committed murder—*she* had.

In the distance, sirens wailed.

seven

A RINGING DRAGGED COLE FROM HIS DREAMS. HIS BLANKETS WERE TANGLED around his legs, and in the dim predawn light, he struggled to connect to reality and not the fuzzy residue of dreaming. Sleep reached out to reclaim him, but the ringing continued. Cole's eyes sought the noise out, only to find the duty phone on the bedside table.

The glow of the cell demanded he wake up.

Cole fumbled for the phone and answered, "Detective Montez here."

The voice on the other end bleated out a whole situation he only half caught. The important bit he heard—there'd been a murder. There would be no breakfast with Isa this morning. Suppressing a yawn, Cole told them he was on his way and hopped out of bed.

After pulling on a button-up shirt and dark jeans, he grabbed his gun and holstered it at his side. He peeked in on Isa and then went out to the kitchen. The coffeemaker hadn't clicked on yet for the morning, and he didn't have time to stop. He'd have to do this sans caffeine. He flipped his prewritten message on the fridge—the one that told Yolanda that work had called him out.

Was this another thing Joan could use against him in mediation?

He worked a lot. He knew that. But he had to make money somehow. Nice for Joan that she didn't have to worry about that, nor did she have to defend her sexuality. Her infidelity had been a poignant point in the divorce, but it didn't matter now.

Not that Michael wasn't worth a little bit of trouble. He just wished the trouble didn't have so much to do with gender.

For the most part, Cole strove not to think about how sexuality complicated things. Officially it didn't matter in court who he slept with. But unofficially? Some caseworkers would take any excuse to thrust the knife in if they thought you were a *deviant*. He had worked with the system enough to know for sure.

That's why he'd transferred out of Seattle PD, the precinct he'd served in during his marriage to Joan. Seattle PD's reputation was anything but stellar, and nothing in Cole's experience contradicted that. King County Sherriff's Office had a reputation for being a bit more understanding and, in a way, he'd hoped to be able to be a little more honest even at work.

Now's not the time for that. Not with Joan grasping for primary custody. *But I won't hide forever. Kids learn from actions, and I don't want mine to say that who I am is shameful.*

Or that I'm a coward.

Cole grabbed his tan bomber jacket off a hook on the wall and slipped out the kitchen door. A light drizzle kissed his face. Above him, the clouds hung low and threatening. He wondered if Michael was up yet.

Ducking out of the rain, Cole climbed into his car and flipped on his police radio. Before he could get his key in the ignition, his cellphone rang. No choice on ignoring that call—it was from the sheriff's office.

"You got more info for me?" Cole asked. He dialed the radio's volume down so it wouldn't blast when he turned the key. "Just hopped in my car. I'm on my way in."

"Don't come in," the dispatch officer said. "Go straight out to the scene. There should already be some squad cars on their way, but it sounds like a volatile situation."

"Just shoot me the address." Cole sighed and rubbed his forehead. Money and murder—too little of one and too much of the other.

"Get out there quickly."

Cole w followed the course set by the glowing map of his GPS, which took him away from the Redmond city center toward Snoqualmie. This early in the morning, avoiding freeways made sense; Redmond–Fall City Road wasn't in deadlock, and it had few lights or major intersections. The evergreens and fields that lined the winding two-lane road would have made it a great drive for thinking if he didn't know he was heading toward a crime scene.

The clouds overhead broke up as he drove. Dawn brought a dim light to the scene—no vivid colors reached over the top of the evergreen trees, and only a slight glow of pink let Cole witness any of the morning's majesty. He wondered if Michael ever watched the sun rise.

No matter how hard he tried, Michael kept resurfacing in his thoughts. *He has me panting after him like a hormonal teenager with a crush.*

Cole made a turn, and his tires crunched over loose gravel. Most of the road was dirt, the rocks having been beaten into the soil over the years, but there was enough grit to give the long drive a bumpy feel. Cole checked his GPS. *Remote place.*

Around the next bend, the gravel ended in a driveway. Four patrol cars ringed the majority of the area, and police tape was being hung. The yellow tape and flashing lights weren't the only things to greet him as he climbed out of his car. A young cop—looked like a kid who wasn't old enough to see a crime scene—dashed over to him.

Cole flashed his badge, and the kid relaxed.

"Where's the incident commander?" Cole asked.

"I guess me for now. Nobody else has arrived to take over."

Meaning Cole got to work with a kid who had no idea what was going on. With four police cars parked there, this kid was the one in charge? He hated bureaucracy. Also, this probably meant the crime scene wasn't properly secured.

"What can you tell me?" Cole asked.

The exterior was normal enough for one of these isolated homes. No evidence of a crime. Nothing out of place, just a bunch of things that had been discarded to rust months or years before. Cole guessed the actual crime had taken place inside the house. Two cars were parked in the driveway: a blue pickup that looked like it belonged there and a red, two-door Hyundai with a University of Washington bumper sticker.

Was some college girl lured up here and raped? Murdered?

"Owner of the house is in there; someone cut him up. The girl won't talk, and what she *has* said makes fuck-all sense."

Cole's shoes crunched over the gravel until he saw the woman the cop had referred to sitting on the front stoop. Hunched over and head buried in her hands, she rocked back and forth. Blood was smeared on her white arms and on her dress—but no obvious splatter that would imply she had been doing any stabbing.

"Any info on either of them?" Cole asked as he ducked under the police line. Then he paused, just out of the girl's hearing.

"Well, the owner of the house, Joseph Bey, has had the cops up here several times on misdemeanor charges, and a girl came in recently with a complaint against him. Nothing that stuck. As for the girl on the steps, we don't know who she is. The car is registered to a Lucinda Grange, but that isn't her."

"Car stolen?"

"Maybe. Lucinda Grange reported it missing last night. But this girl had a key."

That's all but meaningless. She could have swiped it. How green is this kid? "Anything else?"

"Animal control has been called in. There's a python loose in the house."

"A python?" Cole glanced at the rundown shack of a house. There were always complications, but a python was a new one.

"Yes, sir. Mr. Bey kept it as a pet."

"Is the scene secured?"

"Not yet."

"A python? Really?"

"A twelve-footer."

Stupid. Joseph was lucky his pet hadn't killed him. Cole couldn't comprehend why people insisted on getting dangerous wild animals as pets.

"Anything else?" Cole asked.

"Yeah, the girl hasn't said a word since she called 911."

He'd better tread lightly. This might be his key-witness if she wasn't the killer.

Cole nodded to the young cop and crossed the rest of the drive to where the girl sat. Had Joseph tried to rape her? That could be motive. *Best look at the evidence before I start formulating guesses.*

"Get her into a squad car," Cole commanded the kid. "We'll need to ask her some questions down at the station."

The girl looked up. The set of her eyes and her nose was familiar somehow, but Cole couldn't think where he knew her from. Pretty thing, though.

"Are you injured?" he asked.

She shivered like a wounded animal. Sympathy he couldn't suppress and couldn't let himself use welled up. *She's just waiting to be put out of her misery.*

"Are you hurt?" he asked again.

The girl peered into his face, a quizzical expression dispelling some of the blank shock from her eyes. She took in a deep breath as if readying herself. "No," she said. "Joe's dead."

Cole forced his expression to remain neutral. He didn't know what had made the girl break her silence, but he needed to take advantage of it while he could.

The young officer approached her and offered her a hand up. The girl looked at him as if his arm meant to bite her. She'd just been through a huge trauma, but a reaction like that implied either she had been raped or that she had been dealing with residual trauma long before this morning.

She looked directly at Cole. "You're the detective on the case?"

Odd statement. Too calm. Too familiar. Unless she had been through something like this before. He had to get a look at the scene, secured or not.

"Yes. I'm Detective Montez," Cole said to the girl. "I'll need to question you about Joseph, but for now, I need you to go with this nice officer while I look inside. Once the police photographer gets here and captures some shots, I'll see about finding you some fresh clothes."

"That won't change anything." Her voice was vacant. Shock did that to people. But this seemed like more. She sounded defeated. She stood, though, and let the young officer take her arm and guide her off the steps.

On her shoulder blades, between the torn straps of her dress, rose the tops of tattooed wings. Black lines cut jagged edges through the feathers as if they were made of porcelain, ready to shatter. They were different from Michael's snow-white wings, and yet all too similar. Cole grabbed her arm to stop her from leaving.

"What's your name?" he asked.

The girl looked at him, her eyes a honey brown. Blood speckled her pale cheeks like freckles, making her look even younger. A brief, fragile smile flashed across her face. "I know you," she said. "I've seen your picture."

The young cop's eyebrows drew together, but he said nothing.

Shit. Shit. Shit. "What's your name?"

"Gabrielle Cross."

eight

Cole stared at Gabrielle. Michael's sister. *I shouldn't be here. I can't be the investigating detective on this crime. I'll just get her through today, then I'll tap out.*

"And you're Detective Cole Montez," she said. "I didn't recognize your last name."

He dropped her arm and noticed under the smeared blood were scratches. Like someone had clawed at her. Defensive wounds. *I can't be here.*

But who else can I trust? She needs someone who isn't out to crucify her. Yolanda had that same wounded look when I interviewed her in the hospital. If I hadn't been on that case, where would she be now?

Maybe Gabrielle didn't do it. What I need to do is gather information, find out what happened.

"I have to go look at the body," Cole said. "Officer"—Cole glanced at the kid's badge—"Lewis, call for another detective to come out. Request Sera."

Cole didn't like working with a partner, but Gabrielle being here changed everything. When he had a minute and more facts, he'd have to decide if he could stay on the case at all. There was no law against him doing so, but he knew the sheriff would take him off in a heartbeat if he found out Cole was personally involved with the lead suspect's brother. He didn't even want to consider the disciplinary actions.

He ascended the stoop and hurried inside. The first thing he noted was the empty snake habitat in a cage by the wall—the lid pulled askew and a smear of red that might be a handprint on the glass.

He thought, *We'll try to get fingerprints from that* warred with, *Where is the snake?*

Stepping carefully to avoid compromising the scene, he took a few quick snapshots with his phone, though he knew a photographer would be there soon to take official photos.

The trail to the body was easy to follow. Bloody handprints traced the wall—Gabrielle's, judging by the height. She would have been stumbling out of the bedroom. The red splotches were concentrated around the doorway, and Cole picked his way over, snapping pictures of the bits that interested him.

Inside the bedroom, a man's body was laid out on the floor, propped up against the foot of the bed. The python curled on the windowsill was covered in blood—presumably Joe's. But it seemed to be a safe distance away, for now. He turned his attention fully to the body.

The positioning looked intentional, not as if he'd fallen. In fact, there was a trail of red from the window, indicating he'd been dragged. Several stab wounds were evident on his chest. A glance showed no evidence of a knife. Cole moved closer to take more pictures.

The victim's face had been turned toward the doorway. His glazed eyes fixed open. His eyes were reddened by hematomas and bulged like someone who'd been strangled, but Cole saw no marks on his throat. Though there were marks around his mouth and wrists that implied he'd been bound and struggling.

No evidence of whatever was used to bind him. Why would the killer take those off postmortem?

If a slender girl like Gabrielle had wanted to overpower the deceased, binding him first would have been extremely useful. But how would she have bound him? Maybe some sort of sex game? Then he wouldn't have struggled until the murderer entered the scene. In which case, Gabrielle had likely seen the killer.

The killer couldn't be her. It couldn't be Michael's little sister.

The snake twitched, and Cole stepped back, luckily avoiding any of the blood splatter. His mind knew it was a safe distance away; his rapidly beating heart didn't seem to agree. But he couldn't let that rule him. Animal control would be there soon, so Cole wanted a few shots from a safe distance that showed where the snake had been found. He was moving to a different angle when a shout from outside halted him.

Cole's hand flew to his sidearm.

"Elle! Where is she? Elle?" came the booming voice.

Cole's hand tightened around his gun in its holster, and he hurried as fast as he could without compromising anything to the front door.

Just outside the police tape line was Michael—but not the calm, smiling Michael he knew. *Crud. How'd he get here so soon? No one should've contacted Gabrielle's family yet.*

"That's my fucking sister! You will—"

The cop in front of Michael interrupted him. Cole missed the words, but he didn't trust the police officers were calm. Not with the way one of them physically held Michael back and two more had their hands on their belts, waiting to draw.

Cole and Michael had been sparring partners in a gym for months; Michael could take almost anyone in a brawl. He didn't need that kind of assault charge hitting him now, but Cole was more afraid that if Michael tried to throw a punch, he'd wind up getting shot.

He released his gun and endeavored to keep a steady pace across the drive. He couldn't afford to seem excited. *Keep it impersonal.*

What do I even hope to accomplish here? If his sister killed that man, I can't let her get away with it. But I can make sure she's treated fairly and not railroaded into taking the fall for a crime that doesn't fit what really happened.

"Calm down, boys." His voice came out shrill in his own ears. He made eye contact with each of the cops in turn but avoided Michael's eyes. "I know him. He's a social worker who helped me with a case a few months back. Let me talk to him."

Michael glared at all of them but allowed Cole to lead him off to the side—outside the police line. Walking with Cole was the only difference he noted in Michael's behavior toward him versus the other officers. When Michael finished doling out glares, his eyes never left the house, even though he had to crane to see it as he walked.

He's not going to be able to hear anything I have to say in this state, let alone process it.

Before they reached Michael's car, Michael stopped. "I can't! I've got to go to her, Cole. You can't keep me away."

"Stop. You've dealt with enough crimes to know how they work." Cole folded his arms, planting himself between Michael and the house. "That's a crime scene. At best, Gabrielle is a witness, and at worst…"

"Are you arresting her?" Michael leaned forward, the stance threatening.

He could probably take me down. But the anger in his eyes and stance seemed more defensive, as if it overlaid tears. Cole guessed he could talk Michael down.

"Back off, Michael." Cole returned Michael's glare.

Michael's face contorted, as if struggling between one action and another, and then he took a step back.

"We're not arresting her at this point." *But it doesn't look good.* "If you'll wait over there"—Cole pointed at Michael's car—"I'll let you see her as soon as I can. We'll be taking her to headquarters to get an interview. But you can pick her up there."

"She'd better be okay when I do."

The threat in Michael's voice sent a chill through Cole. For the first time, Cole wondered if there was the potential for a killer in him.

nine

THE INTERROGATION ROOM BORE LITTLE RESEMBLANCE TO THE ONE Gabrielle recalled being in as a child. And she'd had plenty of time to inspect it as she waited for one of the detectives to return and continue interrogating her. White-walled with a tan table, the only darkness in the room was the one-way mirror. The table sat with its short side to the window and three chairs lined up moving outward along the longer sides. Gabrielle sat in the corner, with one shoulder uncomfortably near the one-way glass. But it still wasn't as unnerving as what she'd expected—all metal and shadows.

Gabrielle twisted her T-shirt in her hands. It was an old shirt; the police must have asked Michael to bring her clothes. Unless he kept them in his car? She hadn't seen him since leaving the crime scene. She wasn't sure she wanted to after seeing the pure anguish on his face as she was driven away, covered in blood, from the crime scene that morning.

She doubted she'd ever get her other clothes back—not that she wanted them. They would be tucked away in evidence with all the other physical tidbits they'd gotten from her. Including gratuitous pictures of the cuts on her hands. She knew what they were called, defensive wounds. Though who knew how she'd gotten them with

Joe tied up. Gabrielle rubbed at the spot on her arm where they'd drawn blood, her wrist hitting the baggy fabric of her shirt.

Michael wouldn't keep clothes in his car, would he? Is his life that centered on getting me out of messes? And I let it be that way. Covered in blood, I called him and got him mixed up in this.

And it was a huge mess. Anything that landed her in an interrogation room wasn't something she wanted Michael involved in.

Gabrielle had been answering Cole's questions all day, and she was already sick of them. How many times could she explain that she didn't remember anything?

She pushed her chair as close as she could to the one-way mirror on the wall and tried to stare through. Was Cole in there? Or the other detective who'd showed up for this interview? Gabrielle had heard the woman's name, but it didn't stick. She had shown up at the crime scene late and hung back through most of the questioning at the station.

Why'd Cole even call the other detective in?

Before Gabrielle could get too lost in these thoughts, Cole reentered, this time alone. Though that didn't guarantee the severe, female detective wasn't behind the glass watching. If so, she was standing back because Gabrielle couldn't make anything out.

Detective Montez slid into the seat across from her. He put a folder on the table—thankfully closed, as the pictures and information inside were surely distasteful.

He was an attractive man in spite of a little graying at his temples and a few laugh lines around the eyes. Even under the circumstances, Gabrielle understood why Michael had been so excited about this guy. From the dark, thick hair and the deep skin tone, she guessed he might have some Middle Eastern heritage thrown in. He was buff too. If she hadn't already known, she would've accurately guessed they met at one of the many gyms or dojos that Michael went to. Cole definitely looked like a bodybuilder.

At least it's me sitting here—not Michael. Being interrogated by Cole would destroy him.

Only Cole's brown eyes showed any softness. She'd just have to hope the eyes told the truth.

"We need to go over a few of the things you told us about the events at Joseph Bey's house."

Gabrielle nodded. *Doesn't he believe me? I don't know what happened. I want answers more than he does.*

"Your file shows you have a history of blackouts that dates back to your childhood, as you told us. These blackouts seem to be associated with stressful events, and longer ones, like the one you're claiming you had going to the house, have only been spurred by traumatic circumstances. What happened between you and Mr. Bey this past weekend? Please remember that honesty will serve you far better than any lie."

"I-it was a first date. I haven't dated much, so it made me nervous. I talked to my brother, Michael, and he advised me not to go. But he's so overprotective. I wanted to act like every other nineteen year old."

"So why did you go back to Joseph Bey's house?"

"Is that not normal? I don't know." She was sick of saying that. It was a helpless thing to say. She was so sick of being helpless—and even more sick of not knowing.

Gabrielle stared into the mirror, trying hard to see the glowering face of the woman behind it, but all she could see were her own wide eyes and trembling mouth, and Cole's concerned expression behind her as he leaned his chin on his hands and waited.

She lowered her gaze to the table, avoiding looking at the folder. Still, she felt imagined eyes from behind the glass. *That woman suspects me. Maybe that's good. I couldn't have killed anyone. But I will find out what happened this time. I'm not a kid anymore.*

"What else, Gabrielle?"

"We had a few drinks, and then Joe said he'd had too much; he couldn't drive me home. We were out in the middle of nowhere. I started to wonder if he was going to hurt me, but he just kept giving me drinks. After a while, I asked him for food. He said he'd get me some bread, but he didn't. I was scared, but he took me home in the morning."

She paused. That wasn't right. She had experience with murder investigations. Cops liked the exact truth. "No. He brought me to a gas station, where Cinder picked me up."

"Ms. Cross, clearly this is a difficult topic for you, but given there is a homicide involved, I'll need you to be fully honest. You say you were afraid he'd do something. What did he actually do that night after getting you drunk and stranding you at his house?"

"Nothing!" *Too forceful. I need to calm down, or he'll just think I'm as crazy as my file implies.* "I scare easily. I don't know if he even meant me any harm."

"You don't know? Meaning you still think he might have. Why would that be, Ms. Cross?" Cole lowered his hands to the table and tapped on the folder.

"I did what he wanted. I didn't make him force me."

Cole's face tightened, and his next breath came out shaky. "So you had sex with him that night?"

"No. I . . ." Gabrielle forced down a scream that rose inside her as she remembered, and her face grew hot. She couldn't meet his eyes and stared at the tan tabletop instead. "I used my mouth."

"You gave him oral sex?"

Gabrielle nodded.

Cole sighed. "Okay, Ms. Cross. We're going to let you go. But we'll be in touch. Don't leave town. This is an active homicide investigation."

They're not holding me? They have seventy-two hours even if they don't plan to accuse me yet.

Gabrielle stood, the chair clattering back on the cement floor. Part of her expected Cole to stop her; he couldn't mean to let her go. *They suspect me; they just don't have any proof.*

Having been through it more than once, Gabrielle understood the process. They couldn't risk arresting her unless they were sure they had a case. As long as she didn't appear to be an immediate threat to anyone or a flight risk, she could walk free. But surely they had enough evidence to detain her without charging her.

Maybe not. Or maybe Cole was pulling strings for her.

She looked at Cole through her lashes, trying to hide her inspection.

Cole remained seated, watching her; his brown eyes never left her face except for a single flick to her trembling hands. She clasped them in front of her to control her fingers.

Then Cole stood and opened the door for her. An influx of noise assaulted her ears, conversations, ringing phones, and the clacking of keyboards. Gabrielle fled into the crowded room. No one seemed to notice her. Papers shuffled and conversations wound through the air. Gabrielle slunk off toward the door, not letting Cole walk her out.

Michael waited in one of the three hard-backed chairs outside the secure door labeled *CID offices*. He wasn't his usual put-together self, and the slight disarray of his clothing and hair sank into her like the thrust of a knife. Panic seized her throat and filled her mind until it felt like it would burst. Facing him was too much.

She ran out into the parking lot without pausing. Only when the cool air hit her, heavy with coming rain, did her feet agree to slow. The sudden emotions that had swept over her on seeing her brother loosened their grip in the face of the fresh spring air. Footsteps sounded behind her on the asphalt, and Gabrielle held her pace steady to let Michael catch up.

With guilt twisting inside her, Gabrielle realized that Michael only had to deal with this because of her actions. The least she could do was face him. *I caused this. I caused all of this by accepting* her *help.*

That was stupid. In the real world, with a real death, there had to be a real answer.

She squared her shoulders. If she'd caused it. Then she darn well needed to be part of the solution. *And that's why I need answers. I'm never putting him through this again.*

"I'm sorry," she said as he fell into step with her.

"Gabrielle." Michael reached over and pulled her against him in a tight hug. His shirt was still warm from the heated air inside. He got cold easily and often sat near heating vents.

A rush of fondness overtook her at his familiar scent, heat, and the steady beat of his heart. She had to be strong. But just knowing that made something inside her tremble, like a wall breaking down. A hiccupping sob slithered from Gabrielle's throat, and she held him to her as the tears rushed forth. His arms provided a protective barrier from the world. Just for the moment, she accepted his protection and allowed fear to wash over her.

As her emotions conquered her, Gabrielle's knees weakened. Michael held her weight without comment, except an occasional murmur that it would be all right, that he wouldn't let anything hurt her.

But she couldn't let him do that anymore—sacrifice himself. She wouldn't. He could still be normal. Have a normal life. She couldn't let him give up that chance, even as she felt her own chances slipping away.

ten

Gabrielle and Michael stood, frozen in the parking lot outside the county Sheriff's office. A car horn honked, and Gabrielle looked up. Michael gave an apologetic wave at the car trying to get by them. A smile cracked on her face, and she wiped the tears away. Michael guided her out from the middle of the parking lot over to his car and opened her door. She slid into the seat, flopping her head back against the headrest.

The driver's side door slammed, and Michael turned on the car. Rather than backing out and driving, though, he sat, watching her.

When he finally pulled out of the parking spot, his eyes left her to check the road. "What happened?"

"I told you, I don't know. The same thing I told your boyfriend." She motioned to the police station. "The last time I remember seeing Joe—alive—was Sunday night."

"Did he rape you?"

"What is this obsession with that line of questioning? No." *No. No. I made a choice.*

"Because if he did—"

A small burst of anger renewed her strength. She didn't want or need blind protection. Answers were the only way to dig herself out of the pattern of violence that had swallowed her life thus far. "Michael, even if he did *rape* me, and I killed him for it, that wouldn't make what I saw back there at Joe's house self-defense."

"No, but it might help a jury understand."

"You think I did it."

The car moved out of the lot onto the road, and Michael stared at the other cars, intently avoiding Gabrielle's eyes. "I don't want it to be you."

Who else? Her. *It was* her . . . *but that doesn't make sense. Normal people didn't blame dolls for murders. There is a real answer, and I'll find it.* Gabrielle knew from years of therapy that any personification of the doll was just a symptom of her own trauma. To believe otherwise was insanity.

Gabrielle focused ahead of her as they passed under a green light just as it turned yellow.

"Joe has a record of being a real scumbag, Elle. We could get other girls to step forward."

Of course, he knows that. She wished he could understand that some forms of protection weren't helpful. "Michael."

"That and the drug charges against him—"

"Michael! Stop. Stop talking like—like I killed him. Like you already convicted me."

"No, baby. I don't think you did it. I'm just scared they will charge you anyhow. Last time you were just a little girl, but now they're going to *want* to pin this on you."

"I don't feel like I did it, you know?" Gabrielle paused, picking at her jeans. *But I did ask for help.*

"You were nine. You blamed a doll."

I was a child. I'm not this time. There is a real solution. "It's how I felt last time, too, like I was to blame for wanting it, but someone else did the deed." The image of golden eyes and a myriad of tiny cracks surfaced in her mind. *I thought I saw her at the crime scene.* "Where is she, Michael? Did you see her there?"

Michael slowed the car, earning a honk from a driver as a little, black sports car raced around them. He took several deep breaths, and his knuckles whitened as he squeezed them tighter.

She barely resisted the urge to hold her palms over her ears and not hear his next words.

"The damn thing is at your condo like always." He looked up as if testing her for a smile or acknowledgment. "I thought Dr. White was working with you to put it into storage. I knew you weren't ready to get rid of it."

"I thought I saw her."

"I'm hiring a lawyer," Michael said.

"No. They haven't even charged me." *Yet.*

"Who did you talk to yesterday? They're going to interview all of them."

"You. Cinder." She lowered her voice, knowing how he'd feel about the final name. "And Peter."

"Are you kidding me? Last time you saw Peter, you told me he scared you—that he kept going off about government spacecraft monitoring our behavior with alien tech."

"He's getting treatment."

Michael slammed his fists against the steering wheel. Gabrielle jumped and jerked away from him, and then she felt silly. He'd never hurt her.

Her brother's anger didn't fade at her burst of fear. He spoke in a tight, controlled voice. "That's the last person you need right now. Look, I'm sure he's a great guy, but two—"

"Crazy people," Gabrielle snapped. "That's what you mean. You think two crazy people don't make good support systems for each other. You're wrong. Who else understands? Not you." *You still look at me like I'm broken. Peter doesn't. I don't feel broken when I'm with him.* "And right now, if anyone is a danger to anyone else, I'm a danger to him."

"All one-hundred and twenty pounds of you."

"I don't care what you think." Except that Peter brought up another issue. How would he respond to being called in and interrogated? He'd done it once on her behalf when they were thirteen, and he'd stood up for her then. But maybe being pulled in again would just make him think she *was* a killer.

Michael drove in silence until they were less than five minutes out from her place. Gabrielle squirmed, not wanting to leave things like this with her brother. Michael and Peter were the only two people in the world she would have died for, killed for, fought for.

"So," she said, forcing a smile. "That's your new boyfriend?"

"I doubt that's true after today. He thinks we're both crazy." Despite his words, a tiny smile tugged at the corner of his mouth.

He's proud to show off his new beau. A ghost of a smile snuck onto her face to match his.

"He doesn't think you're crazy," Gabrielle said. "Considering the situation, he was kind to me. He didn't have to be. He didn't even have to let me come home. I like him. Last time police interviewed me, they weren't half that gentle."

Michael gave her a quizzical look, and she gazed out the window so he wouldn't see that she was hiding something. Nasty slip of the tongue. Michael only knew about her being in trouble with the cops when she was nine. He didn't know about the other incident.

"It won't work out," Michael said. "And I'm not going to worry about it. I'll have time for a romantic life when this whole mess is done."

Hell no. I won't let him throw this romance out the window for me.

"He's cute, Michael. I'm sure that niceness wasn't entirely for my benefit. I don't want to foul up another of your relationships."

"I do that all on my own. And you need to stop blaming yourself for Evan." Michael pulled into one of the parking spots in front of her building.

Gabrielle flinched. She doubted she'd ever stop blaming herself for Michael's fiancé leaving him.

The small condo stared back at her. Every room on the ground floor was lit up in Cinder and Gabrielle's half of the house, but the other units were dark. *I really wish I could just walk into one of the other condos, walk into another life.*

"I agreed to take Cinder to pick up her car tonight. Will you be okay here alone?" Michael asked. He shut the engine off.

Gabrielle ignored the last question. "They aren't keeping the car?"

"Don't ask me, Elle. Apparently, they don't consider it evidence and have already gone over what they needed."

"You can come in."

"I'd like a minute." He ran a hand through his curls and gave her a boyish smile. "I should call Cole and apologize for acting like an ass. Even if it doesn't work out, I owe him that."

"Good." Gabrielle smiled and opened her car door. Halfway up the drive, she glanced back at Michael. He had his phone out and his brow furrowed.

This is my mess and only mine. I won't let him make it his. Again.

Cinder had the door open before Gabrielle could even reach for her keys. Cinder held her arm across the opening.

"What the fuck happened!" Cinder's sweatshirt slouched to the side, showing the red strap of her bra. Her blue hair made a messy nest on her head. "I got a call from the police asking about my car and then . . ." She looked past Gabrielle. "Where's Michael?"

"Go inside for a sec. I'll explain, and Michael's making a call, but he'll take you to your car." Gabrielle swallowed hard. "I've been in a police interrogation room most of the day. They'll want to interview you"—*and Peter*—"tomorrow."

Cinder dropped her arm but didn't step out of the way. "Shit, Angel."

"A big pile of," Gabrielle agreed and pushed inside. She wasn't ready to mention the murder, especially before she confirmed the doll remained safely in the condo. If it was, then she'd imagined seeing it. Gabrielle would know she was crazy, but she was used to that feeling. She had to go look.

The short foyer was bare except for hooks screwed into the white walls to hang coats on, which served as the duplex's coat closet. Gabrielle headed toward the living room. Every lamp in the place cast its spotlight on her. Against the far wall, the attached kitchen behind the breakfast bar was spotless for the first time since Cinder had moved in.

More damage I'm leaving in my wake. Cinder must have been very stressed to actually clean. Even the stairway beside the kitchen was free of Cinder's scattered clothes.

Gabrielle took the few steps to the living room. The only visual division between the kitchen, entryway, and living room was the change in flooring. The living room sported a worn cream carpet, as did the stairs to the second floor. The entrance hall used a more practical linoleum tile in mint green, and the kitchen had faux marble tiles. Gabrielle felt safer with her feet planted on the carpet.

Without meaning to, she glanced up the stairs at the back. The doll had to be there. Safe. Protected. If the doll was there, then the whole world still made sense.

Gabrielle shied away from that thought. Because the doll being gone didn't seem to prove anything. *Either the doll moved, or I'm irrevocably broken and I moved her. I'm a killer.* And dolls didn't move. "The police will want to do a full interview with you if all they've done is call about the car."

"About?" Cinder hopped up on the outside edge of the couch to start wrestling her boots on.

"Remember Joe?"

"That shithead from two nights ago?"

"He's dead. I found him." *And my messed up insane mind is trying to convince me that a dangerously unhinged doll living with us killed him.* But she didn't say that. She didn't want to be called crazy on top of everything else today.

"Shiiiit. Did Michael kill him in your honor?"

"You're joking." Gabrielle's fingers jabbed into the couch's soft material. No one was going to accuse him this time.

"Sort of." Cinder visibly deflated. An expression that might have been suspicion pulled at her face. "Mostly."

"It's not funny. Accuse me if you want, but leave Michael out of it, okay?" Gabrielle clutched her hands in front of her. She could still remember Michael's face as he went through round after round of questioning after their parents' murder. She wouldn't let him come under suspicion again. Then, to extract herself from this conversation as much as anything else, "Michael's probably ready for you."

Once Cinder was gone, she could look. Make sure the doll was where it should be. She'd asked the doll for help, and now Joe was dead. Whatever that meant, it was up to Gabrielle to shoulder the truth.

"Fine. You're gonna give me details when I get back." Cinder waggled her finger and hopped down from the counter to grab her coat from beside the front door.

"Sure."

Cinder hovered at the door, nibbling on the corner of her lip.

"Go. I'm taking a shower." Gabrielle pushed off the couch. "I'll be fine." *Do I just want her to think that, or am I fine?*

Gabrielle turned and headed up the stairs into the bathroom. Four doors opened off of the hallway beyond: her bedroom, Cinder's, a storage closet, and the bathroom. Gabrielle traced her fingertips over the faded floral wallpaper as she approached the bathroom door.

Once inside, the cramped walls breathed around her. The wallpaper had faded even more than in the hall, leaving ghost flowers to pop up here and there. She sat on the toilet seat and turned on the shower. Then she slumped there, her cheek brushing the thick plastic of the shower curtain.

She waited for the front door to open and bang shut before turning the water off. A shower came next, but first, she had to know. She crept into her bedroom, invisible eyes pricking at her skin.

Cinder's passage through the room Monday morning to get Gabrielle's clothes had marred the orderly space. But other than a few stray items from Cinder's search, everything was in its place. The purple lace of her lampshade converted its light into a soft caress that crept out to the pastel blue walls. Schoolbooks lined a shelf over her neatly made twin bed. But only one thing in the room grabbed Gabrielle's attention.

One spot on that bookshelf was empty. Just a conspicuous blank space, exactly the right size.

No doll.

eleven

A BURNT-OUT CIGARETTE DANGLED FROM COLE'S FINGERS. HE WAS WAITING outside the police station to interview Michael. His Tuesday wasn't winding down any better than it had started, with Sera taking the lead on the interviews with Gabrielle's friends. For the sake of any future criminal case, he had to let her handle Michael's interview as well.

But first, he needed to warn Michael. He had dropped Gabrielle's roommate off for her interview and to pick up her car, but he had disappeared too quickly for Cole to catch him then. Some weird crud came up in that interview that kept rolling in Cole's head, but he'd have to wait to address any of that.

Despite the cigarette in his hand, Cole hadn't smoked in four years. He'd kept up the habit of taking fifteen minutes with some of the beat cops for information and companionship.

But this time, he was alone in the front parking lot rather than in the gated police lot out back where the others took their breaks. Just holding the cigarette was oddly calming, and he twisted the cross around his neck with his free hand.

The deep shadows caused by the setting sun were slowly being blotted out by clouds that promised, but had yet to deliver, rain. His mind drifted back to the crime scene over and over. He couldn't block out Gabrielle's wide eyes from the interrogation earlier in the day—like a doe caught in the headlights. And his interview with Gabrielle's roommate, Lucinda Grange, had convinced him the blue-haired girl had no issue with lying. She staunchly insisted she'd given Gabrielle the okay to take her car and had simply forgotten about it when she reported the car missing to the campus police.

No way to prove her wrong, but also not the most believable lie ever to cross a young woman's lips. Question was, why was she lying for Gabrielle? Did Lucinda Grange know something, or was it just youthful fervor and loyalty?

Peter Cullen hadn't been much better. Other than accusing the cops of trying to frame people and demanding they turn off the security cameras and stop "watching him," he hadn't said anything helpful.

Yet, despite the lies and evasions, Cole couldn't believe that Gabrielle had killed anyone. That soul-consuming fear he'd seen in her wasn't the type a killer showed when they knew they're about to be caught. No. He recognized that expression. It was distinct in his mind; it was the same look Yolanda had given him in the hospital when she'd asked if her husband's kids had been injured in the fire or if she'd gotten them out safely. The look of someone struggling with questions about their own responsibilities.

He'd helped Yolanda when she was accused of arson. And he wanted to do the same for Gabrielle.

His thoughts were interrupted when Michael's green Honda pulled up and parked close to where Cole stood. He dropped his cigarette. It wasn't burning anymore, but he still crushed it.

Michael climbed out of the car with sluggish movements. Cole's chest squeezed tight. Michael already appeared dejected, and Cole had only more bad news for him. He dragged his feet as he came closer to Cole, but he never lifted his gaze from the sidewalk. A big change from that morning, no more avenging fire.

Cole stepped off the curb to meet Michael. There were reasons he'd waited outside for this meeting. Things he needed to say he didn't want Detective Sera hearing, things he didn't want to be recorded.

"Look, Cole," Michael started.

"Wait on that. Whatever you need to say—"

"Mostly sorry." Michael gave a sheepish smile, but it didn't last.

"It can wait. We can't hang out here talking. In fact, if you could avoid mentioning anything about us, it would work in your favor."

"Cole, I know that." Michael reached out for Cole's hand, but Cole took a step back.

"Oh, stop," Cole said, starting across the lot toward the front door of the station, avoiding Michael's eyes. "I'm not mad or ashamed. But I've seen the evidence in this case, and it isn't looking great for Gabrielle. I'm not going to lie or withhold information, but I'll be a lot gentler with her than Detective Sera. She's a good cop—and fair—but she isn't known for coddling suspects."

"And you think you'd be taken off the case if they knew we were involved." Michael's steps sounded as he hurried to catch up.

Cole paused. He should already have left the case. But if he said that, Michael might advise him to jump ship. "*Maybe* not taken off, but at least asked to relinquish the role of lead detective. Yes." He would leave the case as soon as he could get everything settled. If his romantic involvement came out, he'd be off the case in a heartbeat. It would be worse than just being taken off the case if people higher up the chain knew he'd purposely lied about his personal involvement in the case. "I'm not telling you to lie. In fact, don't. If you need to bring something up, do. But if it doesn't come up . . . I also can't be lead on your interviews. Just in case."

"You don't have to do this."

"It's only partially for you." Cole rubbed at a tightening in his temples. "God, your sister looked so terrified. There's more to this case than the cut and dried. I need to see her treated fairly."

"Thank you. Even if it isn't for me. Thank you."

Cole reached the door, and it opened with a swish of air. He motioned for Michael to follow. They walked inside, the heat from the vents buffeting up his pants legs. The waiting area was deserted, and even the girl manning the booth beside the secure entry only glanced up for a second. Cole escorted Michael into the back, where cluttered desks filled the wide room.

"This way," Cole said, heading to a vacant interrogation room. Detective Sera was still wrapping up her interview with Joseph's mother in the room next door. But she wanted Michael planted the moment he arrived. She liked to observe people before questioning them.

Cole motioned Michael into the empty room.

Michael took a seat on the far side of the yellowish table, wedging the chair back into the corner. Cole went to his desk and waited. He didn't have the presence of mind to work, but he could at least try to look like he was doing so.

It felt like ages until Sera emerged with Mrs. Bey. They said a stiff but friendly goodbye and then Detective Sera stalked right over to the interview room that Michael was waiting in. She paused to look back at Cole, one immaculate brow arched as if to say *are you coming or not?*

Cole definitely intended on joining in on this one.

twelve

DETECTIVE SERA OPENED THE DOOR TO THE INTERVIEW ROOM AND HELD FOR Cole. She liked to do those things, grabbing traditional gender roles and flipping them. Some of the other detectives found it unnerving. Cole really couldn't see why it mattered. With a nod to his fellow detective, Cole sat down facing Michael, but on the same side of the table, leaving the seat on the opposite side for Sera. As she entered, her painted red lips curved into an equally painted smile. Other than that, her face was makeup free and nearly absent of any femininity. She wore her black hair slicked back into a bun. Everything about her was neat and orderly, not allowing herself to show any hint of softness.

She held folders in her hands. Though Cole hadn't seen her pick them up, he knew what they were.

"I apologize for being held up, Mr. Cross," Detective Sera said. Rather than sitting, she laid the three manilla folders out on the table, closed but facing Michael. This was an odd place to start the interview. Sera was diving right in with the past rather than questions about Joseph Bey's murder. But Cole had to admit that from a practical standpoint, this was a good way to set a person off their game.

Michael's eyes fixed on the three dates, years apart, labeling the tabs of the folders. Cole had been unpleasantly surprised at a few things in the files. None of it was likely to be more fun for Michael. Each file was a murder in some way tied back to Gabrielle.

Michael set his hands on the desk but nowhere near the offending folders. "Three files? That means three crimes?"

"Why don't you tell me about them?" Detective Sera asked.

Cole set his hand on the table, touching the folder on the left. The oldest of the files.

"I can't." Michael leaned back forcefully in his chair. Then he nodded at the files in turn. "That one is from my mom's murder judging by the date."

He didn't even include his stepfather in that statement.

"That one is dated from yesterday, so guessing it's from that murder scene. But the third? I don't know that date."

"Mr. Cross." Sera nodded, stepping forward and looming over the desk. "You claim you have no knowledge of an incident on this date?"

Michael's jaw clenched, and he gave a slight incline of his head. His posture had stiffened with each word Sera spoke.

"So tell us about the two events you know of." Cole set one hand on the file in the middle. How could Michael not recognize all three cases? Of course Sera didn't believe him. Cole could barely wrap his head around it. It had to mean something if Michael didn't know all three crimes, and it was Cole's job to find out what, but knowledge didn't always make things better.

Especially with loved ones.

Digging deeper just meant you got to the smellier shit faster.

Michael looked down, his gaze dragging over Cole's hand. Then to the date on that file.

"Answer the question, Mr. Cross," Sera said, tapping one short but cleanly filed nail onto the table.

"Go on, Michael," Cole said.

Michael's eyes narrowed at the use of his personal name. He shot

Cole a questioning glance. Cole repressed a smile. Clearly, Michael was not used to concealing secrets. It's all about knowing where to draw a believable line. The station was aware that they'd worked together before—acting overly formal would be a dead giveaway something was being kept below board.

"Start with this one," Sera said, with a nod of her head toward the folder with the earliest date.

"That file is on my mother's murder," Michael repeated. He sat rod straight in his chair and didn't even glance toward Sera. He left out that his stepfather's murder would be in the same file. "I was fourteen, and Gabrielle was nine. I was the primary suspect initially, but I could prove I was at a friend's house when it happened. The police never found the culprit."

Sera nodded.

"The other file has to be from the murder yesterday. But this?" Michael tapped a finger on the middle file. "You brought it into the room to question me, so clearly it isn't a secret. What does it have to do with me or Gabrielle?"

Sera folded her arms. She was probably watching Michael's nonverbal cues, which was her forte, and she had a better angle from a standing position. But Michael had been on lockdown physically since she walked in. Cole didn't know what she could decipher.

Cole slid the folder forward and then flipped it open. The picture clipped to the inside was that of a middle-aged man. The sides of his mouth were bruised and reddened. His throat had been slit, and glassy gray eyes stared out at nothing.

Michael barely glanced at the photo—just a flick of his eyes, which was probably unintentional. Pretty normal. Most people don't want to look at murder victims.

"This is from seven years ago," Sera said. "One year before you adopted your sister and took her out of foster care. Mr. Pritcher was murdered in his basement. Some of those crime details link closely with this morning's crime."

There were an uncomfortable number of similarities between the three crimes, like the post-mortem positioning of the body, the marks on the wrists, which in all three cases were found to be made by some item of cloth already in the home. Gabrielle's father was the only victim included in the files who was not bound. He was the first victim, killed over an hour before the mother, thus dissimilarities made sense. In the mother's case, the ties from the drapes had been inexpertly knotted around her wrists and a sock stuffed in her mouth. With the autopsy and police reports together, he made out that she was probably asleep when the initial attack happened and bound as she died.

The latter two cases the victims were bound prior to their death and tied in a much more expert fashion. If it was the same killer, they'd learned. In Joe's case, torn towels from the bathroom were used and in Mr. Pritcher's, scraps from old blankets. Damage around the mouth consistent with a gag was noted, and yet the gag was nowhere on site at either crime scene.

"That's awful, but what does it have to do with me or Gabrielle?" Michael glanced at Sera—everything about his posture was adversarial.

Detective Sera leaned to plant her hands on the table. "I'm surprised you didn't recognize his name."

Michael's eyes widened as if the information had suddenly fallen into place. He grabbed the folder and pulled it closer. Cole swallowed hard. He'd never considered Michael a particularly good actor, and that type of surprise was hard to fake. So Michael did know the name, even if he hadn't recognized it immediately.

"Tell me about Mr. Pritcher," Cole said.

"That's the last name of Gabrielle's second-to-last foster father," Michael said, his eyes glued to the picture. "She left that house one year before I turned eighteen. She wasn't even in his care when this" —his eyes skipped to the file—"happened."

"And?" Cole prodded. Gabrielle had been the primary person of interest in the case. No charges were filed. No official marks against her, but there had been enough suspicions that this case came up easily when Gabrielle's name appeared at another murder scene. "Please be honest. It wasn't as simple as that."

"I reported him for abuse," Michael said. His jaw clenched before he went on. "Gabrielle told me some things he'd done, but she wouldn't come forward. She was afraid. I couldn't get charges filed. I did manage to kick up enough of a fuss that they moved her to another family. But I don't see what that has to do with anything. He was alive when she left that damn place."

"Yes," Sera said. "But we couldn't find evidence of abuse."

"The police never find proof," Michael snapped.

"I'm sorry, Michael," Cole said, then glanced up at Detective Sera. *I shouldn't have said that. I've got to let her take charge. If I can't do that, I have no business on this case.*

"I'm sorry too." Anger laced Michael's tone, but it died out, replaced by weariness. "I never knew you guys investigated. I thought you ignored me. But if you say you didn't find it, then at least you actually looked."

Cole nodded. Police looked into his original complaint against Gabrielle's dad too. *It wouldn't matter to Michael that the cops believed him back then; they just couldn't prove it. Either way, I can't ask him what sort of abuse happened back then with his stepdad. It's not even the cop in me that wants to know. But, Jesus, how hurt is Michael?*

"If you looked into her foster father's murder," Michael said. "Then you know we weren't there. The fact I was never called in means I was dismissed as a suspect. Why bring this here now, unless it's just to upset me? Any link you have is tenuous."

"I hope for your sake that's true." Sera finally pulled out a chair and sat across from Cole and Michael. "The killer was never found, and we're reopening this case. Now, I have some questions about yesterday."

"I would expect so." Michael managed a personable smile with some trace of his usual humor.

"You arrived on the scene shortly after the police." Sera closed the file and pulled it away from Michael. "What brought you there?"

"Gabrielle called me," Michael said. "She was scared and confused."

"And she asked you to come get her?" Cole asked. *That was leading. I'm not asking questions like an investigator. This is all wrong.*

"No." Michael leaned back in his chair and folded his arms across his chest. "She wasn't looking to flee, if that's what you're getting at. She called 911 first. I came because I couldn't let her be alone."

"She gave you the address?" Sera asked.

"No," Michael said. "As I'm sure she told you, she didn't know where she was. But she's been through a lot. When she goes on dates, I look into the guy."

"How do you look them up?" Sera asked.

"Government computers." Michael sat up straight. "I know it's not exactly official use of resources, but she's my sister."

Well, crud. Now we have two suspects. Him and her. But it couldn't be Michael. He isn't a killer. Could my judgment be that fucking awful? I was thinking of introducing him to Isa.

"Where were you when she called on Tuesday morning?" Sera asked. "Describe the moment for me."

"At work." Michael fidgeted.

He shouldn't be nervous. He was at work when she called, but he must have been at home at the time of the murder, right? Why wouldn't he have been? From the interviews so far, Cole had every reason to believe Michael had been home. Though he still wasn't sure if he believed Lucinda Grange's version of where Michael had been Monday night.

It was insane to him that Lucinda Grange had a version of events that involved knowing Michael's whereabouts. But even with her statements, he should have been home by the time Joseph Bey was killed.

"At the time of death, around four to five in the morning, where were you?" Sera asked.

At home. Just say "at home."

Michael licked his lips before responding. "I was at home."

Good boy. Cole resisted smiling.

"Is there anyone who can vouch for your whereabouts that morning?" Sera asked.

"No." Michael speared Sera with his eyes. "I was alone Tuesday morning."

Sera responded to Michael's animosity with a catlike smile.

"No one can corroborate your whereabouts?" Cole asked. *Come on, Michael, a neighbor who saw you coming home the night before, going out for the mail? Anything.*

"I was alone past 2 a.m. when I left the bar. I drove for a little while, then I came home. I got there by 3 a.m."

Very factual. Also, very hard to verify it since he lived alone.

"What bar?" Sera asked.

"Don't know the name. It's some dive just down the road from my house. Darian's? Damien's?"

Why was he at a bar at all? The only reason that came to mind was sex. *That has nothing to do with the investigation, does it?*

"Do you normally go to bars on Monday night?" Cole asked, framing the question as best he could to be relevant.

"No. Gabrielle called me Monday morning in a panic. I left work to find her, but she wasn't on campus, where she'd called from. After looking for her all day, I was worried, so I went out for some drinks with a friend. I wasn't going to sleep either way."

"We're going to need that friend's name," Cole said.

"Gabrielle's roommate, Cinder."

Cole nodded. Michael's statement matched Lucinda's. Were the two of them friends or was he using Lucinda for information on Gabrielle? Given how protective Michael was of his sister, it didn't surprise Cole that he'd use any avenue to keep tabs on her. Any other case and his mind would have gone to an affair, but his gut told him that was the wrong track.

"How do you know Miss Lucinda Grange?" Sera asked.

"When Gabrielle started looking for a house, I went out and found her a decent place. With her inheritance from her dad, money isn't the issue, but I needed to make sure she had someone to look out for her. I knew Cinder from my college days—I tutored some kids at her high school, and she was one of them, and we kept in touch, Facebook friends level of in touch."

"If you two weren't really friends," Cole asked, "then why were you with her at the bar?"

"We've started hanging out occasionally since Gabrielle moved in with her." Michael fiddled with the collar of his shirt.

Cole wondered if the gesture was due to nerves caused by being in a police interrogation. Or maybe it was a sign that he understood how over the top his attempts to watch over Gabrielle were. Cole already knew the answer when he asked his next question. "And what were you talking about on Monday night?"

"Work. My new boyfriend." Michael hesitated on the word as if unsure whether or not to commit to it. "And Gabrielle. Then some of Cinder's college friends dropped by, and Cinder left with them."

"Did anyone see you when you returned home?" Sera asked.

"I didn't pass anyone in the neighborhood. They were asleep. Am I a suspect?"

I wish I could say no. Sera will answer—then at least I don't have to say it out loud. Cole forced himself not to glance away from Michael and Sera. He couldn't afford to look nervous, even though his stomach clenched inside until nausea rose and fell like the tide.

"At this stage, everyone is a suspect," Sera replied. "Now, you were very agitated when you came to the crime scene. Can you explain why?"

"Gabrielle isn't strong," Michael said. "You have her psychiatric records on file. Isn't it obvious why her being at a murder site would upset me?"

Sera made a scoffing sound.

Cole took a deep breath and opened the most recent file. He leafed through the bloody photos until he found the one he wanted. There was one question that needed answering, especially after the parents' murder and all the things Gabrielle said back then. She'd accused a doll, and the psychiatric reports from the time had indicated an unhealthy attachment between the girl and the antique.

"Your sister drove to the crime scene in her roommate's vehicle," Cole said, showing the photo to Detective Sera. "Lucinda swears she loaned your sister the car after they drove to school, but she had no explanation for why Gabrielle would bring this over to a date's house." Cole shoved the photo across the table.

Taken through the rear passenger side window, the picture focused in on one item. Standing on the seat, its head turned to the window, was an antique porcelain doll. Threads of brown hair clung to the net over its bald scalp, and eyes of a peculiar amber met the camera almost as if the doll saw it. Its threadbare ivory gown, covered with tiny flowers, was neatly arranged over her chubby legs.

"Can you tell us," Sera asked, "what state of mind your sister would be in to bring this object with her?"

"Upset. It's like a security blanket." Michael's voice had lost any trace of warmth, and his eyes closed, his head turned away in denial of the image.

He knows something. Michael's posture spoke volumes. The problem posed by the doll was minor—a question of Gabrielle's mental state. But Michael had to know that establishing that mental state would be very important in *how* Gabrielle was charged if the case swung that direction.

thirteen

GABRIELLE STARED BLANKLY ACROSS THE AUDITORIUM AT HER PROFESSOR. After a long night waiting for Cinder to come home, Gabrielle had decided to go to class. She'd hoped the crowds would keep her mind off what Cinder and Peter might have been through with the cops the day before. To some extent, it worked. Hundreds of other students served as a buffer between her and the flickering eyes of the teacher—but that buffer didn't work both ways. Nothing stopped her classmates from peering sideways and whispering.

My life's always been like this. It's no different now than in high school. They're all whispering that I'm crazy.

Seats stood vacant in a ring around her. She was a lion uncaged to her classmates.

They know. They all know.

I'm sitting in a spotlight; they all see what I am. I'll never be normal.

The professor paced the front of the auditorium, saying something about rock formations—something she'd never wanted to learn and couldn't concentrate on. Instead, her mind went back to why Cinder had stayed out all night, who had the doll since it hadn't been in the car when Cinder drove it home, what Peter must have felt being called in to be questioned by the cops, and what Michael was enduring because of her. Then back to Joe's dead eyes, accusing her. Again and again, her brain slipped into a vision of fleeing the class out into the hall, then out under the spring sky. She would be able to breathe without the accusations that filled the classroom air.

Someone plunked into the seat next to her and leaned close. Gabrielle's attention snapped over to him. The young man grinned —a frat boy smile that announced he owned the world.

"I came in late," he whispered, leaning closer than she thought seemed normal. "What did I miss?"

"Uh, what?" *Could he be serious? Doesn't he know what I am? Doesn't everyone?*

"Oh, c'mon, cutie. You don't want to be sitting all by yourself, do you?" He patted her hand.

She jerked her arm away. *Is he hitting on me? Who hits on a murderer?*

Gabrielle took a quick glance around the room to see if anyone was watching and cackling. Instead, she noted for the first time that everyone else toward the back of the lecture hall sat in small groups or alone. She was far from the only one with a circle of vacant seats around her.

Maybe no one has noticed me at all. It's all in my head.

She glanced to the side at frat boy, who seemed to be listening to the professor.

Either that or this idiot is crazy enough to hit on a killer.

"Can I look over your notes from earlier in the class?" Frat boy leaned closer to ask, though it didn't sound like a question, especially as his hand snuck toward her notepad before she answered.

"No." Gabrielle liked how the word felt. This guy made her uncomfortable. She wanted him gone. She took a deep breath and continued, "Please go away."

She closed her eyes, squeezed shut against light and sound. Frat boy *hmphed,* but she heard the rustle as he got up. The professor droned on up front. Gabrielle's phone buzzed.

Probably Michael again, but talking to him was out of the question until she found the doll. Until she had answers and could safely keep him out of the line of fire.

And if her answers just proved she was crazy? She clearly didn't have a great grasp on reality. She didn't even know if she was a pariah around campus or not.

If her answer was the doll?

I asked her for help. I said I wanted Joe gone. Now the doll is missing, and Joe is dead. There has to be a solution that doesn't involve a killer doll.

No matter how often Gabrielle reviewed the crime scene in her mind, she couldn't prove anything to herself. There were too many questions and no answers. How had she come to Joe's? What happened in the twenty hours she'd lost to the blackout? Who killed Joe?

She brushed her fingers over her arm. The rough edges of scabs scratched her fingertips. *Did he score me with his nails before I tied him up and stabbed him? If that's true, the wounds are proof I'm a monster.*

The questions bubbled inside, never stilling and never turning to steam and dissipating. Answers were a long way off. She'd have to find a way to live with this new set of questions, for now.

She'd learned to live with unlivable doubts before—she wouldn't need to do so again. She'd find out what really happened. Answers weren't something she'd ever had, but they were going to be part of her future.

A hand fell on her shoulder, and Gabrielle squeaked. She turned, ready to tell the frat boy off even more forcefully.

"Gabs?" Peter asked. He carried rather than wore a rain-speckled hoodie.

He must have come in from outside to find her, but she didn't know why he would have. Surely after being dragged to the police station, the last thing he'd want to do was see the girl who brought the situation onto him. But the way her heart briefly fluttered in reaction told her she was glad he had come to get her.

The classroom was nearly empty. The last of the students trickling out gave her strange looks, and the professor stood at the front, eyeing her as he gathered his papers.

Is that because they know I'm crazy or because I've been sitting here zoned out?

"Class is over," Gabrielle said.

"You look out of it, Gabs. How are you holding up?"

She chose not to answer that question. She honestly wouldn't have known how. "I think Cinder is avoiding me, and Michael is hovering again."

"Come on. You need to get away from all of this."

"That's not even possible."

"It is. We'll walk to the bus stop and go someplace far away from your everyday life, and you can escape for a minute."

"No buses," Gabrielle said as she pulled out her phone. Without hesitation she texted Cinder, who wasn't at school today but had let Gabrielle have the car to drive in. But she'd want to know if Gabrielle was keeping her wheels past the usual time. After shooting off a quick text, Gabrielle tucked her phone away again.

If Cinder had a problem with it, she'd say. In the meantime, Gabrielle really needed to decide if she was willing to go off alone with Peter, even if Cinder was okay with it.

Gabrielle stood and shouldered her bag. Leaving with him sounded nice, but she wasn't sure it was actually a good plan. He hadn't even brought up the crime yet. "Aren't you going to ask me if I did it?"

"No. Why would I ask you that?" Peter touched the small of her back and guided her out of the row of seats. "I'm going to ask you what happened Monday night, and hell, Sunday night, too, and who the dead guy was."

Gabrielle nodded and let him escort her outside.

"Where's the car?" he asked.

She looked up into his eyes. The blue washed over her with a warmth that seemed to force back the dread. There was no one she'd rather escape with.

Gabrielle pointed toward the grassy area past Drumheller Fountain, which currently wasn't much of a fountain at all, since it was drained. The lecture halls rose up on either side of the vast empty circle, looking like nothing less than medieval castles to her.

She took the lead and meandered across campus. The most direct route to where Gabrielle had parked the car would have taken her along the sunny path through a wide walkway surrounded by grass, but she preferred the shade and the sense of privacy between buildings. Some of the buds on the smattering of cherry trees had burst open, and a light patter of rain made them bob up and down.

"Why do we need the car or a bus?" Gabrielle asked. "There are places nearby."

"Because you need to get away from the scenes of your regular life." Raindrops speckled Peter's shoulders. His sweatshirt hung over one arm leaving only a T-shirt between him and the spring sprinkle. "That means going farther away than you can walk."

The bus sounded like hell—a box on wheels packed with strangers. She didn't know how Peter dealt with it every day. Even the fancier express buses were nothing but unfamiliar faces.

Strangers always stared. They whispered. Nothing made her feel less comfortable in her own skin than being around strangers. She'd shared Cinder's car since moving in. She paid for gas and insurance and Cinder let her use it pretty much whenever she asked.

Getting your own car and insurance with blackouts in your medical history was a tough sell.

"Where then?" Gabrielle pulled her sweater tighter over her shoulders. Her leggings stuck uncomfortably to her legs, and at even slightest provocation of wind and rain, cold shivers ran through her.

"I'll tell you where to go."

He always gave horrible directions. Most people who didn't drive themselves couldn't give driving directions. But ribbing him about his flawed skills would be far more effort than it was worth. "I can't leave the area."

Peter laughed and shook his head at her. His red hair had formed tight curls in the humidity.

Is he laughing because the idea of fleeing the state is crazy or because he thinks me obeying such a restriction is crazy?

"You'd be driving, Gabs. Even if I led you to the state line, you'd choose whether to cross."

She ducked under the eaves of the building along the evergreen-lined path toward the car. "Just tell me you understand that I'd make an awful fugitive."

"I won't concede that point, but I'm not planning on making a run for it. However, if they charge you with anything, I make no promises."

"I almost wish they would charge me. Then I'd find out if I did it."

"You didn't. It's not in you."

She lowered her head and hurried across the road to the parking spot she'd lucked into. *Then who was it? That was what she needed to know. If it wasn't the doll, and it wasn't her, who?*

"But what if I'm not me?" she asked, keeping her gaze low. "I blacked out. What if in those blackouts, I'm different?"

"You don't have dissociative identity disorder." Peter's tennis shoes splashed in a shallow puddle. "I've seen your blackouts since we were kids. You don't become someone else. You zone out—like you're sleepwalking."

"Sleepwalkers can be dangerous." Gabrielle's mind latched onto that idea rather than addressing the other term Peter had thrown out like it wasn't a massive blackhole of a disorder. "There have even been murder cases where a sleepwalker has gone through lengthy, complicated routines before murdering someone. It wasn't even about wanting the people they killed dead, more like a bad dream. Only they wake up and it's real."

"But you're not a sleepwalker."

"You made the comparison, not me. The point is you can't know." *I can't know.*

"And yet I do. Stop feeding me facts from creepy documentaries and tell me what happened."

Gabrielle hurried ahead of him to the red compact car, clicked it open with her key fob, and swung her backpack into the hatchback. Her eyes briefly scanned the backseat for the doll. But it wasn't there. A wave of weariness swept over her, and she hunched under the meager shelter of the liftgate.

"What happened?" Peter asked again. He remained in the open, a red curl falling across his freckled forehead, but tossed his jacket into the open hatch while he waited for her to answer.

Gabrielle sat on the floor of the hatch and stared up at Peter, haloed by dark clouds behind him, and the words came. She told him about meeting Joe at a party with Cinder and about Joe picking her up and taking her to his place, and she didn't stop until she had described her horror at the doll being missing from her room.

"I'd ask if you were okay, but you seem on the brink of losing it. What can I do?"

"Just get me out of my head. I can't seem to escape thinking that someone is dead and it's my fault."

"Well, it's not your fault. And Joe deserved it." Peter offered her his hand and helped her stand.

"I doubt a court of law would agree," she said.

"C'mon, seriously let's get out of here." He shut the hatch.

"To your new apartment? I haven't seen it."

"No. That's boring."

"Where exactly?"

"You'll see when we get there."

fourteen

"Turn right." Peter fiddled with the dial on her radio until he found something classical—he knew better than to try her presets for anything he liked.

Gabrielle took a sideways glance at him.

He really is doing better. He seems so normal. Healthy. Am I as paranoid now as he was then? I need to try to see all of this like a sane person would. If Peter can be normal, so can I.

Then Peter said, "You're thinking you killed him because you were there and no one else knows where he lives, right?"

"Mostly because I was there." *Please stop, Peter, just stop.*

"But you don't see that anyone else who knew about the other murders could have found him and duplicated them." Peter gestured wildly as they passed the Mountlake Bridge.

"I guess." Gabrielle bit her lip.

"Turn left." Peter patted her leg. "Just look at social media. Anyone who knows you could have found his last name or city, and anyone with any skills could have found his address."

"And the doll? How do you explain that away?" Didn't he see his theory wasn't any better? Because who would care enough to find Joe on her behalf? Only Peter and Michael . . . *And I'd rather be the murderer than have them be murderers to protect me. Maybe Cinder?* After that, Gabrielle's closest friend was Dr. White, her psychiatrist. "I thought you were taking me away from this shit."

"Sorry." Peter paused. "I meant to stop talking about it. You even asked me. No more. I promise."

Gabrielle glanced away from the shop-lined road into Peter's sky-blue eyes. *Tell me I'm not broken.* "It's just, what if the doll did it? What if I was never crazy?"

"No, no. I promised no more. Turn off here." Peter motioned to a swiftly approaching right turn.

Gabrielle had to jerk the wheel and cut a car off to follow his directions. After that, they were on backroads; she could drive more slowly, and it was easier to accommodate his last-minute dictates. As the orchestra on the radio ramped up toward the crescendo, she drove along a hilly residential street winding down a steep slope toward Lake Washington. Between the houses, glints of water flashed.

"Now, park." Peter grinned at her. "We'll walk from here."

Gabrielle surveyed the packed street. There was barely room for one car to pass between the vehicles parked on both sides. She rolled her eyes. "Park where? I should have known better than to take directions from someone who doesn't drive!"

"Go back up the hill. I don't mind walking a bit further."

Gabrielle wondered where he pictured her turning around. Carefully, employing a driveway, she managed what amounted to a six-point turn.

"If I crash Cinder's car, I'm making you pay," Gabrielle commented as she twisted the wheel. She wound back up the hill until she found a spot.

"My parents can afford it." He grinned.

"Where are we?" Gabrielle asked as she set the parking brake.

Peter opened his door and sprang out, motioning in the direction of the water. "There's a great little beach down there."

"Are we allowed to use it?"

He shrugged and closed his car door. "No one cares."

What am I afraid of? Some homeowners yelling for me to get off their private beach? I probably killed someone. This was a minor offense at best.

Peter grabbed her hand and tugged her from the car. With their fingers interlaced, they started along the street in the dappled light of the sparse trees lining the hill. Their hands swung slowly between them.

"So how have you been, anyway?" she asked, trying to push away her own thoughts. "What ever happened to Monica?"

"She's seeing someone else." His voice quieted as it always did when he wanted to avoid a conversation. "They got serious."

Well, screw her. She cheated and then claimed they had an 'open' relationship. Then she left him. And he still thinks she's perfect. "You deserve so much better, Peter."

"It happened a while ago. She calls sometimes and comes around." He jabbed the toe of his worn sneakers into the uneven sidewalk.

"Why would you let her?" Gabrielle's shoulders felt looser already—she was done talking about herself. Focusing on him made her feel better.

"Not everyone believes in the corporate idea of love that you do. Monogamy and eternity are shams."

"My views aren't corporate, they're societal, and this has nothing to do with monogamy. It's about trust, and she's abusing yours. She—"

"I know, Gabs." He squeezed her fingers. "I thought she and I were a couple, and she let me think it until she found better. I'm not looking to be involved with her emotionally, but there's no reason to hold a grudge and not be friendly."

"Friendly?" Gabrielle shook her head and flashed him an incredulous smile. "Is that what we're calling it now?"

"Not all of us are angels, Gabs." He stepped aside to reveal a narrow path. He let her go first, scrambling down a steep dirt incline to the rocky shore.

Gabrielle stepped out onto an empty beach with a few yards of rocky turf between her and the greenish water. The beach was recessed—a rock ledge to the left. Beyond that was a vacant wooden dock. To the right, the beach petered off into a clutter of boulders. But the little cove itself formed a peaceful oasis. The rocks smoothed to pebble-thick sand near the water, and across the vast lake, trees and houses lined the shore. Even farther out on the horizon, the skyscrapers of Bellevue rose, shining against the gray clouds.

Gabrielle picked her way over the rocks to the dock, her sweater pinned to her back by the breeze. Wild roses grew in one of the gardens nearby, and their sweet scent added spice to the gentle tinge of green decomposition from the lake. Sunlight struck only the tip of the dock, despite it being only early afternoon. Throughout the shady area, the water on the sides rippled in dark waves, complicated further by the lake reeds reaching up toward her. Her steps echoed over the wooden slats.

"This is a lovely place." Gabrielle sat on the dock's edge and pulled off her flats. Emerald seaweed danced under the surface of the water. The bottom was invisible beneath the rippling green.

Peter plopped down next to her and dropped his sneakers beside him before lifting his T-shirt over his head and laying it by his shoes.

"You can't mean to get in. The water must be freezing." Gabrielle dropped her bare feet over the edge and kicked down into the water, burying her foot up to the ankle. Goosebumps climbed her legs. "Yes. Freezing."

"We're going in." Peter grinned at her.

"Don't you *we* at me."

Peter stood and unbuttoned his pants. Gabrielle averted her eyes at the first flash of the waistband of his underwear.

"I'm not stripping, Gabs. I'd love to take you skinny dipping, but I wouldn't trick you into it."

"We clearly have different definitions of stripping." Gabrielle smiled and watched his reflection in the lake—too blurred to really see but enough for her mind to form its own picture.

He leaped in, and the cold water splashed up onto her. Gabrielle laughed and held out her dripping hands. She glanced at her water spotted leggings and blouse. The outfit was nothing she could wear in the lake.

"Water's public property," Peter said as he emerged. A broad grin spread over his features. "But the dock is privately owned. Unless you jump in, you're trespassing."

And then he was under the lake's surface again before she could kick water into his face.

As she gathered up his clothes and her shoes, she saw her face reflected in the waves—she hardly recognized herself. Her smile transformed her. *I look just like all those girls I always watch. I look happy—normal.*

When I'm with him, I don't feel crazy. I just feel like me. Joe's dead face slipped through her thoughts, and she shoved it down. *Not now.*

Gabrielle scurried off the dock and stood on the coarse sand. His clothes made a neat pile to the side, and she dug her toes deep into the pebbles.

Peter emerged, standing with the water up to his waist. His hair was slick and dripping in his eyes. Naturally lean rather than gym-crafted, his chest and arms were muscular without a hardened edge.

"Any woman who doesn't want you is crazy," Gabrielle said.

Peter blushed, a reaction that made him once again safe—hers. *Someday maybe. No. I'm the last thing Peter needs.*

"Come in," Peter said, resubmerging up to his neck and treading water. "Let go of your worries, all of them."

"I don't . . . I can't just take off my clothes!" It was Gabrielle's turn to blush.

"Then don't. I'll turn around; you take off what feels comfortable, then come in."

"No, that's silly." Her heart thudded, belying her calm tone, but the words continued to cascade from her. "You don't need to turn around. The point is for me to live, right? To let go of the fear."

"You're safe with me. You always will be."

Gabrielle hooked her thumbs under the waistband of her leggings and slid them down. His eyes remained locked with hers, the same sweet smile on his face that had made her instantly trust him the day they met. His smile told her in a way no words ever could that she was safe.

Between him and the lake, maybe she really could escape for a while.

The cold water bit at her skin as she splashed in up to her thighs.

Peter swam over and lifted her up, propelling her into the water with his arms wrapped around her. And even in the remorseless, unfeeling chill of Lake Washington, his heat cut through.

fifteen

JUST PAST SEVEN, WHEN GABRIELLE WAS GIVING UP HOPE THAT HER FRIEND would come home, Cinder marched into the house. From Gabrielle's position on the couch, she could see Cinder's reflection in the dark television. Cinder held a takeout box under one arm and the doll under the other. She kicked the door shut, and the doll's amber eyes closed and then opened, seeming to focus accusingly on Gabrielle.

Taking a few deep breaths, Gabrielle pulled the throw tighter around her shoulders. She tried to push down the terror that rose inside her throat and drove the fevered beating of her heart. Gabrielle turned away from the muted television and leaned on the couch's arm to fully face her roommate by the door. The doll's sparse, matted hair hung from the net that held it over the sculpted porcelain beneath. From this distance, the myriad of cracks over the doll's chubby cheeks were indistinct. Yet their darkness spread out, giving the entire expression a shadowy appearance.

The doll looked at Gabrielle with lazy, half-closed eyes. If only Cinder would tip her a little more, get the eyes to slide shut, so that the doll wasn't watching, waiting, daring Gabrielle to say something. Gabrielle had seen those eyes at the crime scene.

Cinder moved around the couch, between Gabrielle and the TV.

Don't look at me like I'm crazy. Yell. Please, just yell about the inconvenience. Gabrielle sank into the cushions. Her hair was still damp from her swim with Peter earlier in the day.

Cinder tossed the takeout box onto Gabrielle's lap and then plopped the doll on the couch's arm next to her. Gabrielle froze, feeling as trapped in porcelain as the doll, whose arm now brushed her waist.

"How did you get her?" Gabrielle asked.

"She was in my car at the station when I picked it up."

"And you didn't give her to me? You kept her?" Illogical or not, Gabrielle's stomach turned at that thought. The doll was only safe and happy when she was with Gabrielle. *She's my friend, not yours.*

But that was what a crazy person would think. *I'm not crazy.*

"I didn't want to drive with the thing in my car, so I gave it to Michael. It was actually on the porch just now when I walked up. I guess he left it for you? Dunno. Don't care."

"Why the takeout? I had the car... did you bus with this?"

Instead of speaking, Cinder flopped into the slouched armchair on one end of the coffee table and lifted one leg at a time to take off her knee-high black boots.

Afraid to offend the doll, but also worried at her nearness to Cinder, Gabrielle eased the doll off the padded couch arm onto the cushion between Gabrielle and the armrest.

"The cops think you killed him, Angel." With her boots off, Cinder stood and crossed the room to the kitchen. She poured herself a glass of water, keeping her back to Gabrielle. "Did you?"

"No." Gabrielle's voice came out in a squeak, and she swallowed before attempting to say anything else. But Cinder's long absence implied that perhaps Cinder already thought she was guilty. "I'm sorry I got you mixed up in this."

"You should be." Cinder's voice lacked any emotion. She paused to sip from her glass before finally turning to face Gabrielle. Cinder's blue hair had come free from her ponytail, and wisps paraded over her shoulders. "But mostly because you still haven't told me what I'm involved in. Spill."

Gabrielle picked up the takeout. The container had opened, revealing a hamburger and fries—a full meal, not leftovers. Her heart pinched at the gesture of caring.

A glance at the doll brought another thought. *Cinder brought that too. And of everyone I know, she might actually believe the doll is more than just a doll.*

Cinder had an entire wall of occult stuff in her room and books upon books on spell craft and magic rituals. Along with several texts with spines that displayed things like *The Factual History of Vampires.*

"Seriously," Cinder said. "What happened with Joe? And also, I know you don't want me saying shit about Michael, so I'll avoid that, but did you know Peter was at the police station yesterday? Why was he there?"

"I texted him, and he was the last person I talked to at the U. The police called him in like they did you."

Cinder's lips pursed as she padded across the floor to the couch, hips swinging, so confident and sexual without being comical. Gabrielle had tried to copy that walk. Cinder had laughed, head thrown back, and called her a sex kitten for days.

"Joe?" Cinder asked.

"He wanted me to do things I didn't want to do. That's it." Gabrielle lowered her eyes, and the doll met her gaze. The flaming eyes cut like red-hot brands, cauterizing Gabrielle's aching soul. Gabrielle blinked and realized the doll's eyes were closed.

I must have taken her to Joe's. It's crazy to think dolls walk around on their own.

"Angel, what happened? No bullshit. I have to sleep in the same house as you. You owe it to me to tell me exactly what your brand of crazy is."

"I'm not crazy." *Yes, I am.*

"Everyone worth knowing is a little crazy." Cinder stood over the couch, one hand on her hip, the other holding her water glass. "Now answer."

"I blacked out. I do that a lot. I have since I was a kid and my parents were killed."

"Fuuuck." Cinder paled and took a small step back from Gabrielle and the couch.

"I don't have solid answers for you, Cinder. I don't even have solid answers for me. The last thing I remember is Joe's truck driving up to me on Monday morning. I woke up at Joe's house covered in blood. I'm working on piecing together the rest." *And it has something to do with that doll.* Gabrielle resisted hurling it further away.

Cinder flopped on the couch on the opposite side of Gabrielle as the doll and flipped the top off the takeout box. She grabbed out a fry and poked it in between her lips. "So you don't know if you killed him?"

"How are you so calm about this?" Gabrielle slammed down the takeout lid, the Styrofoam crumpling under her palm.

"I wasn't. After I dropped the car off here, I got trashed at a party then cruised around with some friends all night, trying not to think. I crashed on a friend's couch and almost didn't come home today, but then I remembered, well, you." Cinder stopped to sip her water.

Gabrielle withdrew her hand from the crumpled box. "Sorry."

Cinder continued, "Since the day we met and decided to be roommates, there hasn't been a fucking moment where I've understood you. I admit sometimes I thought you were going to burst out and say you were raised Amish or some shit. You just seemed so confused by the world. Except, well, Michael was clearly not raised Amish."

Gabrielle stared down at her fingers, which clutched and unclutched the air. A queasy feeling churned inside her. She didn't understand herself any better than Cinder did. They both wanted answers.

"I'm sorry I'm not normal," Gabrielle said.

"Normal is a lie told to us by the media."

Cinder reached into the takeout box again. This time she shoved a fry into Gabrielle's face and let it dangle there until Gabrielle took a tentative bite. "The point is, I wanted to hear your side of the story. But so far, you've told me fuck-all. Please."

"You say everyone worth knowing is crazy, but I don't think you've ever known *crazy*. I am. Or I'm not. I don't even know anymore. I spent half my childhood in institutions, drugged up, or rehashing my parents' death and my insane theories with therapist after therapist." Gabrielle paused. Speaking of therapists, she really needed to call Dr. White. Michael must have contacted the office because they'd left a message to confirm an appointment she hadn't made.

"Your parents' death?" Cinder asked. "You've never talked about it."

"When I was nine, my father was killed in my bed, and I was found with my murdered mother in my parents' room."

"In your bed?"

"He never raped me," Gabrielle snapped. The queasiness inside her turned into a painful clutching. She shoved it down, refusing to think about any of that.

Cinder's eyes narrowed, but she remained quiet.

Gabrielle met the doll's mocking gaze, her pretty, painted mouth curled up in a smile, and the room spun. Her father's yell came through the wall—not yell, scream. She covered her ears and curled into a ball. Her legs tucked up to cover her nakedness. Above her on the hallway wall, one of her mother's crosses rocked back and forth.

"Gabrielle!" Cinder kneeled in front of her. The takeout box had spilled on the carpet.

Gabrielle shook her head in a quick, jerky motion. "The doll did it!"

"Did what? What just happened?"

"The doll killed my parents." Gabrielle lowered her face into her hands. The words drove out of her, the pressure causing tinkling cracks to spread over the porcelain inside her. Tiny shards flew off, and Gabrielle tasted their sharp bite on her tongue. A sob tore out of her.

The memory came, and it poured from her mouth even as the revelation took her into it, ripped her from herself into her trembling nine-year-old body.

"Daddy was in my room, and I was so scared. Momma was praying, and I could hear her voice through the crack of my door. He always left it ajar. My pajamas were on the floor. I remember the air being cold, so cold, and I wanted to wrap up in my blanket. Daddy wouldn't let me. Then I don't remember anything past that until I came to in Momma's bed, soaked with her blood. But I was dressed. Someone dressed me, or I dressed myself. And that damn doll—she was just lying on a clean spot of the covers. She looked so innocent, but I *knew* she did it."

Cinder grappled Gabrielle close, squeezing her in a tight hug. The doll watched them with her mockingly innocent smile.

"The cops never found who did it," Gabrielle said.

"Maybe it *was* the doll." Cinder's voice was hard, but she didn't sound like she was joking.

How can she not be joking? The suggestion had to be a trap. No one ever believed. Not even Michael. "That's crazy, you know, to think that."

"Yeah, it is." Cinder paused and chewed on her lip a moment, before picking up in an animated voice. "But you believe it, and there are *tons* of stories of possessed objects or people. I could show you so many articles of—"

Gabrielle tried to push away from her friend. "The doll isn't possessed."

Cinder's arms held tight. "You don't know that."

"I do. It was my great grandmother's doll. She's always been in my family—no tragedy or anything until my parents."

"You don't know that there were no hidden tragedies. I'm sure the cops looked into everything else, but has anyone ever really looked at the doll? Other than you?"

Gabrielle fought free and stood, grabbing the doll by its chubby arm. "Stop it! I don't need to be humored."

Cinder slumped over, burying her head in her hands, and then spoke through her fingers. "Angel, I don't know what to think, really. But I'm not humoring you. I'm not saying the doll kills people either. Just that discounting the option seems silly to me. That *thing* is clearly some sort of trigger of bad juju."

Gabrielle bolted up the stairs and then into her bedroom, slamming the door behind her. She collapsed on the bed. The doll's porcelain arms clinked together as she tumbled onto the bedspread. When Gabrielle looked over, the doll's eyes were closed.

Did I bring her upstairs? Gabrielle shook. The doll's tiny, cracked hand rested against Gabrielle's arm. The immobile fingers brushed over the tattoo of Peter's pearly gates, and Gabrielle watched as the cracks spread out.

Cinder knocked on the door. Knocked again. Then she heaved a sigh, and Gabrielle heard her walking down the hall. Her bedroom door slammed.

Darkness dripped over Gabrielle's eyes, and instead of her bright room and the scent of laundry detergent from her sheets, dust and mildew tickled at her nose. A trickle of light reached her from under a door.

I can't move.

Religious knick-knacks cluttered the kitchen and covered the walls. A picture of a man walking on a beach, two sets of footsteps trailing behind him, was framed above the breakfast bar. Gabrielle stared in horror at the kitchen of her childhood—one that no longer existed.

No. No. I'm not here. This isn't real. Gabrielle screamed, her voice not reaching the scene.

Gabi stepped back from the sink, dragging her adult consciousness along. Everything faded into black and white with an edging of red. Red where her father's lips pressed together as he stalked toward her.

Behind him, on the couch, with the television flickering in front of them, sat Michael and her mother. Gabrielle tried to scream for Michael, but this was a scene frozen in time. She couldn't change it. Instead she backed up, as she had done ten years before, as Gabi wiped the soap suds off of her hands.

Her dad grabbed her arm, the grip tight enough to grind her bones against each other.

"Is this a joke, Gabi! This is how people get sick. Does this water feel hot enough to kill anything?" Her dad's face flushed red. His grip on her wrist held up her prying fingers as she struggled to get free. It wasn't within her power to stop him from dragging her over to the sink and shoving her hand into the soapy water.

Silence is golden when he's like this. Please don't say it. Please. But as Gabrielle had known it would, Gabi's voice burst forth with the feared words. "They're clean! Leave me alone!"

He turned on the spout, still bellowing. The words struck her ears but didn't sink in; the rush of terror blocked them out. Gabi looked to the couch. Her mom regarded the kitchen with a frown but wouldn't meet her daughter's eyes. Instead, her mom sank back and returned to the television, her hand twisting the golden cross around her throat.

Michael threw his arm up on the back of the couch. Fear and anger battled on his features. At fourteen, he was already nearly six feet tall, but as previous occasions had shown, he was not a physical match for her dad.

There was nothing Michael could have done. Gabrielle wished she could leave her own memory and go to him. Tell him that none of this was his fault.

A jerk on Gabi's arm brought Gabrielle's attention back to the kitchen. With her eyes back on him, her father released her arm and reached across the counter.

Steam billowed up as he swept the dishes Gabi had just finished cleaning into the sink. Only the red knob was turned to the on position. Gabi took a few trembling steps away from him as the last of the plates plunged into water so hot even her father thought it killed germs. *What did he think it would do to me? Did he care?*

"Scrub the dishes, Gabi."

There is so much steam.

"I ask so little of you," her father said. "So very little."

Gabi clenched her fists and ran out of the kitchen toward the basement door. Michael stood up and yelled for her father to leave her alone, but her father's anger wouldn't be that easily stopped.

In the basement, at the foot of the stairs, she waited for me, but the house was bright. My fear of her seemed flimsy when facing Dad. In the light, he was my only fear. I should have known better.

The door opened at Gabi's frantic handling. She dove inside and slammed the door behind her. Gabi clamped her hands over the knob.

The doorknob twisted on the other side. She held tight.

"Stay in there, then! You filthy ingrate." And the lock clicked.

Gabi's small hands fell from the doorknob, and she turned to face the pitch black.

No! Wake up!

sixteen

THE BOXING GYM'S WINDOWS CAST A GLOW ONTO THE HALF-DOZEN CARS parked in its small lot. Cole shivered, hands tight on the steering wheel as he debated going in to work out. He needed the release of exercise but didn't want to meet up with Michael inside. With Michael's nightly gym habit, that was a real risk. Cole had turned off the engine a while ago, and the interior was nearly as chilly as the night air outside.

He shot off a text to Detective Sera about the autopsy. He was hoping to see the results.

Two men he didn't know sparred inside, their bodies twisting the light into jabbing rays as they passed the windows. Other than the show of lights and punches, nothing about the concrete building caught the eye.

Cole's phone rang, distracting him from the gym's facade. He pulled out his cell and flinched at Joan's name on the screen.

Screw it all—ignoring Joan will only piss her off and make the situation worse.

He slid his finger over the screen to accept the call.

"What do you want, Joan?" he asked, switching the phone onto speaker and placing it on the dash. His eyes moved back to the men boxing inside the gym's window. The rhythm of their movements helped soothe away the annoyance caused by even the idea of Joan's voice.

"The less you cooperate, the easier this is for me," Joan snapped.

"I picked up the blasted phone. What do you want?" Cole leaned his forehead against the driver's side window and stared out at the gym's light.

"I want not to have to meet with a mediator, Cole. But you're making it impossible."

Cole watched as one man landed a solid punch and the other stumbled back. If only every fight was so simple. He grunted in reply to Joan.

"The parenting plan you suggested is ridiculous," Joan said. "My lawyer literally laughed."

Her lawyer—her family's blasted lawyer. Probably time for me to call my lawyer again.

"I didn't know that prick had a sense of humor," Cole said.

"You know I'm not accepting that plan, right? I'm not signing off that I need to be supervised with Isa at all times. You're acting like I used to smack Isa around. You have no legal standing for this. Is all this fighting really what you think is in Isa's best interest? I'm here now, and I want to be in Isa's life, even if it means having to deal with you." Joan took an audible breath.

"You don't like my terms? Then don't come to see her." *That'll look great for you.*

"Stop being belligerent. I moved back to Washington to be with her!"

Cole's fist struck the wheel. "You don't just get to waltz back over here after abandoning her and be trusted. You're unpredictable. I don't want you to be part of her life. She's better off without you."

"Yes." Scorn and sarcasm hardened her already titanium tone. "Because research has always shown a child is better without their mother. Look, I left to escape *you*. I'm back now. I'm not leaving her again. Ever. You aren't going to stop me from seeing my daughter."

Joan clicked her tongue on her teeth, a habit he used to find adorable in his neat, proper wife. Now it sent shivers of disgust up his spine.

"So come see her," Cole said. He sucked in a deep breath, trying to calm himself. "But it'll be supervised. I don't trust you."

"For now, I don't have a choice. But I'm not signing off on this! I'm taking her tomorrow and Friday. And you will *not* be there."

"Fine." His lawyer had been clear that trying to block Joan would work against him. That didn't mean he had to trust or help her. "Yolanda will supervise."

"You aren't a knight in shining armor, Cole. This habit you have of trying to save injured women won't turn out well."

Cole winced. Was that really what he did? Certainly she'd lump Gabrielle in that category, and maybe she was right. It was ridiculous to try and save Gabrielle. "It didn't turn out well with you." Cole stretched his fingers, trying to loosen the stiffness from having them clenched around the plastic of the steering wheel.

"Because you're a deviant. I was never broken. I'll be there tomorrow, Cole. But expect me to fight this. If we can't work things out there, I *will* take you to court!"

"Coordinate your visit with Yolanda. I'm done." Cole hung up, clutching his phone in his fist.

Now he had to go in. He needed to hit something. Cole kicked open the car door and strode up to the building.

Through the glass, he saw a smattering of people—mostly men—sparring, lifting weights, or throwing punches into body bags. The owner, Tony, a short, brawny man. strutted over the black mats covering the floor.

Cole opened the door.

Tony turned and waved Cole over.

That isn't normal. I just want to work out. Cole hesitated, then with his jaw clenched to keep from swearing, he walked toward Tony.

Tony waved again and pointed off to the side at his office, which was partially hidden by the reception desk.

No choice. Darn it. Cole stalked toward the office after a quick glance around. The groups of active fighters didn't look at him. Cole and Michael's usual sparring area in the back was empty. The mat on the floor looked wet as if someone had just cleaned it. They only cleaned it during business hours when blood got on the mats. At least there was no Michael. That would save Cole one confrontation tonight.

A desk and computer chair served as both the reception area and the wall between the office and gym. In the chair sat a chubby girl with red hair, looking bored. Behind her, the office was dark.

"Hey, Cole," the redhead said. Her right eye looked puffy, and the makeup over it was heavy. Anywhere else, that would set off alarms of domestic violence, but here, it wasn't out of the norm.

"Hi, Lissa."

He had no more time with the girl before Tony reached him, clapped him on the back, and guided him into the closet-sized office.

The light turned on after a brief flicker, revealing a huge glass window facing the gym. Despite the small size of the room and the clutter that further cramped the area, Tony kept everything orderly. Piles of paper were neatly stacked on the floor. The lack of a desk left the floor open to two chairs.

It wasn't a nice place in a way the Joans of the world would appreciate. But the carpet was unstained, and a smell of cleaner hung in the air. This room, this whole gym, showed Tony's love.

Tony closed the door behind Cole and positioned himself in the chair to face out into the gym.

Cole sat with his back to the window.

"What's up, Tony?" Cole had trouble keeping a growl from his voice. He had a feeling Tony had called him in about Michael, and Cole didn't need more problems. But if Michael was hurt, he had to know, so Cole sat and waited.

Michael's absence from the gym screamed that something was off. He came to spar pretty much every evening. The wet spot on the mat wasn't a good sign either. Plus Tony was fidgeting more than usual in his chair. Cole didn't want anyone to be hurt, but he prayed that somehow, this wasn't about Michael. With his sister under suspicion of murder, Michael didn't need more to deal with. Of the gym regulars, Tony was the only one who officially knew about Michael and Cole's relationship, though Cole suspected most of the others had guessed.

He'd spent most of his post-college life in a hetero relationship with Joan. In that time, he'd gotten used to the ease of existing that came with such a relationship. He told himself that he and Michael hadn't been hiding anything from their other workout buddies; it was simply a new love affair. But with Michael missing and Tony looking at Cole, he wondered if both Michael and he hadn't been staying quiet for entirely different reasons.

"Michael was in here earlier," Tony said. His forehead gleamed with sweat.

He doesn't want to tell me. I wish he wouldn't—the last thing I need is more crud to worry about right now.

"Isn't he always?" Cole glared at Tony. Maybe he could stop this conversation from going forward by will alone.

"Things got a bit out of hand." Tony held up his hands in a quasi-shield position as if Cole had shown some aggression, which he was certain he hadn't. "Now, I don't blame Michael."

"Just tell me what happened." *Or don't and let me walk out of here.*

"Some of the guys read about that murder out near Snoqualmie Ridge, and word gets around. I don't know exactly what was said, but it set Michael off."

Tony paused and pressed both hands into his knees. He rocked forward and back, then gazed out at the floor.

If I get up and leave, I don't have to hear the rest. He could imagine how Michael would have responded. And Cole didn't blame him. It was always hell for the families involved in murder investigations. And for Michael, well, he'd been through it before and was probably especially sensitive.

It was obvious from how Tony told the story, with little pauses but no animosity, that Michael was okay and no one else was seriously injured.

"He was sparring with one of the idiots at the time. Michael usually goes easy on kids like that but . . ." Tony held out his arms in a placatory gesture.

Thank God this happened here and not on the street. Cole twisted his finger through the chain that held the cross around his neck. His brain felt fogged with worry and anger. Michael was suffering, and Cole wanted to help. But he didn't need this on his shoulders. Tony could have just stayed quiet. He did his best to shove the anger down under the worry. It wasn't Tony's fault, not really. When Cole spoke, his voice shook with the effort to stay calm and say the right thing. "But the kid's okay?"

"Yeah. He went down, and it wouldn't be an issue at all except Michael kept hitting him. We didn't have to pull him off or nothing . . ."

"But what? Why are you telling me this?" Cole smacked a fist against his knee. "Jesus, Tony."

"Because I picked up that he has some connection to that crime, and he's emotionally volatile. I think it'd be a good idea if he doesn't come in until this investigation is over. I can't afford to have some punk kid die in here. I like you, and I like Michael."

"Then shut up, Tony." Cole leaped to his feet. He'd already stuck around for too much of this. If he stayed, he'd wind up hitting something. "Michael's in a cruddy place right now, but all he did was hit some kid he was sparring with. People get hurt in here all the time."

"And I'm not kicking him out. I just think it would be better for him too."

Cole lifted his hand and jabbed a finger toward Tony. "*You* tell him that."

Tony crossed his arms, visibly unimpressed by Cole's anger. Or trying to seem that way. Cole sighed and rubbed at the bridge of his nose. He didn't feel like avoiding Michael. As hard as Cole's life was, what Michael was going through stunk more. He needed someone.

"When did Michael leave?" Cole asked.

"Ten minutes ago."

"I was in the parking lot." *How did I not see him?* "On the phone," he added as if that explained his delay.

Tony shrugged and gestured with his thumb toward the back door.

Cole nodded a single time. All he wanted to do was go hit something, get some of the pent-up rage off his chest. But Michael needed him, and Cole suspected he'd regret not going after him. Without another word, Cole shuffled out of the office toward the front door with his hands clenching and unclenching at his side. If Michael had taken off only ten minutes earlier, he'd still be on his jogging path. If Cole wanted, he could catch up with Michael before he hit the green belt behind his house and was off the road.

Cole hurried out to his car. When he got in, he checked his phone. A text waited from Detective Sera telling him the autopsy still hadn't come back.

A frown creased Cole's face.

He turned the key in the engine and pulled out of the parking lot. He knew he had to find Michael, but the autopsy was puzzling. Normally they came back within twenty-four hours. What could be so complicated about this one that it was taking days?

Joe had been stabbed to death. Not much there to figure out.

seventeen

Cole spotted Michael jogging alongside the road. His white sneakers caught and reflected the streetlights, though the rest of him was shrouded in darkness. Cole slowed the car as he neared and took a deep breath, trying to dispel the lingering annoyance still heating his blood. He pressed a button to roll down the driver's side window.

"Hop in," Cole said, pulling his car toward the paved bike lane.

Michael slowed his run but didn't stop. The car's tires crunched in the loose rocks and soil that merged onto the asphalt, which made the border between the paved road and the tall wild grasses. The yellow streetlights rolled over them as they traveled.

"I'm on your side," Cole said. He leaned his head out the window.

Michael stopped, turning to face the car. His jaw flexed. Sweat made his curls limp and darkened the edges of his shirt. "You talked to Tony."

Cole nodded. The car tires ground to a halt.

"I wanted to kill that little punk," Michael said.

"You didn't. You aren't a killer, Michael." Cole motioned to the passenger door. "Get in. Talking about it will help more than anything else, even more than beating in the faces of smart-mouth kids."

Michael laughed. It was a cold laugh that verged on either tears or anger. Maybe both. His hands made fists at his side and stepped up toward the bumper. "Someone's a killer, right? Is it really better if that's Gabrielle? You're the cop. You tell me how someone like her would survive in jail."

Cole rubbed the bridge of his nose again, aware he was making this anxious gesture far too often of late, and considered his answer. It was a good thing they'd met in the gym. If a meeting in uniform had been Cole's opener, they never would have gotten past the mutual dislike brewing between the police force and social services. Especially with Michael's seething personal resentment toward cops even stronger than most social service workers'.

This conversation wouldn't go well if Cole took on the role of a cop. Even if he was a cop on Gabrielle's side.

"I'm not accusing you or her of anything," Cole said. *I wish I could say the same of my partner. Bringing that up would do no good.*

"But you want to! I see it in your eyes."

"Shut up." Cole threw the car into park and opened his door. He stood and came face to face with Michael. He naturally fell into a stance from which he could protect himself if Michael decided it was time to start throwing punches.

Michael pressed his lips together and stalked past Cole toward the street.

"I don't want you to be guilty," Cole said. "Michael! I don't want her to be guilty either. All I want right now is to be someone you can talk to."

"Not now, Cole." Michael didn't turn to face him, but his shoulders sagged. "You don't get it. No one does. I have a wall lined with belts from different martial arts. I've been training to fight since my stepdad died—training to defend her. But nothing I do can defend her from any of this. I'm helpless, and I never wanted to be helpless like this again."

Cole paused to digest that. He hadn't seen this room of belts and had a sinking feeling they were kept in Michael's home gym—the one he'd converted from the room where his mother died. Gabrielle was all he had left. "We'll find a way to help her."

"Like hiring a good lawyer?" Michael's tone dripped sarcasm.

Cole felt the residual anger in him rise. Why did Michael have to make this so hard? He was already doing everything he could. "Get in the car. Let's talk. We can figure something out." *Though I can't promise he'll like the realistic options.*

"I'm afraid of what I'll wind up saying," Michael said. "I don't want to be around anyone when I'm feeling like this, especially you."

Cole leaned against the hood of his car. Michael stood immobile for a moment, stiff, angry, and indecisive all at the same time. Then he started off down the street again. Words rose in Cole, over and over again, as Michael ran up the hill to the crest. Words to call him back or comfort him. But Cole never voiced any of them.

The truth was, he couldn't solve Michael's problems.

Not until he got some answers. He glanced again at Sera's text. Maybe answers would be in the autopsy.

eighteen

Gabrielle woke huddled in the corner of her bedroom as the phone chirped its text message alert. Bumps from lying on the carpet all night covered her arms. Her back ached from the unforgiving angles. The doll lay flat across the bed like a queen while Gabrielle unfolded her stiff joints.

Morning light crept in her window to cast a cheerful glow over her neatly made bed. The doll luxuriated in the sunlight, strands of hair spread over the blue comforter. Her spot on the bookcase remained empty.

Did I sleep on the floor all night?

Gabrielle's phone beeped again. She fished it out of her jacket pocket: two texts and a missed call from Michael, and a text from Peter. A smile darted over her face before her general melancholy could kill it.

Peter.

She ran a hand through her stiff hair. The clumped strands smelled of lake water. *All of me must smell like that. I need a shower.*

First, she opened her message from Peter.

-I had fun. See U in class? Or should I bring something by?-

Before she sent a message, she needed to know what to say. She tapped her nail against the phone, making sure not to activate the touch screen. *I want to meet him. But there's no way I'm making it to school. Michael will kill me if I don't call Dr. White's office to confirm my appointment. That was at 10:30?*

The clock on her phone told her it was only 7:13. Cinder would already be gone with the car. So this would be either a day to bus or make the hour-long walk to school. She might be able to borrow the car from Cinder if she could find her on campus.

Gabrielle typed a return message.

-Can't hide. I have to meet with Dr. White anyhow. I'll be there. Meet you in our usual spot at 1-

Nursing the happiness hearing from Peter imbued in her, Gabrielle opened Michael's texts. They asked repeatedly and in no uncertain terms for her to call him. The third emphatically told her Michael needed to talk to her NOW.

Gabrielle concentrated her glare on the porcelain demon lying on the bed. Those brimstone eyes were closed, but its mouth seemed to tease upward in a mocking smile. Could the porcelain antique be possessed, as Cinder had suggested? *Is the doll possessing me?*

Dr. White would hate that I'm even considering this. I need to call Dr. White.

She shook her head. That call could come later. She had more pressing concerns.

Shower. I'll shower, and then I'll text Michael. I can at least let him know I'm okay. I can't avoid him forever but shower first.

Gabrielle skirted the bed, not turning her back to the doll as she approached the door. The weighted eyes stayed shut—not a peep of orange.

Maybe Cinder's right. Maybe she's the curse. The deaths only happen when I want them too, so maybe, somehow, she's just trying to please me. Something about having someone finally believe her, believe her even when she didn't, flipped a switch inside Gabrielle. *Maybe it isn't me.*

I could have a normal life.

I have to do something about the doll. Find a way to communicate with her, stop her.

With those thoughts swirling in her head, exposing her back to the doll proved impossible. The doll would know. The doll always knew. She flicked the overhead light off, leaving only the morning sunlight and the bedside lamp to illuminate the room. The lacy purple shade broke the light into uneven beads, which cast deep shadows from some of the doll's more prominent cracks.

What if she doesn't like me nosing around?

Gabrielle backed into the hallway and closed the bedroom door. Then she fled to the bathroom.

She flipped the showerhead on and stood beside the tub, staring at the mesmerizing stream. Her hand clenched around the blue and green shower curtain. The drops clattered against the white tub. A light mist cooled Gabrielle's face.

She needed information on possessed dolls.

She's connected to me somehow. If I separate her from me, the deaths will stop, right?

If I do, will I remember? Remember my parents' death? The day Mr. Pritcher died? Remember how Joe died? No answer I find could be as horrid as not knowing.

Steam rose from the water, hanging heavy in the air around her, beading on the colored waves of the shower curtain. Even the yellowed walls seemed to be soft ivory.

Gabrielle stripped, letting her clothes pool on the bathmat, and stepped into the steam. The pounding spray stung with heat, scalding away all the pesky thoughts along with the dirt that clung to her. If only the water could reach inside and steam-clean her soul. The water at her feet turned a dingy green. She washed, never quite forgetting how the doll was sprawled out on her bed.

What if it came down to destroying the doll? What if that was the only way to stop her?

Getting rid of the doll will destroy me too. Despite everything, the doll held her together, like glue in the cracks of her soul. Maybe it was just projection as her councilors over the years had suggested. That didn't change that she was emotionally dependent. *But what about Michael? Peter? Cinder? Holding onto this bond with her may destroy them. That's all that matters.*

Gabrielle massaged shampoo into her hair, and cucumber overwhelmed the pungent scent of lake water that had followed her since her swim.

The doll is getting worse, or I am. Before Joe, everyone who died deserved it. But Joe? He scared me, but he never hurt me.

How long until this insanity, mine or hers, goes further? How long until it's Peter? Or Michael? Or someone they love? No. Even if it's crazy, the only answer I have is the doll. Cinder is right. I can't ignore that.

Bubbles swirled around the drain, and Gabrielle shoved her toes into the white frothy mess. Her skin was a warm pink from the heat of the water.

Gabrielle shut off the tap and toweled dry. Then, sitting on the edge of the tub, hair wrapped in a towel and another wound over her chest, Gabrielle read through Michael's messages again. Something was slightly off about them, not what she'd have expected.

Something was wrong.

Gabrielle pressed the button to dial his number. Once the phone rang, she put it on speakerphone and returned to towel-drying her hair.

"Gabrielle?" Michael answered.

"Sorry, yesterday was crazy." A blush climbed Gabrielle's already heated cheeks as an image of shirtless Peter crossed her mind. "What's going on?"

"What happened yesterday?" A thread of panic wove through Michael's voice.

Gabrielle heaved a sigh, loud enough for him to hear. "Not that kind of crazy. Peter took me to the lake to get my mind off things, and then Cinder brought the doll home."

"Oh . . ." Michael's voice trailed off, leaving too much unsaid.

"Just say it." She wrapped the towel around her hair again and stood to stare into the fogged mirror.

"I didn't think we kept secrets from each other, Gabrielle."

"We don't. I told you what happened yesterday." *What does he know?*

"Why didn't you tell me Mr. Pritcher was murdered?"

"Oh. Um." *How did he find out about that?* "You were already so upset. I was just a kid, Michael. I was scared." *Scared I did it. Scared you'd hate me. Scared I didn't do it, and I'd be next.*

"They think it's the same killer, and that makes you look even guiltier." Michael's image on the phone, a picture from a barbecue the previous summer, showed him smiling and cheesing at the camera with a Diet Coke. It didn't fit the angst in the voice coming out of the phone's speaker.

"I know how guilty I look," she said.

"Do you? You seem way too calm."

"No. Not calm. It isn't just the police who worry me. They'll figure out what happened, and if it was me, then I'm better off locked up." Yet her voice trembled on the words.

Gabrielle swept the towel off her hair and hung it on the wall rack. She turned back to her amorphous outline in the steamy mirror. Tiny beads of water formed and trickled down it, leaving streaks of clear glass. *Like cracks where I can see the real me.*

"What worries you?" Michael asked. In the background, a phone rang and someone laughed. He was at work—early.

That's my fault, too, isn't it? He's missed a ton of work and needs to make it up.

On the plus side, that meant he couldn't yell and scream at her answer.

"The doll. I need to get rid of her," Gabrielle said, keeping her voice low.

Two yellow-orange dots stared at her from the fog. Gabrielle spun, but the only thing behind her was the wood door.

"Are you ready?" Michael asked. Something clicked, like a door closing, from his end of the line. "Last time you tried to get rid of it, you had a breakdown. Now might not be the best time to try."

"Does it matter if it's a good time? People are dying."

"Don't do anything yet, okay?" His words came out quick, frightened. "Let's talk to Dr. White first. Did you confirm the appointment I made?"

"There is no 'let's,' Michael. This is about me."

"Like Mr. Pritcher?" Bitterness seeped from the phone.

"Just like that."

"What happened, Elle?" Michael said. "You're not a child anymore. How can I help you if you don't even tell me what happened?"

"Not too long after CPS moved me away from the Pritcher house, Mr. Pritcher accosted me at the store. He said some nasty things. I ran over to Peter's house, which is what I told the cops back then."

"So you were with Peter?"

"That's what Peter says." Gabrielle set a hand on the sink counter and leaned her weight against it. Her hair fell in damp clumps over her face. She paused, gathering her thoughts before she continued.

Michael stayed quiet on the other end.

"I remember," Gabrielle started, then swallowed, "showing up at Peter's place and going out to his treehouse as it started to get dark. Usually Peter left me alone out there. Otherwise, his parents got angry and came out. Then I'd get sent home. But I don't recall what happened that evening. He says he was with me. I went black." *I could have killed Mr. Pritcher. It's only Peter's word that I never left. I never felt like I did it though. Doesn't that mean something?* "When I woke up in the treehouse, I was holding the doll. Michael, the doll has always been there. I have to get rid of her."

"Please wait."

"I have to go," Gabrielle said. Her fingers scratched against the sink top.

"Gabrielle, I only want you to be safe."

"I know." *And I want you to be safe.* "I've got to get to school."

"Gabrielle, if you don't call Dr. White to confirm the appointment—"

"I called and confirmed, but don't come." It wasn't really a lie. She was intending to call. And she needed to placate him. The force of his worry was simply too much. Gabrielle hung up before he could continue. His objections would only steal her confidence, and she needed all of it.

The hallway was silent, and Gabrielle opened the door to her bedroom. She dressed for the day without glancing at the bed. After a fragile shell of cloth protected her, she faced the doll. A thin net of hair stuck out in knots from her head and the cracks appeared deeper and darker than usual.

She's angry.

Dark swept across Gabrielle's eyes and traveled through her veins. The room blurred and faded and then coalesced into a different place, a basement filled with boxes. She held the doll in her arms, and the tiny cracks that ran through the porcelain varnish on the doll's face crawled up Gabrielle's skin, making a delicate sound like ice cracking in water. The destruction spread up her neck and raced across her cheeks.

"No!" Gabrielle tried to shout, but her lips refused to open—they were painted porcelain now, and she stared out of orange-tinted eyes.

Gabrielle's father stared back, blood squirting from his neck as he clasped his hands over the gash, desperately trying to hold his life in. Then it was Mr. Pritcher's face, his huge form lumbering forward, red seeping from his broken scalp and burbling from between his lips.

Gabrielle hit the ground. When she looked up, she was in her bedroom staring at the doll, who pretended to sleep peacefully on the bed. Gabrielle grabbed the demonic antique from the covers, ripping through what darkness remained at the edge of her vision. In her room, lit by the morning, she trembled from lingering fear.

"I'm not a monster. You are," Gabrielle said. Her fingers tightened around the doll's plump arms. "I'm throwing you away." She meant it to be a shout. The words came out closer to a question as the doll's golden eyes stared at her, eyelids fluttering as Gabrielle shook her.

Gabrielle stalked over to the trash can and held the doll over the mess of papers and old food wrappers. *What happens if I do this? Does it free me or just make her angry?*

Orange eyes flickered like a flame in the light and the room seemed to dim around the doll's small body. Gabrielle's heart shuddered, and her chest contracted, making breathing painful.

I need to speak with Cinder.

With a frustrated scream, Gabrielle tossed the doll onto the bed and ran from the room.

nineteen

"DO YOU THINK I KILLED HIM?" GABRIELLE ASKED DR. WHITE. COLD AIR from the vent billowed against Gabrielle's maxi skirt. It fluttered against her calves.

"Did you?" Dr. White flicked her stylus pen several times while staring at her tablet.

Gabrielle held her breath as she watched the pen bob in Dr. White's stubby fingers. The psychiatrist's petite frame was hidden up to the chest behind the faux wood desk that separated them. Even so, she cut an imposing figure for Gabrielle; after all, this was Dr. White's castle, surrounded by her weapons of choice: a computer, picture frames, and books.

The side of the desk closest to Gabrielle was bare. She tapped her nails against the plastic arms of the thin pad that made the chair arms minutely more forgiving.

Potted indoor trees surrounded cushioned chairs, lining the back of the office. Gabrielle could have seated herself in one of them. But then Dr. White would have moved out from behind the desk to sit closer, and Gabrielle needed the barrier of the desk more than a comfortable seat.

"What if the doll killed him?" Gabrielle asked, unable to stand the silence. "She's been doing odd things, moving . . . She was at the murder site! That has to mean something."

"Have you been taking your meds?" Dr. White asked, looking up from her tablet.

As always, the laugh-lines around the psychiatrist's brown eyes deepened her expression of concern. They were the only sign of age on her face; she dyed her hair an immaculate chocolate brown, and if not for the date on her diploma, Gabrielle would never have guessed Dr. White was in her fifties.

Dr. White made a noise, air sucked between her teeth mixed with a sigh, to grab Gabrielle's attention. "Have you been taking your meds, Gabrielle?"

"Mostly." Gabrielle dropped her eyes to the beige-and-cream checkered floor.

"What does 'mostly' mean, Gabrielle? You realize, I'm being asked to give a professional opinion to the police?"

And if I'm not taking my meds, she'll say I'm probably hallucinating. Talking about the doll won't help. Let alone telling her that I'm oscillating on whether the doll is really alive.

"Why are the police asking your opinion?" Gabrielle asked. *They want to know if I'm fit to stand trial. They know I did it.*

"You know that answer already. Are you taking your meds?"

"I've skipped a couple of nights, that's all."

"How many?"

Gabrielle turned to gaze out the window of the office. As if to demonstrate how the facility saw its patients as rats trapped in a maze, the window didn't face outdoors. Rather, it showed one of the building's many hallways. A potted plant with spiked leaves took a warlike stance beyond the half-drawn blinds. It didn't fool Gabrielle into thinking the window served any real purpose, but it gave a place for her eyes to avoid Dr. White's concerned expression.

"How many, Gabrielle?" Dr. White asked.

"A few." Gabrielle watched as the leaves on the plant swayed in a burst of air conditioning.

"Gabrielle, please don't evade the question." Dr. White's stylus tapped on the desk. "I'd like to help you."

"Then answer my question." Gabrielle's eyes snapped back to her doctor. "Do you think I killed him?"

"I don't have the ability to judge that. However, I can say that in the time I've known you, I've seen no violent tendencies—nor are any mentioned in your file. What I believe is you need to be more careful with your meds. Especially now, when you're under so much stress."

Gabrielle bit her lip and flopped against the stiff back of her chair. "It feels like the world is out to get me."

"Go on." Dr. White leaned forward, resting her elbow on the desk and setting her chin on her palm.

"Michael thinks I killed Joe, even though he won't say it. But it's more than just that. Why me? Why does this keep happening to me?"

"This isn't a new feeling for you," Dr. White said. "Is the mantra you wrote working?"

"Not really. I used it on my date, but since then, I guess things got out of control. And I have trouble believing I really do have any idea how to differentiate a real threat from something my mind concocted." Gabrielle's voice lowered, but she couldn't help a strain of sarcastic bitterness from entering her words. "I guess that happens when you wake up next to a dead body."

"So why don't you tell me, in your own words, what happened. How you got to be in a house with a dead body. Anything you remember."

"I was at school. Then I wasn't. I was at Joe's house, and he was dead."

"And the night before? On your date?" Dr. White's pen resumed its bobbing motion, calling attention to the fact it had stopped for a time.

"I shouldn't have gone. I shouldn't have been drinking."

"You were drinking?" Dr. White lowered her arms to lean forward on the desk. The pen tapped against the hard surface.

Gabrielle nodded. She sat up tall and let her chin jut out stubbornly. "Everyone else does."

"Not everyone else is on your medications." A thread of frustration crept into Dr. White's controlled tone. "You realize that alcohol exacerbates your symptoms? That explains why you're hallucinating again."

Gabrielle shoved her face into her hands. She wanted to run from the office screaming. The doubt and disappointment in Dr. White's voice wound around her heart and squeezed—the death grip of a python.

Running would be the same as giving up. Peter was getting better. He was working with the system despite his lifelong paranoia. *He's doing it in part for me. How could I give up on myself after that?*

There was no doubting Peter had been out of his mind that night six months ago when he'd grabbed her. The memory remained fresh, although the surrounding days blurred.

Peter had invited her over for dinner at his parents'. After dinner, she and Peter retreated downstairs into the basement.

Peter started going off about how they were all being watched. He pointed to a crack in the wall and went on some rant about bugs and wires. Gabrielle pulled out her phone—and Peter went crazy. He grabbed her arm and threw the phone across the room.

She had to rip herself out of his grip and run out of his parents' basement. And the whole time, she was terrified Peter had convinced himself that she was someone else. He'd never hurt *her*, she knew that. But she knew a lot about schizophrenia and recognized the signs. It had been on the long list of possible labels to pin on Gabrielle herself. It was a cruel disease, and if he'd convinced himself she'd been replaced by something else, well, then it wouldn't have been her he thought he was hurting.

Gabrielle met Dr. White's gaze—the memory providing her a modicum of strength.

If Peter could come back from that, couldn't she try to make it back too?

"I want to get better," Gabrielle whispered through her fingers. She'd already agreed to meet with Peter at 1:00, she wanted to be able to look him in the eye when she got there. "Peter got better. I saw him after my date with Joe. I feel like I've been working with the system my whole life, and nothing has ever changed. It seemed hopeless. But in six months, Peter has really gotten better."

"How does that make you feel, Gabrielle?"

"Hopeful. Maybe if I want to be well strongly enough, I can get there. But then I remember Joe and I think . . ."

"Yes?"

"How can I get better if I don't know what's wrong with me? How can anyone help me unless they know? If I killed Joe, I need to know. I'd rather be prosecuted and be able to work on getting better than to go free and never feel safe in my own mind. I need to be responsible to heal, and not just let the cracks spread and spread until I shatter."

twenty

Cole opened the computer file on Mrs. Lorretta Bey, Joseph Bey's mother, and stared at the screen. Detective Sera had conducted the interview with Mrs. Bey the day after the crime. She'd chosen to come into the police station rather than be interviewed in her home, so they had a video recording of the whole exchange.

Cole had watched most of the original interview from behind one-way glass before going outside to meet Michael. But something was niggling at him. He needed to listen again.

But even after years on the police force, the sight of a crying woman always brought out his inner protector. And Cole already had one woman on this case he felt driven to protect.

Most of the office had headed out to lunch or milled in the kitchen area. The mishmash smell of frozen Weight Watchers meals, microwave pizza, and coffee made Cole's stomach turn. That could also have something to do with the lineup of images strewn across his desk.

No matter how many cases he worked, some things never got easier.

The pictures were of Joseph's body, mixed with others of the scene and some of Gabrielle, tear-stained and vacant-eyed with defensive wounds on her arms. Each picture fit like a piece to a puzzle, and regardless of how Cole looked at that puzzle, it was not coming together in a way that would reflect well on the Cross family.

I shouldn't need to watch Joseph's mother sobbing to remember that solving Joseph's murder takes precedence. But there's nothing I can do for Joseph now—maybe Gabrielle can still be saved.

He shifted the pictures on his desk to reveal the cover of the manila envelope for Mr. Pritcher's murder. He didn't need to see inside to know exactly what the papers within contained. He had been looking at them all morning. Those contents were likely to be the ones that damned either Gabrielle or Michael—once he figured out how the facts within fit together. There were discrepancies. Ones he needed to look into.

And that was next on his to-do list for the day. After watching the interview, he needed to go check-up on some statements made during the Pritcher investigation.

Gabrielle is a victim too. I don't give a crap what anyone says. Kid watched her parents get slaughtered. What happens if I start to see Joseph as the victim too? What would I do differently? Am I sabotaging the investigation?

Yet he couldn't leave the case. Not as long as every time he looked at Gabrielle he saw Yolanda reflected back at him. Yolanda had never been charged. Her husband's kids were supposed to be at their mother's that night. But according to her statement, she'd heard them yelling when she got home from her night shift. She'd run in to save them. The kids were unharmed. If he could have proved she set the fire, she'd be in jail now. Or he liked to think that's what he would have done.

Now it was time to prove to himself that no matter his internal reactions, he'd work to find evidence. If Gabrielle or Michael were killers, he'd find the evidence and charge them. But first, Mrs. Bey.

With a heaved sigh, Cole shoved on his headphones and pressed play on the taped interview. A low buzzing static was all the sound at first, but on his computer screen, he saw the older woman fold and refold her hands in her lap as Detective Sera leaned onto the table, in a posture Cole was sure she meant to be reassuring. For someone who knew so much about body language, she had no handle on her own.

Detective Sera asked a series of simple questions, all in a simpering voice that sounded patronizing to Cole but seemed to work on Mrs. Bey, as her answers came out with more confidence as the interrogation went on.

Cole looked away from the screen and stared into Joe's glazed eyes. There was something here he'd missed. Maybe at the end of the interview when he'd left to meet Michael?

Joe needed a champion. He had Sera.

Didn't Gabrielle need one too?

Sera started speaking on the video. "Our records show you talked to your son the morning before he died. Can you tell me what was said?"

Cole's eyes snapped back to the video.

"I spoke to Joe in the morning. Yes, that's true. Because of my health, he checks"—Mrs. Bey took a long shuddering breath—"checked in at least every other day."

Detective Sera nodded for her to go on, but Mrs. Bey stared off into empty space.

Cole couldn't connect with her emotionally or even intellectually. He tried to reason with himself to see her side. *How would I feel if Isa was gone? I don't imagine it would be any easier if it happened when she was in her twenties. Losing a child is losing a child.*

"What did you and Joe speak about that morning?" Sera asked. From the camera's angle, Cole couldn't see her face, only her black hair and the looped earring in her ear.

"Some girl he was dating, mostly," Mrs. Bey said. "She came to his house the night before, and Joe had himself in a state worrying about her—he said she freaked out and demanded he leave her at a gas station."

"What was the girl's name?" Sera planted her elbow on the table.

"Don't you know that?" Mrs. Bey snapped. "You've been questioning her."

Cole leaned back in his chair and glanced around the office. Only one other desk was occupied, and that detective slouched down in his chair as if asleep. Cole looked back to the screen.

"I need to know what your son told you, ma'am." Sera used that sickly sweet tone again. Her hand massaged the back of her neck. To him, the touch seemed hard, a gesture of frustration.

"Ella. He called her Ella. Anyhow, he was worried about her state of mind and wanted to go talk to her—straighten things out."

"Straighten what things out?" Sera's fingers stopped moving. An action Cole knew meant she thought she was onto something.

Cole shifted the photos in front of him, moving a shot of Gabrielle seated on the exterior steps to the house. Her doe eyes pleaded with him. He kept his gaze off the recording.

"They'd been drinking, he said, and . . ." Mrs. Bey paused to sob.

Cole covered his eyes to fully block the images on the screen and on his desk. No matter where he looked, he couldn't escape.

"He was afraid," Mrs. Bey said, "of what she might wind up doing. He already has one ex saying nasty untrue things."

"That would be Rebecca Learner?"

"Yes. She's still threatening to file abuse charges, but he never hit her! I know that. She never even implied it until he kicked her out. She's an addict, and that's the start and end of the situation. After six years together, my Joe got tired of cleaning up after her. But if this little Ella got the wrong idea in her head or . . . Oh, I don't know. But he wanted to be sure Ella was okay. He told me he was going to her school to try to talk to her. I asked him not to, but he wouldn't be talked out of it."

Cole spun his chair to the wall, turning his back to the recording. Joe had been at the school that morning? Perhaps there was some video of the two meeting there. Security footage of that meeting could go a long way in figuring out what happened.

The smell of fresh coffee covered the other odors in the air now and wasn't nearly as revolting to Cole.

I can get lunch soon, or at least a cup of coffee, but I can't put off watching this any longer.

"So he went to see her," Detective Sera said. "Did you speak to him after that?"

His headphones pressed against his ears and Cole found it a modicum easier listening to her with the blank surface of the wall in front of him.

"No."

"Do you know if he found her?"

"He's dead, and she was in his house," Mrs. Bey snapped.

"That was the next morning. It's the time in between that we need to fill in," Sera explained. "Did Joe seem angry with Ella?"

"No. Just concerned."

"As close as you recall," Sera said. Her concern sounded less faked when he wasn't looking at her posture. "What did he say about going to find her?"

"He said, 'She isn't stable, Mom. She's a mess. A cute mess, but a mess. I shouldn't have taken her home at all but now, I have to check on her, make sure she's okay.' That's it."

Cole's stomach was a tight knot inside him. *I need to know the truth. That's my job, finding the truth.*

"When are you going to arrest her? She killed my boy." Mrs. Bey's voice rose to a near wail. "He wasn't perfect, but no one is. He didn't mean her any harm, and he didn't deserve that."

Cole closed his eyes. No one deserved what happened to Joseph, but that didn't mean that was all there was to the story. Cole shut the recording off. His head hung over his desk. Mrs. Bey might not need answers, but he did. He knew from conversations earlier that Detective Sera was off pulling records and trying to reconstruct Joe's last hours.

But Cole found another tug was stronger. He needed to know about Gabrielle's past. The pictures of Mr. Pritcher's murder showed similarity to Joe's murder. And he wondered if the autopsy would show even more when it came back. Those two crimes were almost certainly committed by the same killer. However, the murder of the parents was different. Was that an effect of the passage of time? Were all three crimes committed by the same person?

If they were, the only killer who made sense was Michael. Gabrielle hadn't been strong enough to commit her parents' murder. But Michael seemed not to have even known Mr. Pritcher was dead. Cole couldn't really believe Michael was capable of lying so well or, truthfully, of killing someone.

If the first murder was committed by someone different, the list of suspects grew. Gabrielle was certainly one of them but so was her friend Peter Cullen. He'd been close to both Mr. Pritcher's murder and Joeseph's.

Time to answer some questions.

Cole shot a quick email to Detective Sera telling her to stop by the university to check on security footage. Chances were she had put the same pieces together, but why not communicate? In fact, it was odd that she hadn't filled him in on that bit. Sharing a case usually meant sharing information. Then he grabbed his jacket and left the office.

Fresh air, tinted with sweet pollen, filled his lungs. He stood in the secure police parking lot with his jacket over his arm and stared at the dark clouds on the horizon. Blue sky stretched over him, but it wouldn't last.

His car waited across the lot, and after sky-gazing long enough to gather himself, Cole ran over and got in. Almost simultaneously, his phone rang.

Michael.

Cole swiped the screen to ignore the call. He settled Mr. Pritcher's file on the passenger seat and took off. Time to hope that some old leads would get him somewhere new.

twenty-one

Cherry blossoms danced in Gabrielle's vision as she stared up at the branches that crisscrossed over the quad. She'd lain there in peace for nearly half an hour. It wasn't yet time to meet Peter, so she'd settled on the far end of the lawn away from where she'd arranged to meet him. She texted Cinder about the car and let her roommate know where she was.

Truth was, Gabrielle had ulterior motives for seeing Cinder. But she didn't want to put anything in writing about the doll.

Other students passed by, each lost in their own world. No one even glanced at Gabrielle sprawled out on the grass, except one man with a goatee who leered at her.

She'd missed her first class to make her appointment with Dr. White and now, she felt oddly unmoored surrounded by so many people simply going about their ordinary lives. She wondered what it would be like to see inside those lives, to live them.

Did those people know how lucky they were?

Cinder didn't text back.

Why'd I even come? I could've messaged Peter to meet me at the coffee shop instead. No way I'm going to classes. Peter was right; I can't keep my life going as if everything is normal. Gabrielle shoved up on her arms and propped her back against the rough bark of the tree behind her.

A white petal drifted across her view of the buildings and their pinkish stone and then coasted over the gaping black mouth of the huge arched entranceway and the stairs rising within. Her eyes fastened back on the trees. *Is Peter already here? I could get out of here if he was.*

She looked around but didn't see him among the throng of students hurrying over the brick walkway. Of course, she was on the opposite end of the huge yard and didn't have a good view of their meeting spot.

The more she thought of Peter, the guiltier she became. She should be avoiding him, as she was trying to do with Michael. Being around her right now would only settle them in the middle of this Joe mess. But Peter . . . She couldn't get the sturdy warmth of his arms out of her mind, or the way she felt around him.

I'd never do anything to hurt him. Never. I need him, but am I destroying him in the process? He doesn't have the strength to be my support system. But maybe I could be his, if I was stronger, if I was normal.

If I was free of her.

Cinder plopped beside Gabrielle on the grass, lying flat on her back across the manicured lawn with her fishnet stockings displayed proudly as they splayed out.

"These trees set off my allergies like nothing else, but I still just love them," Cinder said by way of greeting.

"Hi," Gabrielle said. Not for the first time, she wondered what magic Cinder had that she could just break all the social rules and somehow still fit right in.

"So, that brother of yours," Cinder said, "is he single yet? I'd be a great rebound."

Gabrielle swallowed several replies. What would one of the pretty sorority girls walking the lawn say to Cinder? Something snarky and borderline mean, something that made it clear both that Michael was not and never would be interested and that Gabrielle had no wish to think about her brother's sex life. But she wasn't sure how to make such a comment. "He still has a boyfriend."

"Okay, okay. You need the car?"

"No. Not really. I need to talk about the doll." Gabrielle glanced nervously around, but no one was near enough to hear her words. Still the hairs on the back of her neck prickled. "If she were possessed or something, what does it mean? What are my options?"

Cinder propped herself up on her elbows. "Cool. Let's do this."

Was Cinder the weird one?

"All my books are at home, but I've been looking since we talked. Basically, it all depends on what sort of possession you have and what you want to do about it."

"What sort of possessions are there?"

"Demonic is the one everyone on the Internet talks about, but there's also spirit possession. Not all cursed or possessed objects are inherently evil."

Gabrielle thought about that while eying the lawn. A heavyset man at the far end walked their way. She hoped he'd turn before reaching them. "What's the difference?"

"Demons are just out for carnage and damage. Spirits are remnants of the person they were—or are."

"Are?" Gabrielle worried her lower lip with her teeth.

"There are cases of possessions from the spirits of still living souls—mostly coma patients or others who lost major capabilities in accidents. Damaged people who can't affect the world in other ways. But most are dead. Either way, they usually have a mission left over from their former existence that they need to accomplish."

"She isn't demonic." Gabrielle fidgeted with her skirt, very conscious of their conversation as a woman with headphones on bopped by. "Every time she's acted out, I've asked her for help. She's protecting me."

"Okay. So who could be possessing her? Your mother. Didn't she die around the thing?"

"Not my mother. The doll always felt alive to me and . . ." *My mother's death is among her crimes.* But that was too insane to say here, surrounded by denim, backpacks, and cherry blossoms.

"How'd your great grandmother die? Dolls back then often weren't made in huge batches. They were more personal. Maybe her bond to the thing lasted after death. And as family, she'd have reason to want to protect you."

Over my mother? But it made a kind of sense. Gabrielle had held the doll, loved her, protected her from the dark, while her mother abandoned the antique to the basement. Gabrielle whispered her secrets into that cracked porcelain ear and held those hard little hands.

"Maybe it doesn't matter who," Gabrielle said. "I don't want to hurt the spirt, just stop them, stop this." *Free me.*

Cinder gave a dirty look to the heavyset man as he finally reached them and slowed his walk. He peered at them, either to ogle Cinder's outstretched legs in their fishnet casing or to listen to them.

"What?" Cinder snapped.

Gabrielle retreated internally, waiting for the man to yell back. Instead, he left.

"Was he listening to us?" Gabrielle asked.

"Who cares?"

"He'll think we're crazy." What would he say to his roommates when he got home? Whispers like that gathered and made clouds that would follow Gabrielle. She'd been through it before.

"Who cares?" Cinder asked.

"They'll lock you up again. You're being naughty," the doll whispered. Gabrielle shook her head to rid herself of the voice.

"We could do like an exorcism on her," Cinder suggested.

"Have you done that before?"

Cinder guffawed, tucking a strand of blue hair behind her ear. "You serious, Angel? No. Obviously no."

"Would it work?"

"It's that or burning her. From what I've read, burning is the most effective."

Gabrielle flinched. "We can't burn her. I don't want to hurt her."

Cinder rolled her eyes and shuffled to her feet. "I read a cool ritual about cleansings that work like exorcism. And burying the object in consecrated soil to neutralize any lingering spiritual presence."

"Thanks."

"I gotta get to class. You want to keep talking? You can walk with me."

Gabrielle shook her head. Peter's class might be letting out.

twenty-two

THE QUAD WASN'T TOO CROWDED WITH PEOPLE YET, BUT IN MOMENTS, IT would be. Gabrielle hurried over the walkway, past the sandstone benches in front of one of the buildings, as she headed up to find Peter. Her flats made a dull, echoey sound.

The early afternoon air smelled of pollen. Dashing out onto the paths twisting under the cherry trees, she breathed in the sweetness. Most of the blossoms were white now, having fully bloomed, but a few pink buds lingered in the puffy cloud over her.

She scanned the trees, but though there was a scattering of people reclining under the canopy of leaves and flowers, none of them was Peter.

Gabrielle pulled out her phone. A message from Peter waited for her. The time stamp put it at five minutes old.

-Detective is here. The woman.-

Gabrielle texted back.

-Where?-

She hovered on the sidewalk, and people scurried around her. Out here, she was anonymous. The other students went about their simple lives, laughing, chatting, holding hands—and paying no mind to the cracks swiftly spreading through her life.

Something acidic coiled inside Gabrielle. *A life like theirs, like each of them take for granted, is all I ever wanted, and I'll never have it. How is that fair? Why does everyone else get to live and I get this?*

Is getting rid of the doll really the choice? The way to get from where I am to normal?

Her phone beeped with a link to the Allen Library and a message from Peter.

-Here. Near the fountain.-

Gabrielle started across campus toward the library, keeping her eyes lowered to the ground, hoping to escape notice. As she went, she chewed on her thoughts. But no matter how long she mulled, her ruminations became no more palatable.

The laughter of her fellow students as they ate lunch or threw a Frisbee on the lawn outside the student union building left Gabrielle cold. None of them knew there was a homicide detective on campus. None of them cared. It didn't touch their lives.

Who could the police be here to see? Was there another suspect? Or did they have evidence on her?

As she neared the location Peter had sent, her life fell into a split screen.

She walked beside herself and the ghost of Joe. This reflection of her past self and a dead man strolled together in an amiable fashion, smiling and relaxed. Only two days had passed since that day, yet everything had changed. And that change had all started with this event parading along beside her. She didn't recall ever walking with Joe here, but the moment felt true. This had actually happened.

We talked. What did we say?

But although she could see this image, it made no sound. Joe held a cup of coffee—or something in a Starbucks cup. She held the same.

I don't seem frightened at all, just childlike.

Gabrielle glanced at the buildings they passed between. The walkway was wide, but with other students crowding it, she was forced to walk practically on top of her past self. Her phone beeped, but she didn't check. Peter would be telling her where Detective Sera had moved on to, or Michael would be calling to fret. The latter she didn't want to hear, and the former she already knew.

She followed the ghostly figures.

Maybe I didn't kill him. Tears flooded Gabrielle's eyes at the thought. Next to her, as the scene played out, she saw no aggression, no sign that violence was building in either party. Nothing existed in that casual walk that could have foretold where she and Joe would end up only a handful of hours later.

Monday's Gabrielle spun around, hands held to the sky. She giggled. Joe seemed relaxed, his thumb hooked in his jeans. He didn't impinge on the personal space of Monday's Gabrielle.

Maybe getting my memory back wouldn't be bad. What if . . .

Then Monday's Gabrielle turned, and her eyes shone in the sun —not brown but yellow—faded and brightened in turn by time and hate. Gabrielle wasn't in those eyes. Something else was, something pure in its wickedness.

Gabrielle stopped, letting the apparitions parade on without her. Tears, moments ago warm, spilled as cold as a lonely mountaintop over her face.

Something evil lives in that doll. She's followed me my entire life and nothing has ever changed or gotten better. I gave her access to the world, to play, to kill.

"Ms. Cross?" Detective Sera's voice startled her.

Gabrielle looked up through tear-glossed vision. The apparitions were gone, as was the crowd of students. Only Detective Sera stood on the walkway.

Gabrielle recoiled, a small gasp escaping her lips.

Sera had planted herself, legs slightly spread, her hand pulling back her jacket to rest on her hip—the move displayed her badge and a glimpse of her gun. A dubious expression settled on Sera's makeup-free features. Her forehead wrinkled. The only softness about the woman was a few strands of black hair that danced in the breeze, having come loose from her ponytail.

I can't handle this woman's questions. She won't believe anything I say. "Is Detective Montez with you?"

"No. I came to review some security footage." She held up some evidence bags.

I can tell her I remembered meeting with Joe. But she'll assume I knew all along and am telling her because she has those tapes and can prove it. Telling her will make me look guiltier. If only Cole were here, he'd understand.

"I found some interesting images," Detective Sera said. "Why don't you come to the station later and we can discuss it?"

Gabrielle winced away. *She's not demanding I accompany her. Not arresting me. That has to be a good sign, right?* "Will Cole be there?"

"Cole?" Sera stressed the word and arched an eyebrow. "At the moment, I'm doubting Detective Montez will be there."

Be honest. If I want to know the truth, it's best for me to give the truth. And I do want to know, don't I?

"Ms. Cross? You don't look well." Detective Sera didn't appear or sound overly concerned.

"I may be able to fill in some of the blanks for you. That's actually why I'm here. I've remembered meeting Joe—or bits of it."

"Oh." Detective Sera smiled, her thin lips nearly disappearing in the expression. Somehow, she seemed more aggressive. "Follow me back to the station, Ms. Cross. We can discuss everything you've just 'remembered.'"

Gabrielle nodded. "I don't have a car."

"I'll drive you."

The detective started out walking with Gabrielle. As they rounded a bend, Gabrielle saw Peter watching from a doorway and shrugged.

I have to know what really happened. If this is how I find out, then I'm going to go.

twenty-three

Cole drove in silence. The sunlight heated the interior, and sweat dampened the back of his shirt. Dangling in his view, a bracelet of blue beads hung from the rearview mirror—a present from Isa, a present she'd made and given to her mother. But Joan hadn't wanted the reminder when she left. At Isa's heartbroken look, he'd claimed he'd always wanted it anyhow.

Isa had settled her hands on her hips and said, "Is that really, actually, true?"

"It is," he had said, resisting the urge to use "really, actually" in his reply for fear she'd think he was mocking her.

He'd kept the bracelet and hung it where Isa could see the prize displayed.

Joan doesn't care about Isa.

No. If this was really about Isa, Joan would be desperate to make up for her abandonment—not making demands. This was about the same thing as everything she did: herself.

Nestled in a low-income housing apartment in Kent, Cole arrived at the current address for Mrs. Pritcher. The dreary look of the place was enough to pull him out of his personal pinwheel of worries.

The sidewalk in front of the building was cracked, and old rusted bikes leaned against the exterior. Cole got out of the car and gave a purposeful nod to the eyes peeping out from behind blinds. After double-checking the apartment number in his files, Cole approached 6B and rang the bell, but heard no sound. Assuming it was broken, he rapped three times on the metal door.

"Who are you?" snapped a rough, female voice behind the door.

Cole lifted his badge in front of the peephole. "You're not in any trouble, ma'am. I have some questions for you."

The door creaked open, and a woman peered at him. Her hair was tied back severely in a bun so tight she looked like a TV sitcom nanny. Her otherwise wrinkle-free face scrunched with worry. Age spots littered her hands and exposed arms, leading him to think she was somewhere in her sixties. The odor of cat piss and mildew leaked from the interior, along with a strong scent of cooking oil and spice.

"You're here about my late husband. I know, I know." She crossed her arms under her breasts, cutting in half the cute cat face dominating her shirt.

"Yes."

"This is about that awful Cross family."

Cole nodded, yet no matter how he tried, he couldn't apply this description to Michael or Gabrielle. Who was seeing the situation wrong? Her or him?

"Devil take them both." Mrs. Pritcher waited, eyebrows both lifted expectantly.

She wants to know I'm on her side, that I condemn Michael and Gabrielle.

"May I come inside? I have a few questions."

She glared. "I've given all my answers."

Okay, I'll play her game.

"They might be connected to another murder," Cole said. "I'm hoping to gain some insight."

"They killed him, my husband, you know."

Really, actually? Cole resisted smiling and motioned inside the house.

"That's why you're here, right? No one could prove she did it—but she did. And him, Michael, the things he accused my husband of! Alvin never did any of those things, but you all were sure quick to bury his murder. Real quick."

"If you want answers, then cooperating with me is a great place to start."

Her nostrils flared, but she stepped aside to allow him through the cramped hallway into the dimly lit living room.

"That little bitch ruined everything. Everything," Mrs. Pritcher said, going to sit on a sunken brown couch.

Cole picked his way over the newspaper-littered floor. Discolored watermarks speckled some of the musty paper. Probably mice. Dried up hairballs gathered in the corner and coated the furniture.

He'd been in plenty of low-income homes that didn't look like this. Mrs. Pritcher's apartment screamed of despair and loneliness. This was a woman who'd given up on life.

Cole chose a rickety wooden chair nestled in the mess and sat. "I assume you mean Gabrielle?"

"Yes."

Behind Mrs. Pritcher was the apartment's tiny kitchen. A pot sat on the stove, giving off a heady garlicky odor. He was thankful for its mask over the other, fouler fumes lurking in the air.

Cole adjusted himself so he faced Mrs. Pritcher directly and met her eyes with a steady gaze. He needed to seem attentive; someone like her was used to being ignored and wouldn't respond well to disinterest of any kind.

"Can you tell me how long Gabrielle lived in your house?"

"Only a few months. Yes, a few months."

"And what sort of child was she? Was there anything of note in those months?"

"Quiet. I barely heard her speak the whole time. Snotty too—when she did talk it was always about her things and what we were permitted to do with them." She snorted. "Like that hideous doll. We didn't listen though—it scared the other kids. So we put it away."

"Did you ever meet Gabrielle's brother?" Cole averted his eyes. His face might give him away at her answers, and he needed to keep her talking. "Did he come around the house a lot, or speak with either you or your husband?"

"No. Cowardly, bastard. Never even saw us but thought he knew us. Knew us! Accused my husband without ever looking in his eyes."

"Did you ever see Gabrielle after she moved out?"

"Certainly, certainly. The day she murdered my husband."

"I would love it if you'd tell me, in your own words, what you saw the day of your husband's murder." This is where new clues would be. Because Mrs. Pritcher was correct, her husband's murder had not been as exhaustively investigated as the double homicide of Gabrielle and Michael's parents.

"Oh, that's easy! Alvin was real upset, real upset." Her hands gesticulated wildly as she spoke. "He had been so fond of Gabrielle, you see. She was his favorite of the kids we'd taken in. So when that horrid brother of hers accused him of being more rough than he ought, he took it real hard. Real hard."

"And the day of the murder?" Cole asked. He noted her verbal tic of repeating herself had gotten stronger, implying to him that her agitation was not in any way forced.

"I saw Gabrielle peeping in the windows of our house—I chased her right off. Right off. I didn't want her there after all the trouble she'd caused. I figured she'd come for her creepy doll, and I told Alvin so. I told him! We had to take the thing away from her because it scared the other kids."

"So you told your husband that she was at your house? What did he do?"

"He went to talk to her about it, I guess. I guess that's what he did. I hated that thing. Hated it. I swore it watched me every time I went to get something. You see, I had to go up there and see those awful eyes, yellow eyes. Awful, awful eyes."

"This was after Gabrielle left? The doll was still with you?"

"She left in such a hurry you know." Mrs. Pritcher huffed.

Cole leaned forward. Given her psychological dependance on that doll, confirmed by every source he could find, it might have meaning that it had been kept by the Pritchers after Gabrielle left. "Did your husband hold a grudge against Gabrielle?"

"No." The woman paused and shook her head, her tight bun bobbing. "No. Like I said, he was real shook up about her brother's accusations. Angry like, you know? He loved Gabrielle so much, like a daughter. And that little bitch killed him."

Cole waited, not wanting to fill the silence with empty words. It would be better to simply let her talk.

"The last time I saw Alvin he was headed off to find her. Then they found him there, just lying in the basement." Mrs. Pritcher sat up completely straight and said her next words as if throwing darts into a board. "And the only thing missing from that basement was *that* doll. That damn doll."

And only two people had a reason to want that doll. Michael and Gabrielle.

twenty-four

AFTER WASTING A FEW HOURS AT THE POLICE STATION WAITING FOR Detective Sera "to be ready" for her, Gabrielle was relieved to see Detective Montez. He entered the interrogation room with Sera and stayed while Gabrielle was questioned. By the end of the interview, she doubted her splash of memory had done them any good. But on the surface, both detectives believed her.

Sera had been sitting with Gabrielle the whole interview, but as it came to a close, Cole stepped up to the table and leaned down. Detective Sera's face hardened.

There is tension there. Am I causing him problems? If Michael and he don't work out because of me, I'll have to live with stealing another shot at happiness from my brother.

"I went to see Mrs. Pritcher today," Cole said.

Detective Sera's eyes widened with surprise. Her mouth tightened. Gabrielle's eyes flicked between the two. She was unsure what to make of Sera's reaction.

"I'd like you to answer a few questions," Cole continued.

Gabrielle nodded.

"You previously said that on the evening Mr. Pritcher died, you were with your friend Peter Cullen, in a treehouse at the back of his

151

parents' property, correct?" Cole's hands lay flat on the interview table, which made his muscular arms stand out. She doubted he meant it to be a threat or intimidating, but Gabrielle couldn't help but imagine how impossible it would be to escape those arms. Like iron bars, they blocked her way.

"Yes." Gabrielle glanced at the clearly steaming Sera. "Though I never claimed to remember all of that time."

"To your knowledge, were you alone during that time?"

"Not to my knowledge. Peter said he was with me."

"What do you remember?" Cole asked.

I wish I knew what he was driving at. I would give it to him. "Peter took me out to the treehouse, and I lay down on the back bench."

"Did you have the doll?"

"No." *Oh. That's where he's going.* She'd been on this merry-go-round before.

"But pictures show you had it when the police found you at Peter's."

Gabrielle nodded. She'd been through this so many times she could have played her part *and* his with ease. How if, as Peter claimed, she was with him the whole evening, had she gotten the doll? Had Michael been checked for this murder? Cole couldn't remember from the files.

"Look, detectives," Gabrielle said, lowering her eyes to her hands, which were clasped in her lap, "I don't have the answers you want. I wish I did. Maybe Peter's mom went to get the doll, or maybe . . . I don't know."

"Are you certain you didn't have it with you when you arrived?" Cole asked.

"As I told them back then, I don't believe so." Gabrielle tugged at the sleeve of her sweater until it covered her hand. "Mrs. Pritcher had the doll locked up. I was supposed to get it back when I moved houses, but Mrs. Pritcher claimed she couldn't find it in the attic."

Cole nodded. "You're sure she said the attic?"

"Yes. That's where she kept all the breakable stuff she didn't want the kids near." Gabrielle eyed Cole from under her lashes. She flicked the edge of her sweater sleeve with her fingertips. This was new. Different. What did he know—or think he knew? Obviously, he wasn't going to tell her. Could this mean answers might finally be on their way?

"How did you get the doll back?"

"I don't know. I didn't have her, then I fell asleep or something. When I came back to myself, I had her."

Cole nodded and stood up straight, effectively ending his line of questioning.

"Thank you," Detective Sera said. "We'll be in touch." Her chair scraped against the floor as she rose. She motioned Gabrielle toward the door.

Gabrielle left the room, all the while feeling Sera's gaze biting her back. She walked out into the lobby and then directly outside to find Cinder and Peter waiting for her—Cinder sitting on the dirty sidewalk next to the door and Peter further away.

Gabrielle hadn't been outside since she walked with the shadows of Monday Gabrielle and Joe. The sun had dropped near the horizon in the intervening hours. The blue sky of earlier in the day had faded, a flurry of deeper colors populating the sky. The moon made a pale sliver over their heads. Without looking at her phone Gabrielle guessed it was closing in on five o' clock.

Cinder had dressed as if attending a rave, not visiting a police station—her blue hair was spiked, and her corseted top left little to the imagination. Peter, on the other hand, had sunk into his hoodie and held a hand beside his face as if protecting himself from surveillance.

"Hey there, Angel," Cinder chirped, tucking her cell phone into her cleavage and leaping to her feet. "What happened?"

Gabrielle shook her head, not wanting to share. "How did you know I was here?"

"I told her the detective brought you here," Peter said. His voice sounded strained. "I needed a ride."

"What happened?" Cinder repeated. "All Peter knew was some bs about the detective being at campus security and you leaving with her."

"That's what happened," Gabrielle said. The expectancy in Cinder and Peter's faces made her nervous. She didn't even know what to think herself about what had happened in the interrogation room. Divulging it was out of the question. "I don't want to talk about the rest. I need to digest it myself first."

"Are you okay?" Peter asked.

"Yes, but let's get out of here, please," Gabrielle said. The air pricked at her like needles and her feet ached as if conspiring with her skin to pressure her away from the door.

"Happily," Cinder said.

Peter shuffled after them, eyes shifting nervously. *With all his conspiracy paranoia surrounding police and government, he came here, on purpose. For me.*

Gabrielle grabbed his hand, hoping her touch would help calm him. Peter jerked at the contact and started to pull his hand back. Then the burst of fear faded, and he tightened his fingers around hers.

"Is there someone whispering from over there, Gabs?" Peter asked, quietly, his head motioning slightly.

"No." She squeezed his hand.

From what she knew of his disease, questions like that were actually a good thing. It meant he was making a real effort to differentiate between the voices in his head and reality. And better yet, he wasn't acting belligerently, which he had been last time she saw him in a police station. He hadn't dealt well with being questioned about Mr. Pritcher's murder.

She let their hands swing between them. The three of them headed further into the parking lot.

Peter pulled his hand free and crossed the parking lot quickly, getting them as far from the building as possible. Gabrielle trotted to keep up. With a little distance between them and the police station, they all slowed as they headed toward Cinder's car.

"Why did you come here?" Peter asked, then without pausing. "Are you really okay?"

"I'm fine. They found some video footage at the school of me and Joe. And I *really* don't want to talk about it."

She took in a deep breath and recalled that flash of orange in her past self's eyes. She hadn't mentioned that bit to the detectives, but it was the one piece that haunted her. Had that been real?

"Cinder?" Gabrielle said when they were halfway across the lot. "Earlier today you were saying some things about demon possession?"

Cinder grinned. The gleam of excitement in her eyes did worlds to calm Gabrielle. She wouldn't be this excited if she was just playing along with Gabrielle. No, this interested her.

"Yeah," Cinder said. "There's a huge history of possessed objects. All different sorts actually, but the type you have—"

"What the fuck!" Peter shouted. "She doesn't have a demon possession."

Gabrielle grabbed for his hand, but this time Peter rejected her attempt to placate him.

"Shush," Cinder said, pursing her lips. "She asked me."

"So?" Peter snapped, a red flush hiding the freckles on his cheeks. "Do you really think you're helping, feeding into her delusion?"

"Peter," Gabrielle said, reaching an unclaimed hand one more time toward her friend.

"What, Gabs?" Peter turned to her, and they stopped, sandwiched between two unknown cars. "This talk isn't helpful. It's the opposite."

"You sound like Michael," Gabrielle said. Internally she winced at the statement. Michael would have a lot more to say about it. Most likely he'd go on about committing her again.

"Good! Of the four of us, he's the sanest," Peter spat.

"What does it hurt for Gabrielle to address the possibility of a possessed doll anyhow?" Cinder asked, hand planted on her hips, her tightly corseted waist swaying. "Even if demon possession *is* a crock, which I don't believe, what does it hurt?"

"Because this is a delusion Gabrielle's been trying to overcome for ten years! You talk to me about it when you've been there for years of her weeping or watching her struggle to figure out what's real and what's a nightmare." Peter looked at Gabrielle, concern in his blue eyes.

And she understood his point. It's how she'd felt when people talked around Peter about the government surveilling all calls—and that was before they'd had the blowup where he shattered her phone. He tried hard enough to stay functional, to tell reality apart from the misfires of his brain—he didn't need people feeding his delusions.

Is that all the doll is? Everyone keeps saying so. Except Cinder.

And if there is any chance at all . . .

"This is different, Peter," Gabrielle said. "People are dying. I have to do something, or I'll go crazy. Literally."

"Not this." Peter crossed his arms.

"What then?" Cinder asked.

The three stood silently in the parking lot, Peter staring Cinder down and Cinder refusing to break eye contact.

"Enough," Gabrielle said. "I just want to get out of here."

"Well, I'm going home," Cinder said, at last, tossing her keys in her hand. "Gabrielle, we should continue our research. I can show you some books and websites on possession, even how to destroy said objects."

Destroy her? I don't want to destroy her, just stop her. "She wasn't always evil—just innocence bent and broken, cracked until the ugliness spilled out."

"She's a *doll*," Peter said. "Don't go home, Gabs. You don't need more time in that house with that doll."

"What do you suggest?" Cinder asked. Then with a jeer in her voice, "Going back to old favorites? Gabrielle's told me about you. Maybe you were thinking dumpster diving?"

Gabrielle's shoulders relaxed, and a smile crept up her face. Cinder might not understand Peter, but he and his brand of spontaneity were exactly what she needed. They *had* gone dumpster diving once—at a bookstore. Though she didn't recall telling Cinder about it. They had lain amid the piles of old musty books for twenty minutes laughing, before picking a few at random. Then they'd read passages to each other in a local park.

Gabrielle decided. The idea of running away from her problems for an evening with Peter sounded perfect. Even if it meant taking the bus. She could manage the crowds with his arm to cling to. "I'll go where you guide me."

twenty-five

"You're late." Joan tapped her watch with one perfectly manicured nail as Cole climbed out of his car. She stood on the front porch of his home, which they'd once lived in together.

What was she still doing here?

She wasn't wrong. His interview with Gabrielle had kept him, and now Joan had that ammunition. He'd arranged to be home at seven, and it was nearly eight after finishing up paperwork and the deadlocked drive home. Every muscle in his body tightened at the sight of her, but he'd be damned if he'd let on. "You didn't have to stick around. Yolanda would've taken care of Isa."

Joan let out a sigh of derision and flicked a lock of platinum hair off her shoulder.

Cole cracked his knuckles, staring at her vampiric nails. No choice but to face her.

He started across the driveway past her pristine BMW. Joan sneered. With a number of choice phrases on his lips, Cole took the first porch step and stopped.

Isa's little face peered out of the living room window, only eyes and nose above the sill. Yolanda must be in there with her, but Cole couldn't see her.

"You couldn't have called?" Joan's lip curled up as she spoke.

"I was working. You wouldn't know what that's like."

"Oh, I remember very well how incapable you are of keeping decent hours. I'm sorry to see Isa is still suffering from it."

From the bitch who abandoned her for over ten months? If Joan wants to see fucking suffering . . .

Cole grabbed onto the column supporting the porch's awning to keep his hand from forming a fist. Joan would be sure to notice such an aggressive gesture. After a few moments, he felt capable of speaking again.

"What is it you want, Joan? Or did you stay just to lecture me?"

Joan pulled her hair back over her shoulder. The motion wafted the scent of her expensive perfume toward him. The scent, some exotic mix of oils, seemed overly sweet—a poison disguised as a fruit. "I want Isa overnight on Friday."

Cole's stomach cramped. He directed his attention back at the window, hoping for Isa's face to remind him to stay civil, but she had disappeared, leaving only the rippling curtain, which quickly stilled. Even if he couldn't see her, she might be in there listening.

Cole shook his head. "You know the deal."

"No! This isn't about our 'deal.' This is about Isa. She told me there was a mother-daughter campout with the church last summer."

Cole remembered. It had broken Isa's heart not to go. Yolanda had offered to take her, but even at her young age, Isa knew the difference between a nanny and a mother. He and Isa had rarely attended church since. Isa felt her mother's presence there, and Cole felt the judgement from all of Joan's old friends.

A glance at the curtains showed him that Isa hadn't returned. "What's your point? You can't go back in time and be a good mother."

Joan's face flushed, and her mouth parted as if to yell. Instead, she jabbed her finger into his chest. "I'm taking her camping as a do-over. I need her overnight."

"I'm not concerned with what you need or want." Cole glared back into her snapping blue eyes. How dare she talk about her needs. His hand slid down the post but didn't let go. "You get her until seven. Figure it out."

"Please, Cole."

Cole resisted smirking at "please" slithering from her lips. "I didn't know that you knew that word. The answer is still no."

"Well, then." Joan gave him the meanest smile he'd ever seen. "I'm sure the mediator will love to hear how summarily you dismissed a simple request. I can wait two weeks."

Two weeks? He hadn't processed that mediation was so close. *I need to call my lawyer.*

"Fine, Joan, if it means that much to you. Not overnight, but you can keep her late on Friday. I'll let you have her until ten? I'll stay out and come home well after she's asleep. It's too cold yet to have her sleep outside anyway. You can do whatever you need to do in the house."

"If it's not overnight, I'll do it on Tuesday. I have other things to do on Friday."

Cole clenched his jaw. Joan's constant desire to one-up things and "win" had always been annoying and was more so now. "Tuesday? That's a weeknight—"

"So? Isa doesn't have school the next day, and I'm free."

"Fine," Cole growled. He pushed past Joan to the door. Her footsteps traveled the other way, but he didn't feel safe until he'd entered his house and shut himself inside.

He leaned his back against the door and took several deep breaths. The entrance was unlit, and the playroom and kitchen on one side had been tidied and closed for the day. On the other side, the living room was lit by a lamp and the TV, which was turned to an almost inaudible setting and displayed a cartoon lion dancing.

Joan's BMW roared to life outside.

I could've handled that better.

"Mr. Montez?" Yolanda asked. The waxy smooth burn scars all over her brown face scrunched as she talked.

Cole glanced over into the living room, but she wasn't there. His eyes found her in the hall next to Isa's bedroom door. The fact her door was shut meant Isa had been put to bed. That wouldn't last long since she knew Daddy was home. She was probably jumping on the bed waiting for him to come in.

"Do you need anything?" Cole asked Yolanda.

Yolanda sidled down the hallway. Her dark hair fell loose down to her shoulders and shielded her face from view, just as her shapeless house dress hid any trace of what the body beneath might look like.

"Sorry I'm late," Cole said. "Sorry that I left you with Joan."

Yolanda let out a barking laugh and stopped walking a few feet from him. "I hate that woman."

"You're not alone."

Yolanda nibbled on her lip, pulling the scars taut. Cole knew that mannerism. Yolanda had something to say, and she didn't think he'd like it. Which also made sense of why she'd put Isa in her room this early and right when Cole got home.

"I know I shouldn't say this because she's Isa's mother. But she is a horrible, horrible woman."

Cole nodded. Nothing yet that he had any objection to.

"But there is something I should say. You need to hear." Yolanda gave a swift jerk of her head that resembled a nod.

"Go ahead." *It's been a long day. All I want to do is say goodnight to Isa and then take a shower. But Yolanda has been putting up with Joan. I've got to shoulder whatever blow she needs to deliver.*

"Mrs. Montez is awful, but she's Isa's mother."

What? A hole seemed to open beneath his feet threatening to swallow him. Yolanda had to be on his side. He couldn't go through this without her. Cole held up a hand to silence her. Yolanda went on.

"Give her a chance to be the kind of mother Isa needs." Yolanda sighed. "Make a deal."

"As soon as she says something reasonable."

Yolanda shook her head, clucking her tongue in disappointment. "This is about Isa, not you and not me. Not Joan either."

<h1 style="text-align:center">twenty-six</h1>

WIND PLASTERED THE THIN FABRIC OF GABRIELLE'S SKIRT AGAINST HER LEGS in rippling sighs of silk as she climbed a metal ladder. Peter climbed above her, seemingly fearless as he approached the third and final story of a partially constructed office building. Though the ladder was on the interior of the abandoned site, the walls were not completely built, and below her, the second story was nothing but metal girders waiting for the flooring to be applied. With each movement, she was conscious of not getting caught in the air's battle with her clothing. The fall would do more than knock the wind out of her if she slipped.

Her hands clung to the aluminum rungs of the ladder. Peter knelt on the rooftop, a hand offered to her. She gripped it and let him help her the rest of the way up.

"What do you think?" Peter asked, his eyes wide and hopeful. It had been his suggestion to come here. They'd started their Friday evening after leaving the police station with dinner and a walk. By then it was nearly eight, but she hadn't wanted to go home. He'd brought her here on the bus, to show her something that helped him relax.

"Let me actually look at it first." Gabrielle smiled.

Through the scaffolding, Gabrielle saw the litter-strewn floor three stories below. People had once had high hopes for this building, she was sure. What made them abandon the project, not even half-finished?

She hurried to the center, leaving behind the ladder for the relative safety of a wider wooden platform built onto the scaffolding for construction workers.

The wind pierced through Gabrielle's thin jacket and whipped her hair around her shoulders.

Peter never glanced down as he crossed the boards after her. Instead, he tilted his face up to the stars. Gabrielle tried to do the same, but she wondered if they'd ever see the same thing when gazing at the heavens. The purple tinge at the horizon glowed like a leftover caress from the sun. The stars twinkled playfully, pausing in their endless game of tag across the sky to flirt with the earth. It was all just a mass of wonder and beauty for her, but she knew her friend well enough to know he saw something more sinister.

Government satellites floated up there, closer than the stars— and for Peter, this had always been a point of concern.

Peter grabbed her hand and led her to the edge of the center platform so that the toes of their shoes crested the drop. Cold fingers of air shoved at her back, encouraging her to take one more step. The view of the city swept out in front of them, but all Gabrielle noticed was Peter's fingers wound in hers. The image of his silhouette cut out against the city lights belonged in an art gallery.

"Michael thinks you're bad for me," she said. *I wish he could see us now. The only time I feel safe is with Peter.*

"Maybe I am, Gabs. Two broken people don't fit together to make something whole. If I'm hurting you . . ." The wind swallowed his words.

"You're not, Peter. You're all I have." She shuffled closer and turned to him. She set a hand on his bicep, and his muscles were firm under her touch—tense.

He faced her, a careful distance between their bodies.

"When we were younger, I always thought we'd end up together," she said, gaze fastened on his mouth, not quite daring his eyes. She hadn't thought of those feelings in a long time, not since well before their falling out. "Growing up, I mean. I hated your girlfriends. None of them were ever good enough. I just wanted it to be me, but it never was. Why didn't we?"

"Remember when we were twelve?" Peter smiled. The starlight caressed his face, and in the moonlight his shadow toppled over the edge of the platform onto collapsed, mildewed cardboard boxes below.

"Our one date?"

"Yeah." Peter smiled sheepishly. "I wanted to kiss you. I actually dreamed about it, planned it the night before, but then you were there and—and I just couldn't."

"But you could have." Gabrielle reached out and touched his cheek. *I would have let you. There wasn't anything I wanted more.*

"Maybe. It's been like that for eight years. There was always a reason not to, and I never wanted to mess things up." Peter motioned between them. His feet scraped on the oil-stained boards, but he didn't move away from her. "Sex is just sex. You and I are more. I want you there every day of my life, and sex, it complicates things. You have enough complications right now."

"I wouldn't know." Gabrielle forced his chin up slightly so she could see his expression. The scattering of freckles was hardly visible in the light. His jaw had tensed, and emotions warred behind those eyes.

Kiss me, please. What if this is the only time? I may not have another chance. The chill wind blew over her body, making her want the heat of his touch even more.

"Sorry, Gabs." He gazed over her shoulder out at the city.

"Don't apologize." *No, don't look away from me.* She moved her hand back to his face and traced his lower lip with her fingertip.

"Gabs." His voice came out thick and throaty. "You need someone stronger. Not me."

"I don't want someone stronger." *I want you.*

He turned and held her shoulders. Then slowly, he leaned down, seeming to reconsider with each inch, until his breath touched her lips. Indecision washed over his face. Before he could rethink it and take this moment away from her, Gabrielle lifted on her tiptoes and kissed him.

His stiffness melted at her touch. Hands that had been hesitant to even touch her moved down her back, fingertips making a river of sensation along her spine. They slid along the band of her skirt.

She sighed and locked her fingers behind his neck. *My Peter.*

He crushed her body to his. A soft moan escaped him, eliciting a flash of warmth through her body. The jolt of sensation chased away her thoughts, and her lips parted to his seeking.

Gabrielle opened for him. Her arms encased him, her mouth welcoming. Her flesh proved that her doubts about her abilities in this dance were wrong; she knew the steps. They started with a flame, a hungry desire that quickened inside her, driving her hands and igniting her body so that every touch, every point of friction, brought a frenzied craving until there was nothing left but his tongue, his lips, and his hand pressed into her. Every solid inch of his body that molded against hers sang to her, and yet he was not close enough.

"Peter." She sighed. "I know you think it's silly, but I'm going to get rid of the doll. Evil or not I don't need her. I need to be normal."

A siren whirred in the background. Gabrielle's eyes flicked over to the flashing lights. Fear spiked inside her. And buried in the dark behind him, Gabrielle saw a pair of orange eyes burning.

"*You are mine,*" a voice said.

Then everything went black.

Her feet slipped in the warm wet. She opened her mouth to scream, but liquid copper surged into her mouth—choking her. Far away, yellow eyes burned, getting closer and closer.

"You're mine. Only mine. You swore."

Gabrielle felt the cracks moving up her arms, across her shoulders, and blood seeped from the lines. Then a sharp pain flared in her back as the cracks bloomed out, marking her.

"We're only safe together. He'll only hurt us," the high, tiny voice screeched. Then softer, *"My friend."*

twenty-seven

GABRIELLE RECOGNIZED THE SHADOWS OF HER NINE-YEAR-OLD ARMS AS THEY clutched at the basement door handle. She stood in the dark, clinging and waiting to hear her father on the other side.

The doll waited in the basement at the bottom of the long, dark flight of stairs. The light switch at the top was broken, so Gabi would have to run down in the dark and turn on the light before the doll woke. The doll wasn't kind in the dark, only in the warmth of the light. Gabrielle felt a foreign desire, belonging to the younger version of herself, to cradle the doll. She was young Gabi's one true confidant.

From the bottom of the stairs, out of Gabrielle's sight, porcelain ears listened patiently. Gabi believed the doll loved her as long as the light was on, and Gabi loved her ivory dress and tiny painted mouth. But even then, Gabi had feared the doll, too, just as she doted on her.

Gabi's hands clamped over the knob, clutching tighter at the sound of her father's approaching footsteps.

The doorknob twisted on the other side. She held tight.

No. Please, Dad. But it was no use begging the past. And the darkness eyed her back.

"Stay in there, then. You filthy ingrate." The lock clicked.

Gabi's hand fell off the doorknob, and she turned to face the pitch.

Don't go down there. Please. Don't, don't. Gabrielle screamed from inside the memory, but no matter how loud her voice was, it simply ricocheted around inside her mind.

The doll's gaze was different in the dark, and Gabi imagined sharp little teeth under the porcelain lips. The doll was afraid of the dark and hated living in it.

The rush of water from the sink reached her through the door. She could almost see Dad standing over it, waiting to force her hands under the stream.

"I'll tell her about Dad, and she'll agree that little hands burn faster than germs," Gabi whispered, her voice soft and high as only a child's could be. "Locking a child in the dark is evil. She understands that better than anyone."

But first, Gabi had to make it all the way down the stairs. To young Gabi's mind, it would be simple for the doll to reach her in the dark and let her tiny teeth rip open Gabi's throat.

Michael's voice burst from upstairs. He yelled. Gabrielle wished she could push her younger self to go up the stairs and listen, but she had no control over the body she rode in. *Had Father picked a fight with Michael, or was Michael trying to defend me?*

Sitting down in the middle of the stairs, young Gabi waited for the doll to come up the stairs. "I don't want to be afraid."

Gabi's hands pressed to her ears. The shouting muffled, but the fears that she wouldn't hear the doll approaching swept through Gabrielle.

She never came for me before, Gabrielle thought, unsure why that day had been so different. *Maybe she saw my cracks that day and forgave me for living in the light she was denied. Was that what happened? Only that's crazy. I just told Cinder it's crazy to blame the doll, and it is.*

From the house, there was a crash. A small squeak that intended to be a scream erupted from Gabi's lips, and she ran down the remaining stairs. Her hand swatted at the light switch.

She missed.

The physical presence of the darkness closed in. Gabi tried not to be afraid.

"The doll likes the taste of fear in the dark," Gabi said. "And she'll forget we're friends."

Would the doll's voice be as black as her time-infected cracks or the same violent yellow-orange as her eyes? Gabrielle couldn't see them glimmering in the night, catching the light as they always used to right after she turned off the light in the basement.

No. This was the basement. *No, no, not now!*

Gabrielle knew this moment. Right after her father had thrown her in the basement for cold dishwater. That was the night he died. A shrill scream escaped Gabi's throat. No one would come. Dad wanted her to be scared, and Michael was no match for a full-grown man. Gabi hated Mom in that moment. She knew her mom loved her, but she wouldn't contradict Dad. Calling it a "unified front" was her excuse not to see.

Gabi's young heart hated Mom most. Gabrielle wished that even now she could fully forgive her. After Mom inherited the doll, Dad didn't want the antique in their room, and Mom always caved to his desires, afraid to lose the money and security he gave her. *It was her job to take care of all of us.*

If Mom had done her job, the doll wouldn't have so much hate. Do I believe that now? That it really was the doll?

Gabi's hand went for the light switch again and missed. She sniffled and then suppressed the sound. The doll didn't like tears because she couldn't cry. "Please don't hurt me."

Gabi jumped at a low scraping sound.

Was there a sound? There cannot have been a sound. There was no one in the basement except me.

"Please," Gabi said again. This time her seeking fingers found the switch, and the light burst on. It flickered at first as the old bulb warmed.

The doll was not on the shelf.

Gabi rotated, looking for her. Back then, she'd firmly believed that if she could see the doll, the porcelain monster couldn't hurt her. The stairs creaked, and Gabi's eyes moved to the source.

Finally, Gabrielle saw the doll crouching by the bottom step. One fist rested against the post and the other on the stair. Young Gabi sat, mostly because her legs refused to support her, and touched her porcelain companion's remaining hair with a trembling hand. "You almost reached me this time."

Gabrielle gasped, realizing what might have happened. The doll would have killed her.

And then, I thought of asking for her help, and I picked her up. Gabrielle stared out of her own eyes and helplessly wished just this once the memory would progress differently.

Gabi scooped the doll into her arms.

"Tonight," Gabi whispered to her, and the doll was her co-conspirator, "Tonight I'll put you upstairs. I'll put you near Dad. If Dad was gone, you could sleep in the house every night. You could live in the warmth and the light."

I suggested she get rid of him. Even back then, I was telling her to kill.

Upstairs, Gabi heard the familiar tread of Michael's heavy shoes and the sound of the lock clicking open.

Gabi cradled the doll closely and switched off the light. She hoped the doll would let her reach the top of the stairs. Even back then, Gabrielle knew the doll liked the taste of fear, but she had been fool enough to think the porcelain monster liked her caresses too.

I had to trust she could see my cracks. What choice did I have? At some point, you have to trust someone. And now how do I go back? How do I trust someone else? How do I get rid of her?

Gabrielle struck out at the orange eyes—at the cracked face of the doll. Her hand sprayed blood across the aged ivory dress, making the faded flowers flare a bright red. The doll flew backward from the force of her blow.

A thud reached Gabrielle's ears followed by a distant scream and crash.

Her knees hit hard wood, and her palms scraped against unfinished boards. The night around her glowed with city lights. She blinked, looking from side to side over the empty rooftop.

Empty. Peter.

She shoved herself up, ignoring the rushing in her ears, and turned in a circle. No matter how hard she looked, she was alone on the roof. The edge of the platform showed a black abyss that called to her.

"Peter!" Her scream tore into the air, echoing and then fading into the night.

Gabrielle darted to the edge of the boards and peered at the inconclusive mass below. Construction material made looming monsters across the floor, that, three stories down, buried in shadow, could easily have hidden the single form she searched for.

"Peter, please!" Gabrielle screamed again, her hands wringing before her. Somehow she knew she would hear no response. And her legs set off back toward the ladder before her mind caught up to the impetus.

The doll pushed him. No, she isn't real!

I pushed him. Me.

No! No. It was her. It must have been her.

Gabrielle sobbed as her feet slipped on the rungs of the ladder, and then continued the downward climb. The cold metal bit into her palms.

I wouldn't. I would never hurt him.

Her feet hit the concrete floor, and she scampered toward the center of the room.

The gaping holes in the roof of the abandoned construction project provided the only light for Gabrielle to see by. The stars, which had seemed so playful and bright minutes before, were distant and cold now. She could barely make out general outlines around her.

Still, Gabrielle knew where something would have fallen from the platform above and she stumbled in that direction, toward the pile of junk.

The dark formation in the center of the room remained still. The scattered garbage around her smelled of piss, but with each step she took, that odor lightened, letting in the undertones of mildew.

Peter might be in that pile. My Peter. No.

Never again. My life is my own. If I hurt him, I'll throw myself *off the goddamn building.*

An image came to her of Peter six months before, as she had confronted him at the top of his parents' stairs. They'd both gone to the Cullen's house for a dinner, but it hadn't turned out the way anyone intended. She'd accused him of being dangerous, of being schizophrenic. Her wrist had ached from where he'd grabbed her, and his parents came running at them shouting. She could still see the hurt and anger in his beautiful eyes.

He went against everything he believes in and took the damn pills. To make me feel safe. To make sure he was mentally stable. If I'm a danger to him, how can I do less? I'll cut out any part of me that could hurt him! "Who" is doing this doesn't matter. It's stopping it that matters.

Her thoughts raced at lightning speed. As fast as her feet moved toward the moonlit patch, her mind plunged on ahead. *The doll. I'll get rid of the damn thing. If that doesn't work, there are plenty of ways to die.*

But first, she had to find out if he was all right. Or if . . .

She reached the pile of trash and stepped into the mess.

"Peter, Peter!" Something sharp jabbed into the sole of her shoe, but she pressed on, fighting through rusty beer cans, corroded bits of metal, and disintegrating cardboard. A bottle clanked and rolled off the edge of a box. Gabrielle flung herself toward the movement. Peter lay on his side, facing her, eyes fluttering. She pushed past the splash of red spreading out on the cardboard under his head. Panic shot like electricity through her body. He had to be okay! She knelt beside him. Her hands rested by his torn pants leg. His knee was contorted and already swelling.

Alive. She fought to that word and held it.

"Peter, I . . ." She stopped as his eyes closed. Her breath hitched. She looked at her hand on the boards next to him. His fingers had moved to hers, curling against her skin.

Get it together. After forcing herself to breathe, she pulled out her phone. *It doesn't matter* what *happened. At least not for now. I've got to get help.*

Habit led her fingers to Michael's name, but she pushed it aside. She dialed 911 and clung to Peter's hand. She hardly heard the operator or her own words. Gabrielle watched Peter's chest, reassuring herself every instant that he was breathing.

A few minutes later, an ambulance pulled up. The red and white lights flashed, searing into Gabrielle's eyes. With each pulse of red, the thick scent of blood rose in her memory.

How can I believe any of these crimes are a coincidence? They have one thing in common—me. Unless I change, I'm dangerous.

Gabrielle stared blankly as paramedics reached her. Their voices were a blur across the darkness of her mind. Hands pulled her away from Peter. She watched as Peter was loaded into the ambulance— even heard the squeak of one of the gurney's wheels and the clatter of the stretcher being loaded in the back.

Then the paramedics shut the double doors.

twenty-eight

THE NEXT THING GABRIELLE KNEW, SHE WAS IN THE HOSPITAL. THE TIME IN between blurred together. Yet she instantly knew where she was, and what the waiting room around her meant. Peter was alive. They wouldn't have her waiting here otherwise.

The smell of the hospital covered her, bleaching out the remaining ammonia odor of urine from her nostrils. She watched in numb silence as the doctors and nurses passed by. The waiting room was on the small side, with three rows, back-to-back, of green padded chairs, all locked together at the arms. A small table held several magazines, each at different angles, seeming to imply that people read them. Of the few people in the waiting room, no one was reading them now. No one there met her eyes except one old woman, a rose handkerchief twisted in her gnarled hands.

"You all right, dear?" the woman asked, leaning forward.

"I think I pushed my boyfriend off a building." *And killed some guy I barely knew. Oh and murdered my parents and my foster father. That or my doll did.*

Gabrielle started laughing—hysteria making the sound high and uneven. It was that or cry. The old woman's smile melted. Then she averted her eyes. *And now I'm scaring little old ladies.* The urge to laugh receded as quickly as it had come.

Maybe fifteen minutes later, a doctor escorted the old lady away. Gabrielle huddled down in her skin. Her phone rang. She ignored it.

Once the phone stopped ringing, she lifted it to see Michael's name on the screen.

I may not be picking up for my family, but what about Peter's? Have they been called?

Gabrielle thumbed through her contacts and swiped to call Peter's mother, Sharon. Someone picked up, and the phone made an audible click. Light classical music played in the background, and the hum of distant conversation and laughter drifted over the line.

"Sharon?" Gabrielle asked.

"Gabrielle? Dear? Are you at the hospital?"

Gabrielle nodded.

"Gabrielle?" Sharon asked.

"Yes. I'm here. They called you?"

"Yes. Has something changed?" Sharon paused for a split second, not long enough for Gabrielle to formulate an answer. "We'll be there as soon as we can. I got a voice message from the hospital. Can you imagine? It was horrid. Just horrid. I only wish I'd heard the phone ring!"

"Okay. As long as you know . . . I just wanted to make sure." *Because, you know, your son is in the hospital and you aren't fucking here!* Gabrielle stood up from her seat and paced over to the far wall, wanting some distance from the smattering of others seated in the waiting room.

"David should be off asking to have our car pulled around," Sharon said. "You'll call if anything changes?"

"Yes."

"Thank you, dear. This is all so upsetting."

Gabrielle could find no words to return to that.

The line went dead.

She couldn't help but think that if it was her child, she would have been *running* to her injured son if need be. But of course, Sharon couldn't be rude, not to whatever random wealthy people she was hanging off of. Maybe if Sharon had actually sounded upset, it would have been easier to hear.

Is this all Peter has in his life? Parents who couldn't give a shit and me?

I can't afford to judge anyone. I'm a monster. Gabrielle struck out at the white hospital wall with a closed fist. *No, I can't think like that. It doesn't matter what I am or what I'm not as long as I stop this insidious violence.*

Gabrielle trudged back over to her chair and lowered herself into its stiff embrace. She tucked her legs up onto the green seat, hugging them close to her body.

As she sat, rocking herself back and forth, a police officer approached from down the hall. Not either of the detectives, but a younger man, slightly thick around the middle, with eyes that squeezed together in the center of his face.

"I need to ask you some questions, Ms. Cross," the officer said, standing awkwardly in front of her. "Come with me."

Gabrielle nodded. Here it came again, an interrogation with questions she wanted to answer but couldn't. She followed him into a vacant room and sat down in a chair exactly like those in the lobby. The officer positioned himself across the room and eyed her as if she carried a plague.

I'm a monster.

"Why don't you tell me what happened?" The officer hooked his thumbs under his belt, the posture making his stomach stick out.

"I don't know." Gabrielle averted her eyes. *Michael would be laughing at this guy. I wish I could. I wish I could blame the cops, vilify them in my stead.* "I'll give you any answers I can."

"Don't you remember?" The officer pulled out a pad of paper.

"I remember fine," Gabrielle said leaning away from the officer. The stiff green cushion under her resisted her attempt to gain distance. "No, I don't. We went up there and talked, then he was gone. I found him below."

She paused as the cop scrawled something onto a pad. The scratch-scratch of his pen scraped against her eardrums. They'd have her in cuffs soon.

"Will he be okay?" Gabrielle said the moment the sound of writing paused. *If I did push him, put me away. I don't want to hurt anyone.*

<h1 style="text-align:center">twenty-nine</h1>

Cole passed the first sign for Harborview Medical Center, Sera sitting shotgun. Parking was usually a hassle, even with the hospital having its own lots. But due to the late hour on a Friday night, finding a place to leave his car was the least of his worries, so Cole lingered at the crosswalks, heading slowly toward the 8th Avenue entrance. Despite it being nearly midnight, he'd rushed out the minute he got the call about Peter Cullen "falling" off a building. If this had to do with the Bey case, he couldn't afford to put it off.

Sera remained unusually quiet, a heavy quiet charged with something Cole hoped to ignore. He had enough on his mind between Michael and Gabrielle and Isa and Joan. Shoving Peter into the mix made the tangle seem unmanageable. Whatever made Sera silent was one more problem on a list Cole already couldn't handle.

The garage was barren, and he found a parking spot quickly. The cool, blue-tinged light from the elevators leading into the hospital gave the area in front of the car a chilled look as if they were in the middle of winter. Before he could open the door and get out, Sera grabbed his wrist, immediately releasing him.

"Look, Cole." Sera smoothed her hands over her slacks, ridding it of imaginary wrinkles. Joan had always done the same thing when she had something unpleasant to say. "We've known each other a while—since you transferred."

"Yeah." Cole tensed, his muscles going rigid as if to freeze him in the moment.

"The Bey case is getting messy," Sera said. "Joseph Bey's mother is making waves and talking to the press. The higher-ups have suspicions about you and Michael Cross. This isn't just about personal choice. Your decisions might damage the case."

That's an understatement. And not a conversation I want to have.

"I can handle myself." Cole pulled on the handle, popping the door open a crack.

"The Sheriff isn't happy you stayed on this case, and right now there's a general feeling in the powers-that-be that, well, anything solid on you and Michael and you're gone."

"Off the case?"

"That and more, depending on how much you misstep."

Hearing it voiced gave Cole a queasy feeling as if he were standing on the edge of a precipice with the wind pounding at his back. "You're saying that they'll take my badge? They can't do that. I pulled you in on the case to cover my bases." He knew it was bullshit —bringing her in was a token gesture—but it was all he had to defend himself.

"That's why they haven't done it yet. In my opinion, I doubt this would be happening this way if Michael was a Michelle, and that's why I'm telling you. But they don't like the position this puts us in, or what it could do in court. If you drop the case now, you may be able to avoid the fallout."

"Thanks for the warning." Cole tried and failed to keep the growl out of his voice; he couldn't help wondering if the sexuality bias came from her. He'd never seen any evidence of that sort of thing affecting those in charge of King County. Seattle, sure, for an otherwise liberal city, it had a sordid history of bigotry: enough of a history that the city had undergone a major reorganization of the top levels of law enforcement. The reorg was supposed to have helped, but he still found it easier to buy that the Seattle precincts would be the ones who dismissed him at the first excuse.

She opened her car door with a kick of her foot and glanced over at him. "Just think about it, Cole."

Cole nodded and got out, but he had no intention of thinking about it—at least not for now. He pushed the conversation far to the back of his mind as they took the elevator and then walked into the brightly lit hospital. One problem at a time, and for right now, what had happened to Peter Cullen was the thing he needed to be concerned with.

That and why the autopsy hadn't come back yet.

But first, go interview the most recent person to get hurt around Gabrielle.

The clean stink of the hospital sunk into his lungs as a nurse bustled past him. Sera strode in the lead, looking straight ahead, hands tugging at her slacks. In the better light of the hospital, he could see the cheap polyester fabric—not something Joan would ever have worn. And a tiny stain marred the gray cloth near the waistline. Her mannerisms might be like his ex-wife's, but he had to remember there were differences too. Her warning probably came from a desire to help, not a desire to gain anything.

The last person Cole had interviewed in a hospital was Yolanda, and illogically, he glanced into every room for her face. That was the last case he'd been involved in on an emotional level. And if he'd left that case to people like Sera, who were out for bloody retribution, rather than justice, Yolanda might be locked up.

If I do the right thing, and leaving the case would be the right thing, Gabrielle may get thrown under Sera's boots. I'll never forgive myself if that confused girl goes to jail because I gave up on her.

But the freedom of a relative innocent wasn't the only thing at stake this time. Custody of Isa hung in the balance. *If I lose my badge because I stubbornly cling to this case, chances are I'll lose Isa.*

He needed to leave the case. He knew it, but somehow, he couldn't seem to make that decision.

Cole glanced over into a random hospital room. A large glass window dominated one wall, showing a view of the hospital's other buildings. In the moonlight, the pale stone of the exterior glowed an eerie yellow. The smells and sounds weren't the same as the burn unit, but visually there wasn't much difference.

Sera looked at Cole over her shoulder. Her steps over the nondescript blue tile slowed to almost a halt as if intentionally trying to let Cole catch up to her. When Cole stopped walking entirely to compensate, she shrugged and resumed her original stride.

Cole slouched and followed Sera's slender form. The next time she slowed, Cole drew up to her.

Sera cleared her throat as they approached a waiting room. "We'll talk to her after."

Her? Cole focused on the hospital and saw Gabrielle seated in the waiting room. He cursed under his breath at her tearstained face. He hadn't meant to get sucked into those thoughts. Gabrielle and Peter both deserved his full attention.

Okay. Concentrate.

Detectives Sera and Cole passed the waiting room and stopped to talk to the uniform near Peter Cullen's room.

"They've both been questioned?" Detective Sera asked, motioning to Gabrielle in the waiting room and then to Peter's door.

"Ms. Cross has. Everything is recorded, but he," the cop nodded his head toward the room, "just regained consciousness when we called you in. He hasn't talked to anyone."

"Just regained consciousness? How long was he out?" Cole asked. In his experience, an extended period of unconsciousness after a head injury was something that needed to be considered in an interview. Who was to say that, even awake, Peter was in any condition to talk to them?

"A few hours. You could talk to his doctor."

"Good. Thanks," Sera said. "We'll do that after we check in on Mr. Cullen."

Cole nodded to the uniform on the door and gave him a smile.

The poor guy looked like he hadn't slept in days. Guarding a hospital room was a thankless, boring duty.

Cole followed Sera into the room. Peter Cullen's immediate glare was good evidence he was in his right frame of mind. Machines crowded around, but other than the bandage on his head and leg, Peter appeared like the same distrustful kid he had been during their last interview. Certainly, nothing about his expression screamed "victim."

Sera went and sat in the chair by the bed. Her body language altered, softening.

"How are you feeling, Mr. Cullen?" she asked.

Peter glared directly at her. With the fresh bruises and scratches on his face, he seemed more sullen than threatening.

"We'd like you to go over tonight's events for us, okay?" Sera said, still using that soft, sweet voice.

Peter glared harder.

Sera's shoulders tightened, and Cole thought it was time to step in.

"You're not helping Gabrielle by staying silent," Cole said, still standing back from the bed. "Whatever she actually did can't be worse than what it looks like she did."

"She didn't push me," Peter said. He shifted his gaze toward the IV in his arm.

"We're not there yet, Mr. Cullen," Sera said. "Let's start after you left the police station. Can you describe the events that occurred after that?"

Cole folded his arms and watched the stubborn jut of Peter's chin. *No way this kid is talking to us.*

"We can't make you talk, but," Sera glanced down, "that means we have only Gabrielle's word to go on."

Clever.

Doubt crossed Peter's face, and he clenched his jaw. "What is Gabs saying?"

"That's not something I can discuss with you," Sera said.

Cole resisted smiling.

"Gabs and I left the police station with Cinder," Peter started, resentment brimming in every word. His head twitched to the side, and he glanced over his shoulder toward the shuttered window. He seemed to be listening to something, though there was no audible sound outside the machines, which filled the space with white noise and periodic beeps.

"Go on," Sera prodded.

"Then Cinder went home, and Gabs came with me to a Hawaiian sandwich joint in Ballard. Then, when it got dark, we headed to a construction site. They ran out of money for it a while back, and so the building is just standing there. Climbing up on the roof was my idea."

Sera nodded.

"Then when we were up top, I slipped," Peter said defiantly.

The amount of aggression in his tone made Cole certain the kid wasn't telling the truth, or at the very least, not all of it.

"It was stupid," Peter continued, "but *an accident.* Gabs had nothing to do with it."

"Nothing else happened?" Sera asked.

"Nothing that's your damn business." Peter folded his arms across his chest. A long scrape ran up his arm, standing out against his pale, freckled skin.

Sera stood and looked over at Cole. "Detective Montez, shall we go follow up with Ms. Cross?"

"Wait," Peter said. He started to sit up, winced, then lay back. "She blacked out. I can tell when it happens because her face changes. She never does much when she's like that, just stands, walks, looking vacant. It creeps me out a bit; that's why I stepped back."

Cole bit back his questions. Gabrielle's blackouts seemed very pertinent, but neither Sera nor he would get more answers from Peter.

"Ms. Cross never touched you?" Sera asked.

"She had nothing to do with me falling."

Sera headed outside, and Cole followed her. The hall was cool, and most of the doors to patient rooms were closed. Once they'd passed the officer and were out of earshot, they stopped beside an unoccupied nurses' station.

"Do we need to interview Gabrielle?" Sera asked Cole, resting one arm on the spotless white ledge that surrounded the station. "We can't force Mr. Cullen to talk, and we can't get anything to stick without him."

"It's all linked together," Cole said. "The important part to know is that she blacked out. We already have a statement from her about this incident?"

Sera nodded.

"Then we don't need to interview her tonight. Let's see how close her statement and Mr. Cullen's are. We'll call her in later if we need to."

"You get home. I'll talk to the doctor." Sera stared down the hallway toward the waiting room. He could practically see the scales weighing in her mind. "Earlier, when you questioned her about Mrs. Pritcher, what were you digging for?"

"Mrs. Pritcher said in her original statement that the doll was in the basement. She corroborated that again today. Then, she admitted to keeping a lot of valuables in the attic but that the doll creeped her out. During the murder, the basement was ransacked, the attic was not."

"So how did she get the doll the day of the murder?" Sera rocked back on her heels.

"Maybe someone else is involved. Peter Cullen seems the most likely. He's already lying for Ms. Cross." Cole patted Sera on the shoulder. Time to go home and get this case off his mind, which was going to be hard, considering how tightly his home life was linking in with work.

Sera glanced past him at the waiting room again and tapped her finger on the white ledge of the nurses station next to them.

"Gabrielle killed Joseph Bey. I know it. This is all about finding out how."

Cole gritted his teeth wanting to point out how biased her police work sounded. But he knew he didn't have any right to talk. He shouldn't be on the case at all. "If she's guilty, you'll prove it. That doesn't mean I can't look into other theories."

Sera sighed, loudly. "Because she's your boyfriend's sister? You realize this is the sort of thing that's only going to make the higher-ups even more suspicious, right?"

"I'll dig a little deeper. Get some statements from the other kids who lived in the Pritcher house."

"Either way, not tonight." Sera glanced at her watch. She and Joan were the only women he knew who wore analog watches. "Seriously, go home. I've got this. I'll catch an Uber."

Cole nodded. Her push for him to leave didn't seem emotionally driven. He doubted she cared. She just wanted him away from the case, away from Gabrielle and Michael, and he couldn't blame her.

Sera turned around to talk to the uniform about Gabrielle's interview or to catch the doctor. He started off down the hall. But the long empty corridor gave him pause.

Sera's only trying to help me. She might resemble Joan in ways, but she wasn't.

Cole spun back. "And thanks. I don't know what my plans are, but thanks."

Sera tipped her chin as if tipping a hat.

How could he drop the case? Sera was a good detective despite her hang-ups, but she already believed Gabrielle was guilty. *What chance does Gabrielle have of a fair investigation if I leave? Sera won't fabricate evidence, but she may not dig deep enough or try hard enough.*

I could just call things off with Michael—that wouldn't solve the issues with the case, but if this is really about the brass's hang-ups, it might help. It wouldn't be enough. I have to leave the case.

Cole grimaced. The idea of having to tell Michael that didn't sit well with him either. Maybe a breakup would be enough, and maybe Michael would prefer it.

I always swore I wouldn't back down. That I'd show Isa it's okay to be who you are and that good people come out on top.

But something had to change. Otherwise, he was heading to certain disaster.

thirty

GABRIELLE KEPT GLANCING DOWN THE HALLWAY TO PETER'S ROOM. SINCE the detectives went in, she couldn't seem to look away. Before entering, Cole briefly glanced at her but didn't make eye contact. *He thinks I pushed Peter. They all do.*

She rang her hands together and twisted on the hard cushion of her seat. The cops watched her. Given everything she'd said, she had expected to be in cuffs by now. But instead, she was just sitting there.

Peter's parents still weren't there. It was past midnight, and the accident happened at nine!

Detectives Montez and Sera left Peter's room. They headed down the hall away from the waiting room. Gabrielle was certain they'd want to interview her as well, but no one had put her under arrest yet.

Peter's doctor approached her.

"Looks like they're done. You can have a couple of minutes with Peter, he's been asking for you. Come right this way,"

She didn't need more prodding than that.

Gabrielle slipped inside Peter's hospital room. Her heart pounded, but on seeing him, the weight that had been crushing her chest lifted. He was alive. Injured but alive.

"I'm so sorry!" Gabrielle said, dashing over to his bedside.

Peter's face was bruised and scratched, looking like he had been mauled by raccoons. The pristine white bandages on his head didn't help the guilt eating at her, nor did his elevated leg.

"You have nothing to apologize for." Peter sounded sincere but wouldn't meet her eyes.

"Did I push you?"

"No." Peter stared at the IV in his arm.

"Don't lie to me." Gabrielle sank into the seat beside him and twisted her hands in front of her, not daring to touch him. "I felt something. What did I do?" *Tell me it was her.*

"Nothing."

"I don't believe you. I want to, but I don't. If I pushed you, I need to know."

"Gabs." Peter sighed and his eyes closed for a moment. "I'm not going to talk about this anymore. I can't."

Gabrielle choked back more questions and glanced at the door behind her. "Your parents aren't waiting out there to see you."

"Really?" his voice dripped sarcasm. "Makes sense. Why would they bother to disturb their night?"

"You know your parents. They *will* come." *They should have been here with me, waiting all night. At least they know they didn't push you. Shit. Even* they *are better for you than I am.* "The doctor and the police guarding your room won't let me stay long We only have a few minutes."

"So, where were my parents all night? The movies?"

"A dinner party, I think." Gabrielle rolled her eyes. "And of course, your mom had to go home and change. You know, she had to look properly distraught, and one can't do that in silk!"

"Were they upset with you?" Peter stroked her hand.

He shouldn't be comforting me. Gabrielle pulled her hand back.

"No," she said. "I kind of wish they were angry with me. Maybe if someone else was blaming me, I could stop blaming myself."

A light rap sounded on the door and then it opened a crack.

"Time's up," a nurse chirped from the doorway.

"Gabs." Peter reached out and touched her face. "This was a shitty end to a lovely night. I meant what I said. I love you. I always have."

Gabrielle's lip trembled, and she clutched at her chest. Pain ripped through her. A crack spread inside, not visible but deep and wide. How was she still breathing? She could have sworn her heart had torn in two. "You and Michael . . . You're the only people in this world who really matter to me. I can't take it, Peter. I can't stand thinking that I might have hurt you! And you didn't fall. I know you didn't."

"Forget it," Peter said. "You'd never hurt me."

I won't forget it. I'll find a way to protect you. Gabrielle leaned down and brushed her lips over his.

The nurse beckoned from the doorway.

"Call me when they let you out," Gabrielle said.

Peter smiled. "The moment I get home."

"Come along," the nurse said, a little less cheerily. She held the door wide.

Gabrielle walked into the hall as the nurse ushered her out, with a cop standing at the edge of the doorway. Peter's parents hovered only a few feet away, talking to detective Sera. Gabrielle averted her eyes. She couldn't take a conversation with them, however brief. Detective Sera probably couldn't arrest her if Peter was insisting he fell, but she didn't want to test that theory. And despite their issues, Sharon and David loved Peter, and Gabrielle was certain in her gut that she was to blame for him being hurt.

Even if it was the doll. It was her doll. She'd brought it into his life, and she'd failed to get rid of it.

She ducked her head and hurried down the hall, past the waiting room, away from them. No one stopped her.

Someone in one of the rooms ahead of her was crying. Gabrielle slowed momentarily to absorb this siren call to the clenched yearning inside her. Then the door shut, and the only remaining noises were the tap of shoes on the floor and the hum of distant voices.

Gabrielle trooped out of the hospital and crumpled on the ground, arms wrapped around her knees, leaning against the exterior wall near the door. Every once in a while, people passed, preceded and followed by the swish of the automatic doors. Gabrielle buried her face in her knees and tucked her legs as close to her chest as she could. The scent of Peter still clung in her nostrils, holding on even through the cool cucumber of her hair.

Peter was lying. She didn't know what about, but her gut told her with certainty that he was. And chances were that meant she had pushed him off the building. And the doll hadn't been there. Couldn't have been, they had walked to the building. *But I saw her eyes.*

What does that mean? Either the doll really was there and brought herself or . . . Gabrielle was imagining it all? But the latter couldn't be true. Gabrielle would never hurt Peter. Never. It had to be the doll because she would never push Peter.

It had to be her.

Either way, she is mine. As long as she's mine, I'm dangerous. The best thing I can do for the people I love would be boarding a plane and never coming back.

She clutched her knees tighter, pressing her face against the fabric of her skirt. The walkway under her was unforgiving, and her tailbone protested every movement.

I deserve the pain. Maybe I should slit myself open.

No. Not that. The point was to protect Michael, not hurt him. He'd just blame himself if she died. The key was finding a way to neutralize whatever threat she posed. Her dream of being normal, of having a normal life had gone up in smoke. And waiting for answers before proceeding might lead to others getting hurt. Inaction had led her to this place, and that couldn't keep going. Gabrielle had to pick a path and stick to it. Any action had a better chance of success than continuing to do nothing.

Having come to this conclusion, Gabrielle stood and meandered the walkway toward the street where she'd find a bus or give in and call an Uber. Her tentative footfall echoed on the pavement. Yellowed light cast a sickly glow over the ground.

Gabrielle checked her phone. Calls from Michael, of course, since she'd texted him to say she was coming here. But he hadn't shown up at the hospital. Why? She had been too distracted to think about it, but now that she had a moment, the idea was preposterous. What in the world would have kept Michael away?

She opened the app to summon a car. Truth be told, she was not in the mood for a bus ride and strangers sitting next to her. Then she stared at Michael's missed call.

Time to break the silence and make sure he wasn't in any trouble.

She dialed his number. His phone rang to voicemail, which at least got her the sound of his voice. Gabrielle hung up and texted him to let her know that he was okay.

Michael had to be okay. There would be a simple explanation. The important thing was that she make sure he stayed okay, and he wouldn't unless Gabrielle protected him from her, from the doll.

Her ride arrived.

She was hardly conscious of the drive home; she stumbled up the walkway to her door, completely exhausted but determined. Inside the house, the living room light beamed, and Cinder lay on the couch. Her mouth hung open, and a damp spot spread on the cushion under her face.

Gabrielle shut the door behind her as quietly as she could and turned, but Cinder had already sat up and rubbed her eyes.

"You're late," Cinder said. Her blue hair stuck up in clumps and mascara was smeared under her eyes.

"Sorry?" Gabrielle forced a smile. She crossed over to stand on the opposite side of the coffee table from her friend. Cinder turned in her seat to face Gabrielle, and her legs slipped out from under their blue throw blanket to the floor.

"Is Peter okay?"

"He is." Gabrielle dropped her gaze to her feet. Then a thought occurred to her. She hadn't told Cinder how the evening with Peter ended. She hadn't even thought to call her. "How did you know he was hurt?"

"Michael called me. He was worried."

Michael? Why would Michael have called Cinder? It didn't matter. She needed to deal with the doll first. The rest could wait. "I need your help ensuring Peter stays safe."

Cinder tossed off her blanket and patted the couch next to her.

"I need your help getting rid of the doll," Gabrielle said. She remained standing, moving her weight from foot to foot.

"Okay. I did a bit of research, and a cleansing should work to put the spirit at rest."

"You said before that destroying the cursed object works the best." Gabrielle swallowed hard and glanced up the stairs toward her bedroom door. "I feel like she's listening."

"Let's go get her, then. At least try a cleansing first."

"First, fine. But burning is the preferred method. We probably need to do that." The doll's eyes burned with anger in Gabrielle's mind, and she tasted bile. "What if that goes wrong? What if it just pisses her off?"

"Hmm," Cinder said as she stood. "Good reason to go with the cleansing. Why would that anger her?"

It wouldn't, but it didn't feel final enough. Peter and Michael were the ones who mattered, and she felt the tattooed wings on my back expand. She had to be their angel. Protect them. Even if it meant betraying the doll, even if it meant facing her anger. "If the cleansing works, then she won't be there to be angered by the burning. And if it doesn't . . ."

With the idea of burning being spoken, Gabrielle felt the need to see the doll, to know exactly what the little demon was doing.

Gabrielle went upstairs to her bedroom, Cinder behind her. The door wasn't fully closed, and Gabrielle pushed it open with her fingertips. Someone had turned off the purple lamp that she always left on. The room inside was dark, only a bit of light from the streetlight across the way filtering in through the window.

Yet on the shelf, the doll's eyes caught this light, reflecting it back like the gaze of an owl. *I didn't leave her on the shelf.*

"Did you move her?" Gabrielle asked. She tried to take a step back and bumped into Cinder.

"No." Cinder gave Gabrielle a shove forward. "Fuck, no."

Gabrielle switched on the light. The room displayed its usual mishmash of purples and blues, and the doll's eyes burned like a flame from hell amidst the cool colors. *When I threatened to throw her away, Peter got pushed from a building. I have to assume it's linked. What if burning her doesn't work? What if that just angers her . . . or sets her free?*

"Cinder?" Gabrielle asked, folding her arms around herself as if for warmth. She glanced away from the doll, back at her friend. "I need her burned, but I can't . . . I don't think I can do it. She'll stop me. Can you do that part?"

"You sure?" Cinder asked, leaning her shoulder into the doorframe. "Once she's cleansed, we could just bury her. That would work."

Gabrielle flinched and her eyes leaped back to the doll, who sat impassively on the shelf, a spiderweb of cracks over her chubby face.

"No." *There is no halfway. I love her, but she needs to be destroyed.* "We burn her."

"Cursed objects sometimes can't be destroyed," Cinder said matter-of-factly. "They just find their way back."

"That's why we cleanse her first." Gabrielle spun and gripped Cinder's arms. *I asked for her help when I was a child. I started this. The doll protected me when I was too little, too scared to protect myself.* "She wasn't always evil. She wasn't. So we do what's needed to set her free. Please."

Cinder's face bunched in thought, and her cheeks puffed before she let out a burst of air. "I'll burn her for you, Angel."

Gabrielle sighed and nodded emphatically. From the corner of her eye, she thought she saw the doll's faded skirt rustle. A high, taunting laugh rang inside her mind.

This would work. It had to work.

<h1 style="text-align:center">thirty-one</h1>

THE NIGHT SIPHONED ENERGY FROM COLE. HIS DRIVE HOME FROM THE hospital seemed to drag out longer than normal, and he opened his window to let the crisp air keep him awake. Each red light stretched for ages. By the time Cole reached his house, the dashboard clock told him it was nearly two in the morning. Friday had slid into Saturday.

Leaving the Bey case should have been an easy choice. And it was —until he really considered it. Gabrielle was lost, and she needed someone to find her. Dropping the case would be abandoning her to the wolves. This wouldn't be like the other murder accusations she'd faced; she wasn't a child anymore. The pattern of deaths was too defined. Everything pointed to a multiple murderer and to her being the culprit.

She wasn't innocent, but she wasn't the cold-blooded killer Sera saw either. Justice was a fickle mistress, and sometimes the clear path was hard to see. Cole couldn't let Gabrielle get lost on that road. She wanted answers; she kept saying so. Nothing he did would make her more or less guilty, but the idea of abandoning her rankled.

As his car rolled to a stop in his driveway, Cole bent his head over the wheel. All he wanted to do was give his sleeping daughter a kiss and crawl into bed, no more late-night calls to drag him from under his warm blankets.

Cole shoved open the car door and stretched his legs. Exhaustion throbbed deep in his bones. The porch light splashed out over the driveway, leaving tendrils on the sidewalk, and the TV's lights glowed from behind the curtains. Yolanda was awake, or at least had been when she sat down.

She waits up for me like a mother.

The night had a chill, and Cole plodded toward the front stoop, crossing his arms over his chest for warmth. The light coming from the house made the dark outside seem deeper.

"Cole!" It was Michael—Cole recognized the voice instantly. He pulled his hand away from his sidearm where it had automatically gone. "Cole?"

Cole waited on the porch as Michael approached from the dark. His head hung, obscuring his face, but his pants were wrinkled, and his shirt looked slept in. That was enough to tell Cole what sort of emotional shape he was in. How long had he been waiting out there? No point in asking how Michael found his house—he'd already explained how he found Joseph Bey.

"Why are you here?" Cole asked. Too much accusation came out with the remark, but he was too tired to care.

"Shit." Michael slumped, hand gripping the porch railing. "You know, I have no idea. Everything I could say sounds like a horrible excuse."

"Why didn't you call? Rather than lurking in the dark." Cole glanced at the houses across the way. All the lights were off.

"I know how messed-up this situation is. Honestly, I thought you'd turn me away. If I were you, I wouldn't want me meeting Isa right now."

"She's four, Michael. She's in bed." Cole sat on the porch step and motioned for Michael to sit beside him. "Thank you for considering that, though. Are you aware that Gabrielle is at the hospital?"

Michael paused and glanced behind him into the night, toward where Cole supposed his car was parked.

Shit—I should have said she wasn't hurt.

Yet when Michael turned back, his face showed no surprise and no additional worry. "I know."

He joined Cole on the wooden step. Cole lifted a hand to brush Michael's cheek. Even in the dim light from the house's windows, the shadows under Michael's eyes were deep. Nor did he look as neatly dressed as his norm—wrinkles slashed across his shirt, and one of the lapels on his jacket curled upward.

After a moment Michael said, "Gabrielle texted me. She hasn't been answering for the past two days, though. I went to the hospital and saw her there but just left. I couldn't see any way to help. All I seem to do recently is make things worse for her. Whenever I do talk to her . . ." He stopped and swallowed. "You won't answer my calls either."

"I've just been busy." That wasn't entirely true, but this wasn't the time to sort through the possibility of breaking things off with Michael. Right now, Michael needed an ear. Cole could do that at least, considering that a few days before, he had been imagining moving in with Michael and sharing a life.

"We both know that isn't true," Michael said with a sad smile. "I should be backing off, but . . ."

"We can't talk about the case. I'm already in deep shit." *I shouldn't have said that, either. Why even bring the case up?* But rather than the slip of his tongue adding weight, Cole felt a sliver better.

Michael set his hand on the wooden step in between them. "Thank you for staying on the case. That's more or less what I came to say."

"Don't say it yet." Cole rubbed his forehead.

"You're not staying on?" Michael tugged at his collar. "But yesterday you said you could help Gabrielle."

Cole dragged in a deep gulp of the night air. "Look, Michael, I'm going to be honest with you. More than I should be."

Michael tucked his legs closer to his body. The moon defined the masculine angles of his profile and his arms. The cool light even danced over the stubble on his usually smooth jaw.

"Joan is suing for custody," Cole said. "Or threatening to. We're set to meet with mediators, but she won't back down. She's going for the jugular."

"Oh, wow. I'm sorry." Michael shifted over so their knees brushed and put a hand on Cole's shoulder. "Any way I can help?"

"That's the thing. Me being on this case puts me on shaky ground at work. Any misstep and they could suspend me—that'd be like handing Isa to Joan on a platter." *Now's when I should mention the relationship angle. But what if he decides to end it for me?*

"You're saying that we are the problem?"

Ouch. But it had to be said. "Then there is the case itself and our personal involvement being against policy. We could stop seeing each other. Then our involvement would be less likely to come out and harm Gabrielle's case. But not seeing each other wouldn't change the fact we had a personal relationship, and if it came out, it would still ruin my career and the case."

"So leave the case." Michael sounded disappointed, but his hand gently massaged Cole's shoulder. The warmth of the touch loosened the emotions curled tightly within Cole.

He tried to say something, but for a moment couldn't form his thoughts and feelings into words. Could Michael really be okay with him giving up? "Shoot, Michael. I wish it were that simple. Gabrielle might have pushed her friend Peter from a building tonight. She needs someone on her side. I don't want to be the sort of person who would abandon her just to cater to bureaucracy. I'm the only one on the case who doesn't want her to be guilty—because it's neater if she is."

"She didn't push him." Michael didn't sound convinced. That was a change, but Cole tucked it away to ponder later.

"That's what Peter says. But everything in his voice and body says he's lying." *I need to stop talking about the case, but I can't hold this in. How is he being so calm and so kind?* "I want to be in Gabrielle's corner. I'm having trouble seeing how."

"Cole, there's no blame from me either way. Bear with me a moment." Michael pulled out his phone and sifted through. He showed Cole a picture of him standing with another man. Both wore suits and held glasses of champagne.

"That's Evan," Michael said. "Several years back, we were engaged. But some stuff with Gabrielle blew up, and she wound up back in treatment. I canceled some events that mattered to him so that I could be there for Gabrielle. Evan said that he wasn't going to spend his life competing with my crazy sister, but I wouldn't abandon her. So he left me."

"I'm sorry—"

"No. Don't be." Michael pressed the side of his cellphone and the picture disappeared. "Gabrielle isn't my kid, but I get the devotion. Isa has to come first. I know what it's like to have to make that decision. I don't want you to think that you have to choose between me and Isa. Isa would win and *should* win. I'll find a way to take care of Gabrielle—I always have. You take care of you and Isa."

Cole reached out to brush a finger down Michael's face. *What if taking care of Isa means ending this?* His hand trailed to Michael's chin and turned his face so that Michael fully faced him.

Michael gave him a ravishing half-smile. Cole leaned in and brushed his lips over Michael's. The contact was brief, and as their lips parted, Michael's hand moved behind Cole's head to pull him back in.

I shouldn't do this. It's not fair when I'm considering walking away.

Yet Cole's body played devil's advocate, and he parted his lips. His arms wrapped around Michael and the flexing muscles of Michael's back. The taste of Michael's mouth and the pressure of his fingers on Cole's neck made thinking difficult.

And thinking hurt, anyhow. Everything about being in Michael's arms felt amazing.

"Come inside?" Cole asked. His hands slid down Michael's back and lifted the bottom of his shirt, nothing demanding, just enough to stroke his fingers across flesh.

"Are you sure?" Michael's mouth moved only inches from his, making a primal hunger curl up inside him. The porch wasn't a good place for this.

"Oh, absolutely sure." Cole stood, his skin prickling at the cold places where Michael wasn't.

When Michael stood, Cole kissed him again. But he wanted more than kisses. He wanted Michael. If he was honest, a night wasn't enough. Letting go of this feeling, of this man, would be sheer madness. There had to be another way.

"Inside?" Michael asked, an adorable, taunting smile on his face. "I'm happy to stay out here, but those are your neighbors, not mine."

Cole chuckled. "You would not be happy to stay out here."

"Really?" The twinkle in Michael's eye was unmistakable. He stepped back and lifted off his shirt, leaving his chest bare to the night. Every inch of smooth skin was perfect. "You wanna try me?"

Cole wanted nothing more, though not in the way Michael meant. The moonlight did Cole no favors but fanned his hunger by further outlining every defined muscle in Michael's revealed chest.

Prying his eyes away, Cole unlocked the front door and walked inside.

A light buzz of unintelligible speech niggled at his ears. Yolanda sat in the living room, asleep on the brown leather couch. The TV flickered on the wall.

"Just a moment," Cole said and motioned Michael into the hallway. He crossed the room and grabbed the remote to turn the TV off. He leaned over Yolanda and tucked a blanket up around her chin. Then he turned back to Michael. Cole held up a finger for silence.

The two men snuck back into the hall, and Cole led the way into his bedroom.

"Am I going to have to sneak out the window?" Michael laughed. "I feel like we'll get in trouble if your nanny sees us."

Cole looked at Michael, then at the bed. He thought of the sealed envelopes with suggested parenting plans and mediation dates. And he made a decision. On Monday, he'd resign the case.

It's just a first step, but it's something. I don't know how yet, but I'll find a way to keep all the people I love.

And I do love him.

"No. I'll introduce you in the morning. To her and Isa."

thirty-two

The greasy smell of bacon filled the air. Cole opened his eyes and sat up.

Michael stirred beside him, rolling over and flopping an arm across Cole's lap with an unintelligible mumble. Cole's sheets were tangled around Michael, and they lay together in the center of his bed, the edges chilled from the open window. Cole wanted to take more of the Saturday morning to sleep in. Yet something wouldn't let him relax.

No telling for sure under the smell of bacon, but he'd put money on Yolanda having made pancakes as well. If he knew her, she'd have a full spread laid out. She always knew when someone was in the house.

Cole glanced down at Michael. Breakfast smelled wonderful, but he was loath to disturb the peacefully sleeping man beside him. With everything going on, who knew how many calm moments he and Michael would get any time soon?

A tentative knock sounded at the door, followed by, "Daddy?"

"I'm up, Isa."

"Nana says to go knock but not open the door. No. No. Breakfast is ready. Are you up? Come to the table."

Cole smiled at the long-winded burble. "I'll be out in a minute."

When Cole glanced down again, Michael's eyes were open.

Isa's footsteps pounded away outside the door. Cole wished he had that sort of drive and energy for life. He was certain the child never walked—everything was a run or a sulky trudge.

Michael stretched out under the sheets. The brownish-maroon coverlet lay crumpled at the foot of the bed. "It isn't too late for me to sneak out the window."

"Oh, it is far too late." Cole motioned toward the door and took a whiff of the grease-tinged air. "Do you smell that?"

Michael lifted his head, sniffed, and then nodded.

"Yolanda doesn't cook like that for me. Maybe on birthdays. She'll kill me if I don't introduce you to her. Plus, there are probably pancakes."

Cole slipped out from under the sheets. The wooden blinds on the window were open, letting light fill the room, and Cole crossed to the dresser beside the door. The closet, where all his button-up shirts hung, was on the other side of the room, the door standing slightly ajar.

He felt Michael's eyes on him as he pulled on a fresh undershirt and grabbed socks.

A quick glance showed that Michael's clothes, though still wearable, would scream the fact that they'd spent the night crumpled on the floor. So he searched to find anything that stood any chance of fitting the taller man. The button-downs would be no good, but Cole had a light sweater that might be presentable. He tossed it over to Michael on the bed.

"Fresh shirt for you."

"Thanks." Michael kicked off the sheet, and it joined the coverlet at the foot of the bed. "I used to carry a spare outfit in my car, but I haven't needed anything like that in a long time."

After they were both presentable and had made the bed at Michael's insistence, Cole took Michael's hand. They walked out into the hall.

One of Isa's plastic baby dolls sat guard outside the door. Cole scooped it up and, as they walked by Isa's room, tossed it onto her garishly pink bed.

Isa bounded around the corner, wearing a fancy pink dress with a ridiculous number of flounces. Out from under this monstrosity of femininity poked dirty bare toes.

Michael tensed at the sight of her.

"Hey, sweetheart. Come here." Cole motioned to her, and she skipped over, lifting her sticky face to Michael. Her lips gleamed with beads of syrup.

"Hi," she said.

"Isa, this is my friend Michael."

Isa nodded, blonde hair bobbing. "There are really, actually pancakes. Really, actually!"

With this revelation off her chest, Isa ran back into the playroom.

"She's not shy," Michael said.

Cole chuckled. "No."

They stepped into the playroom, which was divided from the kitchen only by a low breakfast bar.

Yolanda had her back to them in the kitchen, her thin frame dressed in a baggy robe. She stayed in constant motion as she grabbed and stirred and scraped. A low rumble of music came from speakers she had set up on the counter, and a high sweet child's voice sang about Noah's Ark. A spread of food was set out on the counter behind her, waiting to be served up.

Isa sat at the breakfast bar, looking small and breakable on the tall stool. Toys scattered over the floor made the place resemble a warzone, and Cole picked his way toward the other seats. Michael shuffled after.

"Help yourself, Mr. Montez," Yolanda said, flipping something on the stove before turning toward them. "And you must be Michael. I'm Yolanda."

Michael scooted toys out of the way with his toes. "Good to meet you. Then again, you did open with bacon and pancakes."

Cole imagined that Michael winked in the brief pause in his speech.

"And is that fresh orange juice?" Michael asked.

"Nope. Just from the carton."

"Honestly, boxed is better," Michael said. Cole still couldn't see his face, but if he hadn't been winking before, the flirt was certainly doing so this time. "The fresh stuff is too sour for me."

"Me too!" Isa said, bouncing on the stool as if this proved they were soulmates.

"Next, you'll be encouraging her to use boxed pancake mix." Cole reached the counter and grabbed a plate.

"Why not?" Michael grabbed a piece of bacon, skipping the nicety of a plate. "It tastes the same from a boxed mix, and it's easier."

Yolanda laughed.

"It does not taste the same." Cole loaded a plate. *I never imagined things going this smoothly.*

"Mr. Montez!" Yolanda's eyes twinkled and her scars bunched as she smiled. "You're very picky for a man who doesn't cook. Now, go eat with Isa. I'm going to have a chat with Michael."

"But, Nana!" Isa objected.

"He'll come play with you later. Right, Michael?" Yolanda said, directing her twinkling gaze at Michael this time.

"Of course." He matched her wicked smile.

Cole couldn't get Yolanda to meet his eyes. He wasn't entirely sure he wanted them colluding.

Still, he let himself be ushered away both by Isa's enthusiasm for him trying the pancakes and by Michael and Yolanda refusing to acknowledge that he might have any other option.

The dining room had its own doorway from the playroom, and Cole took his usual chair at the dining table, which unfortunately put his back to the kitchen. He glanced behind him through the doorway as he sat down with his plate.

"Daddy!" Isa's tone grabbed his attention. She kneeled on her chair across from him, hands on her hips.

He recognized when he was defeated and asked her about her dreams the night before.

But the whole breakfast, he found himself straining to hear what was being said in the kitchen. By the time Michael came to join him at the dining table, Cole's stomach was clenched into a ball of stress. Michael looked lost in thought.

Even then, there was no chance to talk to Michael because Isa took over.

When they were all through eating, Yolanda gathered Isa up to go get her washed. Alone at the table, Cole waited for Michael to say something about his chat with the nanny.

Instead, Michael pulled out his phone, checked the screen, and put it down in frustration.

"Still no word from Gabrielle?" Cole asked.

"She called me last night from the hospital, but when I tried calling her back a few minutes ago, she didn't answer. She never answers anymore."

"Why don't you go visit her?" Cole asked. "Who knows what's going through her head right now, but I'm sure deep down she wants to see you."

Michael stared at his plate and then pushed out his chair and stood up. "If I'm going to do that, I'd better go. She usually wakes up late on Saturday, but there's no telling where she'll go during the day."

"Understood. I'll walk you out."

The two of them meandered outside, neither starting a conversation but neither really trying to hurry to Michael's car.

"Cole, if I had information that related to the case . . ." Michael paused on the bottom porch step, and when he glanced up at Cole, there was something tortured twisting in his eyes. "No, never mind."

Cole sucked in a quick breath. He hadn't even thought about the case all morning. Had his plan to leave lifted so much from his shoulders? But until he had filed the paperwork, Cole had to do his job. "Do you know something about Joseph's murder?"

"Not really. There's just something I've been chewing on since I found out about Mr. Pritcher. Look, it's not fair to lay this on you, and I know that."

Cole leaned against the porch railing. "You aren't telling me anything."

"I'm sorry. I'll call you, okay? I just need to parse through how to say this before I blurt everything out wrong."

"Michael . . ."

"Bye." Michael hurried down the driveway and to the curb.

Cole watched as the car started and then disappeared. What secret was Michael hiding? Why did this whole thing have to keep getting messier? Why couldn't one thing go right, make the path clear and easy?

Isa's laughter rang out from inside and then she burst from the door. Her little feet skidded to a halt. "Where's Michael?"

"He just left, sweetie."

"He didn't say goodbye!"

Cole ruffled her hair. "Don't worry, he'll be back." Cole paused, fingering the cross around his neck. If Michael had a confession, maybe that was something that he needed a safe place for. "Maybe I'll even invite him to church tomorrow."

There. One more thing was decided. Michael would stick around. It wouldn't really solve anything to get rid of him now, anyhow. Cole just needed to follow through on his decision to leave the case.

<h1 style="text-align:center">*thirty-three*</h1>

Morning hit Gabrielle like a sledgehammer. As soon as she woke, she recalled what had happened the night before with Peter's fall. She curled into a ball under the covers and threaded her hands into her hair. The light coming in through her shades forced its way through the barrier of her arms and through her scrunched eyelids.

She could still feel Peter's lips on hers, and a reflection of her own desire rippled through her, followed by the well of sadness that came with knowing it was only a moment. Peter was not an option for her.

I can't let my selfish desires get him hurt, again.

An ache spread over her chest that came with a tightening, a pull inward.

I wish I could just implode, rid this world of me.

The sunlight insistently called to her. And low voices through her door knocked at her consciousness, demanding admittance. But only when she recognized Michael's voice did she unwind from her blankets and sit up.

Michael was here. Her heart hammered, and she felt her secrets like sweat popping out over her skin. Gabrielle took a quick glance at her phone—it was nearly eleven on Saturday morning.

The doll watched Gabrielle from her place on the shelf. Gabrielle refused to meet her eyes. She'd know what Gabrielle planned.

"I'm being as kind as I can," Gabrielle said.

"You can't survive without me."

She pulled on a sweater and sweatpants before leaving her room and dodging past discarded items of Cinder's clothes to get to the stairs. At least Cinder's mess hadn't made it onto the steps this time. Gabrielle descended.

Michael sat in the living room, sprawled across the couch. The sound of plates told Gabrielle that Cinder was in the kitchen.

What if Cinder told him about the doll? He was so upset the last time I even suggested getting rid of her. He'd stop me.

Gabrielle sucked in a breath and walked into the room.

"Good morning, Gabrielle." He sat up, making room for her beside him. "Don't be mad. I had to check in on you. I tried to give you space. Are you okay?"

Gabrielle swallowed and then nodded. "Did you get my message?"

"I did, but at the time . . ." His grin told her what he didn't say. If it hadn't, the sweater he wore, which she'd never seen before and hung a little baggily around his shoulders and chest, would have told her. "How's Peter?"

"He's pretty shitty. I don't want to talk about me." As she said the words, Gabrielle realized how often of late she'd been saying them. She couldn't pretend to be normal anymore, but at least she could avoid constantly talking about how messed up she was. So instead, she focused on Michael's sweater and gave him a good direction to let the conversation go. "You were at Cole's. Why aren't you still there?" She smiled and tucked an errant strand of hair behind her ear.

"Gabrielle, it's well past ten. I stayed there for breakfast, met his daughter. It was fun." And he was saying his goodbyes. Michael was already planning to leave or be left, to lose everything once again, to protect Gabrielle.

He was always her guardian angel. But she needed to be his.

She crossed the room and sat on the couch next to her brother. Cinder hovered by the stove and made an obvious effort not to look at them. The smell of cheese and potatoes drifted out.

Giving us the semblance of privacy without leaving earshot.

"How are *you*, though?" Michael took up Gabrielle's hand.

"I *don't* want to talk about it, and thank you for not leaving Cole's. I can't even explain how much it means. If this case takes over your life, I—I just want you to be happy."

"You're an adult now, Elle. I get it. You don't need me hovering."

"It isn't that." *If only it were. That sounds like a perfectly average teenage rebellion against an authority figure.*

"Just start answering my calls, okay?"

Something moved at the top of the stairs.

"Okay," Gabrielle said, glancing at the stairs. There was nothing there. "So tell me about your night? I could use a distraction. What's his place like?"

Michael shook his head. "It's a house. Nothing special. I met his nanny, though—his daughter's nanny."

"Yeah?" Gabrielle leaned in closer.

Michael grabbed his phone and searched for something on it as he spoke again, softly. "I think I love this guy, Gabrielle."

Good. "What does that have to do with the nanny?"

Michael looked over at the television, which was off, serving only to give a reflection of them sitting there and Cinder holding a spatula behind them. Then he turned the phone to Gabrielle showing a news article about arson. "The nanny, Yolanda, told me about it, not him. Apparently, her husband died in this fire."

"And she's his nanny?"

Michael nodded. "He was one of the detectives on her case."

"Seriously?" *Is this guy as crazy as me?*

"She was never charged."

"We both know that doesn't mean she didn't do it."

"Yeah, I know." His attention snapped back to her. "Cops just decide who is guilty and make facts to prove it. Can't trust their investigations for shit."

"So?"

"I recognized her name—it reminded me of something. So when I left, I looked up the case." Michael waved a hand at her laptop. "Apparently, her husband had kids from a previous marriage. She found out he was abusing them and reported it."

"I bet that did a lot of good."

"The point is," Michael said, "that's why they suspected her. But the interesting part is that she got caught in the fire—and so did his kids. She saved them and, in the process, got burned pretty badly. Third-degree burns had her in the hospital for weeks. When she woke up, those kids were the only thing she was worried about."

Gabrielle twisted her head to try to get a better look at the article, but all she could really make out without more time was a blur of words and the title screaming arson in the suburbs. "So she didn't light the fire?"

Michael wrapped an arm around Gabrielle and squeezed her in a hug. "She'd hardly tell me if she did. But she seems to love Isa, Cole's daughter. And Isa clearly loves her. Maybe her bastard of a husband deserved to die. Should I care if Yolanda killed him?"

A frown creased Michael's forehead. He released Gabrielle and turned on the couch to face the kitchen. She pulled his words apart in her head.

He never said he thought Yolanda didn't light the fire.

"You sure you don't need help in there, Cinder?" Michael said. "I'm a killer cook."

"I bet you are." Cinder winked at him. "Is there anything you're bad at?"

"Minding my own business." He grinned.

Michael stood up and joined Cinder in the kitchen. The two of them chatted. Their voices formed a background buzz as Gabrielle curled her legs against her on the couch. The blanket was warm from Michael as she wrapped it around her shoulders.

Michael seemed happy, but he was hiding something. The more she thought, the more odd it seemed that he hadn't pushed her for more information on Peter. He might be all smiles and charm, but that didn't prove anything about what he was really thinking. How could she push him on it when she was hiding so much more? She couldn't tell him she was plotting with Cinder to destroy the doll. She already knew how he felt about that. Nor could she tell him the doll had pushed Peter from a building.

Would he condemn me or support me? Which is worse?

A few minutes later, Cinder brought out three plates filled with omelets and hash browns made from frozen Ore-Ida potatoes. She plunked the plates down on the coffee table and pulled a worn armchair a bit closer and sat down. Michael sat with them, and he and Cinder made conversation around Gabrielle's silence.

She kept checking for movement on the stairs. She knew she was really checking for the doll and those vengeful eyes. Then, each time, she'd sneak a glance at Michael to ensure he was still okay. The less he was involved in all this, the better.

Finally, after breakfast, he excused himself.

Cinder and Gabrielle remained around the coffee table, their dishes nearly empty. Michael raised his voice to say goodbye. The door clicked closed. After he left, Gabrielle fidgeted with her fork. Cinder pushed a leftover blob of egg around her plate.

"When do we burn her?" Gabrielle glanced at the door of her room. It was closed, but she imagined the doll pressed against the wood, listening. She imagined the fiery eyes staring as they heard those words. "We should hurry. She's angry about this. I feel it."

"Tomorrow." Cinder stood and grabbed the three plates, carting them into the kitchen. "I need to buy some things."

I just want it gone.

I want it never to hurt another child. Even if all it means to do is help.

"Well, I'm out. I have lunch plans with Kate. You could come if you want." Cinder stood. Her short skirt had turned to the side, and she wrenched it back. When Gabrielle didn't answer, she went on. "You sure you're not coming?"

"Maybe someday I'll join you. I can't concentrate on being social with murder charges hanging over me." *And why would any of Cinder's friends want to hang out with me?* Gabrielle could already hear their snickering laughter in her mind.

Cinder tugged a crop jacket on and went out the door. It closed with a final click that left the room in a deep, aching silence.

Gabrielle reached out to the keyboard of her computer. Maybe it was time she do her own research, but even before she got to the wiki page, the pictures that came up with the search term *evil dolls* turned her off the quest. She already had one doll to haunt her; she didn't need more.

Her phone buzzed, and she pulled it out, glad for the distraction. A text from Peter.

-They'll be releasing me Monday.-

-How are you feeling?-

-Plenty of drugs. I feel fine.-

-Give me a call when you're home.-

She lay back on the couch, facing the ceiling with the phone held above her and waited for his response.

-K. Cops R gone. Makes everything better.-

-Get some rest.-

Her mind went back to the doll. Maybe a cleansing would be enough? Maybe they didn't need to burn her. As long as the doll didn't find more children to "protect" no one else would be harmed. It hadn't hurt anyone prior to that night in the basement when Gabrielle suggested getting rid of her father. Before that, it had been harmless, and it'd been in her family for generations.

No. She had to be certain. Peter and Michael had to be safe.

"You can't get rid of me," a high voice whispered.

thirty-four

Cole pulled up to the church early Sunday morning. Coming, despite Michael's refusal to accompany him, had been a spur of the moment decision, but he knew it had everything to do with leaving the Bey murder case. If God wanted to have a say in this, he'd give the Almighty a chance.

The lot was nearly empty. He parked in the shade of a large pine as Isa sang tunelessly in the back seat. Blackberry vines crawled up the trunk of the tree and spilled out toward the curb. The shady spots always filled up first on sunny days. His need to be timely had caused fights between him and Joan when they'd attended together, since she was constantly late.

But now he came without her. Cole smiled as the shade rippled, making dots of sunlight parade over his dash. The beads Isa had made for Joan swung on the rearview mirror, sending tiny lights dancing. He reached for the key to shut the car off.

"Can we please listen?" Isa waved her arms at the stereo from the back seat. Her request was a familiar one, to wait until the end of the song on the radio before he turned off the car. Cole usually had none of it, but Yolanda must give in to requests like these since Isa wouldn't keep asking if she never received a yes.

"Pleeeeeease," she begged.

Cole sighed. *Why not? We're early anyhow.*

He dropped his hand to his lap as a woman's voice soared out of the speakers. The song ended five seconds later, but Isa's beaming face was worth the compromise.

"Shall we invite Michael to come out to brunch with us afterward?" Cole asked as he opened his door.

"Yes. He's my friend!" she burbled.

That would give Cole a chance to tell Michael he'd made a decision. Saturday had gone by without further contact between them, and an after-church brunch seemed like a safe option. Though he acknowledged it was cowardly to use Isa as a shield in that conversation. But Isa was the reason he had to make the decision, and maybe her being there would keep Michael understanding.

Before he lost the confidence to do it, Cole shot off a text to Michael, inviting him out.

He shut his door and went back to open hers. Isa's voice flooded out the minute he did. When she was speaking that fast, even being her father, Cole couldn't make out what she was saying.

"Mmhmm," he said and leaned over to unbuckle her from the car seat.

"Why he not come to church with us?" Isa asked as she hopped onto the asphalt. The air was heavy with moisture, but the clouds were fluffy, and the sun would beat away the remaining wet soon.

"Not all people like church, Isa. Many people believe differently than we do."

"Why?"

Cole scooped her up and started toward the front of the church. His parents would have told Isa those people were horribly misguided, if not evil. Joan probably would have too.

"There is no proof of God," Cole said. "So we have to trust our faith. Many people just don't have that faith."

"Why?"

Cole could see this conversation stretching on for a while. He couldn't foresee her understanding any of the answers. "It doesn't matter why. We just need to accept that people can be different and still good."

"Why?" The question seemed unfocused this time, and Isa's face turned up to the sky.

The church's steeply sloped roof dragged his eyes up to the top, where the building ended in sky. "There is room in the mind and heart to accept and love things, even if we don't fully agree. The important thing is to remember that whether someone believes the same thing you do, they deserve love and respect."

Isa swatted at a leaf on a tree branch as they passed. She giggled and swung her chubby arm again.

That went over her head. But she stopped asking, so—win.

One of the church's double doors stood wide open. He walked into the lobby and set her down on the worn carpet. The room was mostly empty, but a few people stood around, absorbed in their own worlds. Two women looked up and smiled warmly in greeting. As he entered the sanctuary, an older man seated in the front row of interlocking chairs waved at him.

"Good to see you here, Cole," the man called.

"Good to see you, Mr. Weir." Cole nodded and ushered Isa in front of him.

He scooted her into a row just a few in from the back. There were only about a dozen people in the sanctuary so far, but they were all seated toward the front or in the very back row. Cole picked a seat at the center of the row.

Numerous windows brightened the sanctuary, and though the room had no fancy adornments, the glow of the sunlight made it anything but dull. The wooden pulpit at the front was etched with a large cross and behind that hung a silk tapestry of a brightly colored cross.

His phone beeped. After taking off his coat, Cole checked the message. From Michael, begging off going out today. He said he had to catch up on work while the office was empty.

Was Michael avoiding him? Cole decided there was no point in jumping to conclusions on this. If Cole had already left the case when they talked, maybe the conversation would be easier on both of them. He tucked his phone away.

Cole had barely settled into his seat when Reverend Alice entered. Isa jumped up and down on the seat next to him. Before he could stop her, she climbed up over his lap and crawled along the line of empty chairs away from both the adults.

She's not hurting anything.

The pastor spotted him and waved, but rather than leaving it at that, she ambled down the aisle toward him.

"Cole, it's good to see you here," Alice said. Her mousy brown hair fell in wisps across her sharp, brown eyes. "How have you been?"

"Pretty decent."

"I heard Joan moved back to the area," the reverend said softly, laying a hand on his shoulder. "If you need to talk, I'm always available."

It felt wrong to hear that when it was here that he and Joan had done their counseling before the divorce. In fact, it was in this church, with this pastor, that the whole marriage fractured. Oh, they'd been having problems already; that's why they'd gone in. But Cole could pinpoint the moment of no return.

And Alice had been there to witness it.

When he'd mentioned that Joan was one of the few women he'd ever dated, and Joan's eyes got wide, it was all over. She'd been instantly angry. Cole thought Joan had always known about his history; he'd made a point when they were first dating to mention his past boyfriends.

Maybe he'd done it all wrong. Could Joan have assumed that when he mentioned Al, he'd meant Alison? He'd thought he'd been clear from the start, but Joan made it obvious very quickly that she hadn't heard him right.

And everything fell after that. Joan started blaming all their issues on Cole being gay—which wasn't how he thought of himself —saying he'd tricked her. Then she'd cheated to "make herself feel wanted."

His sexuality was something she couldn't forgive.

Her infidelity was something he wouldn't forgive.

Reverend Alice had had prime seats for it all. And now, she stood there, hand on his shoulder, no judgment in her eyes. He'd kept coming to church at first, but he'd felt like everyone was judging him. Shortly after the fiasco with the Mother-Daughter camping trip at the tail end of summer, Cole had stopped regularly bringing Isa.

How is it Reverend Alice can still look at me like nothing has changed? My own wife thought I was an affront against God.

"Has Joan been back?" Cole asked quietly, trying to keep the question out of Isa's hearing. Whether she heard or not, he had to know the answer. Seeing Joan wasn't on his to-do list for the day.

"No, although she would be welcome here." Alice paused as Isa ran past to the aisle and flung herself to the floor to tug at a string loose on a chair.

"This was her church first," Cole said. "I don't want to drive her off."

He realized as he said it, though, that having her driven off would bring him only joy.

"You aren't driving her anywhere. She's a grown woman and can make her own choices. Everyone is welcome here—and that includes your new boyfriend." Alice smiled. "I hope to meet him soon."

Cole leaned back. He knew he'd mentioned Michael to a few of the other parishioners in passing over his infrequent attendances, but it surprised him that the reverend knew. "Michael."

She nodded.

"I doubt he'll be coming anytime soon." Cole fiddled with the cross around his neck.

"Well, whenever he does decide to come, introduce us." She paused as if debating her next words. "I like seeing you happy. The whole congregation does, and he makes you happy. If you've felt anything different, I apologize. We've missed seeing you. Let Michael know he's welcome here."

Cole nodded.

She walked away to greet some congregants coming in, and Cole watched Isa as she intently played with the string coming from the back of a chair.

Then he watched the stream of people enter. A few avoided meeting his eyes—he knew some of them had taken Joan's side of things strongly. Many, however, met his eyes and smiled. Several rushed over to greet him. The request to bring Michael was repeated nearly a dozen times.

It would be good for Michael to see this more tolerant side of religion. Maybe heal some of his scars. *But how would I ever convince him?*

thirty-five

A FEW TREES, A MOSTLY EMPTY PARKING LOT, AND THE WINDING DIRT PATH broke the view of muddy wetland. The sparsely traveled landscape felt further removed from the city than it was. Really they were only a five-minute walk from the parking lot and Cinder's car. The feeling of isolation did nothing to alleviate Gabrielle's sinking feeling of being trapped with the doll and her intention to be rid of the thing.

This was the third location she'd asked Cinder to travel to for the cleansing ceremony, and Gabrielle's roommate was starting to get anxious about the delay. Her first class that Monday morning was at 10:30, and Cinder expressed repeatedly her desire not to miss the lecture. Gabrielle would like to believe there really had been something wrong with the other locations. Given the snake of fear moving through her now, she doubted it. The problem was within her; it was with her paralyzing terror of burning the doll and what consequences that would have. What if she survived? What if, what if, what if?

"Is this far enough from home?" Cinder lugged her backpack with her supplies from her shoulder to a dry patch of ground. There was a stone circle with old ashes within a few yards—proclaiming this was more than a perfect place to ensure the doll never harmed anyone again.

"Where are we?" Gabrielle asked.

"Snohomish."

"I don't know this area." *Neither will the doll. It's perfect, or as perfect as getting rid of her is ever going to be.* Gabrielle looked down at the doll, who nested in an open box held awkwardly in Gabrielle's arms.

The doll's chubby face seemed to rest peacefully, reminding Gabrielle all too much of the comfort the wicked thing once brought her. "Let me find a good place to set her down." *And say goodbye.*

"I'll have a smoke while you wrap this up." Cinder strutted towards the murky water and pulled out a cigarette. She was old school. No vaping.

Gabrielle felt the cool morning air against her bare hands as she set the box on a patch of dry ground near the firepit. There was no hiding from this task. Cinder lit up, not glancing back toward Gabrielle. Her jeans were decorated with fashionable holes through which peeped out fishnet stockings.

She looked cold.

Cinder is never concerned with fitting in or being normal. Is that what it's like to not be all messed up in the head? Maybe someday I won't have to worry about it, either.

As Cinder stood, smoke streaming along in the breeze, Gabrielle stared suspiciously at the doll's eyes. The whole thing still felt like a trap ready to be sprung.

Yellow eyes stared up at her from within the box, filled with accusation and fury. Gabrielle blinked to make the illusion go away. The doll's weighted lids were closed.

Cinder returned. "It's time."

Gabrielle turned her back and shoved her hands into her jacket pocket, twisting a little string around her finger. Was this place hidden enough?

Having briefly looked over Cinder's cleansing ceremony,

Gabrielle couldn't make heads or tails of it. Cinder laid out a big book with symbols all over the cover—she'd insisted those symbols were not demonic, but Gabrielle couldn't see what else they could be.

Cinder drew a circle in the dirt with a stick, centering the circle around the doll. Then she placed objects at four points, using a compass to identify the directions. Gabrielle watched the doll. She wasn't moving. Something was wrong.

"Stand in the South corner," Cinder said.

Gabrielle went where indicated. Cinder insisted on doing the cleansing, but all Gabrielle cared about was the burning. Destroying the doll would set whatever spirit was bound there free. That felt right. This magic words and objects stuff didn't.

She closed her eyes as Cinder began reading words from the book.

"I protect you."

Destroying the doll was all that mattered. Gabrielle's wings itched between her shoulder blades. *I don't need a guardian angel, especially not a bloody one.*

Michael and Peter are my angels.

The odd cleansing, a mishmash of pagan and Christian symbolism went on. Cinder burned herbs, chanted, and lay "sacred" objects inside the box. Objects like an old necklace of Gabrielle's, a picture of the siblings as children, a rock from the house Gabrielle grew up in.

Guilt gnawed at her. But the doll had come to that rooftop. She'd attacked without being asked. It was Gabrielle's turn to act.

Cinder continued with the ritual, but Gabrielle's mind spun, vision blurred.

Could she really do this? Burning the doll could not be undone. *We were friends for so long—she was my protector. What am I without her?* Fear mounted in her gut.

The doll lay in its box at the center of the circle, those demonic eyes closed. If the cleansing worked, it would be just a doll by the time she burned. Then the burning wouldn't really matter, would it?

"You think you can destroy me without destroying yourself?"
Stop whispering in my head.

Cinder started flicking water from a special silver box and droplets sprayed the doll's face. Gabrielle moved forward to do the same at Cinder's bidding.

The water was warm on her fingertips, and she painted a cross on the doll's forehead. Gabrielle might have no faith, but her mother's family had. The gesture was one of good will.

"It's done." Cinder touched her arm. "You're shaking."

"We need to burn her."

"We don't have to. We could bury her."

Gabrielle wavered. Staring down at the doll, she felt too many emotions all clamoring against each other. "It must be done. Light the fire."

Cinder pulled some logs from beside the firepit and some paper starter bits from her backpack. Then adding some firelighter, she lit it and waited for the flame to build.

Gabrielle stared into the velvet-lined box, as the shadow-light of the flames flickered over the doll.

"I won't leave you in the dark; light will take you," Gabrielle whispered. *I'm not breaking my promises to her. I'm just sending her somewhere else.*

I don't even believe myself.

Gabrielle folded the excess velvet over the doll and the light padding all around her, to keep the fragile antique from cracking during transport. Cracking *further.*

Pain sliced through her skull, and she gripped it, letting her eyes close.

Strained, gasping breaths filled the air. Black. *Oh, god. Oh, god.* Wood stairs supported her feet, and a darkness so thick its tendrils crawled over her skin.

Gabrielle climbed up the basement stairs she recalled from her youth—expecting to feel an icy hand latch onto her and drag her down. The top of the stairs and the crack of light from under the door grew no closer, though she hurled herself forward.

Cracks sizzled up her legs.

Wings flapped behind her—the wings of an avenging angel. Blood sprayed off them.

She opened her eyes but saw nothing.

"*Weak girl,*" the doll's voice hissed. "*You couldn't even manage to say the word no. That's why Joe's dead. You could have stopped everything, but you're useless. How can you ever defend yourself in this world? You need me. You're weak.*"

A flicker of light entered Gabrielle's vision and a flash of gray sky with the smell of smoke.

"Fire's ready," Cinder said. The tone of her voice asked once again if Gabrielle was certain.

Gabrielle's fingers crushed the corrugated cardboard until the small ridges popped, leaving her finger marks across the box's flaps. Gabrielle shut them tight, forcing the darkness away.

"I can stop this," she whispered.

If this doesn't work, she'll kill me for the attempt.

Gabrielle gazed directly to her newest tattoo—the pearly gates.

Peter. I hurt him. She hurt him. He's not safe as long as I cling to my promise to a doll.

For Peter.

The smell of smoke reached Gabrielle on the wind, and a moment later, Cinder's boots clumped up to her.

"Do you need help carrying that?" Cinder asked.

"No." *This is my burden.*

Gabrielle hugged the box to her chest. Her pulse hammered. With each beat, it commanded her to run.

"Yes," Gabrielle whispered. "I can't put her in the flames."

"We don't have to burn her."

"*It doesn't matter,*" the doll's familiar voice whispered into Gabrielle's mind. "*I'll be coming back. Do you think it'll be this easy?*"

Gabrielle gasped for air. And stumbled back. *I can't do this.* "I can't even watch Cinder, I can't. I can't!"

"Let me deal with this," Cinder said, stepping in and taking the box. Suddenly seeming much more willing to burn the doll. Gabrielle didn't care as long as it happened.

Gabrielle fled the clearing and down the path to the parking lot. Her lungs burned and black ribbons swirled before her eyes, threatening to plunge her into the hell of her past. She bent down, curled over her knees, and struggled to breathe.

As long as it keeps Peter safe, it's all worth it.

A plume of smoke reached up over the trees.

thirty-six

Cole stood under a light drizzle in the parking lot. There were few cars in the police station lot at ten on a Monday morning, but the emptiness felt fraught with tension. A cigarette hung from his fingers, making a trail of smoke into the sky. He'd been absorbed in slowly watching the cigarette burn down, trying to get up the courage to file the paperwork that he was leaving the case, and why.

His cell phone rang.

He took in a deep breath before fishing it from his pocket. What were the chances this news was going to be any better than anything else that had happened in the last few weeks?

"Cole here."

"We have news from the coroner's office," Detective Sera said.

"Really? It's about time." *Crud. Regardless of what it says, I can't change my mind.*

"Yeah. And Cole, you have to hear this." Sera's voice lowered. "Get into the station. Now. Our whole case just changed."

"I'm *at* the station." And all the paperwork he needed to leave the case was piled neatly on his desk, just waiting for him to reenter and turn it in.

"Then get over to my office." Sera hung up.

Cole held the phone in his hands for a few long moments before dropping his untouched cigarette and grinding it into the pavement with the tip of his shoe.

He trudged into the station, keeping his eyes on his shiny shoes to avoid having to speak with anyone. Since Sera's talk with him on Friday night, he couldn't help feeling that everyone there was watching him.

Certainly at least some of them are. And they're just waiting for me to slip up.

He reached Sera's desk and walked up to her. Positioned in the corner of the room, and with the desks around hers currently empty, there was a sense of privacy.

Mascara darkened her eyelashes and, in addition to her red lipstick, this was more makeup than he'd ever seen her wear. Any femininity that it might have added was wiped away by the scowl tightening her mouth and scrunching her eyebrows together.

"That was fast," she said.

"I told you, I was already here. Just outside." Cole leaned against her desk. "Where's Joseph Bey's autopsy report?"

Sera slapped her fingers down onto a folder and shoved it across the desk toward him.

Cole flipped it open. He scanned the document, jumping from one segment to another: crushed ribs and asphyxiation, far less blood loss than expected from the knife-wounds. It didn't take long to get the gist. It seemed Joe had died from asphyxiation, with crushing injuries seeming to occur prior to the knife wounds—injuries more consistent with being crushed by a giant snake. And given the giant python free in the room where he'd died, this manner of death was being given serious credence.

Joe was crushed to death.

Gabrielle hadn't killed Joseph Bey, or at least, she hadn't dealt the death blow. That had been the snake.

Apparently attending church does work miracles. No one can say that Michael's sister is a cold-blooded murderer now. A killer maybe, but the complications made proving murder beyond a reasonable doubt a long shot. And Cole could be free of the case with no guilt. Things were working out perfectly.

He slapped the folder shut. Sera's tight shoulders tensed even more. *Well, she'll still say Gabrielle is at fault, and the courts may even try to prove it. But the DA would be a fool to charge Gabrielle with first degree murder.*

He forced himself not to smile. Finally, he understood why the autopsy had taken so long. There were contradictory narratives telling stories over Joseph Bey's body, and the coroner had to be especially careful to gather each little bit of information.

"What does it mean?" he asked, though he was pretty sure he knew. Gabrielle would still be charged with stabbing him, but a good lawyer could sway a jury that she'd only been trying to stab the snake. With bad aim. Very bad aim. Reasonable doubt.

Sera pulled the file back, opened it, and looked down as if she were reading it over for the first time. But judging from the scowl that still hadn't dissipated, it was more likely she was hoping the words had altered.

A picture frame on her desk had been bumped askew by the rapid back and forth of the folder. Cole's eyes lingered on Sera's smiling face and that of the man beside her. The man, who held a dressed-in-white Sera against him, looked more effeminate than she did. Soft face, soft hands, diamond earrings.

A pang of jealousy rippled through Cole. No matter how things went, he'd never have a picture like that of Michael on display. Within the precinct, it was fine to be proud of your partner, to display them like a trophy, no matter how off the norm they were—unless they were the same sex.

Or is that me, making excuses for myself?

Cole straightened the picture and lifted his hand.

Sera *hmph*ed.

"I'm leaving the case," Cole said.

"The autopsy findings mean nothing," she said. "You know I think Ms. Cross killed him."

"I do."

"And you know I will continue to try to prove it." Her voice lacked its usual strength. Sera wasn't giving in. They would catch Gabrielle for assault, probably a first-degree manslaughter charge.

He'd had cases where he felt like that. Where he knew the person was guilty but the evidence just wasn't there. Letting someone like that walk hurt. "I know how you feel."

"Then get out. I have work to do. Take the report if you want to look at it more but make me a copy." Sera turned away from him and pointedly set her hands on her keyboard.

Cole grabbed the autopsy report and stepped out into the hall. Time to drop the case. Everything was going to be okay. Hell, this was a glorious day.

The snake had saved him. Now, everything would work itself out. Cole grinned.

More importantly, the news gave him back a real shot of having the life he wanted—a life with both Isa and Michael in it.

He went directly to his office and gathered up all the physical files he had belonging to the Bey murder case. With one more glance over the autopsy report, he stacked it on top, picked the stack up, and headed out of his office.

Time to talk to those higher-ups Sera had been worried about.

<h1 style="text-align:center">thirty-seven</h1>

"I still need to talk to you," Michael said over the phone. "Meet me somewhere?"

Cole looked at his desk, still covered with paperwork, but far less of it with the Bey case gone. The clock said it was earlier than he'd feared, only eleven. Only an hour had passed since he turned in his paperwork to leave the case. Still, there was a lot more paperwork to go through, and it wasn't the best day for a meeting with Michael.

But seeing Michael was the one thing that could make an already fantastic day better. Sure he had confessed that he had some information, presumably related to the case, that he needed to share, but even that didn't dampen Cole's mood. Things were finally starting to look up. He felt as if he'd been buried beneath a landslide and suddenly a rock had moved, giving him a glimpse of light.

Why someone had stabbed Joseph Bey as he died was a separate issue, and one Gabrielle was still likely to be tried for. But it wasn't a murder case. There really wasn't any better turn the case could have taken, short of a second person showing up covered in Joseph Bey's blood.

"Cole," Michael said. "I really do need to talk to you. I tried calling you Sunday."

"I know, I'm sorry. I took Isa to church and after we went to lunch, she got really sleepy. I took her home for a nap and got caught up in legal paperwork. I didn't see your call until late."

"Can we meet today?" Michael sounded nervous, tight. Cole imagined him having a vice grip on the phone.

"Yeah, sounds good. I have something to tell you too."

"Are you leaving the case?" Michael's voice fell flat. If it had any emotion, it hid in the deadpan tone.

"I did this morning, but I'll meet you for lunch. I have good news." Though who knew if Michael would see it that way.

"You sound really happy."

For the first time since this mess began, he was.

"Dick's?" Michael named a nearby drive-up burger joint, a local institution and one of the places closest to being equidistant between their two offices.

"No. I don't really want to sit outside or in my car." *Not to discuss a murder investigation. Going to a diner kind of sucks too, but it has to be somewhere.*

"Okay . . ." Michael dragged out the vowels and took a long pause as if the rejection of this location mattered far more than it should. "There is a place. I'll text you the info."

"See you in an hour?" *I should be in a hurry to hear whatever Michael has to say after how he left Saturday morning. But, God, please don't let his revelation ruin things.*

"Sounds good."

Cole hung up and rose from his desk. Detective Sera smiled at him from across the room and walked over to him. A red blouse peeked from under her black blazer. He really had never imagined her as the color sort of person, but he supposed they all hid parts of themselves at work.

"I didn't think you'd really do it." She leaned against the edge of his desk. "Word came down you left the case."

He nodded.

"I've got to warn you, that autopsy doesn't exonerate Ms. Cross.

The point of the matter is Joseph was stabbed repeatedly. Some of those wounds are—"

"Don't tell me." *The snake killed the victim. And it would be impossible to prove that Gabrielle orchestrated or planned that. She is off for murder one.*

Sera shrugged. "Just don't be shocked. We aren't dropping the case."

"She'll be charged with something, I'm sure. But it's none of my business anymore." Cole nodded at her and then walked outside. There were plenty of other worries to face, but at that moment, he couldn't stomach any of them. He wandered out into the parking lot and enjoyed the feel of fickle spring sunlight on his shoulders. Clouds rimmed the horizon. The good weather wouldn't last.

Sliding into his car, he reached up to touch Isa's beads. Things were going to get better. They were. He smiled and turned the car on. His phone beeped, and he checked the text from Michael. He put the address into his GPS and started the drive.

He arrived more than half an hour early and sat in his car. The heat slowly built up as the sunlight was amplified by the glass, and only when the car was too stuffy to stand did Cole open the door and climb out.

It was still a good fifteen minutes before Michael was due, but he headed inside anyway and ordered a coffee. He was on his second cup by the time Michael strutted in. His eyes sparkled, and he seemed back to his usual dapper self. Not an eye in the place didn't lift to him.

Michael didn't appear to notice the flirty looks of the hostess or the sideways glances of other patrons.

I guess it'll be like that most of our lives. Cole smiled. *Wow. Fuck. When did this become so long-term to me? And how can I let myself feel like that when I know he's about to drop some awful bombshell?*

Michael grinned when he saw Cole and headed toward him over the red-and-white-tiled floor. He scooted into the booth beside Cole instead of taking the opposite side. Cole almost commented on it—

not that he minded having Michael close, but this wasn't typical behavior.

He's doing it to reassure me he doesn't blame me for leaving the case. Or is it something else?

"You said you had good news?" Michael laced his fingers with Cole's. Their legs touched.

"I do. But I think yours might be more important."

Michael slouched away, everything about his earlier gregarious demeanor changing. He even dropped his eyes to the faux-wood tabletop, as if interested in the skewed sugar packets.

"No," Michael said. "Let's start off with you."

"Just before I left the case, the autopsy came in. The contents were good news as far as you and Gabrielle are concerned. It appears that Joseph Bey was killed by his snake, not the stab wounds. The investigation will keep looking into Gabrielle. But the cause of death is going to give defense a leg up and makes murder one an unlikely charge."

Michael lifted his gaze to give Cole a quizzical look. "He wasn't stabbed to death."

"No. He was stabbed *too*, but he was squeezed to death. Joseph had a pet python."

"But they'll get her for something." Michael perked up a little, grabbing up one of the sugar packets and shaking it by the corner. "I don't know that some time in a psychiatric facility wouldn't do her good. That's what's most likely to happen, right?"

"It's hard to say. Pleas of Not Guilty by Reason of Insanity are really hard to pull off. If it had been a murder charge, I'd say no, she probably couldn't convince a jury. But aggravated assault or whatever they stick to her? Maybe."

"You did everything you could."

"I wish I could have done more."

"Look, that's actually one of the things I needed to see you about. I need your help." Michael tapped the sugar packet against his palm, then against the edge of his empty coffee cup.

"Okay. I'm listening," Cole said. Michael's eyes weren't scrunched, and his shoulders were relatively relaxed. So Cole guessed this wasn't the same news Michael had been so worked up about.

They paused as the waitress approached, holding two pots of coffee, one with an orange mouth and one with black.

"Another coffee?" she asked.

Cole nodded.

"Anything for you, sir?" the waitress asked Michael as she poured from the black-mouthed pot.

"Coffee and whatever your special is." Michael's usual chipper tone returned as he spoke. He turned up his cup from its paper coaster, and the waitress filled it to the brim.

"Anything to eat for you, sir?" The waitress smiled vacantly at Cole.

"Cheeseburger."

She nodded and scooted back off toward the counter.

"Go on." He took a sip from his fresh coffee and waited for Michael to continue.

"Gabrielle and Cinder exorcised the damn doll. Gabrielle wanted to burn it."

"The doll isn't evidence. We don't care."

"I'm not concerned about the police." Michael ripped open the sugar packet. "It's about Gabrielle. She can't destroy that doll; her psyche is too dependent on it. Now maybe it'll all turn out for the best, and she'll be right that getting rid of it will help her. But it might completely wreck her."

Michael peeled open two creamer cups and dumped them in.

Cole swallowed a mouthful of black coffee, and thoughts jumbled around in his head. "Why do I get a feeling you already did something?"

"Cinder called to tell me, and I sort of retrieved the doll." He sipped his concoction.

The way Michael said that sounded guilty, and Cole decided that digging in was not in anyone's best interest. "She is an adult, Michael, not a child. Do you realize how this sounds?"

"Yes. But you didn't see the damage it did last time she tried to give the thing up. She was institutionalized for months—she thought she was the doll. Gabrielle is . . . Did I tell you about the tattoos?"

"The bloody wings?"

"She was involuntarily committed. That's when Evan left me. We got our wings after she came out of the mental hospital as a reminder of where we come from—that God left us to this world of blood and death—that all we have is each other. When we were going in for the tattoos she said, 'We are the only angels left.' So I am her guardian forever. I literally swore to it in ink on my body."

Cole had a sinking feeling. "I'm guessing you aren't telling me any of this out of an overwhelming desire to open up."

Michael nodded. His hand wrapped around his coffee cup, though he seemed to have lost interest in drinking it.

"You need something from me."

"Yes. I can't keep the doll." Michael shivered, a brief look of fear crossing his face. "I know it's stupid, but the thing terrifies me. Every time I see it, I just see them, my mom, Gabrielle's dad, covered in blood and . . . That's what I came to ask you. Can you keep it? Just in case—for a few months. If Gabrielle doesn't relapse or get worse, we can get rid of it. If not, I'll come to get it from you."

Cole took a gulp of coffee to allow himself a moment to think. He didn't like the idea of a doll that was so central to Michael's sister's psychosis staying at his house. But it wasn't particularly a logical feeling. The doll could just be stored in the garage as far as he was concerned. And doing the favor might give him a level of sway with Michael that could only come with trust.

Cole touched the cross around his neck.

Michael fidgeted. "I'll have Cinder drop it off at your place. Just leave it on the porch, no trouble to you."

"I'll store the doll for a bit. But I have a request of my own. You come to church with me next Sunday. I'd like you to see that it doesn't have to be bad."

Michael looked away, then down, then away again. He was hiding something. That much was obvious. But what?

"I haven't been entirely honest with you, Cole. I don't belong in church. I'm not a good person. Even if I wanted to believe in God, I doubt any god would have me."

Now here it was, the real thing that Michael needed to tell him. "Tell me what's going on, Michael. This isn't all about a doll."

"I can't. I thought I could discuss this here, but I can't. Not now." Michael took in a deep breath and met Cole's eyes. Indecision washed over his face, but then hardened. It was the look of a man who had made a difficult choice. "Tomorrow night, come over to my place. Isa will be with Joan doing the camping thing, right? I'll tell you everything. Then you can decide for yourself. But you'll hold onto the doll still?"

Cole nodded. "One more thing?"

Michael's hands tightened around his cup.

"I have a date set with Joan and the mediator to talk about Isa's parenting plan. I was hoping maybe you could drive me there? I don't want to go alone. It wouldn't be smart for you to come in, but maybe you could keep me company on the ride there?"

Michael reached out his hand and placed it on Cole's knee. The heat from the coffee seeped from Michael's palm. "If you still want me to when this is over, of course I will."

<h1 style="text-align:center">thirty-eight</h1>

THE EMPTY SPOT ON THE SHELF BEHIND HER BED STARED AT GABRIELLE. Its dark void seemed ominous. Something would fill that space or creep out of it. She flopped back on her bed. Cinder's music pumped through the bedroom wall, losing all melody and retaining only a steady, demonic beat.

With the doll gone, Gabrielle should feel lighter—free. Instead, her hands shook. Something bad was coming, and the stench of sage didn't help. She was stranded on a train track, immobile, staring at the approaching engine. She had wanted to escape so badly. She'd dreamed that by now she'd be at her proverbial train station, awaiting a train to the real world, not about to get crushed by it.

Gabrielle tossed onto her side and glanced at her clock. Peter should have been released by now. He had said Monday. But dinner time had come and gone. It was past 6 p.m. Was he home? Why hadn't he called? He hadn't seemed upset with her at the hospital, but that could have changed. Maybe he'd realized how dangerous she was.

Would that be for the best?

No. I can't lose him. This can't all be for nothing.

She reached for her cell.

The phone rang, and she drew back, fingers curling. But at the sight of the caller ID, she swiped her finger over the screen to accept.

"Peter! Are you okay? Are you home?" She clutched the phone to her ear with both hands as she sat up, throwing her legs over the edge of the bed.

"I'm fine." An undercurrent of anger sounded in his voice. "Gabs?"

Her jaw clenched as tears, which had been far too free and loose recently, rose in her eyes.

"Can you do me a favor?" Peter asked, that thread of anger gone, leaving only exhaustion.

"Anything." *He needs me. I can start to make it up . . . somehow.* Her heart sang in her at the sound of his voice, asking for her. Wanting her.

"My parents were supposed to come get me hours ago. But my dad just called. Apparently"—he sneered this last word, enough venom in his voice to rival any snake—"Mom's having an anxiety attack. She had a meeting with one of her fundraising groups and didn't want to miss it. She's worried about seeming pitiable to her friends, about how missing the meeting will look."

"How it will *look*?" Gabrielle's nose flared, and her mouth turned in a sneer of its own. *Screw his parents. He doesn't need a family like that.* "Of course she is."

"Dad said he knew I'd understand and that I could find another ride."

"Me? Peter . . ." *I shouldn't. I should keep my distance. But the doll's gone. Wasn't that the point? Peter is safe now.* Gabrielle stood and looked out her bedroom window. Cinder's red compact car was sitting in the driveway. "I'm on my way."

"Thanks."

"Why me?" Gabrielle rubbed her socked feet over the carpet before shoving them into the black tennis shoes she'd been wearing earlier. "I mean, you have plenty of friends who would come if you asked." And it was true; despite his eccentricities, Peter had a sizable social circle—most of them druggies, but still, he wasn't alone in the world like Gabrielle.

"You're the only one I want to see, Gabs. You don't mind, do you?"

"Oh, Peter." The warmth spreading inside her flowed out of the words. As if she'd ever mind him wanting her around. Gabrielle closed her eyes, cradling the phone as if to keep the words close. "No. I don't mind. I'll be right there."

"See you."

"Bye." Gabrielle hung up and then grabbed her oversized sweater off the bed to put it back on. She bolted over to Cinder's room and knocked. After a brief exchange, Gabrielle had the rights to use the car for the night. Cinder said she'd be staying over at a friend's anyhow and wouldn't be home until after school the next day. Gabrielle raced through the house and out to the car. The sky sported a rich glow that implied twilight was just around the corner. Peter hadn't been kidding; his parents really must have been due hours before.

She climbed into the car and started out of the neighborhood, picturing what the day must have been like for Peter. How long had he waited after signing himself out? No way he would have called for a rideshare of any kind, but still, sitting in a hospital couldn't have been easy. And his parents just left him there.

But am I any better? He wouldn't have called me if I pushed him, right? It was her, and she's gone.

I can be what Peter needs. Normal. Whole. Just one of those smiling girls on the street.

Gabrielle rubbed her palms over the wheel and gathered her scattered thoughts. She drove past the gas station next to the pink house where Joe had dropped her off. She eyed its exterior. Had it been just last week she sat there, falling apart over what seemed now to be a non-event?

She merged onto I-5 and threaded into the constant traffic. At least at this time of evening, slightly past 7 p.m. the traffic moved—a little. The cloud cover above was an angry gray, threatening rain; it also brought the twilight on early. Taillights extended out forever, row upon row of angry, red demon eyes.

They looked hungry.

Gabrielle turned the radio on, and the nasal whine of a local folk singer filled the car—a steady beat to guide her heart.

The doll is gone. I can live my life. I have to believe that—it's the whole point.

Michael can live his life.

And no one else dies.

She smiled. And she looked into the car window beside her. A father drove the vehicle with two kids in the back. One of the kids was gesticulating wildly, and the dad looked annoyed and tired. Gabrielle could almost imagine herself as the mother they came home to—just another person living an ordinary life.

Gabrielle's exit was coming up, so she merged right. The blue hospital sign signaled the correct exit to her even if her GPS hadn't been chirping alerts.

How could Peter's parents not have come? And what on earth could his mother have been afraid it would look like? That Peter had attempted suicide? That she cared about her son? What did it matter what any of her wealthy friends thought? Mothers weren't supposed to be like that: selfish and needy. Parents were supposed to protect their children.

Why did the world never work that way?

The meek shall inherit the Earth. Her mother had loved that phrase when cautioning Gabrielle to be obedient. But it didn't feel true. The world didn't look out for the weak. The world expected people to protect themselves, and if they couldn't, well, that was their failure.

"*I protected you,*" the doll's voice sang out.

Gabrielle swerved, veering far too close to the cement barrier that flanked the exit.

Yellow eyes swelled up in her rearview mirror, seeming to lurch from the back seat. No. *She* was gone. Destroyed.

The car careened the other way. Cement loomed up and black threatened to encroach on her vision. The doll's illusionary hands pulled her down into the past.

thirty-nine

Peter's treehouse surrounded Gabi, and she lay on the floor, tucked up under a warm blanket. Then Mr. Pritcher's red angry face leered down at her. He shouted, spittle flying from his mouth. Then she was in a basement surrounded by boxes, a knife in her hand. Mr. Pritcher lurched down the stairs toward her. Gabrielle felt herself smile and adjust her grip on the blade.

A horn blared.

Gabrielle slammed on the brakes.

Her tires squealed.

Her eyes closed.

The brakes engaged, and the car stopped, sending her flying forward. The steering wheel jammed into her sternum. Breath wheezed from between Gabrielle's parted lips, and tiny white dots popped in front of her eyes.

The horn continued behind her. Then stopped.

Panic sped her heart and her breath, but a terrifying clarity speared her mind. If Mr. Pritcher had been at the treehouse the night that he died, then Peter had lied to the police. The question was, how much had Peter lied? The fact she'd also recalled being with Mr. Pritcher later and holding a knife didn't imply good things.

"Are you okay?" someone asked from outside her window.

Gabrielle lifted her eyes.

I'm blocking the exit.

Her bumper stood less than an inch from the cement divider that had kept her from plowing onto the freeway. The doll laughed, a high-pitch squeal of glee.

She looked up at the man outside her window. She needed him to go away so she could parse the vision and consider the ramification of it having come after she got rid of the doll. But the man stared in at her with concern. "Sorry," she mouthed.

Unable to think of something better to do, she pulled fully onto the shoulder and turned on her flashers.

"Are you okay?" the man asked again.

Gabrielle nodded, rolling the window down. "I'm headed to the hospital. Just give me a second." She was afraid he'd stick around, but after another worried glance, the man backed off and got into his car.

She leaned against her steering wheel. The ache from her chest pulsed, and she focused on that, ignoring the rest. For now.

The pain laced through her, allowing her a moment's respite from the single pounding fact that kept trying to rise up. Gabrielle had been in the basement with Mr. Pritcher where he died. She'd been holding a knife.

She had killed Mr. Pritcher. And the doll had been there. She hadn't seen it in the vision, but the knowledge rang as a truth inside her.

Gabrielle felt the cracks covering her spread and deepen until she feared she would shatter. The doll was gone. Cinder had destroyed it, but Gabrielle was still broken. So if she'd killed Mr. Pritcher before, which seemed like the only possibility, then she could well kill again now. Destroying the doll hadn't made her safe or free.

The cement divider outside her window mocked her. Just a few moments more and she would have been dead, and that might have been better for everyone.

I'm dangerous.

Gabrielle tucked her knees up under her chin, pressing her legs to the steering wheel and buried her face in her hands.

She imagined moving her foot to the gas pedal, removing herself and whatever danger she posed from the world. Would her body break apart like porcelain shattering on a stone floor? In her mind, she saw the cracks inside her rising to the surface, fissures along her skin until her limbs flew off at jagged angles.

But if she shattered, what happened to the evil still lingering inside her? If Gabrielle was alone in her mind, and simply crazy, her death might end the violence, but it wouldn't provide anyone with answers.

Finally, the thought of Peter forced its way through her fingers into her mind. He was waiting. Gabrielle might not know what hope she had left for herself, given she was apparently an insane murderer, but she could at least fulfill her promise to him.

She turned on her blinker and pulled back out onto the road. The sky above had dimmed, leaving the darkened streets a grayish-black. The city lights cast a sickly pall on the clouds hovering low over the buildings. The stars and the moon couldn't break through the cover.

Gabrielle glanced at the clock on her dashboard. It was already closing in on 9 p.m. Not quite able to believe so much time had passed, she checked her phone to confirm. She had a few missed calls. It hadn't felt like she'd sat there for over an hour, but clearly, she had.

As she drove, she pondered the new facts.

Given her presence in the basement and the knife in her hand, she could assume she had killed Pritcher. And given that she had a history of murder, she must assume she had killed Joe. But Peter had given her an alibi for Mr. Pritcher. One that didn't seem to hold up. Why would he lie, and how much did he actually know about what happened with Mr. Pritcher?

Peter knew that Mr. Pritcher had been at the treehouse and must have known that she'd left it that night. Gabrielle mulled this over as she turned her car onto Jefferson Street, between the towering buildings that composed Harborview Hospital. How was her foster father's presence at Peter's possible? When had Mr. Pritcher gotten there? She rolled the memory around in her mind but couldn't make heads or tails of the little snippet. All she knew was that it didn't fit into the version of events that Peter had been feeding her for the past six years.

Peter had sworn to the cops he'd been alone with Gabrielle in the treehouse all night. And sworn that he'd never met Mr. Pritcher. His lies stank of her guilt. Did he know what she'd done? It seemed that way. Maybe he'd have answers to fill in the gaps. He had been there with her and Mr. Pritcher at the treehouse. Could Peter have been involved in the murder itself? No, she dismissed that thought. But he must know more than he was saying.

Just like he knew more about how he came to "fall" off the building. Peter had answers for her, answers she needed before she made any further decisions. Only getting him to let go of his secrets wouldn't be easy.

He thinks he's protecting me. But what does he think he's protecting me from?

forty

GABRIELLE TURNED ONTO 8TH AVENUE BETWEEN THE WEST HOSPITAL AND A little grassy park that extended out past the helipad landing. Rather than waiting for her at the hospital entrance, Peter was sitting on the steps leading down into the park—as far from the building as he could get and still be next to the road. A crutch rested on the ground next to him. She parked at the curb and turned on her flashers again before getting out.

Her questions stuck like briars in her throat, refusing to come loose. He looked so broken. It was her turn to protect him, if only for a moment.

There were several other cars pulled up to the building on the other side of the road, waiting. Motion bustled behind the glass doors and the streetlights reflected off the decorative windows on the bridge between two nearby buildings. Several pedestrians bustled along the sidewalk and hopped in and out of cars.

"Sorry it took me so long," she said, offering her hand to help Peter up.

The bruising on his jawline and his temple had faded slightly, but the purplish tint was still visible. Gabrielle found herself staring, tracing each mark on him to add its weight to her soul.

As she gazed at him, Peter inspected her face.

She'd hurt him. Just like she'd killed Mr. Pritcher and Joe. *What do I do now?*

"What happened?" he asked.

"I almost crashed the car. I . . . Can we talk about it? Maybe at your place. I don't know if I'm safe to drive all the way back to my place anyhow."

"Are you safe to drive to *my* place?"

"It's only a few blocks. I'll hold it together." She offered her hand again.

Peter accepted and stood, grabbing the crutch off the ground. "I was getting worried something had happened to you when you didn't show up. I texted."

Gabrielle looked away and swallowed against the thorns still lodged in her throat. Angling herself beside Peter to help him walk, she managed to avoid meeting his eyes. "Sorry, I didn't see your text. And I'm not so sure that worrying is the wrong reaction, but for now, let's get you home."

She helped Peter into the car and then got back in herself. Her hand hovered over the key, but she couldn't force herself to turn it. He reached out and set a hand on her shoulder, rubbing his fingers into the tense muscles.

"We can just pull into one of the lots and wait it out, Gabs."

"No." She turned the key, its resistance straining her fingers. "I want to get out of this damn car."

Peter's hand remained on her shoulder as she drove. She'd have to circle around the hospital complex to get back to I-5. As scattered as she was, she couldn't afford to react to Peter until she was out of the crowded, pedestrian-ridden area. Though he watched her, he didn't demand answers. He waited, and the words bubbled and frothed inside her, demanding to be spoken.

"Cinder and I destroyed the doll first thing this morning."

"Why?"

"That's not important." Gabrielle steeled herself to say what came next. She had to tell Peter all of what happened. He had to know so that just maybe, when she asked, he'd tell her the truth about the night Mr. Pritcher died. But first the roof. That was easier. No one had died. "On the way here, I heard her, the doll," Gabrielle said. "Then I saw her eyes in the rearview mirror. She's angry at me for getting rid of her. Whatever connection she has to me hasn't been broken."

"Of course not, Gabs," Peter said.

"I thought getting rid of her would fix things, that it would make me safe to be around." *But I've never been safe to be around. And you've known all along.*

"There's never been a proven case of demonic possession. The doll is just a doll. Getting rid of her is a cheat. You can't fight problems in your brain by addressing unrelated external factors."

Gabrielle sped through a yellow light. "All I know is that Cinder cleansed and then burned her, and then I saw her eyes and things went wrong. What if I've been possessed by whatever evil lived in that doll all these years, and now, the spirit's mad at me? Now she wants me dead?" *It can't just be me. It can't. Please.*

"No. Calm down. You suffered a major trauma as a child. These blackouts and hallucinations are just your mind's way of dealing with it. Getting rid of the doll stressed you out. It's the stress that's affecting you, not the doll's absence."

Gabrielle clenched her jaw and continued to drive. She was a killer. But if he was right, it was her own fault that she was a killer. At least if it was some unquiet spirit, there might still be a way to salvage her life.

After a tense silence, she turned onto a residential road, crowded with cars parked on both sides.

"Then how do you explain how I act when I'm in these blackouts?" she asked. "How I acted on the roof?"

"That's how your brain is dealing, Gabs."

Headlights approached on the opposite side of the road.

Gabrielle pulled over to the side, between two parked cars, to let the car pass, then pulled back out.

"So that's your explanation?" she challenged. "Dissociative Disorder?"

"It isn't demon possession, that's for damn sure. Dissociative Identity Disorder can be treated, *if* that's what you have."

"You realize that there has never been a 'proven' case of DID either, right?"

"That's different. They just haven't had a chance to prove it. Most scientists think the old 'possessions' were things like schizophrenia and DID."

"Proof is proof, if that's what you are going to demand." Gabrielle tried to temper her tone as she pulled into the lot for Peter's apartment. The cracked pavement made the car bump, and arrows of pain moved through her chest.

"Is that true? Gabs, if I'm willing to trust in the medical institution, why can't you?"

She pulled into a tight space in the cramped lot. The cloudy sky still withheld the rain it promised, but the darkness hid the threat of the clouds. Peter's words functioned just the same, hanging overhead, threatening and heavy, promising worse. Trusting the medical system was something she'd been doing for years, and yet, here she was with problems growing. She needed him to trust it, but for her, it was different. The doll made it different.

"Don't you see that it doesn't matter which it is?" She switched off the car and tucked a lock of her hair, which had come free of her ponytail, behind her ear. "Either an evil spirit really is angry at me or another part of my brain, that I can't control, thinks it's an evil doll, and *that's* punishing me."

Can't he see that at least if it's a demon possession, I'm not a killer? "I need to know what I've done, Peter. What things have you seen me do when . . ." Gabrielle paused, trying to find the words that he would accept, even if they didn't align with the truth she wanted.

"When that side of my personality takes over? I need you to tell me. It's important."

Peter shook his head. Gabrielle clenched her hands in frustration, gathering the fabric of her skirt into a tight ball. He couldn't just refuse to tell her, not when she needed to know so badly. Unspent tears pressed against the back of her eyes.

Outside the car window, Peter's building nestled at the bottom of Queen Anne Hill. Though the facade was old, cracked, and dirty, the doors leading in were of shiny glass and metal with a fancy intercom system. This was the only quality system she'd ever noticed in the building. The elevators inside worked less than half the time, and the air conditioning stank like rat droppings. She tilted her head up to look at the fourth floor, where his apartment was. A few rickety balconies jabbed out.

"Come inside, Gabs."

"No. I'm a danger to you." *I'm pouting. Why do I need him to understand, to believe so badly?*

"You're really not. Plus, I need help up the stairs." He gave her a wry grin and motioned to his crutch.

"You don't need help." Gabrielle found a smile cracking her face and forced it away. "Okay, you want my help, then at least tell me what really happened on that roof." She crossed her arms. "You can lie to the police all you want, but don't lie to me."

"I already told you." Peter's blue eyes lowered to the glove compartment.

A quicksilver anger took over Gabrielle's tongue. "You lied."

Peter sighed. "I told you the important part."

"No, you didn't."

"Look, you weren't you. I saw it in your face. It's like your eyes changed, and you were somewhere, or someone, else. You shoved me, but it was just to get me away from you. It was like you panicked, and it's my own stupid fault for kissing you by a giant hole three stories up."

Does he think kissing me was a mistake? "A mistake?"

"Yeah."

Her lip trembled as she tried to hold her expression blank. If he thought that kissing her was a mistake, he was probably right. She was a wreck, and hurting Peter was the last thing she wanted. But her heart refused to believe that, and she was afraid if she spoke, she'd start crying.

"Come up? I think I could use help up the stairs, seriously. I'm not used to the crutch yet." Peter touched her face. "Gabs?"

"Sorry, I . . ."

He leaned over the center console and brushed his lips over hers. "Kissing you wasn't the part that was a mistake."

Gabrielle dared a deep breath and to look over at Peter. "Aren't you scared of me?" She eyed the purplish bruise on his temple and the discoloration around his jaw.

"No. Like I said, falling was an accident, and it was *my* fault. Now, my head really hurts, and I'd like to get upstairs and take something."

What about that evening in the treehouse, and then in the basement, with Mr. Pritcher? She couldn't bring herself to speak those words. Gabrielle got out of the car and stared up at the building. "You could take the elevator."

"Oh, what fun would that be?"

She shrugged, not really wanting to resist keeping him company anyhow. Gabrielle met Peter on the other side of the car. She gazed up at him, trying to prove to herself he was there, that she hadn't managed to screw this up yet.

This is why I got rid of the doll. So I could be here with him. I know it can't last—I'm dangerous, but one night, that can't be too much to ask.

Then, I'll find a way to stop me.

forty-one

Consciousness had not fully settled on Gabrielle. Awareness came in lazy waves—a heavy warmth next to her, the press of a too firm mattress, and the earthy smell of marijuana mixed with a garlicky curry aroma. Both scents jarred with the cinnamon incense that fought for precedence in the air. She scooted back into the heat at her side. Unfamiliar blankets brushed her, leaving pockets of cold as she turned.

Her eyelashes lifted, allowing her to see the world through a fringed veil. Morning light and bird song serenaded her senses. Peter's apartment made a comforting clutter around her.

Peter's studio apartment. She was in Peter's bed. Though everything was clean, the lack of furniture led to piles of books stacked against one wall and the pure quantity of clashing fabrics gave the appearance of a mess.

She turned slightly toward the warmth beside her and assured herself that it was just Peter, nuzzled under the blankets with her. Gabrielle's arms wriggled free, and she adjusted the sleeves of her sweater to cover the goosebumps that immediately rose on her arms.

The window on the far wall was open several inches, and the

invasive touch of the breeze cutting through the room reminded her why she never left windows open.

Yet her own wakefulness reminded her of more. She desperately needed to get Peter to talk to her. He'd refused the evening before when they made it up to his apartment. He'd been exhausted and went to lie down. Gabrielle had gone with him after texting Cinder about the car. Once she had her truths, she might not have another chance for little moments with Peter.

She rubbed at her arms, trying to ward off the cold. Turning her attention to Peter, she saw his eyes were open, and he watched her back. Gabrielle inspected his head for where he'd struck it in the fall. The doctors said he'd landed first on his leg, and the head injury came later with far less impact. Still, she remembered the blood on the ground clearly. His hair partially covered the bruise that traced along his temple, and the morning light softened the harsh purple at his jawline.

"I can turn on the heater," Peter said. He sat up, his T-shirt creased from sleep.

"Why not just shut the window?" She curled closer against him, not ready for him to get up nor ready to broach the subject of the murders she logically must have committed. Mr. Pritcher's murder had lain dormant in her mind for years. It could wait until she had a chance to properly wake up. Her skirt had bunched around her legs —maxi skirts were the worst to sleep in. The fabric of Peter's pants brushed a patch of her exposed skin. He pulled himself fully into a sitting position.

"What do you have against fresh air?" He hugged her carefully to his chest.

"Ha!" Gabrielle motioned to the incense and then the bong resting on the loft apartment's only table. "I'm fine with fresh air. I don't usually fill mine with smoke."

Peter shrugged.

"You shouldn't be smoking that anyhow, you know," she said. Depending on how the rest of this day went, she might not be around long to help protect him from mistakes like his casual drug usage. "Schizophrenia symptoms are exacerbated by pot."

"That hasn't been proven," Peter said lightly with a familiar half-smile.

"Yes, it has!" Gabrielle tried to keep a straight face, but his smile worked like a spell on her. "Your arguments are outdated. They have proved a causal relation."

He grinned. "Gabs, are you lecturing me on properly dealing with mental illnesses?"

She fumbled for a response, but silence seemed to be the only appropriate comeback.

"I'll get the window." Peter let her go and picked up his crutch from the floor. He then swung his casted leg awkwardly from under the blanket.

"Peter, let me do it."

"You can make us tea. I need to learn how to use these things." He shook his crutch, then stood and clumped over to the thermostat, clicked some buttons, and turned on a space heater near the foot of the bed.

Gabrielle stood and headed into the kitchenette. Tea was a good idea to warm up her body and ready her mind for the coming conversation.

Music clicked on from the speakers against the wall—something Celtic, the only type of music they ever agreed on. Gabrielle lit the stove and set a kettle over the flame. She pivoted on her heel to face Peter as a woman's voice rose from the speakers, filling the air with a song of repressed longing.

He dropped his crutches and used the wall to help him sit down on the mattress, which lay directly on the floor. Even so, the check-ered sheets and jumble of mismatched blankets looked appealing. Better yet, Peter's scent clung to the fabric, along with the fading odor of morning breeze laundry soap. She trailed across the room and sat next to him, ignoring the wooden chair beside the table and the beanbag chair.

"Peter . . ." She let her voice trail off, tasting his name.

"Gabs." Peter grabbed her hand. "What happened to you on the way to the hospital—that's just your imagination."

The music's mournful tones seemed to disagree as they dragged on in lament.

"And what about what you saw on the roof?" Gabrielle asked.

"You didn't mean to hurt me," Peter said.

An internal cold washed over Gabrielle. So she had hurt him. If it had been someone or something else, he would have phrased that differently. His fall wasn't just some accident. And if she could hurt him once, she was capable of doing it again.

Peter squeezed her fingers and let go. "Look, I want you to get whatever help you need, and maybe getting rid of that doll was the first step, but you can't expect perfection overnight. At risk of sounding like Michael, you should call Dr. White."

"I don't . . . I just . . ." She paused. Dr. White couldn't help her now. Gabrielle needed to know what really happened during her blackouts, and years of therapy hadn't accomplished that. Some truths Gabrielle had to find on her own. And some truths, she didn't know if she could face. Maybe her brain had hidden what occurred with Mr. Pritcher for a reason. Maybe unearthing it fully would break what little remained of her. The truth mattered, but not as much as protecting Peter and Michael from her and the porcelain cracks that spread out from her. "Do you think you could get me a train ticket out of here? Just away somewhere."

"For us?"

"No, just me."

"You want to make sure you're not a danger to anyone." His blue eyes burned into her.

I need to know I'm not a danger to you. Screw "anyone."

"But you don't get that from cutting people out of your life," Peter said. "You can't isolate yourself. That's how you wind up raving in a gutter. Maybe running off would protect me, Michael, but it's suicide. We believe in you, and we're capable of making our own choices of whom to love."

Love. There it was, that word.

The song from the speakers switched to something spritely—hopeful. The sound jarred with her despondent mood but fit the gleam in Peter's eyes.

"I don't want you out of my life," Gabrielle said. "But I don't want to drag you down with me either." She stared at their conjoined hands. "That's why I got rid of the doll. I wanted *us* to be a possibility. I'm just afraid having her gone isn't enough." *That Michael may have been right, and I made everything worse. And if I'm ever going to know, I need to ask Peter about Mr. Pritcher. Why can't I get the words out?*

The kettle interrupted them with a hissing squeak, and Gabrielle leaped up to dart across the room. Making tea was simple. That was something she could do. Even now. She grabbed two mugs as the squeaks turned into a squeal and then a sharp whistle. The kettle's screams melted with the Celtic woman's soaring voice until Gabrielle turned off the gas. She filled two tea balls with leaves and dropped them into the cups, then poured water over both.

Brown leaked from the holes in the metal, staining the water, ballooning out. The tea leaves contaminated every drop within a few moments.

How much of a danger am I? I can't see my own contamination spreading. If only it was all as easy as watching tea steep. But it isn't.

"I need you to tell me the truth about some things," Gabrielle said, turning with both mugs in her hands.

"What things?" Peter reached up for one of the mugs and moved an ashtray from beside his bed on the floor between them to hold the tea balls. His casted leg stuck out in front of him at an awkward angle, belying the relaxed ease of the rest of his posture. His uninjured leg bent up in front of his chest, making a perfect rest for the mug.

"You're not protecting me by lying." Gabrielle sat beside him, careful to position herself on the opposite side from the worst of his bruising and averted her eyes. His tousled hair and blue eyes would undo her in an instant, especially if she witnessed any sign of his injuries. Instead, she watched the steam pour out of her mug. "Michael does that enough. I don't need it from you. I need you to trust me with the truth."

Peter held his mug out in front of him, arms resting on his knee. Even with her peripheral vision, she saw him roll the cup along his palms. A sure sign of nervousness. A lull in the music gave the moment an eerie stillness.

"I did tell you the truth," Peter said. "Last night. Remember?"

"Not about the rooftop." Gabrielle took in a deep breath—inhaling the steam of her tea. "I need the truth about what happened that day with Mr. Pritcher."

"What do you mean?"

"I remembered something in the car, just a flash, but it means that one hundred percent, you lied about what happened. Mr. Pritcher showed up at the treehouse. I remember him in front of me and hearing you shout. What happened?" *Did I kill him? Did you know?*

He rolled the mug back and forth, holding his fingers out straight and stiff. "I'd gone inside the house for dinner. I didn't see much of whatever happened with him because I wasn't with you for most of it. I snuck back out to check on you, and I heard him. I ran into the treehouse and told him I'd shoot him." Peter paused. "Of course, I was holding a stick so that clearly wasn't going to happen."

Peter turned to give her a weak smile. Gabrielle returned it, hoping hers had more strength.

"Please, go on," she said.

"Then your eyes changed. I'd seen you have blackouts before, but not like that. It felt like something was staring out from behind your eyes. Your body was stiff, not relaxed, and the corners of your mouth turned up just slightly. But that *something* behind your eyes was the same something I saw on the roof before you pushed me."

"Pushed." Gabrielle gagged on the word. Of course that was what happened, but to hear it. She was a monster.

Peter took out the tea ball and placed it on the ashtray between them. He then lifted his mug to his mouth and sipped. The singer's voice warbled.

Gabrielle swallowed. She needed to know how much of a monster she was.

"Peter, please, I need to know everything." Gabrielle plunked her tea ball by his and then leaned against his shoulder. She stared at her own steaming tea.

"Are you sure you want to hear more?" Peter's free arm moved around her.

"Yes." The heat of the tea seeped into her palms, and Peter's arm worked the chill from her back.

"When Mr. Pritcher came to the treehouse, you were smiling, Gabs. Smiling broader and broader as the moments passed. And your eyes never left Mr. Pritcher. I escorted him off the property, or more accurately, he stormed off and I followed to make sure he left. When he was gone, I went back to the treehouse, and you had disappeared."

"So you didn't see if I killed him." Her chest deflated. *I did. I killed him in the basement. There is no other explanation for the knife in my hand. But if Peter didn't see what happened in that basement, then I still don't really know.*

"I don't know where you were, Gabs." He sipped again as if taking a break to figure out his next words. "I didn't think so. As the police said, there was no blood on you or the doll. When I came back to the treehouse, you were gone. I assumed you'd snuck out there for the doll, and the murder was a coincidence. You weren't even gone that long—to my mind, not long enough to kill a man, trash his house, and magically keep your clothes clean and wash any blood off."

"You told them I was with you the whole night and that we never saw Pritcher. You lied for me."

"Of course." Peter smiled before taking another sip of his tea.

But that shouldn't be an "of course." People shouldn't lie to the police in a murder investigation. He'd been carrying the weight of that guilt all these years. The guilt was hers to carry.

She put her cup down. It would be a while yet before it was drinkable. The warmth of Peter was enough anyhow.

"What if I killed him?" she asked.

forty-two

Gabrielle looked at her hands, feeling the weight of the question. *What if I'm a murderer?* But that wasn't the only question embedded there. Also *what does it mean that you covered up for me?*

Peter's hand, hot from the mug, fell on her leg. Her heart thudded, and she caught her breath as the heat seeped through the thin fabric of her skirt.

"Mr. Pritcher deserved what he got, Gabs. He hurt you and probably others. Let it go." He turned to meet her eyes. "I wish I'd thought of killing him myself."

"Peter, avenging my wrongs and becoming a murderer isn't the life I want for you."

"Really? You pictured my life?" He shrugged. "Schizophrenia doesn't go away; and who's going to trust a guy who hears voices? I doubt I'm bound for anything spectacular."

"Who needs spectacular?" Gabrielle smiled and stared at her tea mug. Maybe a sip now? No. Still too hot. "I never dreamed of being a movie star or curing cancer or being president. Why does everyone think being special is so amazing? You know the life I always wanted?"

"Hmm?" He took a deep drink from his mug.

"I wanted to be a housewife," she said. "Three kids—two girls and a boy. Maybe four kids, maybe two. The number wasn't important. I wanted to spend my days taking care of my children, loving them like kids in the movies are loved. Not like my parents treated me, or your parents treated you. Really, *really* loving them."

The Celtic singer's voice seemed to echo Gabrielle's own hopes but not the hopelessness in her heart.

Peter twitched and then glanced into the shadowy corners of the room, his face tightening. He rubbed at his ear. "I'd be scared to have kids. I don't know how to be a dad."

"That can be learned." Gabrielle followed his gaze to the corner. She wondered if she should assure him there was nothing there.

"Do you hear someone in the bathroom?" he asked, his voice barely above a whisper.

"No."

There was a wistful expression on his face. "I don't think me having kids is a good idea."

"The point is, I don't want something fancy. I want the life that people think of as 'normal'—a life that I've never actually seen. A husband who loves me and loves our children, a home. Maybe a part-time job to make ends meet. My own toned-down version of the white picket fence."

"I think that's a life you could have, Gabs."

"I doubt it." She dared a sip of her tea. It scalded her tongue, and she lowered the mug to the floor again. She was a killer. Even if Mr. Pritcher deserved it, Joe hadn't. Her parents, well, that was debatable. And she'd killed Mr. Pritcher; it was time to accept she'd probably killed them all. "I'm scared I won't have any life."

"Maybe start small. And that goes for both of us. Start with making ourselves healthy."

"Peter . . ." She wished her heart would slow, but instead her mind insisted on remembering the feel of his lips on hers as they'd stood on the windy roof. She'd been whole with his arms around her.

"I'm scared too." Peter set his cup down and leaned over to her, pressing his forehead against hers and cupping her face in his hands. "What scares me is losing you. This, right here, is the life I wanted, Gabs. Simple."

I'm sitting on his bed. The pressure of his palms wove through her body.

Gabrielle lifted her lips to his. The bitterness of bergamot caressed the inside of her mouth, driven by his breath. Then a gentle touch of her tongue brought the taste into her. Gabrielle's arms snaked around his neck, and she turned to fully press against him.

Peter sighed, the sound penetrating her. Her whole body responded to the stir, and a tight warmth spread through her. If only he would hold her tighter, closer, maybe she could forget the rest.

One of his hands moved from her face to her shoulder, and the path of his touch brought flame. Every inch of her burned. His breath mingled with hers.

When their lips parted, Gabrielle couldn't form a thought. Her chest rose and fell quickly, and air rushed from her parted lips. All she wanted was to wrap herself in his arms and be lost, if only for an instant. Surely she could allow herself that—a taste of the life she wanted—before whatever would come.

"I love you," Peter said. He looked away.

No, stay with me. This might be her last chance, and she wanted the memory of more than a kiss. "I love you too. Please, hold me. I don't know what comes next for me, but I want this now. I want you."

Peter's breath hitched, but he turned and wrapped his arms around her, pulling her against him. He winced and adjusted but didn't let her go. His heart pounded in time with hers. She lifted her face, and he kissed her with ferocity, not gentle as before but desperate. His hand moved over her stomach and the feel of cloth separating them became her focus.

She wanted his hands on her skin. She needed it.

Gabrielle pulled away and lifted her sweater and shirt off.

"Shit," Peter said, his eyes glued to her body.

Gabrielle reached back to him and lifted his hand, placing it over her bra so that his fingers trailed on her breast. She leaned in and kissed him again, her hand moving on his good leg.

Peter ripped himself away, turning his face from her to the wall. "Gabs, I'm not going to do this. Not now."

"What?" Her voice quavered. She wanted nothing more than to be with him. She'd been so afraid of physical touch, but with him, it just felt right. His refusal didn't make sense. Didn't he want her? This was what men wanted—life had taught her that. "I thought you wanted me."

"I do. More than anything."

"Then, please. I'm *choosing* to share this with you." She set her hand back on his leg.

He leaned away from her as if her touch scalded him. "No! I mean, I hope someday, but not today."

"I don't understand." *Today is the only day. I can't go on like I have, not knowing that I have blood on my hands.*

"You deserve better than this," he said. "You're scared and looking for comfort. I'm not going to take advantage of you."

But he wasn't. This was the first time she'd truly wanted this. He was the first man she'd known down to her bones would never hurt her. Gabrielle reached out and turned his face to her. "I say it's okay."

"And I say it isn't. Your whole life, bastards have been telling you that this"—he motioned to her exposed body but didn't lower his eyes to look—"is what you are to men, that this is what we expect from you. And I refuse to corroborate the idea that your body is your value. Not to me. I want to sleep with you. God, I do. But what I want more than to have sex with you today or tomorrow or even next month, hell, ever, what I want more is just you. I can't do this today because you have to know that sex has nothing to do with why I love you. Not until you know you don't *have* to. Not ever. Not with me."

I don't understand. It's not like he hasn't done this before. Why? What's wrong with me? But the line of thoughts would get her nowhere. There was no point in trying to argue with him. He didn't have the right to make her choice for her, but part of her understood why. Gabrielle picked up her sweater.

"Then we don't do that," she said. "Hold me? Please? I don't know where the world goes from here. Knowing I could have killed Mr. Pritcher changes everything, but I don't want to think about it. I want you."

Peter pulled her back into his arms and kissed the top of her head.

Will he ever hold me again? Something is wrong with me. I can't hide from that. If I want a future, any future, I have to get better. That meant facing her crimes.

forty-three

THE DAY EASED BY, HIDING BEHIND THE WALLS OF PETER'S STUDIO apartment. The world outside his window moved as if nothing had altered, as if it were an ordinary Tuesday evening. Time slipped through her fingers and with every hour, the protection Peter's place offered seemed less and less. She couldn't keep hiding. The drugs he was on made him sleepy, and after they shared some vegan gumbo for dinner, he lay down and closed his eyes. Gabrielle had snuggled in the bed beside Peter but couldn't manage to sleep.

So, she'd risen and stood by the window, staring out over Seattle.

Gabrielle kept picturing Mr. Pritcher's enraged face as it had been in her vision on the exit ramp. She'd said all along she wanted answers. And she needed those answers to protect Peter and Michael as they'd always protected her. Knowing she'd killed at least one person, if not more, she had to go to the police with the information. No matter what it would mean for her.

Time to end this.

"It will never be over."

Peter's breathing was even, and she was reasonably certain he was asleep. She stood by the side of the bed, gazing down at him. He showed no signs of waking.

Do I look peaceful like that when I sleep? Do I look innocent?

Gabrielle found a notepad and scrawled a note with the first writing implement she found—a green sharpie. Each time her hand paused in its work, the green bled into the paper and darkened, but finally, she completed the note.

Peter,

Thank you for everything. I know you won't understand, but this is for the best. I'm going to Michael's to tell him about Mr. Pritcher. He deserves to hear it from me, but then I'll go to the police, to Detective Montez. I will confess. If I'm innocent, they'll find out. And if I'm guilty, I need to pay for my sins before I can try to move past them.

Gabrielle

She taped the note to the edge of the table and grabbed her purse.

"I'm sorry," she whispered, but she couldn't let that feeling stop her. She'd love to stay in the cocoon Peter provided, but that wasn't the real world, and the world would break in eventually. If she wanted to deserve him, to deserve a life, and be able to live with herself, she had to push this comfort aside and step out into the fire.

In the back of her mind, she heard the doll's laughter.

She had to know.

Even if it kills me.

Gabrielle hurried out of the apartment and down the carpeted stairs to the lobby. She shoved open the door and dashed into the parking lot. Gabrielle wove through the cars to reach hers.

Fearing another victim would come to haunt her in a vision, she barely dared to breathe until she reached I-5. With the car on track toward Michael's house, Gabrielle felt committed to her course.

In the fire-colored sunset, the other cars appeared extra predatory, worse even than on her drive to the hospital the evening before. These weren't cars; they were stalking demons. Gabrielle couldn't help but feel like she was fleeing from them. The swelling headlights that crept up behind her and then passed, leaving glaring taillights, all exuded a depraved hunger. Just disembodied glowing eyes filled with an unquenchable evil.

By the time she crossed the I-90 bridge and left the city, tears further clouded her vision.

As soon as she could, she got off the highway. Luckily, with it closing in on eight in the evening, most backstreets on the Eastside were vacant—only the occasional car demon to stalk her along the asphalt. As she approached Michael's, the porch stared at her with gleaming lit windows.

She slowed out front. Only Michael's car was parked in the driveway, but she couldn't bring herself to pull in. A ghost of blood and death hung over her childhood home. So much so that she rarely managed to park in front of it. Her foot always found the gas pedal.

Half a block farther, she pushed through the resistance from her bones. She switched off her lights and hunched over in her car. Echoes from the past haunted her. Her father's gurgles as blood seeped through his fingers, which were laced around his throat. Her mother's screams for help ricocheted around in her brain.

After all these years, after living here with Michael, why does the sight of that house still do this to me?

With a cry of frustration, she opened the door and flung herself out into the failing sunlight. She could just see the glow from Michael's house spilling out onto the sidewalk.

Am I ready to tell him about Mr. Pritcher? He'll try to talk me out of going to the police. Can I stand up to him?

Yes. I have to learn to speak my crimes. I killed Mr. Pritcher. I have to be strong.

Her leaden feet refused to move, and the sidewalk stretched out before her, unconquerable. She turned back to the car and jerked open the door.

"You're too weak."

I can't turn around.

She shut the car door again and shuffled a single step on the sidewalk.

But I can't go this way either.

Slowly, she walked away from her childhood home. She looped around behind one of the houses, taking a game trail that, in her youth, had been a dirt path along a hedge, until she reached her old neighbor's back fence.

A greenbelt behind the houses stretched out in front of her. Where she stood, a wide ledge and a subtle drop led to a dry creek bed below, but back, by her old house, the strip of land shrank to a slender snake and the ground plunged like a cliff. Still, walking this path in the dark did not turn her stomach as the sidewalk did.

She viscerally hated this house; she'd have to sneak up on it.

Gabrielle crept forward, stepping over overgrown greenery and brambles. Clearly no one used this path anymore. She knew the treacherous trek well, having used it since she could remember to sneak *away* from the house—usually to hide out at the neighborhood park until her father calmed down, or later in life, hiding until the memories of him subsided. The path was hidden within the undergrowth but still passable, a good sign that Michael still walked back here on occasion, and proof that at least a third of the time she approached the house she couldn't manage the front walk.

Thorns pricked at her, but she forced her way forward. Something was here, a memory on this path. Something she needed.

Peter lied about me being with him on the night Mr. Pritcher died. Somewhere in my head, I know what happened.

As she came up to the back of Michael's house—her parents' house—she peered over the fence. Her old bedroom window up on the second floor was dark, and beside it, her parents' old room. All the curtains on the ground floor were drawn, but light spilled through the curtains of Michael's room. On one side of the lit window was the sliding glass door that led into the darkened living room.

The light had been on when she drove past.

Gabrielle reached a rock that sat up against the fence and used it as a step to pull herself up onto the wooden barrier. With one leg flung over, she paused. From the fence-top, on the hill, she could see into her old room.

The familiar black didn't swarm her mind, carrying her off into a memory she couldn't control, but the memory still came. It ripped through the scarred walls of her psyche. Jagged edges opened up, leaving the space between clear, but—no connections. Just a flash.

She had been in her room and Father had been yelling. Gabi's fists had curled around her blankets, wanting to draw them up to cover her body but not daring to anger her father any further. Yet she shivered in the cold and turned her face away from Father's angry mouth—his red, drunken eyes. She had looked out the window.

And Michael had been climbing over the fence. Rather than seeming like her savior, she'd feared his return would be another trigger for Father's anger. She wished Michael away—wished him safe. But young Michael saw her too, and his face froze in a twist of anger.

With the wall in her mind torn down, these events rushed back at her.

That was the night her father and mother had died.

And Michael had been there. He'd handed her the doll. They'd both been covered in blood in the hallway. Their mother had been weeping in the other room, her tears loud and desperate. The sound burned her ears.

The doll didn't think she had the right to weep.

Gabrielle gasped, not sure how to apply this memory but sure it mattered somehow. How could it be true that Michael was there? Whatever had happened that night, she couldn't let Michael suffer for it.

She swung into the yard. Under Michael's care, the garden was impeccable, and she felt a stab of guilt as her foot crushed one of his flowers, snapping the tender stalk and grinding the petals into the dirt. *That's how I live my life. I destroy things without even meaning to.*

She opened the sliding door and switched on the lights. Gabrielle paced through the living room toward the kitchen, stopping at the window next to the front door. She peered out at the driveway. Michael's car was gone.

She couldn't move on to the police until she'd spoken with him. He'd done so much to protect her over the years; the least she could do was tell him before she threw herself onto the sword.

Gabrielle crashed onto the couch in front of the coffee table, facing out into the woods beyond the sliding glass door. A half-empty glass of wine rested next to Michael's laptop. Michael was too neat to have just left it out, so he was intending to come back. She'd have to wait.

She scooted to the edge of the couch cushion and jabbed the space bar on the open laptop to bring it out of sleep mode. If she was going to wait in *this* house, she'd better keep herself amused. Apparently Michael hadn't been away long enough for the password to be required. She had a moment of joy before she saw what was on the screen. Gabrielle stopped cold.

An email chain glared out from an open browser tab—an email about the doll. Her hand shook as she scrolled over the text. The chain was between him and Cinder. She hadn't burned the doll at all, just left it there in its box and messaged Michael. She'd wanted to swing by and drop it off at his place. In his response, he refused that offer and gave her an address to drop the doll with instructions to just leave it on the porch.

An all too calm voice asked what car Cinder was using. But she had enough friends—she'd find someone willing to lend her a car or drive her. Yet Gabrielle clung to the idea. Maybe the doll was still in the woods.

Why was Michael doing this? Was it just about protecting her?

Or something deeper. He'd barely been willing to acknowledge the doll their whole life, but that night he'd handed it, covered in her father's blood, to her.

Oh, god. I've got to get out.

Gabrielle ran to the front door, her fingers fumbling with the lock. *How could this be?*

She spun back to the house, looking past the kitchen and living room down the hall toward the den and the upper floor.

The darkness of the staircase laughed at her and just beyond that, the door leading down into the basement.

The doll's not in there. She couldn't be.

Gabrielle could almost feel her mother's presence in the kitchen observing her, whispering, "*My little angel, what have you done?*"

Then she froze. It was too much to hope that the doll was still waiting by that boggy firepit. She crossed back over to the computer and highlighted the address. She entered it into her phone.

I have to see where that cursed thing went.

But what she wanted to do was see Michael.

Gabrielle paced the living room. She couldn't trust Michael, not now. He thought he knew what was best for her, but she couldn't be the child he protected forever. She had to face her past. If he wouldn't let her do that, she'd do it without him.

The doll was supposed to be gone. If it wasn't, and clearly it wasn't, that explained her near accident. *It's not me; it's her.*

Gabrielle shut the computer and gave one last glance at the wine. He'd be right back.

But she couldn't wait for this mess to solve itself anymore. She couldn't sit back and let Michael take care of her, cover it up—like he'd hidden the dark secrets of this house. Mother's kitchen of religious knickknacks all redone in stainless steel and her parents' room upstairs gutted and filled with workout equipment. But her brother couldn't erase what had happened here, and no amount of his efforts could erase whatever evil followed her.

The meek don't inherit the Earth.

If she wanted any of them to be safe from the doll, she had to take action.

Gabrielle reached up over her shoulder and brushed her fingers over the tip of the wings tattooed there. Time for her to be the guardian angel. Some things never washed away; you could try to hide them, but they were there. She'd washed blood off her body plenty of times, but it stained the soul.

That was the stain she needed to wash away.

This time, she took the front door and crept along the sidewalk back to her car. Each step was an effort of will. The last thing she wanted was to see the doll again. But she had to get the demonic thing back.

She slid into the car and as her phone's GPS calculated her route, Gabrielle pressed her palms into her face. Whatever she found out about these new visions and Michael's part in them had to be better than going on like she had been.

Knowing had to be better than not knowing. And the key was the doll.

forty-four

Cole texted Michael.

-I'll be over in ten-

The trendy Kirkland waterfront restaurant around him made a blur of noise punctuated by the chink of glasses and an occasional bout of laughter. The sad remnants of his hummus plate sat by his elbow, one lonely piece of celery sticking off the edge. It wasn't much of a dinner, but with Joan having her Tuesday night "camp out" with Isa, he'd needed to be out of the house.

At least he had Michael's promise to meet with him tonight, and with it being almost eight, it was time to call in that promise.

Cole hunched over the bar counter, waiting for the waitress to return with his card, turning his glass in his hand so the ice spun at the bottom. Under the dim illumination of the bar, the motion flowed magically, and the ice reflected glints of the white bulb lights hung around the room.

His phone beeped with Michael's reply.

-I'll run out and grab some more wine. Make it 20?-

Cole typed in a message declining the offer. Having more to drink was a bad plan. At some point, he had to go home. Joan was *supposed*

to stick around until late. No matter how tempting a few extra drinks sounded, he had to stay sober in case Isa needed him.

A waitress strode out from behind the bar, balancing a tray full of tapas and cocktails on one hand. The scent of truffle oil wafted from the platter.

Cole's finger hovered over the send icon, but he didn't press. He'd only had one drink at the bar. The location had been more of a hiding place after work since he'd only get nasty and make things worse if he was face to face with Joan.

One drink with Michael wouldn't be too much, and the idea of sitting on Michael's couch with a glass to sip was appealing. Maybe they could go back to how things had been between them before the Bey murder.

Except Michael still hadn't made his confession, and he said it related to the case. *I need to know. Otherwise, we can't move forward. But damn. Everything else is going so well. Maybe his secret won't be as bad as he's made it seem.*

Cole deleted his first message and wrote a new one.

-Should I pick anything up?-

The answer came almost immediately.

-No. I have some nice cheese and fruit.-

The bartender slid Cole's card back to him with a receipt and a pen. He signed and turned to the buzzing room. The strangers all seemed so happy, but they weren't. Happiness was one of those elusive things that people seek their whole lives.

It's time to get back to a place of mind where I can be happy.

He texted Yolanda.

-How's the visit going?-

He slid his coat on and ambled out onto the street. He'd parked a few blocks away at the Marina. It would be a good place to spend his extra ten minutes—stroll along the docks and stare across the water at Seattle's lights. The street was packed with cars but light on foot traffic.

He passed a well-dressed couple—the woman with gleaming

blonde hair and a pressed jacket. They hurried around him. Life had been like that with Joan, a rush of wealth and order, at least on the outside.

I don't miss it.

The lake's waves shimmered in a mix of shadow and light from the setting sun, but the ripples lapping at the edge of the pebble beach were dim and cloudy. Cole walked to a bench sat. From there he had a good view of the rocky beach, the docks with their boats, and the expensive condos along the lake edge, and across the water, a few high-rise buildings jutting up from an evergreen-covered hill.

He checked his phone.

-Goin well, Mr. Montez. Don't worry. We're going to roast marshmallows in the fireplace.-

He shoved the phone into his pocket and glared at the frothy edge of the lake, where a small collection of broken bottles lined the rocks.

If Joan really wants to be in Isa's life, I have to let it happen.

But just the idea of "making up" for deserting Isa over the summer, after breaking a slew of promises, made his rationale fade into emotional flares. Joan shouldn't get off that easily. But as Yolanda advised, it wasn't his job to punish Joan.

He couldn't let himself forget that in less than two weeks, they'd be discussing this with a mediator.

For a few more minutes, Cole stared out over the water. A group of noisy twenty-somethings poured down the stairway into the parking lot by the Marina.

Cole retreated to his car. The drive to Michael's house was quick. When he pulled up, Michael didn't seem to be back from the store yet.

A car passed him from deeper within the cul-de-sac.

Whoever that is, they're weaving like they're drunk. I should call in the plates. But he didn't. He was done being a cop for the night.

Cole parked on the street. Then sat, tapping his fingers against his knees. He climbed out only when he saw Michael's car pull into the driveway. They met on the doorstep. Michael lifted a shopping bag between them with his perfect smile on his face.

"Shall we drink to things working out?" Michael asked.

"We don't know they have yet," Cole said. *I sound like a grumpy old man. However this night goes, I can't let being grumpy about my ex ruin it.*

"Your meeting with Joan is the week after next, right? We'll know then." Michael smiled, but his eyes didn't sparkle. His mind was elsewhere.

"If Gabrielle needs you—I'll understand if you can't drive me to the mediator's office."

"I'll wait around after I drop you off," Michael said, completely ignoring the offer to let him off the hook. "Then, either way, you'll have someone to talk to."

"Let's head inside," Cole said. Talking about Isa and Joan could wait. He didn't want to give Michael any excuse to turn this meetup into anything other than an opportunity to tell his secret.

Cole watched Michael retreat inside and head into the kitchen. Cole tugged at the cross around his neck. Only truth could help him heal Michael. *Question is, can I handle the truth?*

It didn't matter. Too many secrets were wedged between them. They couldn't go forward like this. Cole crossed over to the living room and sat on the leather couch. Evergreen branches twitched in the wind outside the sliding glass door, creating an odd sense of life in the dark backyard.

"Michael?" Cole asked.

Michael returned with a corkscrew and sat beside Cole on the couch, a single fresh glass held in his other hand. One half-empty glass already rested on the table.

"Before we celebrate anything," Cole said, "I need to know this secret that has you so freaked out."

"I see no reason we can't have wine for a discussion." Michael's voice remained light, but his shoulders tensed. Cole tried to force down his annoyance at Michael putting his confession off, yet again.

Sometimes people needed a moment to get up their courage, and the least Cole could do was give Michael that.

Michael opened the Merlot and poured a glass for Cole. Then he retreated behind the breakfast bar. Cole threw his arm over the back of the couch and watched Michael. The picture of Michael in the kitchen woke something warm inside him. He didn't really want to know. *Let it wait just a moment, just a moment to enjoy this.*

Cole sipped his wine, swirling the red liquid around in his glass.

Micheal's phone rang.

"It's Cinder," Michael said. "I've got to get it. She's my only lifeline to Elle right now."

He looks relieved. How bad is his news, that a phone call interrupting is a good thing? But it couldn't be that bad—Cole wouldn't believe it. "Don't answer it."

Michael stared at the phone until it stopped ringing, but he didn't answer. Then he pulled out two blocks of wrapped cheeses. His hands were shaking.

Cole took another sip of the oaky wine. Sitting here with Michael was so comfortable, so easy, and he was so beautiful. Maybe it really could stay like this. Cole just had to have a little faith in Michael.

"Okay," Michael said, taking a deep drink from his wineglass then leaning his hands against the breakfast bar.

This is it. Everything in Cole narrowed to a single point of focus, like a child who hears noises from the closet. As the handle turns and the closet opens, the child knows that whether a mouse or a monster is found, nothing can be as awful as what they've pictured. *This is finally it. The moment I get to know him.*

"I don't know what Gabrielle has been doing or what her insane boyfriend is up to," Michael said, "but I can tell you that she didn't kill her father. Because I did."

forty-five

THE CONFESSION LAY LIKE A MINEFIELD, SPREAD OVER THE DISTANCE between the couch where Cole sat and the breakfast bar that stood defensively between them.

Michael had killed Gabrielle's father. Both of her parents? He hadn't stated that but confessing to one seemed tantamount to confessing to the other. The words were something directly out of a nightmare, but the plaintive expression on Michael's face made Cole want to listen. *If he's killed, I need to know why.*

But he couldn't even nod to encourage Michael to continue.

"What I told the cops was true," Michael said, his eyes focused on the wine in the glass in front of him. "I went over to my friend's house. Around ten o'clock, his mother fell asleep. I started to regret running out of my house and leaving Elle. I didn't want to be around my stepdad, sure, but I kept picturing Elle locked in that basement. What if he hadn't let her out? She'd be sitting there, crying, shivering against the basement door."

But according to the interviews in the case files, Michael's friend's mom insisted Michael had been at her home the whole time. Is this some sort of sick joke? Please. Cole downed his wine, but the bitter warmth did nothing to calm the spinning of his thoughts or stop Michael from talking.

"I snuck out of my friend's house. He was absorbed in some game, I think," Michael continued. "His mom didn't even stir as I left."

Cole's heart hammered. He grabbed his knees. *I don't want to know this. If I know, I'll have to turn him in.*

"When I snuck around back of the house and hopped the fence, something was off. The light in Elle's room was on. And I saw her father. I couldn't see much, but I could tell he was still yelling. I ran inside."

Michael's expression darkened and the anger boiling inside him rose to the surface. Before he went on, he crossed the room and sat down on the couch, keeping a few inches between them. Michael's next words came out filled with venom and hate.

"I went upstairs and passed my mom's bedroom, and I heard her praying inside. I didn't stop because Elle's door wasn't closed—not all the way, and that asshole's voice took all my attention."

Michael formed a fist, and Cole reached out and laid his hand over it. Their eyes met, and both flinched away, but Cole maintained the physical contact. *Whatever happened is done. He can't undo it.*

But I'll have to tell Sera. "Michael, before you continue, I can't promise that this stays between us."

"I know." Michael nodded and cleared his throat. "But I'm sick of running from it. I'm sick of letting that one night control my entire life. I need to tell someone. I knew that the minute you showed me Mr. Pritcher's file."

Cole lifted his hand, which shook, and poured himself another glass of wine. He didn't drink it.

"I looked inside Elle's room." Michael's voice changed, soft now, every word little more than a breeze. Each syllable dropped separately as if his mouth had to force it out. "My stepdad, I had accused him of abuse, but he never hit me. He yelled and told me how worthless I was. Sometimes he'd push me or throw something. He'd break my stuff, and if I cried, he'd laugh. But compared to the stories I hear every day, it was nothing. That isn't what I saw in Elle's room."

"I'm sorry," Cole said. *How meaningless sorry is. Michael killed his parents.* Numbness spread over Cole. The words repeated in his head, but never connected to his heart. Still, he needed to know. "But the investigators didn't find any evidence that any harm had been done to Gabrielle that night."

Michael gave a low laugh. "They wouldn't have. He was great at not leaving marks. At doing everything but. She was naked on the bed in front of him. And he fucking touched her while he . . . I can't. I *can't* say it, Cole."

"You have to." The weight of the confession leaked in through the brief silence. *Michael killed his parents. Michael killed his parents.*

"The worst part is," Michael said, "I don't even know if that was the first time. In that moment, it didn't matter. All I wanted was to unsee it. Like when you wake up from a nightmare and you're so happy to be back in the real world. Then the nightmare continues, and you know you're still asleep. There's this endless stretch where you try to wake up again and don't know if you're dreaming or if your nightmares have followed you into life."

"What was he doing to her?" Cole repeated. The answer seemed to be the only thing that could lessen Michael's guilt, and Cole wanted to believe in Michael despite everything he was saying.

"I didn't help her," Michael went on, as if Cole hadn't spoken. "I turned around, and I ran downstairs. If I didn't see them, if I didn't know, then it hadn't happened. Then these golden eyes hit me from the top of the basement stairs. Elle must have brought the doll up, set her there. But it looked like she was watching. Judging me."

Cole bit back a response. It seemed both siblings had demonized that doll, not just Gabrielle.

"I don't know how to explain other than the whole situation felt like a nightmare I couldn't escape. I was hallucinating. I was trapped in this horrible fantasy, and I would have done anything to make it end. On the counter I saw a paring knife. I grabbed it."

Cole saw the pictures of the murder scene in his mind. All the blood . . . he didn't want to know any more. Even answers about Gabrielle wouldn't help change the cold reality of what had happened. "You don't have to tell me any more."

Michael didn't respond to Cole. Not a flinch or a glance, and he continued in a dead voice. "I went back to Elle's room, and her eyes. She stared at me where I stood in the doorway, with those wide, pained eyes. Tears rolled down her cheeks, but she didn't fight him. She lay there like a corpse, so stiff. I knew right then I wasn't going to threaten him. I stabbed him in the back of the neck, then I reached around and slit his throat. I could have stopped then."

Cole had never heard a murder confessed so coldly, with so little emotion. It was like Michael had sunk into himself.

"I didn't. Elle barely moved, but she let out this choked sob. I went and got the doll. I gave it to Elle to hold—she had this weird bond with the creepy thing. I should have just stayed with Elle, maybe gone to call the cops. But I was so angry. I wanted to know if Mom knew, if she'd say it was just God's plan, the way she'd excused everything that bastard did to me."

Cole shivered despite himself at the image those words conjured.

"She didn't. She said, 'What have you done?' Elle had followed me into the master bedroom, holding that damn doll. I don't even remember killing Mom, but must I have. That or Elle did, but that's worse. I don't recall anything that happened after I saw Elle standing there until I was out on the street running."

The report seemed sure his mother had been asleep when she was struck or, at the very least, lying down. If Michael left with her awake, maybe he didn't kill her. Either way, he'd killed his stepfather and watched the woman who was meant to protect them both try to pray the damage away. And there was the core of Michael's hatred of God and religion.

"I ran away and left Elle," Michael said, his expression still blank and distant. "I don't know how no one saw me going back to my friend's. I must have been covered in blood. My friend hadn't even noticed I was gone. What I didn't expect was that Elle would blame the doll. Or that Ralphie's mom would be so unaware of time. Apparently, she thought she didn't fall asleep until midnight. She attested to my whereabouts."

Cole shuffled through that. The old autopsy reports said that their mother died nearly an hour later than their father. And she'd been asleep. They only had the friend's mom's word that Michael had been at her house the whole night, and it seemed like an insane coincidence that two different killers struck the same house. But Cole really wanted to believe it.

"You know what the worst part is? Was it him or me who broke Gabrielle? I don't know, do I? All I ever wanted to do was save her, but I destroyed her in the process. If she did kill Joe or Mr. Pritcher, I might as well have been the one holding the knife. If it weren't for me . . ."

Michael stopped and looked over to Cole.

Part of Cole wanted to reassure him that he hadn't broken Gabrielle, to say Gabrielle wasn't a killer, that there must be another explanation. But he didn't believe it. Like the avenging angels they had immortalized on their shoulders, the siblings dealt in bloody justice. It was not something Cole could reason away.

Michael had murdered his stepfather and possibly his mother too. The crime scene photos ran through Cole's mind in a montage of blood and hatred. Michael had stabbed his stepfather fifteen times. *And I slept next to him.*

"I can't build a future with anyone, Cole. I'm a monster." Michael dropped his face into his hands and leaned into his knees. "I destroyed my sister, trying to save her."

"Michael." Cole's arm moved, wanting to take Michael's hand, but his mind denied him, spinning on Michael's words.

"If I'd known about Mr. Pritcher's murder," Michael said into his palms, "I would have come forward, Cole. You have to believe that. I didn't know anyone else had died. It was just me and Gabrielle. Me trying to fix what I broke. I don't deserve to have a life, and I never did. And now more people are dead."

The words echoed in Cole's mind. Capturing them and putting them in a sensible order exceeded Cole's mental ability. For a moment, he felt as empty as Michael's eyes looked. Michael paused and rocked back and forth on the couch. Cole shivered and watched as Michael's phone vibrated. The caller ID said it was Cinder again.

For a moment, Cole said nothing, did nothing. Everything Michael was saying was horrible—like something pulled from the more disturbing files in the homicide department. But Cole couldn't focus on that. He just heard the love in Michael's voice. *What would I have done if I found someone hurting Isa that way?*

"Gabrielle killed them," Michael said, ignoring the phone. "She killed Mr. Pritcher, and she killed that guy, Joe. And that's on me."

"No, it's not." Cole reached out and wrapped his arm around Michael, pulling him close. Whatever came next, he could be there for Michael in this one moment. "You aren't a monster. I don't know what happens now, but we can figure that out later."

Michael's phone rang, and he looked down at it.

"It's Cinder, again," Michael said.

"Answer your phone." Cole didn't really know why he said it except that he needed a minute without Michael looking at him to process. It was probably the same reason Michael wanted to answer it. Anything to get away from the conversation they were having.

"Cinder?" Michael said.

"Hey Michael, is Gabrielle there?" Cinder's voice sounded worried, and a beep came through the speaker, like a car being unlocked. She was talking too loudly, loud enough for Cole to make out her voice.

She's getting into a car? How is that relevant right now? Michael killed his father. Fuck me.

"Why would she be here?" Michael sounded vacant.

"Peter called me," Cinder said. Then a bunch of mumbling that Cole couldn't make out.

He took a sip of his wine. It didn't have any taste anymore.

"Okay, so why are you calling?" Michael's movements were jerky, unsure, as he fidgeted beside Cole.

Cole set his glass on the coffee table next to Michael's closed laptop.

He focused on the movement in the trees outside the sliding glass door. It was open a crack. He wanted to stop noticing these things, but it was like all his brain could handle was the little details.

"Cinder?" Michael's voice rose. But he leaned closer to Cole, letting him hear Cinder's next words.

"Peter was worried," Cinder said. "Really worried. He's an idiot, and he told her some shit he shouldn't have."

Michael stood and walked across the room. "What did he tell her?"

Then, "You didn't ask?" Michael half-yelled. "She *isn't* here."

He killed his parents, and I'm just sitting here. I'm not even processing it, just sitting. Why was Cinder calling Michael to report on Gabrielle anyway? That paired with the fact they'd been at a bar together the night that Joseph Bey died had to mean something.

"Call me if you find anything out. Yeah. She doesn't know about the doll. How could she? I already said . . . Fine. Bye." Michael hung up, and the phone drooped between his fingers.

"Michael," Cole asked as gently as he could. "Why is Cinder calling you with this?"

Michael froze for a moment. "That's not the point right now."

"Tell me."

"I pay Cinder's rent in exchange for her keeping tabs on Gabrielle. We've had the deal since before they ever moved in together."

Michael was right; it didn't seem to be the point right now. More important was what the call had been about. "Is Gabrielle coming here?"

"I don't think so. She should've been here a while ago if she was. I'm sorry, but I need to find her."

The last thing Michael should be doing was chasing after his broken sister. How much could one person give up to protect the self-destructive people around them? Drawing in a deep breath, Cole shifted his eyes from the glass to Michael's face.

"Can you help me?" Michael said. "I get you may never want to see me again or turn me in or any number of things, but I don't know where she could be. She could be a danger to herself or—"

"Michael, we need to call the police first. Especially if what we're doing is chasing after Gabrielle."

Michael didn't meet Cole's gaze. "I need to find her. Then you can do what you want. I won't run. Not from you, not from this."

"Stop that!" Cole slammed his fist into the coffee table. "I've put everything on the line for you and your sister. I can't see how I could justify keeping a murder confession a secret. And despite it all, I will help you find her."

Michael turned away from the tentative light streaming from the standing lamp, but the glow still slid over his face. His profile tensed. "I can't protect her anymore. I've crossed every fucking line there is trying. It's time to stop."

"This isn't about protecting her." Cole swallowed. "This is about protecting you. She's out there. If these murders are hers, we've got to stop her. Based on the past victims in the murders, chances are she isn't a danger to anyone, but we still need to get her off the street."

"She was supposed to come here." Michael motioned to his living room, his hand sweeping over the top of the closed laptop.

Cole inspected the room. "The sliding door, it's not fully closed, and don't you usually leave your laptop open?"

Michael stared at the closed laptop and then flipped the screen up. He clicked the spacebar to bring it to life. His screen lock code didn't come up. Something must be running in the background to keep it from sleeping. "Oh, shit."

Cole leaned over and read the first few lines of the email that had been left open on Michael's computer. His address was highlighted in the body of the email.

"Shit, shit, shit," Michael chanted. "She may have gone to your place for that damn doll."

Isa was at home. Gabrielle wouldn't hurt a child, would she? It wasn't something he wanted to test, especially not with Joan there. His ex-wife wasn't exactly sympathetic or gentle. She'd only make things worse.

"Cinder dropped it off earlier," Michael said.

"It's just a doll."

"Not to her," Michael said.

There was something in the sound of his words that made it clear that the porcelain doll wasn't just a doll to him either, even if he hid it better than his sister. No matter what the doll was or wasn't, the idea of Isa stuck in between the siblings and the heirloom chilled his blood. "Then let's go. You drive, I need to call Yolanda."

Michael stared at the email, the same blank expression he'd worn for most of the conversation on his face.

Damnit! There wasn't time to deal with his trauma. "Let's go! Now."

forty-six

GABRIELLE GRIPPED THE STEERING WHEEL AND FOCUSED ON THE POOLS OF her headlights. Her foot was jammed into the brake as if the car would simply rocket through the red stoplight if she didn't battle with it.

Anyone could live at that address. What if they have kids and its already got its hooks in them?

Gabrielle shook her head to dislodge the thoughts. *No. No. I have to stop the doll.*

Time to burn the thing herself. And if that didn't work?

I'll turn myself in.

Yet it mattered who the doll had gone to. Perhaps the poisoned cracks had already infected its new home.

The light turned green, and Gabrielle's foot sluggishly shifted over to the gas.

I guess I could knock and see who answers. Ask them for the doll.

Gabrielle's phone buzzed beside her on the seat. She ignored it.

Pulling off the road into another cul-de-sac, Gabrielle rolled toward the address on her GPS. The sun had sunk low enough that she needed her headlights to see the numbers on the mailboxes and the corresponding ones above the door.

She parked at the curb a few houses away from the address she wanted. Her phone flashed with numerous notifications beside her. Probably Peter. Perhaps Michael, too, if Peter had called him. When she glanced down, it was a message from Cinder that showed.

-We're driving there now-

The message didn't make any sense to Gabrielle, and a horde of other messages lurked below. She ignored them.

Peter represented the life she wanted—a life she could never have based on the evidence of what he'd told her. Hearing from him might tempt her to try again.

And Michael represented all she had lost and destroyed on her path here. How many times had he thrown himself under the bus for her? Not this time. Not now. She remembered now. He'd been there. He'd tried to save her. Even when they were children, he'd been her angel.

"No." She pulled up harder than necessary on the parking brake. "I'll never be free, not as long as that godforsaken monstrosity exists in this world."

Gabrielle clicked off her headlights and climbed out of the car. She approached the house, her fingers hooking under the buttons of Peter's old flannel jacket and twisting. The porchlights were on, and two cars were parked out front—one an older vehicle with dents in the bumper and the other a freshly waxed sports car with low tires.

The sports car was perfectly clean inside except for a sunglasses case sitting in a cupholder. But on glancing in the older car, Gabrielle nearly pulled a button from the jacket. She pressed her face close to the glass.

A car seat sat in the back, with a sippy cup of water.

Michael had seen how that doll destroyed their family. Hadn't he? Except Michael always thought he knew better than her. If another child was in danger, she'd melt the doll down to char, even if the heat shattered her along with the antique.

Gabrielle rushed to the front door and lifted a finger toward the doorbell. She stopped. She could almost hear the doll's laugh in her mind. She couldn't force herself to press. What would she say?

She lowered her arm.

Maybe she could check without the people inside ever knowing she was here.

Through the window to her right, all the lights were on, and Gabrielle guessed someone was in that room. From the flickering quality of the light, that someone was probably watching television. It almost seemed like the flickering of a campfire. She moved left of the front door and peered into the darker room. Nothing of note inside.

I should leave. But I can't leave the doll here. It's time for me to protect myself and break whatever connection ties me to the doll.

Gabrielle crept around the corner of the house, carefully stepping on the springy grass to minimize noise. She slowly progressed until she came to the first window on the side of the house. A collection of recycling bins and a trash bin blocked her direct path, but just beyond them were a side door and tiny concrete path. A light burned inside. Resting a hand on top of the garbage bin, Gabrielle lifted herself to peer into the window.

It was a kitchen and then beyond a breakfast bar and a playroom. No denying that a child lived there, what with the miniature chairs and tiny princess table covered with several half-completed Melissa & Doug puzzles.

At the kitchen counter, facing away from the window through which Gabrielle peered, was a woman. Her dark hair was pulled into a bun and shapeless clothes made it impossible to tell much about her. Her hand was wrapped around a streaming ceramic mug. Two more mugs rested on the counter, one a child's size.

The idea of innocence existing in the same space as the doll left Gabrielle shivering. Not a shiver of cold, but how her body had quaked when her father locked her in the basement, a shiver of powerless acceptance. She needed to act.

What next? Gabrielle pressed her eyes closed and tried to force herself to turn around and go to the front door. But her feet didn't listen. She couldn't go in the front. No sane person would ever let her in. But she couldn't leave the doll here with a child either.

I need to find it. Get it away before it wrecks this family. And then find a way to destroy it before it continues demolishing mine.

Gabrielle continued her circuit of the house. At the next window, she faced into a bedroom. The light spilling in from the hall was enough to show her a bed made in a utilitarian fashion that implied masculinity to her. Not the bed of a married couple, but the three steaming cups from the family room implied two parents and a child.

I'm no detective. Whatever made me think I could make sense of any of this?

Just find the doll.

Rounding the next corner to the back of the house, she saw only one small window, too black to show anything. But the first window on the final side of the house stopped her. Gabrielle found herself looking into an office, lived-in but clear of many knick-knacks.

Gabrielle started to move on when a picture frame on the desk caught her eye. The frame itself was pottery of some sort and messily painted, a mass of color at one end and untouched baked clay at the other.

Gabrielle lowered her eyes to her feet and took in a deep, wheezing breath.

"*I don't like your interference,*" the doll whispered somewhere in the back of her mind. "*You're not irreplaceable. You can't save anyone.*"

Gabrielle leaned in and pressed her face to the window. The picture was of a little girl and her father, a father who looked like—

Cole.

forty-seven

THE DOLL WAS AT MICHAEL'S BOYFRIEND'S HOUSE. WITH HIS DAUGHTER.

Gabrielle stood on her tiptoes and peered further into the office. She found nothing to contradict the picture. This was a single man's room. And the woman in the kitchen must have been his nanny. Michael had told her about this.

The woman who lit a fire that killed her husband.

"Yes, it's a perfect house for me," the doll whispered.

Of course Michael would send the doll to his boyfriend's. It made sense. That way, he could get the wretched object back if he needed to. Hopefully, that meant that somewhere in the office the doll hid, discarded in the corner of a closet, locked away from that precious child.

If that was the case, Gabrielle could come back for the doll. Michael could help her retrieve it.

She searched for the reassurance of orange eyes to confirm the doll wasn't with the little girl. But if the doll was in the office, it was secreted away. Gabrielle continued her walk, her feet falling heavily on the grass.

The next window had frilly pink curtains, pulled shut. Unfocused shadows danced behind the curtains, not managing to form a cohesive picture.

A woman's voice seeped through the wall, not understandable, but clearly annoyed. She caught the words "S'mores" and "hard floor." Gabrielle couldn't make out enough words to decipher the meaning, but the woman's speech was followed by the heart-wrenching sob of a small child.

"Please!"

Gabrielle stepped away from the window.

A crash came from inside the room, and the child's sobs cut off abruptly.

Her own tears, as years before she'd hidden in the dark basement of her father's house, echoed in her ears. Memories surfaced of a teenage Michael being shoved into the bookshelf and the wall, memories of him mouthing off to her father and then going silent at the elder man's flare of temper. She recalled things breaking, fear so great it silenced ordinary tears.

The child in Cole's house was in danger.

Gabrielle's hand lifted to her head, her fingers digging into her temples, as if to drive out the confusion. Then the crying in the room resumed and a second voice, also female, joined. The voices faded quieter and then dissolved in the distance, leaving only the child's tears.

Gabrielle wove her hands in her hair, and she stumbled out in front of the house, standing on the edge of the yard next to the neighbor's hedge of cone-shaped evergreens. That little girl. That poor little girl.

"Go home. You aren't part of this," the doll's voice said. *"Perhaps I'll leave you alone, now that I have someone so precious to play with."*

But I planned to confess to Cole anyhow. Even without the doll, Gabrielle being here had a use. The child inside couldn't be in the kind of terror she was imagining. *Surely, Cole wouldn't let something like this happen to his daughter.*

He did hire an arsonist who killed her husband as a nanny. I don't know him. Does Michael?

Gabrielle shrank back into the hedge. The door seemed to darken and flicker with shadows. Inside the lit front room, a fire blazed in the hearth. Why would someone light a fire this time of year?

An arsonist and fire. This was no house for the doll. *I've got to get her out of there—protect that little girl from at least one thing.*

But how? I knock and say, "Hey, I'm that girl who may have killed someone. You have my doll. I'd like it back."

Before Gabrielle could force herself one way or another, the front door opened. She shrank further back into the hedge. The green scent filled her nostrils, and stiff tendrils tickled at her skin. She couldn't see the door or the woman anymore.

"I can't deal with this! I wanted to camp out overnight, not just play around a fake campfire. What am I supposed to tell Isa? She's upset, and I can't exactly say we can't have a sleepover because her father is an asshole. Why should I bother?" The speaker stepped out into Gabrielle's view, another woman, dressed in designer lounge pants and a perfectly fitted sweater. "Aren't you here to supervise immature little me anyhow?"

"I'm here until Mr. Montez says you aren't a threat to his daughter."

"*My* daughter, you fucking freak."

"I hear you. But it's your choice to leave." The first woman stepped out of the shadow of the doorway, but loose wisps of dark hair hid her face. Gabrielle recognized her as the woman from the kitchen. "If you make a fuss, I'll make sure Mr. Montez brings it up with the mediator when discussing your parental plan."

"I'll bring *you* up. Cole is insane to invite a murderer to watch our child."

"Stop, Mrs. Montez. I'm not going to argue where Isa can hear. You're raising your voice, and I'm not having it."

"Fine." The younger woman stalked down the steps and over to the sports car. She never glanced up as she slid into the driver's side and backed up.

The front door shut again.

Tiny branches scratched against Gabrielle's exposed skin and rustled at her every movement. The light from Cole's house reached into her hiding spot.

I have to get the doll out of that house. Gabrielle clutched her chest. There was no correct path. The only answer seemed to be leaving without doing anything. That would allow her time to figure out what this whole situation meant. But how could she do that? Waiting might mean it would be too late for that little girl.

I can't sit back and let life just happen to me.

Fleeing would mean leaving a little girl in a house with the old doll, an arsonist, a likely abusive mother, and a father who allowed all the rest. How could she walk away from that? Maybe the nanny was safe for now, as Michael believed, but for how long, under the doll's influence?

If the nanny didn't set the doll off, the mother would.

I have to get my doll.

"You just can't live without me," the doll snickered.

Gabrielle exited her cramped prison of branches and walked back around the side of the house toward the little girl's room. The blinds were still closed, but the light was off. No way she'd gone to bed that quickly.

Gabrielle reached up and touched the glass, pushing to the side. The window slid easily. She listened through the crack. Not a sound. No books laid out or any sort of evidence of bedtime ritual. With one finger, Gabrielle pulled the curtain back an inch and peered inside. Empty.

Gabrielle opened the window fully and set her hands on the sill. Golden eyes bore into her from atop a toy chest. The doll's cracks appeared darker, filled with shadows that seeped out to infect the room.

"Are you coming or not? You always were rather helpless."

Gabrielle shoved herself up onto the windowsill and then tossed her legs into the room. A plastic toy bin sat against the wall directly inside the window, and Gabrielle's foot knocked against it, sending a ball bouncing across the carpet.

Gabrielle spun her head toward the open bedroom door, both hands planted on the window behind her. Her heart slammed in time to the ball's bounces.

She held her breath.

I just want to get out of here with the doll. No one needs to be hurt. No one.

The ball rolled into the hallway.

I bet there are guns in this house. Cops always have guns, right? Would the nanny shoot me?

Gabrielle strained to hear anything. Then she took a long stride away from the window. She met the doll's eyes, which were lazily half-closed as the doll's body slumped.

"You won't destroy another family, another little girl," Gabrielle whispered.

"*You were destroyed before me. I am the glue that holds you together.*"

"Then let me fall apart." Gabrielle grabbed the doll, her fingers digging into the stuffed middle.

Golden eyes flicked shut as the doll flopped back in her grip.

Gabrielle turned and saw even though the hallway was brightly lit, the overhead light wasn't on. So why was it so bright? The illumination seemed to be coming from around the corner and it undulated, growing dim and then bright.

Fire.

Even if I take the doll, that little girl is alone with a killer. A murderer who uses fire.

The fire in the fireplace. She needed to look, to reassure herself that the child was okay.

Gabrielle staggered out of the room. Suspected arson—that's what Michael had said. *She got off on a lack of evidence, like me. But I'm guilty, aren't I? So who says she isn't?*

Fire.

Gabrielle reached the curve in the hall and faced into the living room. There was the nanny, kneeling in front of the fireplace, poker in her hand. The fire's angry colors danced as the flames threw themselves in rabid bursts. On the far wall, on a couch that dwarfed her, sat a little girl. So frail. So helpless. So terrified.

Isa's eyes bore into Gabrielle's, and her curious stare sparkled with innocence. An innocent who Gabrielle needed to protect.

Gabrielle clutched the doll to her chest.

The nanny looked up. Her face was monstrous, twisted in the fires of hell—puckered red scars covered one side of her cheek.

"*I can protect that child,*" the doll whispered. "*You know I can.*"

"I must help her," Gabrielle said.

The nanny took a step toward Isa.

"*You're useless. Always were,*" the doll said.

Then the nanny pushed the child back and walked backward toward the office, keeping her eyes on Gabrielle. She reached up onto a shelf just above the office door and pulled down something metal. A box. The nanny pressed her finger to the lock. "You'd best get out. I don't want to shoot you."

Gabrielle heard screams, and the world went black. And in the darkness was Michael's face, covered in blood, a knife clutched in his hands. The two of them stared at her father's body and tears dripped down her cheeks.

The memory twisted and warped. Demons surged around the room.

Fresh, wet blood coated the wings sprouting from Michael's back. Gabrielle leaned over and ran her cracked hands through the wetness and then reached back to spread it over her own budding wings.

forty-eight

Boom.

The noise exploded throughout Gabrielle's blackness with a brilliant flash, and the sound reverberated in her bones. Her ears rang with the gunshot, and she screamed. A knife with a clean, shiny blade thunked to the floor from her fingers. *Where did that come from?*

She didn't recognize the floor. Carpet.

Whose floor?

She blinked, still trying to get her eyes to focus. Everything beyond the circle of carpet at her feet was just a mash of color and light. Where was she? A plastic building block with the letter *L* emblazoned on it lay just beside her foot.

This is Cole's house.

Shit.

Gabrielle stumbled back a step as the burst of color formed into a room. A woman, the nanny, was unconscious and gagged on the ground to Gabrielle's right. The nanny's wrists and ankles had been bound. There was some blood in her hair, but she appeared otherwise unharmed. Panic forced Gabrielle's emotions to retreat as vague flashes of memory came to her: the woman pulling out a gun, a child running, an overwhelming feeling of fear at the flickering flames in the fireplace, and wrestling with the nanny, cold steel, impact. The flashes didn't coalesce perfectly, but it was a clear enough picture to tell Gabrielle that she'd attacked this woman and come out on top. Behind the nanny, a hungry fire burned in the fireplace. Between them, a brown leather couch had been pushed askew: one end so close to the fireplace it appeared a jolly, dancing orange.

No evidence of the little girl in the room.

The doll's porcelain face leaned against Gabrielle's skin, its clothed body resting in the crook of her arm.

A muddled noise that resembled her name sounded behind her.

Gabrielle spun.

Peter stood, one arm holding a crutch under him and the other gripping a pistol, pointed up at the ceiling, which dripped chunks of plaster. The sound had come from him. Clunks muted by the buzzing in her ears made dulled vibrations against her awareness. The pistol seemed to be the same one the nanny had held in Gabrielle's flashes of memory. A coffee table lay on its side, the corner at a diagonal angle between them. It must have gotten pushed there at some point during her blackout. One sharp corner jutted out into the path between Peter and her.

Gabrielle's hands flew to her mouth, and the doll flopped to the floor.

"The child, is she okay?" Gabrielle asked. She couldn't hear her own voice, just a garbled mumble.

Peter's mouth moved. "She should be—Cinder just ran in her room with her."

The bass tones of his words reached her. His arm, still pointed upward, trembled and his eyes had fixed behind her on the nanny.

Gabrielle stepped toward him, her foot hitting something soft, the doll. Golden eyes stared up at her, mocking. Gabrielle crumpled to her knees, fingers prying at the ivory dress. Her hand touched cold metal.

"Gabs," Peter said. He lowered the gun, setting it beside him on the coffee table's corner. He held both arms out to her, a crutch propped under one arm. "Gabs, come over here, please. Come away from the knife."

"What happened, Peter?" She glanced over her shoulder at Yolanda. The fire flickered over the woman's blackened eye. The skin on her wrists puckered under knots that were far too tight. "Did I do this?"

Don't be an idiot, Gabrielle. Of course you did this.

"Gabs, leave the doll and the knife and come over here." Peter hobbled a step forward.

"Call the police, Peter," she said. She stared at her clean, dry hands. *I'm covered in blood. It'll never wash off.* "Call 911."

"Cinder did. I'm getting you out of here. Let go of the knife."

That was his second mention of the knife. Her spinning mind couldn't quite pull the pieces together. There had been a knife. "I'm not going anywhere." Gabrielle started to rise from the ground, then froze in a crouch with her head swimming. "I was going to stab her, wasn't I?"

"Yes, then slit her throat. It's the right choice to free the child."

Peter reached out to her. His fingers trembled.

"No!" Gabrielle yelled, her voice stinging her still aching ears.

"Put the knife down," Peter said. He took one more step in her direction. His crutch wobbled on the thick carpet.

I'm not holding the knife. Gabrielle glanced down. One of her hands clutched the doll. She released it immediately. When had she grabbed it again? The other had fastened around the hilt of the knife —a knife from the kitchen. She had yet to lift it from the floor.

"Please," Peter said.

"He's weak. He can't protect you," the doll hissed. *"Did you really think you could function without me? With him?"*

"I don't want anyone to die." Gabrielle scooted away from Peter, lifting her hands to hold her head. The broadside of the blade pressed against her temple.

"Too bad," the doll said. The cracks on its face seethed until Gabrielle could almost see the horror that lay beneath the porcelain.

Peter's mouth moved, but the sound that came out was breaking pottery and a barking yell. Her vision swirled, taking away Cole's house, wiping it away like a dream on waking.

When the swirl of dark cleared, Gabrielle stood in Mr. Pritcher's basement, surrounded by the stink of damp and mildew. She stepped off the last stair onto the concrete floor.

Help me. She struggled against her body. She was in her own mind and her own physical form, just as she was in most of her mental regressions into her childhood. But unlike those childhood flashbacks, she didn't recognize the mental state she'd plunged into. The blank emptiness and the seething hate beneath were foreign to her.

Her body, controlled by this unknown entity, stepped past an old vase with a chip in the top and around several rusted filing cabinets. The awkward bulk of a kitchen knife jutted out from the waist of her jeans. The blade threatened to slice her open at each step. She stopped at the back of the Pritcher's basement wall in front of shelves filled with boxes of holiday decorations and outdated baby clothes—each labeled in black sharpie.

"Don't move or I'll shoot. You little bitch. Think you can just break in here." Mr. Pritcher's voice nagged at Gabrielle, but it didn't matter to whatever controlled her body. All that mattered were the glowing eyes that stuck out of a cracked plastic laundry basket. The doll was here.

Gabrielle took a few steps to the basket and reached out. The doll's demonic gaze greeted her from beneath a stained baby blanket. Her hand slid into the basket amid moth-eaten blankets and brushed the smooth porcelain of the cracked, chubby face.

My doll. Gabrielle trembled inside flesh she didn't control.

"Get out," Mr. Pritcher growled. From the sound of his voice, he was still standing on the stairs. "Don't you come in here, thinkin' you're owed something after you and your brother accused me last year."

"You kept things that are mine." The voice that issued from

Gabrielle wasn't quite hers. It rang higher and had a playful lilt that didn't fit the inherent threat in her words. "That was naughty of you, very, very naughty."

Her fingers fastened around the doll's soft middle. A heartbeat pulsed against her palm, and as the doll crested over the top of the basket, its eyes shifted to reflect Mr. Pritcher standing behind Gabrielle.

No. Oh god, no. I don't want to see this. Gabrielle tried to close her eyes but was instead carried along inside a memory that wasn't hers.

"I'll make you pay for this!" Mr. Pritcher yelled.

She spun to him, doll clutched to her chest.

"No," she said. Her voice came out singsong and high once again. Her free hand went to the knife in her waistband and pulled it free. "You're going to pay, Mr. Pritcher. You're going to pay for everything."

This isn't me. I didn't do this.

But Gabrielle's body slashed out, regardless of her intent. She leaped forward and slammed the blade in. Mr. Pritcher fell, screaming. Gabrielle's face formed a smile, and she turned to grab the first cloth item she found on the shelves.

"Now, we'd better tie you up. I wouldn't want this to end too quickly."

Then the world blurred. And the memory faded into flashes of a golden-hued vision. Golden as if tinted through the doll's wicked eyes. Mr. Pritcher tried to rise, but he must have failed. The next thing she saw was the slamming of his head into the step, her hand gripped in his hair as the *thunk* traveled up her arm. Then pinpointed moments of her binding him, sliding a gag between his teeth, moments of her stalking around the body.

The stink of oil permeated the air, and Mr. Pritcher's head bled onto the already stained basement floor. Gabrielle could feel the tiny cracks spreading over her flesh but had no more control over this past moment than she ever did. This was what it would feel like to truly be made of porcelain, to have no control over the world, to simply watch and endure.

Then Mr. Pritcher woke up.

The thing that was Gabrielle giggled and hopped in place, clapping her hands.

No. This isn't me. Gabrielle couldn't handle what she knew came next. She'd seen the crime scene photos. He had been stabbed sixteen times. *I didn't do that!*

"*No. You are useless, helpless. You couldn't protect Gabi. I had to,*" the singsong voice said into her mind. "*I've done that all along. At least Michael tried to protect her. You. Are. Worthless. I think you've been in charge long enough.*"

forty-nine

A STAB OF FEAR SANK DEEP INTO COLE AS HE AND MICHAEL DROVE UP TO Cole's house. His home looked peaceful through the windshield, but he knew that was only a facade. He tore out of the car before the tires fully stopped moving. His ears buzzed, and the swirl of thoughts inside him added a leaden weight to the beat of his heart.

Isa was in there.

Isa was with a killer.

Only the weight of his gun in his hand served as a reassurance.

A strange car was parked in his driveway, and Cinder's car out on the street. These details fell aside under a whirl of fears centered around Isa. Nothing mattered until she was safe.

Cole bolted past the car. Michael's footsteps sounded behind him.

From inside the house came a scream—deep, not a woman's scream. Definitely not a child's.

Adrenalin surged through him, and he lifted his gun. There were more firearms in the house. Yolanda knew where they were and how to use them, but what if she hadn't had the chance to arm herself? He could hear his heart beating in his ears.

He yelled for Isa or thought he did. His voice disappeared into the cold reality. If he handled this wrong, someone was likely to die. It was time to focus. No emotions, just facts. Deal with the facts.

Another male scream came from the living room. Cole followed the sound into the house, Michael trailing after him.

His brain parsed the scene.

Gabrielle, holding a knife, perched on top of someone's prone form.

No Isa visibly present. Good.

A gun lay on the floor near Gabrielle. The gun had been fired judging by the scattered plaster from the ceiling.

On the far side of the room, Yolanda sprawled on the floor. She was tied and gagged but breathing. Cole saw no sign of blood on her.

That made Gabrielle and her weapon the focus.

He aimed his gun at Gabrielle.

"Freeze," Cole said. "Put down the knife. Slowly."

She didn't move. Under the knife's blade was Peter Cullen. He must have been the person screaming. Blood seeped from a wound in his shoulder. From the kid's slack body, Cole guessed he was sinking into unconsciousness.

Michael came up behind him. Cole's mind had halted, and he existed at the center of the hurricane, straddling that tentative point of clarity. Michael could wait. He was not important now. Years of training took over his rational mind. Later, he could think.

This boy would die if they didn't stop Gabrielle. He couldn't live with that. Everything else had to come later.

Michael moved past him—he bent to the ground near Gabrielle and swooped something up. Cole's eyes flicked to him. Michael stood near the crackling fire in the fireplace and held the doll away from his body. Its eyes sparkled merrily in the firelight.

"Elle," Michael said, pleading.

"Peter's been a bad, bad boy," Gabrielle said, but her voice didn't sound like her. The pitch was higher and tauntingly playful. All he saw was her profile. She looked at him out of the corner of her eye.

Gabrielle smiled. This wasn't the girl Cole had met before. This was someone else entirely. The smile and the voice jolted him, threatening to pull him from the eye of the storm that allowed him to focus. There was less than a yard between them, but he couldn't cross the distance without risking spooking her.

Michael had frozen by the fire. He'd taken on a fighting stance, but there was nothing here he could battle. His hand made a fist around the doll's middle. And he kept looking from it to his sister as if he could find the answer to one from the other.

"Lower the weapon," Cole repeated.

Peter moaned. His shirt was soaked with blood, and his face swollen. A crutch stuck out at a jagged angle beside him.

Gabrielle laughed, a high squealing sound. Instead of lowering her arm, she lifted it to strike.

Cole fired.

Simultaneously, porcelain shattered against the stonework surrounding the fireplace. Michael swung the doll's limp body a second time into the stones, and the sharp white shards flew through the room.

Gabrielle froze, her body stiffening. A new red spot bloomed on her shoulder—almost a matching wound to her victim's. But she didn't seem to notice that. She stared at Michael and the doll.

Michael's gaze lowered to her shoulder, and he took a step toward her, then stopped.

Cole held his finger over the trigger, keeping it steady on Gabrielle. If he fired again, he'd have to shoot to kill.

"I was wrong, Elle. It's hurting you. There is no fucking doll," Michael said. His eyes pleaded as he looked at his sister. "If she's gone; you're free. Put the knife down! Please, look at what you're doing."

Gabrielle gasped.

Michael tossed the doll's body into the flame and moved toward his sister, slow, as if afraid she'd run or shatter in porcelain shards as the doll had.

The doll's dress caught fire. The knife fell from Gabrielle's fingers and clattered along the side of the coffee table and onto the carpet a few feet from her bent knee. Cole let his finger slip from the trigger.

She blinked. Michael pulled her into his arms, holding her for a moment before Gabrielle wrenched free. With desperation, she shoved Michael back with both hands, even as blood seeped down one arm, leaving scarlet streaks over her skin.

Then she screamed, throwing herself away from Peter.

Michael reached toward Gabrielle.

"Back off, Michael." Cole waved him off and moved up to her. Michael froze, not moving away from or toward his sister.

"Keep your hands where I can see them," Cole said to her, though her blank stare implied she wasn't hearing him. Cole kicked the discarded gun on the floor out of reach. A few strands of red hair stuck to the pommel. Had Gabrielle hit the boy over the head?

That didn't matter. A quick glance around the room still showed no evidence of Isa. Inside the eye of the hurricane, he felt the desperation to move, to find his daughter. Years of training and conditioning told him he needed to secure this scene first.

Isa was okay. She had to be okay.

Gabrielle made sharp, gulping sounds. Her face had that pale grayish quality that he'd seen often on people about to collapse.

Cole heard a step off to the side. "Michael, stay back!" Then because logical or not protecting both Michael and Isa mattered. "Please, go check on Isa. Make sure she's okay."

Checking if Michael listened wasn't possible. Maybe he'd listen. But Cole wasn't sure that anything would be enough to peel Michael from Gabrielle's side right now. Cole didn't dare take his eyes from Gabrielle. She had to be restrained. Immediately. That was next on the list. *One step at a time. Restrain Gabrielle and* then *find Isa.*

Jesus, let Isa be okay. If she's hurt . . .

"Is Peter dead?" Gabrielle sobbed. "Did I kill him?"

Cole reached for his cuffs.

"Peter!" she yelled, looking from one man to the other. "Help him!"

"On the floor," Cole said. *Isa. I've got to get to Isa.* Then he repeated, since he doubted she heard the first time, "Keep your hands where I can see them."

"Cole," Michael said. "Please, she—"

"Just stabbed her boyfriend," Cole said and held out the cuffs. So Michael wasn't going to leave her side, but Cole could appeal to his need to protect another way. Cole motioned with his head to Peter. "If you want to help, see what you can do to stop his bleeding."

"Hurry." Gabrielle held her hands behind her back. "Hurry."

Cole cuffed her, and Michael kneeled by Peter. He was better suited to help with injuries, anyhow. Once the cuffs were secure, Cole left Gabrielle slumped against the coffee table.

"You didn't have to shoot her," Michael said.

Cole looked at Michael, allowing himself the digression now that Gabrielle was restrained. He didn't actually respond, because deep down, Michael knew that his statement wasn't true. "She's alive."

"Thank you for trying to help her," Michael said softly. "You going to cuff me now? I won't fight."

"No." Cole reached out and touched Michael's cheek. There was no statute of limitations on murder, but Michael had been a child. Right or wrong, he'd already paid for his actions. "If I was on the case, I'd have to. I know that I still should. But as a person, I don't blame you, Michael. I'm on your side. Whatever else happened today, you aren't alone."

He did a circuit of the room, checking for Isa. Along his path, he kneeled by Yolanda. She was out cold, probably with a concussion, but alive. He'd been wrong about there being no blood on her, some matted in her dark hair. He reached for her ties to unbind her, but the emergency calm that had held him broke.

"Isa!" He stood.

No answer.

"Isa!"

Oh God, Isa . . .

Don't think about what her not answering could mean. Not yet.

"Is it safe?" came a woman's voice from the hall. "Peter? Fucking hell!"

Cole looked up to see the blue-haired roommate, just outside the door to Isa's room.

He choked on words and rushed over, trying to get a good look inside his daughter's room.

"The kid's okay," Lucinda said, catching the direction of Cole's eyes. "Fucking scared but okay."

"You kept her safe," Cole said. Then he saw Isa curled on the floor by the bed, holding a teddy and rocking back and forth. He pushed past Lucinda into the room and scooped up his daughter.

She was okay. Her hair smelled like burned marshmallows.

"I'm so sorry, baby," Cole said into her hair.

Isa sobbed into his shoulder, her arms tightening around him.

All his worries from before seemed trivial. Happy and healthy, that was what mattered, not whom she lived with. He'd rather she be indoor camping with Joan every day for the rest of her childhood than see her life in danger ever again.

Cole stroked Isa's hair, the soft silk slipping between his fingers. Her quiet sobs reminded him with every heartbeat that she was alive —and that she might well not have been.

fifty

Sirens sounded outside. Gabrielle stared at the shattered remnants of the doll by the fireplace. Tiny shards of porcelain and black scraps of cloth engulfed in flames. Her shoulder hurt. She deserved worse.

Little cracks ran the entirety of her skin. But no one else seemed to see that she was a moment away from shattering. And no one else could see the awful rot inside the cracks.

The doll was gone but the damage was done.

"They can't take you away from me, Gabrielle," Michael said, his voice softened by the distance between them and the ringing in her ears. He held something against Peter's bloody shoulder—the physical form of her crime between them. "This is all my fault."

"Stop, Michael," Gabrielle said. Her back pressed painfully into Cole's coffee table, and her arms were twisted awkwardly behind her. Her fingers were sticky, and though she couldn't see the blood, she could feel it seep like a poison inside her. It had been poisoning her all along. Blood and fear did that, rotting inside her, turning to poison. Time to let it out in the open, to finally cleanse the wound. "I know what happened to Mother and Father. I've always known it was you, deep down. Who I am—what I am—isn't your fault. Stop blaming yourself."

Cinder came into sight as she walked past the doorway and headed over to the nanny. She gave Gabrielle a wide berth, shoulders slumped, and face lowered.

Gabrielle made no attempt to move. She didn't even turn her head to follow the other woman's progress. Another person she'd hurt. Cinder had brought the doll here. She'd caused this, but Gabrielle couldn't be angry. She never should have trusted someone else to destroy the doll.

Michael remained by Peter. His hands were now covered with blood, but his eyes never left her. She suspected the angel wings on her back were now splattered with real blood as well as ink. But she wasn't the guardian angel, she never had been.

He was. He'd saved her again and again.

"I can't stop blaming myself," Michael said. "I did this to you."

"No, you didn't." She glanced at Peter. The rasp of his breath seemed even. "You and Peter were the only people who ever tried to take care of me. I think now, I need to do everything I can to take care of you, to keep you safe."

"But the doll's gone," Michael said. His voice choked with fear as he looked at her.

"I was broken either way." Gabrielle tried to shrug, only to have her wounded shoulder inhibit the movement. Michael didn't really believe it was the doll. He just knew she did. They would never agree, but it didn't matter. She needed to be somewhere safe. Somewhere she couldn't hurt them. Destroying the doll had stopped it, but too late. She couldn't find the words. The blood was on her hands.

The doll had killed Mr. Pritcher, but she'd used Gabrielle's body to do it. She didn't remember killing Joe, but it made sense that had gone down the same way. Someone had killed their mother, she still didn't recall who. Her? The doll? But Michael had killed Gabrielle's father, and she wouldn't let him take the fall for it. If it came to that, he'd done it to save her. He'd only failed because she'd already sold herself to the doll.

I'd already let her in, asked for her help.

They would put her away, but knowing that made something deep inside her relax.

The front door opened, and two police officers rushed in.

Gabrielle lifted her face and watched the men in blue.

Then she turned her head and spoke to Michael. If only she could make him understand. It was time to earn her wings. And to do that, she had to have them clipped. For as long as it took. Forever. "Now it's my turn to protect us. And I choose not to fight."

The officers lifted her up by her arms. Paramedics filed in.

She spoke again, though she didn't know if Michael would hear her. "It's enough that you stopped me"—*stopped her*—"That Peter is alive."

The officers pulled her to her feet and began to march her out the door. In the hallway, she saw the little girl and Cole. He held her close, and her fingers made a vice grip around Cole's neck.

Tears streaked down Michael's face. "I'm so sorry."

"It's okay." Gabrielle managed a tremulous smile. The burned smell of the doll's remains stung her nostrils. It was finally over. "Look at me. Do you see my cracks?" But she was Humpty-Dumpty. Some things could not be put back together. And some things could. "You're not broken, Michael. You have wings."

fifty-one

The necktie resisted Cole's every effort to make it straight. He glared into the mirror mounted on his bedroom closet. Ten days since a kid had been stabbed in his home and the shadow of that blackened the already dark prospect of mediation with Joan.

All Joan has to do is point out that I almost got Isa killed.

Cole froze. It occurred to him how self-indulgent such thoughts were. This wasn't about him—custody was about Isa. He'd understood that finally when he'd thought Isa's life was in danger. He grabbed up the parenting plan from the dresser.

He sighed and trudged out into the hallway. Isa's laughter sounded from back in his office, where they'd set her up on the computer with ABCmouse. The plan was for Yolanda to watch her while Cole drove down to the mediator's office and meet Joan.

He wished he didn't have to go alone, but he hadn't seen Michael much over the past few days—and only then when Michael was there to see Detective Sera. She seemed to have finally eased up now that she had Gabrielle in custody.

He had Isa to deal with.

And Michael had to deal with Gabrielle right now.

Cole slumped back; his hands tight around the parenting plan he'd made up with his lawyer—probably moot since the attack. He'd let Gabrielle into his child's life, and his foolishness could have gotten Isa killed. His gut told him this was the end.

Joan's been saying it ever since she came back. She never hurt Isa. She never put Isa in danger.

Cole stared down at the papers. Looking at all the little details that he'd insisted on, especially the supervised visits. The requirements, and the anger behind them, all seemed silly and counterproductive.

Isa needed a mother and a father. His duty was to make sure that's what she got.

Yolanda stepped into the hallway, dishrag in hand, and looked Cole over. "You look nice, Mr. Montez."

"I need a pen," he said, more to himself than to her.

"Easy enough." Yolanda shuffled off toward his office. She disappeared inside and then returned with a pen. "What's it for?"

"I need to make some changes to this before I leave." Cole wasn't sure until he said it out loud. But the words felt right and strong. He walked to the kitchen counter and began a brief revision, changing a few words and numbers here and there and crossing a section out. He carefully initialed beside each change.

Finished, he stood, holding the freshly edited document. There was no telling what the mediation would bring from Joan's end, but he'd be coming into it with a clear conscience. When he turned toward the doorway to the hall, he found Yolanda leaning there, dishrag bunched in her fist.

Why wasn't she in with Isa? From the serious look on her face, he guessed he was about to get a talking to. But she didn't say anything for a long moment.

Cole took a few steps toward her and cringed at the fading bruises on her thin wrists. "Are you certain you're okay watching Isa today?"

"I'm fine." She paused and rubbed the dishcloth extra hard over her hands. "You're fine. You didn't put her in danger. I know you feel that way, but you didn't."

"I put you in danger too."

Yolanda rolled her eyes. "Detective Sera wants to meet with me again this evening."

"I'll be home."

"I'm not worried, Mr. Montez." Yolanda shook her head slowly and clucked her tongue.

"You should testify against her, Yolanda."

"I'll tell the truth." Yolanda reached up and fingered her scars.

Cole resisted heaving a sigh at her. He'd heard Yolanda's supernatural ravings several times already. She swore that Gabrielle's eyes had changed, and it hadn't been her at all. But every time the word demon came up, Cole couldn't help scoffing. Lots of people wanted to blame trauma on impossible things.

He dealt in facts. So did the rest of the homicide department.

And Gabrielle was the one who had hurt both Yolanda and Peter. He was about to say so when the doorbell rang, followed by a swift knock.

Cole jumped but didn't turn to the door. He didn't want to talk to anyone.

He adjusted his tie and tried to hold onto his conviction that it wasn't the end of the world if Joan took Isa.

What's done is done. Now, I just have to accept the consequences.

Yolanda walked past him toward the door. She seemed to have returned to her old self, stubbornness and all.

Luckily, she wasn't likely to have to deal with a trial. The DA had made it clear that additional charges wouldn't be filed if Gabrielle would take a guilty by reason of insanity plea to second degree murder. Gabrielle was better off accused of that than first degree murder. Michael hadn't liked the charges, but Gabrielle accepted them without argument.

Isa pattered out into the hall behind him, her wireless headphones still over her ears.

If anyone deserved an insanity plea, it was Gabrielle.

A knock sounded again.

"Coming!" Yolanda said.

Isa grabbed onto Cole's leg and peered around him. Fear showed in her blue eyes—a fear that had never been there before.

Yolanda opened the door. Michael stood out in the morning sunlight. Cole's heart leaped at the sight of him before reason interfered. Michael shouldn't be here. He had other things to worry about.

"Michael?" Cole asked in surprise.

"Come on in, Mr. Cross," Yolanda said, a twinkle in her voice. She must be fond of Michael to be using his title like that. How was it she was so resilient? Cole's soul still felt bruised.

Isa dropped her vice grip on Cole and gave a little jump-wave at Michael.

"This okay? I promised I'd take you to the mediator's office," Michael said, raising an eyebrow at Cole. Then Isa streaked across the floor and hugged Michael's legs. He laughed and kneeled to scoop her up and toss her into the air.

Isa's laughter filled the hall. Michael caught her, and she gave him a kiss, arm around his neck.

"I know you said you'd drive me," Cole said. "I just figured you had other things to do."

"Actually, I could use something to distract me for a bit. You ready to go?"

No. "Yes."

"No!" Isa pouted.

"Another time, princess," Cole lied, hoping, wishing it wasn't really a lie. He leaned over to kiss her forehead. "Love you, and I'll be back this afternoon." *I hope.* Legal proceedings could take a long time.

Michael handed Isa over to Yolanda with a pat on the head, and the two men headed out to Michael's car in silence. The car's motor hummed to life, and Michael steered away from the house.

"I've been thinking," Michael said, filling the silence that had settled under the sound of the engine. "I'm going to sell my house. There are too many memories there."

Cole looked over. Despite the black rings under Michael's eyes, he was still gorgeous. "You've been thinking that, have you?"

What was he getting at?

"Yeah." Michael glanced to meet Cole's eyes for a moment. "Maybe, you can bring Isa for dinner at my new place?"

"That's it? Dinner?" That sounded marvelous and impossible. Like it belonged in a fantasy world that had very little in common with this one.

"I'm trying to say I want to move on with my life," Michael said. "I love you."

Instinctively, Cole reached for Michael's hand. His heart returned the sentiment, but he couldn't form the words in response. There was too much else.

"I'm tired of waiting to build a life," Michael went on. "I've spent so long under this cloud, trying to make up for everything to Gabrielle, trying to protect her."

Hiding a murder. Cole sighed. He either had to let that go or turn Michael in; anything in-between didn't make sense. And he had promised to let it go. But he couldn't let what happened with Gabrielle go. He couldn't, no matter what his heart said.

Cole tugged at his tie. "There are a lot of complications to us being together. I want it to work. We'd need to talk about Gabrielle first. She'll do time, but even after that, I'm not having her around Isa. I can't. Ever."

The flowers along the side of the road showed the full face of their open blooms as the car passed. They made the houses seem like women in party frocks. But so much could hide beneath, Cole couldn't afford to be unaware of that again. Innocence could be deceiving. Heavy clouds hung overhead, but that did nothing to dampen the flowers' joy as they bobbed in the breeze. Color and darkness existed together so easily in nature—light and shadow in harmony.

"I know," Michael said. "She'll be in some psychiatric institute for years, but she'll get out eventually, and I won't be able to abandon her. I know what she put you through, your daughter through—"

"That's it, then. I'm sorry. If she's going to be around in any capacity, I can't be." Cole reached out and brushed his hand on Michael's cheek. He wanted to say that they could make it work. But they couldn't. Cole could admit it now. It had always been Michael that he wanted to protect, Michael he'd needed to save, not Gabrielle. But Michael didn't want to be saved, and Cole had to let go.

"Can I still drive you home? I'd like to know what happens with Isa." Michael paused. "I'd like to know that we didn't mess that up for you."

"We'll see." Saying that hurt more than it should have.

Michael reached over and took Cole's hand.

"Call me when the meeting's over. I won't be far," Michael said. "There's a Starbucks around the corner."

Cole laughed bitterly, but somehow even that slight levity cut through some of the bitterness and sadness. "Do you actually know that? Or are you assuming?"

"I'm assuming conservatively. Chances are there will be a Starbucks on the ground floor of the building."

Cole looked up as the click of heels sounded on the tile floor of the wide hallway. His lawyer waited in a nearby room with the mediator, but Cole sat outside the room that currently housed Joan's lawyer. He needed to talk to Joan in person before the process started. The plan was to have the mediator travel between the rooms, communicating to both parties. Cole hoped his new plan would make the entire thing go a lot faster.

Joan approached, her hands compulsively smoothing her slacks. When her gaze moved to Cole, where he sat on the hard plastic chairs outside the office, she paused. Her perfect, French-manicured nails tugged at her jacket, adjusting the seams.

Joan's cold blue eyes speared him. Like the specter of death, she strode toward him, ready to end everything. And then she stopped in front of him, not taking one of the chairs, just standing.

"Cole?" She motioned to the office behind him. "Glad you're here. Before I go in there, we need to talk."

His old anger snapped inside of him. "You want to gloat?"

"Actually." Joan tilted her head, her posture softening. Before she spoke again, she took the seat next to him. Her legs turned toward him, nearly brushing his knees. Her next words came with a tense tone that implied she was fractions away from gritting her teeth. "I admit when I first heard . . . but then, I don't know. I moved back to Washington because I want to be with my daughter. This was never about punishing you."

Cole scoffed.

"Well, not at first." Joan gave a sneering sigh with a small smile. "I admit that in the process it became about us again. I want to hurt you, but Isa matters more."

Grudgingly, Cole nodded. That was true. He hadn't always been reasonable. That was the whole reason he was sitting where he was, clutching a hastily revised parenting plan.

She licked her lips. The lipstick had worn off of her bottom lip—that only happened when her nerves got the better of her.

"I rewrote *my* parenting plan." Joan tapped the papers in her lap. "I already sent this to the mediator. I suggest you take a look. You're not in a great bargaining position."

She offered the paper to Cole, but he shook his head.

"Oddly, I did the same but without the lawyer," Cole said, lifting the plan in his hands. He'd already bent so far to accommodate her. What horrors could be in that new plan of hers? "You tell me, Joan. What more are you asking for? I'm not giving you primary custody."

"Shut up!" Joan snapped. She slapped the papers on his knee. "I don't want primary custody. But I don't need supervision to see my daughter."

The words spun, not coming together to form a crisp picture. Cole opened his mouth. Closed it. Then, Cole's thoughts raced as he gingerly took the packet. He handed Joan his, with his hastily scrawled alterations, but neither looked at the documents. "What *are* you asking for? My new plan gave a lot more rights to you, but there are some things I can't compromise on."

"You know, you've never even bothered to ask before. What I want is every other weekend and Tuesday nights. No more supervision. I'm her mother, not a criminal."

Cole dropped his eyes to the packet of papers. He opened the folder, but all the neatly typed words blended together. "Joan, I'm sorry, I don't understand why you're doing this. I understand why I'm backing down, but your position just got stronger."

"I left early. I walked out of your house mad because of your stupid terms. I left Isa there, and she got hurt. I don't want to put her through any of this. She needs you—even if I don't. We don't have to like each other, but I know how much you love her. I just deserve the right to prove the same."

Cole managed a weak smile. "I'll look through your plan, you glance through mine. But I get the feeling we can come to some sort of accord."

As he finished speaking, the office door just down the hallway opened, and a pudgy man peeped out. "Mr. Montez?"

"Yes," Cole said.

The man waved him toward the office. "Come on inside."

Joan stood and set a hand on the door to her lawyer's office.

Cole stood. Could it be this easy? "You could have gone for the gullet."

Joan smiled. "I wanted to."

"I know. Maybe it's time we let it go. I hope you find what you're looking for, Joan. You deserve to be happy." The last part hurt coming out, but deep inside, he knew it was true.

"I sure do." Joan stepped into the office.

Before turning to the room where his lawyer waited, Cole glanced over at the windowed door leading out of the offices. Nearby, just out of sight, just behind the green sign, Michael waited with a goodbye that Cole really didn't want to say. Deserved or not, happiness was something to be worked toward. As long as he had Isa, there was no reason he couldn't make a future he wanted to live in.

Even if it wasn't entirely the future he wanted.

fifty-two

THE AUTUMN BLUE SKY SEEMED TO PLAY WITH ITS SCATTERED CLOUDS AS THEY moved slowly across Gabrielle's view. She stood, hands by the glass, observing the soft beauty of the morning. How happy the world outside her little window looked from inside her locked room. After half a year in Western State Hospital, she could almost imagine the world was like that. If only life outside really matched the sunny scene—playful clouds, orange hued trees, and leaves dancing on the wind—maybe she could be in it.

A knock sounded on her door, a light flutter of knuckles. "You have a visitor," came the cheery voice of her favorite nurse.

"Tell him to go away." Gabrielle buried her face in her hands and plunked down on the single bed beside her window. *I wish Dr. Lewis would stop authorizing these visits. I don't want to see anyone. I won't!*

"I haven't even said who it is, hon," the nurse chirped.

But I know. Peter's the only one it could be. It wasn't Michael's day to visit. Gabrielle dropped her hands onto the thin, scratchy blanket as the nurse cracked the door and peeped in.

She was a pretty woman, who reminded Gabrielle of Michael. Her dark skin and green eyes gave a base comfort that Gabrielle didn't really understand. But despite the nurse being older than

Michael, with a sprinkling of gray in her hair, the similarities between the two of them always gave Gabrielle a feeling of being safe.

Spending time with this nurse who reminded her so much of Michael was the closest Gabrielle let herself get to her brother. At her request, her psychiatrist had set up a system for them to visit without ever having Michael in arm's reach.

There was no other choice because Gabrielle wasn't safe to be around. For a moment, when Michael broke the doll, she'd felt free. But the insidious poison crept back. She never should have believed the doll could be destroyed. *It's wounded. But it's already inside me.*

The doll would want revenge on him, and Gabrielle couldn't give her the chance. Michael came at the same time every week.

These visits were short, and he never smiled the way he used to. It hurt knowing that Michael still thought he could save her. He asked every time if she'd had blackouts or heard the doll's voice. Gabrielle told him no every time. So far, the demon hadn't returned. But she had felt the evil inside her, and she knew beyond a doubt that it wasn't gone, just sleeping.

No. The doll would push her way back in. It couldn't be killed. Gabrielle understood that now. The evil had seeped too far into her.

Her psychiatrist kept telling her to see people. Telling her that he needed to be honest with herself and look at the events for what they were. He told her she was safe here.

And she was safe.

But it was her psychiatrist who couldn't see events for what they were.

Michael was the only visitor she allowed—the only one she could handle.

Sometimes, she asked about Cole. He was the best thing that had come into Michael's life in a long time, and she'd ruined their chances. She let herself hope maybe Cole would come back, but he never did.

Things that shattered didn't really get repaired. Not in real life.

Cinder had come for a while. Michael had admitted to placing her in Gabrielle's life, but that didn't matter. Gabrielle could see how much Cinder cared and how much she tried. The best thing Gabrielle could do for her old roommate was push her away. Eventually, Cinder stopped coming and went back to her own life. Everyone had.

Except for Peter.

"You should see him, hon," the nurse said. Her hands thrust into the pockets of her neat, blue uniform. "Otherwise, someday, he'll stop coming."

"Good," Gabrielle said. Michael should stop coming too, but she couldn't bear to push him away. They were each other's angels, even if she was fallen, shattered in a bloody feathered heap on the ground.

"Then tell him that yourself. Don't waste his time." The nurse paused. "He's a good friend—keeping him in your life will be healthy for you in the long run."

And bad for him. I tried to kill him, if I can't move past that, how can he?

I'll never touch him again, never. And as much as that hurt, it was the only safety she could ever give Peter. He would have to live for both of them. And she couldn't be part of that.

The nurse held the door open and motioned Gabrielle out into the empty hallway.

Gabrielle resisted. This day was no different. But her pounding heart declared her desire to do otherwise. The days Peter visited were always the worst. She'd stay up late into the night torturing herself, picturing him.

How was he? Was he stable? Healthy? Happy? Was he still in school? Did he have a girlfriend?

I want him to have a life.

Tears burned at her eyes.

Maybe, just this once, I can tell him to stop coming and see for myself that he's doing all right at the same time.

But she couldn't. She could never see him again.

The nurse frowned and waited, holding the door open.

Peter didn't need the shrapnel of her company. If he had forgiven her, he shouldn't. And if he hadn't, she didn't think she could bear to see it in his eyes.

"No!" Gabrielle let out a sob and covered her mouth. The emotions wrapping around her squeezed tightly like her ribs were crushing in against her heart. Each beat of her heart hurt.

Gabrielle stepped back from the open door and wrapped her arms around herself, gripping her elbows.

"He's waiting for you, sweetie," the nurse said.

He's still my Peter. No. Not mine.

He'll never be mine.

I stabbed him. He got in the way of me and someone the doll wanted to kill, and she *stabbed him. I don't deserve forgiveness.*

"Tell him to stop coming here. Live his life." *Without me.*

"Sweetie," the nurse said, but she took a step back. She'd let the door close soon.

"I'm dangerous. I'd rather die than hurt him." *Than let her hurt him.*

The nurse sighed and let the door shut.

Gabrielle wasn't getting out. She knew that. It would be years, if ever. Though her doctors and lawyers seemed to think she stood a good chance of eventually being released. They were wrong. *She* would come back before that happened.

The doll could still be waiting out there, or inside of Gabrielle, just lurking. Burning her wouldn't last. Breaking her certainly wouldn't. *Because she infected me.*

The psychiatrists had other words for it. Talked about defense mechanisms and terms like DID that Peter would have liked. Gabrielle knew better. She was infected with the doll's evil.

She closed her eyes, and inside her mind, she saw Peter. Bleeding, he reached out for her.

He leaned forward, pushing his outstretched arms closer to her. His blood dripped down slowly from his fingers.

Gabrielle unclasped her hands. She wanted to reach out. But

even in the safety of her mind, there could be no contact. Who knew how the doll could travel? As long as Gabrielle was trapped, the doll was too. They were linked, and it needed her. She saw that so clearly now. Just as it said she needed it. The connection was two-way. As long as Gabrielle stayed locked away, everyone was safe.

"That future doesn't exist." She opened her eyes. It stung too much looking at him, knowing she'd never really be able to do so again. But the image of him, hands outstretched, remained.

The air in the room seemed thin. Gabrielle's hands lifted as if to touch him. His offered hands remained extended—a lifeline she didn't deserve.

Gabrielle looked into his blue eyes, the sweep of freckles across his nose. And she knew. She'd always known. Her heart broke from knowing. "I'm not coming near you or Michael. Not ever."

He stretched out his hands plaintively toward her—hands of flesh—and she knew he wasn't like her; he wouldn't shatter. He would bleed. She curled her arms away, trying to hide the cracks in her porcelain veneer.

Want more just like this one? Sign up for our newsletter so you don't miss out on the adventure. You'll get:

- A free book for signing up
- Advanced notice of new releases
- First word of books on sale
- Opportunities for free books
- Most up-to-date information on author appearances.

We're busy and know you are too. We won't send more than one newsletter a month.

Register below.

acknowledgments

This book pulls enough from my real life that it is impossible to begin anywhere except with the doll. That old, cracked porcelain thing that used to sit in the garage, so frail and innocent, begging to be held. But something about her eyes haunted me at night. Some childhood terrors have a sort of poetry to them, and that doll has traveled with me my entire life, riding in the back of my mind and begging to speak her piece.

Secondly, there are actual people without whom this book simply would not have existed (even with the aid of a doll's ghostly song.) My husband has supported me through all the insanity of my writing, and my son wholeheartedly tells me I'm the best author in the world whenever I doubt. I couldn't ask for a more supportive family or better people to help balance the insanity that is me.

My close friends and critique partners gave me faith in Gabrielle, Michael, and Cole even when I started to lose it—this would not have been a pleasant process without you Tracy, Ligia, Tiffany, Cassandra, Steve, Chris, and Abigail. Tracy and Ligia, thank you for being my best friends, emotional support, and for not letting me doubt Peter or Cole, even when I wanted to. Thank you, Tiffany and Abigail, for not letting me doubt myself or shy from including the painfully personal. Thank you, Cassandra, Chris, and Steve, for believing perfection is attainable and driving me beyond my comfort zone.

And last, but never least, my wonderful editor and publisher

Kelly and the crew at Cursed Dragon Ship who took a chance on me and have made this process nothing but wonderful!

Coming from a long line of storytellers, and as a busy mom herself, Jesse Sprague writes for others looking for an evocative escape. And her debut novel, *Spider's Kiss*, took the shapeshifter trope in a new direction with sexy spiders in space. Her sci-fi series *Beneath 5th City* explores what happens if there are no heroes to step up in an alien invasion. Her previous stories have appeared in anthologies with award-winning and New York Times bestselling authors.

To Jesse, words are magic—they might be the only real magic left in this world. Find Jesse Sprague at JesseSprague.com.

facebook.com/JesseSpragueauthor

instagram.com/jessespragueauthor

www.ingramcontent.com/pod-product-compliance
Lightning Source LLC
Chambersburg PA
CBHW061628190726
48289CB00006B/1526